Devlin leaned over her, his lips finding the corner of hers.

He murmured against them. "Tell me your link with your Blade is closed." He needed to know it was. He didn't want to share this part of her with anyone.

"Yes," she whispered, her breath hot against his lips. "We closed both sides as soon as he was healed. It didn't help. I'm still burning up."

"I can help you. Let me help you, Avera." He settled his mouth over hers, swallowing her whispered assent. His tongue slid across her lips, pushing inside easily, delving, seeking, mating with her own.

For a while they simply fed off each other in long, panting kisses while Devlin's hands worked their own magic on her needy body.

Kudos for *BLOODSWORN: BOUND BY MAGIC*

BLOODSWORN Placed in 2009 Tampa Area
Romance Authors contest—Paranormal category.

"Kathy Lane creates a mouth-watering hero in
Devlin Tragar and a heroine you can root for in
Avera St. John. *BLOODSWORN*—take the plunge
into the exciting new action-packed story on the
magical world of Avalyr..."
~*Sharron Houdek, author of TO KILL A VAMPIRE*

Bloodsworn: Bound by Magic

by

Kathy Lane

Bloodsworn: Bound by Magic

COPYRIGHT © 2010 by Kathy Lane

Cover Art by *Tamra Westberry*

The Wild Rose Press
PO Box 706
Adams Basin, NY 14410-0706
Visit us at www.thewildrosepress.com

Publishing History
First Faery Rose Edition, 2010
Print ISBN 1-60154-822-2

Published in the United States of America

Dedication

To my niece, Darelle, for dragging me to my first writer's conference and thereby re-kindling my urge to write. Thanks for all your love and support and for keeping at me until I actually finished something. You're my angel.

And to my Mother, who has always believed in me. I'll always be your angel.

Acknowledgments

Getting a book published is a lot of work. It starts with one's imagination, for which I can only thank God for giving me a generous portion.

Then there's the time it takes to write the story. Thanks, family, for understanding the long hours I spent at the computer.

Getting the attention of someone in the business comes next, and I can only thank my editor, Frances Sevilla, for sitting through my very nervous pitch at RT and deciding my story was worth a second look. Thanks, Frances, for being such a wonderful editor, mentor, and friend.

Chapter One

Earth, Northern California, Six Months Earlier

Panic sped through Avera St. John's veins like a drug, making her heart race and her whole body tremble. She lay on her side, lungs burning for oxygen despite the air she sucked in through her nose and around the gag in her mouth. Her arms strained against the cord binding her wrists behind her back, muscles tense with the urge to fight, to break free.

Stay calm. Don't let panic overrun your common sense. Panic will only get you killed.

The memory of her father's commanding voice washed through her, dulling the sharp edge of fear enough to let her catch her breath. He was so right. From the moment she'd felt the knife at her throat she'd let panic make her a victim. She hadn't used any of the moves her father had taught her. Hours of self-defense lessons gone to waste.

Stop whining and use your head, Avera. From the moment a Marine is captured he's planning his escape. Don't just lay there, think about what you can do to put the bastard down.

I'm not a Marine, she screamed in her head. *I'm not one of your recruits. How am I supposed to do anything when I'm trussed up like somebody's Sunday dinner?*

1

Heavy footsteps drew near.

Avera bit back a groan as a hand grabbed her and rolled her roughly onto her back. With the blindfold on, she couldn't see, but she could feel. Pain shot down her arms, from her shoulders all the way to her cramped hands pinned beneath her. The sour smell of old sweat filled her next breath. She didn't think she'd ever forget that odor as long as she lived. Which might not be very long if she didn't use her brain and think of something.

The man who'd attacked her as she was unlocking her apartment door came closer. She could feel him kneeling over her, a knee pressed to each side of her legs. He leaned forward and laid a hand on her chest, his breathing hard and fast.

She wanted so badly to struggle, to throw him off. Instead, she waited, trying not to feel the press of fingers against her neck or their slow drag down the middle of her chest. Bile rose in her throat. His roving hand moved back up her body and he leaned forward and squeezed her breast.

Something inside her snapped. Her knees shot up, one slightly higher than the other, and rammed into his crotch. She jerked her head and shoulders to the side as he fell forward, a stream of strangled words pouring from his lips. She wiggled hard, trying to get out from under him, straining against the cords wrapped around her wrists and ankles. The cords suddenly gave. She kicked her feet free and shook her wrists loose as she rolled to the side. She ripped off the blindfold and scrambled to her feet. Needles of pain almost took her down again as blood rushed back into her limbs. She staggered and caught herself. The man rushed her, a knife in his hand. She ducked and threw her arms up shielding her face and chest from the quick jabs and slashes. The knife fell again and again. Oh God, he was going to kill her. Cut her up into little bite sized pieces if she didn't do something fast.

Don't just stand there, run! Get to the gun in your nightstand!

Her father's voice echoed in her head as the knife rose again. She dove under the man's raised arm, twisting to avoid crashing into her coffee table. Fingers tangled in her hair just as a blast of cold, wintry air brushed across her back, making her shiver. Her attacker cursed. The fingers snapped open and she jerked away. Sprinting down the short hall, she wheeled into her bedroom and slammed the door shut.

No lock, but she'd take the few precious moments the closed door offered.

She rolled across the bed, hit the wall, and scrambled on hands and knees to the nightstand. She jerked the drawer open and reached inside. The bedroom door flung open, banging against the wall. Snatching the small revolver out, she turned and fired.

His body jerked, but he didn't stop coming for her. She squeezed the trigger again. The big man grunted and staggered back. He made a futile grab for the bedpost as he fell, grunting harder when he hit the floor. The knife—that oh, so sharp knife— flew out of his hand and skidded across the hardwood floor.

For a moment, all she could hear in the sudden quiet were her own ragged breaths. Desperate pants of fear and anger coming too quick and shallow. She gulped and tried to slow her breathing to keep from hyperventilating. She couldn't pass out now.

Avera pushed up, back pressed against the wall. Her hands shook as she held the revolver, waiting for him to move, to come at her again. He just lay still, taking one shallow breath after another. Slowly, she slid along the wall to the window. She reached out a shaking hand and opened the blinds.

Moonlight flowed in, bathing the patch of floor where the man lay. Her breath caught.

Something white glistened in his eyebrows, lashes, and scraggly mustache, fading slowly as she stared. She bent and pressed the barrel of the gun to his head before touching one cautious finger to the white stuff. Cold nipped her skin, melting away as quickly as the strange substance when she rubbed it between her fingers. Her gaze shot back to the man's face in disbelief.

Ice. His face was covered in ice. Or more precisely, frost. How was that possible? Where had a blast of air come from in her apartment cold enough to frost a person's face?

She remembered the brush of cold air against her back. Replaying the moment, she realized the cold, wintery air had smelled strongly of snow and fir trees. Her apartment was in the middle of a city and this was the middle of March. No snow or fir trees for miles.

She sniffed. A hint of evergreen still lingered in the air.

Her heart started pounding again. She stood, but had to quickly move to the bed to sit down. Her knees trembled. The rest of her body just felt numb. It didn't take a medical degree to know she was going into shock.

Get help now, worry about freaky frost later.

She flicked the bedside lamp on, reached for the phone, and froze.

"My God," she whispered, gazing in horror at her arm. Both arms, she realized, holding the other out in a macabre comparison.

Blood covered her from elbows to hands like a pair of long, fingerless gloves. She couldn't tell how many times she'd been cut, or where. As she stared, fat red drops fell to the floor, slowly at first, but getting faster. Dime-sized splatters on the light-colored wood quickly grew to quarter-sized puddles. The sight made her stomach heave.

As if waiting for that moment of awareness, the pain hit. Not just the sharp stings from the wounds on her arms, but the throb on the side of her face where he'd hit her and the burn on her scalp where he'd torn her hair out by the roots during their struggle.

She shuddered, feeling the pressure of tears behind her eyes. He'd been so strong. If she hadn't been able to get to her gun...

Avera glanced again at the man on the floor. He still breathed, but hadn't moved. She kept the weapon pointed in his direction as she reached again for the phone. She punched in nine-one-one and waited for the emergency operator.

A year ago, she would have called her father first.

"9-1-1 operator, what is your emergency?"

"I...I just shot someone." Self-pity and hysteria hovered, just waiting for her to let her guard down. If, or rather when, it got loose, she was going to be a mess.

"Are you all right?" The operator's voice sounded more focused.

A wave of vertigo made the room spin. "Yes. No." She took a deep breath and tried very hard not to go to pieces. "My arms are cut. I'm bleeding." Later, she promised herself...she'd go to pieces later. Right now, she had to get help.

"I have your address, ma'am. I'm sending an ambulance. The police are on their way. I want you to stay on the phone with me until they get there, okay? What's your name? Is there someone I can call for you?"

"Avera St. John, and no, there's no one to call." No family, no close friends, no one who might care whether she lived or died tonight.

The bleak epiphany shook her, made her realize that after losing her father she'd literally cut herself off from the world and buried herself in her work.

Her dad would be so disappointed.

Chapter Two

The Planet Avalyr, Realm Illian, Castle of the Tragar, The Present

"Are you ready to die?"

The unexpected question, uttered in a deep, gravelly voice, sent a shot of adrenaline surging through Devlin Tragar. His mind snapped a shield of magic around him before he could even jerk his head up to identify his attacker. The reaction was the one the questioner probably hoped for, he realized, instantly recognizing the grinning warrior pointing a naked sword in his direction. The urge to wipe that amused expression off his friend's face tempted him. Devlin settled for glaring instead.

"You're early, Karess. I'm not scheduled to do any dying for at least another hour."

Karess Si-Faderan relaxed his threatening pose and shrugged, lips stretching into a wide grin. "You know how grumpy your First Blade gets without his favorite victim. Fate is cutting through the ranks of your guard like a scythe. The ones he hasn't challenged yet paid me to come fetch you so he'll leave them alone. Mind you, if you're worried about facing him, I'm willing to risk his wrath and let you try to kill me instead." He executed a short series of training moves before freezing in another menacing pose, sword high over one shoulder. The pose might

7

have worked if not for the laughter twinkling in his gray eyes. Karess was hardly ever serious.

Humor replaced irritation. Devlin leaned back in his chair and raised a disbelieving brow. "I didn't realize you were in such a hurry to die."

Karess brought the sword down, twirling it with a flourish. "I did say *try* to kill me. I doubt I'll be in much danger considering your lack of practice lately. You're probably so rusty you'll squeak when you move." He crossed the room, his sword slicing the air in restless arcs. It was apparent he'd already been sparring for several hours. His training leathers were stained dark with sweat and smudged here and there with the pale sand of the practice yard. More sweat darkened his blond hair and gleamed on his skin. A fresh bruise bloomed purple on his left forearm.

Envy flashed through Devlin. He'd spent his morning in meetings with his advisors and going over message scrolls needing his attention. As head of Clan Tragar and ruler of Realm Illian, his duties kept him busy to the point he was lucky to pick up a sword once a week. He wasn't about to give in to Karess' goading, however. "You are the one getting rusty, old friend, else you also think me out of practice at handling your insults. Which, I assure you, is not the case."

The constant flick of the sword paused. "So, is that your way of saying you'll be ignoring your faithful Blades yet again just to sit here the rest of the day reading boring message scrolls?" Karess snagged one of the scrolls out of the stack on the desk with the point of his sword and flipped it end over end into the air. With a deft stab he caught the spinning scroll again, this time flicking it at Devlin. "Or are you going to come out and play?" he challenged, his expression unrepentant.

Devlin caught the small scroll against his chest

and returned it to the pile on his desk. Boring or not, the messages needed to be read. And there was the treaty with Realm Mystia he had to go over before their delegation arrived tomorrow. And—

"Come, Devlin, be reasonable," Karess said, his voice full of impatience. "Would you really rather I sic Fate on you?"

Devlin raised his brows at the dire threat. Fate An-Derrith, First Blade and Captain of Devlin's personal guard, was far less easy going than Karess. The tall, dark-skinned Feyune male had a way of pressuring Devlin into doing things if he thought it was for his own good. "You would do such a thing to me? Your own Bloodsworn? Where is your loyalty, my Blade?"

Karess slapped a hand over his heart. "There is no question of my loyalty if you could but see it so, my Bloodsworn. As your Second Blade, I hold your safety and well-being dearer than my own." He slipped into a fresh grin. "That's why I am here first instead of old stone face. If you don't decide to come with me peacefully, it will be his turn to convince you. And since we both know you've been neglecting your sword work, Fate is likely to drag you bodily through the palace halls to the practice yard whether you want to go or not. Not very dignified behavior for a Clan leader much less a Realm's ruler. Imagine the gossip. Your image as an immovable force when it comes to negotiating would be ruined."

"And let's not forget my image as First Bloodsworn of Avalyr," Devlin added with a feigned grimace. "If I cannot control my own Blades, how can I be expected to control the outcome of the prophecies? Luma would have me replaced before the sun set."

His Second Blade sighed dramatically. "No Bloodsworn office, no Realm, and the Clan would banish you out of embarrassment. We will all be forced to take to the road to earn our living. Damn, Devlin, I'm too old to be a homeless waif."

An image of Karess squeezed into childish clothes flashed into Devlin's mind. He chuckled at the mental picture, feeling the tight muscles in his neck and shoulders relax noticeably. He'd needed this interruption.

"And this is your solution? To abduct me at sword-point from my own study?"

Karess' face lit with mischievous glee. "Yes. Great idea isn't it. You can tell anyone who asks, you were taken against your will." He waved the sword in front of Devlin's face for emphasis.

Devlin stared at the dulled practice blade and rubbed his chin. The prospect was tempting. But while he could put off his other duties, there was still the matter of the message he'd been stewing over when Karess had come in.

"My mother has returned early from the Oracle," he stated baldly. He nudged the message scroll delivered to him a short while ago. "She brought the translation for the Seventh Prophecy."

Karess' grin faded. His whole body tensed, as if he'd spied an enemy. Devlin appreciated the reaction even knowing there was nothing Karess could do to help him with this battle. Not when the enemy was words on a piece of paper.

"She still thinks this Prophecy will name your bride, doesn't she," Karess said, his words more a statement than question. He continued, his tone cautious. "Would that be such a bad thing, Dev? I mean, you must marry and produce an heir soon anyway. Churian is good in a fight but you and I both know your brother doesn't want to rule."

Devlin's teeth ground together but he managed to keep his mouth shut. Anger burning inside him, he launched himself to his feet and began pacing. "Damn Churian. If he'd just stayed home I could have...." He didn't bother finishing the sentence. What was the use? Even if Churian accepted Devlin naming him as heir it would make no difference, not if the Seventh Prophecy demanded he wed some strange female. He would simply have to accept not only the responsibility but the consequences. Considering the last two prophecy marriages, those were consequences he would rather avoid.

"Maybe she's wrong," Karess offered. "This prophecy might be about our treaty with Mystia or Realm Suterra's disputed succession. Or it could be about something we aren't even aware of. Maybe you're worrying for nothing."

"Perhaps." His pacing took him to one of the tall windows overlooking the practice yard. A break must have been called as the men were gathered in the corner near the well. He easily picked out his First Blade from the crowd. Fate stood to one side, talking to a young warrior who looked more boy than man. "How is Kedrick doing?"

The seventeen-year-old male had arrived at the palace gates two days ago, half dead and half way to mad. Like Karess and the rest of Devlin's Blades, Kedrick Gu-Carine had contracted the blade-illness, a devastating sickness that stripped its victims of the ability to absorb the essence of Avalyr's magic on their own. Without the help of a Bloodsworn— someone like Devlin who could take the magic essence and mentally feed it to others—Kedrick would have died.

"Why ask me? Why not query Kedrick yourself through your blood-link? You did say his mental path was a strong one."

Have you forgotten how uncomfortable it made you to have me in your head those first few days? Devlin sent the question straight to Karess' mind through the mental link they shared before switching back to verbal speech. "New Blades have a

11

lot of changes to deal with. I've learned it's best not to overwhelm them."

Karess made a dismissing noise. "You give him too little credit. The boy is fine. He asked if you would be at today's practice. I think he wants to thank his all-powerful Bloodsworn again."

Devlin turned from the window, groaning and running a hand over his face. The only part of being a Bloodsworn that made him uncomfortable was the period of intense gratitude most new Blades went through. Sometimes the feelings even bordered on the worshipful. He had never been able to understand why. True, he saved their lives by linking with them, but he did so because fate had granted him that ability. As Bloodsworn, it was his duty to help any plague-stricken man who crawled to his door. The roles could easily have been reversed.

"Very well. Give me half an hour to clear my schedule and I'll join you. Tell Kedrick I look forward to meeting him again. I assume if he is up to attending sword practice he's recovered enough to lift one himself. Do you know if he has had any training?"

Karess flashed a grin and shrugged. "I haven't asked him and Fate hasn't even let him touch a sword yet. Guess we'll both find out today." He started toward the door but stopped before he reached it. He stood still for several heartbeats before turning around again. There was a strange look on his face, a mixture of apology and pleading. "Uh, Devlin, would you mind?" He waved a hand toward a corner of the room, wiggling his fingers. "I'd really rather not take the chance of running into your mother."

Devlin arched one brow. Yes, his ability as a Bloodsworn allowed him to bend Avalyr's magic to his will, to call forth magical gates between one place and another. The question was, would he? He hadn't forgotten Karess' teasing remark about being rusty and figured he owed his friend a little teasing in return. He stayed quiet, drawing out the moment.

"Devlin, please, we both know your mother will flay me alive with her tongue if she catches me inside the palace half-dressed and filthy. Do you really want my blood on your conscience?"

Another long moment of silence.

"Fine," the warrior snapped, swinging around toward the door. "When you find my broken and bloody body in a hallway somewhere just remember you've only yourself to blame. Between your lady mother and your First Blade I'll be lucky to survive the day."

Devlin laughed. "All right, when you put it that way I suppose I have no choice. Can't have you bloodying up the palace floors." He waved a hand toward a corner of the room. A shimmering oval appeared, slightly taller and wider than a full-grown man. Beyond the golden edges of the gate lay a swath of the practice yard brilliantly lit by the afternoon sun and filled by pairs of men engaged in mock battle.

Karess' exaggerated sigh of relief lightened Devlin's mood almost as much as the prospect of sparring with his Blades. He chuckled and walked closer to the gate, intending to push Karess through. The faint sound of clashing swords seeped back through the magic.

For the second time in less than an hour Devlin was caught off guard. This time, it wasn't trepidation that swept through him, making his heartbeat quicken, but anticipation. The warrior in him rose, pushing aside the diplomat and ruler until he could almost feel the sword in his hand and smell the dust hazing the warm air.

He met Karess' questioning gaze and let the

smile on his face stretch into a conspiratorial grin. Magic surged, changing his loose pants and shirt into supple training leathers. Karess' eyes widened and then he grinned in return. For a moment the two of them were once more just a pair of young boys sneaking off in search of an afternoon of adventure. Before his sense of duty could call him to heel, Devlin took three long strides and slipped through the gate, Karess hot on his heels.

Chapter Three

Earth, Northern California, The Present

Avera drove through the security gate at Barrett Chemicals, pulse pounding in excitement. Only a few cars dotted the main parking lot. She spotted Dutch Wilson's little red Audi right away and grinned. Of course he'd come in early, too. Serum 23 was one of the more promising theoretical formulas tested at Barrett Chemicals since she'd been hired. If perfected, the medication derived from the serum would be a major step toward correcting chemical imbalances in the brain, one of the most common causes of mental illness.

So much for her plan to get to the latest test results first.

Too full of anticipation to let it bother her, Avera parked her car and gathered her purse and sack lunch. She checked to make sure her long sleeves were pulled down over her scarred arms before she got out. After so many weeks, the action came automatically, which suited her just fine. The first few weeks after that traumatic night had been rough. She'd lost count of the times she woke up with a scream lodged in her throat. If not for the strength she'd inherited from her father the depression might have taken her under.

Her work as a research chemist kept her mind

busy during the day, analyzing chemical formulas and coming up with test scenarios. Too busy to dwell on unpleasant memories. Moving to a different apartment had helped with the nighttime hours.

Her little revolver had changed lodgings, too. It had its own compartment in her purse now and spent the night under her pillow instead of in the nightstand.

She hurried out of the car and into the main building. Her footsteps echoed through the vacant lobby and empty hallway, the sound overly loud in the early morning quiet. She pushed open the lab's heavy fire door, her gaze automatically going to the glass window of the climate controlled server room. Inside, the SGI Altair 450 looked half asleep, only a few of the indicator lights visible through the grill of the front cabinet door. She hesitated, wondering if Dutch had had time to pull the results yet.

"In here, Avera."

Following the voice to her own office just off the main lab, she found her co-worker, Dutch Wilson, bent over several pages of printout scattered over her desk. He straightened when she came in and pointed wordlessly to a tall Styrofoam cup on her desk as he picked up its twin. "You're going to need that."

His tone brought her excitement down a notch, but she quickly emptied her arms and picked up the cup of coffee. One sniff told her it was her favorite, vanilla mocha with just a touch of cinnamon. She flashed him a smile. She'd liked the transplanted Brit the moment they'd met. At least twice her age, he was quite brilliant when it came to chemistry and had the most wonderful offbeat sense of humor. As far as she was concerned, Dutch should be heading Barrett's research department, not stuffy Taylor Morrison.

The normal twinkle in his eyes was absent this

morning. He peered at her over the top of his reading glasses, eyes red-rimmed and tired, as if he hadn't had enough sleep. His silvery-gray hair appeared even more tousled than usual. Unease swept through her. "You're starting to worry me, Dutch, what's wrong? Did the new simulation program crash?" The SGI wasn't that old and should have been able to handle the new software without any problem.

"No. The program appears to have run perfectly. I dare say Morrison will be ecstatic over its improved efficiency."

"Then why the long face?"

In answer, he handed her a single page of printout. She took the sheet, her gaze skimming over the dark lines of data. What she saw pretty much ruined her day. She flopped down into her desk chair. "Well, damn."

"My sentiments exactly, my dear," Dutch agreed. Any other time and his lovely British accent would have made her smile. Now, all she could do was frown, feeling sick to her stomach.

"Eighty percent fatal? Eighty percent? How is that possible?" None of the earlier tests had even hinted at something so catastrophic. When Dutch didn't answer she looked up. He appeared deep in thought as he stared through the office door at the server room across the lab. Hoping he'd had an epiphany, something that would save the project, Avera said, "You've thought of something. What is it?"

"Well," he drew the word out slowly, "I didn't say anything to you at the time. I told Morrison, of course."

When he didn't say anything more, she prompted him again.

"Told Morrison what, exactly?" Dutch had a tendency to lose himself in his own thought process

17

sometimes. He'd manage a sentence or two, but it was like listening to a one-sided conversation. Most times she found the habit endearing, but not today. She was too impatient for answers. "Dutch?"

He shook himself as if coming awake and sat up straighter. "Ah, yes, I was just thinking. About a week ago I came in very early and found one of the computers running."

"I didn't..." she began, aware her job could very well be on the line. Security at Barrett Chemicals was extremely tight. Even if a computer was left on by mistake the paths to the database and testing program were encrypted.

"I know you didn't leave it on," he interrupted, waving a hand at her before she could get going on her defense. "You've never once left a computer running that I know of, and you're very conscientious about logging off even when you're just stepping out of the lab for a moment."

"The computer was logged on?"

"Indeed."

"All the way?"

He nodded.

It was possible, however unlikely, that she might forget to turn off her computer. But she *knew* she'd never leave for the day without logging off completely. Instead of feeling relieved to know it wasn't her fault, Avera felt a little sick. Whoever had been in the lab had had access to everything, from preliminary test results right down to the formula itself.

"What did Morrison say?"

Dutch made a disgusted sound. "He said he would look into the matter. Then he came to me the next day insisting one of us must have left it on. Apparently nothing out of the ordinary showed up on the surveillance videos, so I didn't argue with him."

"Well, I would have," she said, anger replacing the sick feeling in her stomach.

Dutch chuckled. "Yes, I have no doubt you would have. That's one of the reasons I didn't say anything to you about it."

Avera made a face at him and tossed the disappointing printout in his lap. "So why tell me about this now?"

He sighed and ran a hand through his messy hair. "Just looking for a scapegoat, I suppose. It's not going to be easy explaining this degree of failure on a project we've spent months on."

"You think someone might have tampered with the formula?"

He shrugged. "Anything is possible, but without proof I suppose it's best not to even bring up the computer incident again when I talk to Morrison. It's just that I've never put much stock in coincidences. For good or bad, things usually happen for a reason." He sighed. "I can't help thinking I should have seen this coming, though."

"Hey, this isn't your fault, Dutch." She put a hand on his shoulder and squeezed. "You and I were both monitoring everything, and Morrison was getting weekly updates. No one saw this coming." Least of all her. She'd been too excited, deliberately focusing her entire concentration on the project. Serum 23 was supposed to be a breakthrough in the field of mental illness. Never mind the favorable repercussions such a success would have had on her career as a research chemist. This was her chance to make up for not being able to help her mother. A chance to keep some other child from losing a parent to an illness that literally sucked the life out of them.

Dutch patted her hand and gave her a smile probably meant to reassure her. It didn't help.

"Don't worry, my dear," he insisted. "I'm a tough

old bird and you're a stubborn young chick. We'll both weather this little storm, mark my words."

She tried to remember his prediction while she waited for him to get back from Morrison's office. She spent the time comparing the file they'd used to set up the simulation to one saved two weeks ago, hoping to find something to vindicate Dutch's suspicion. Unfortunately, the only changes she found were those tagged by either Dutch or herself. When he walked back into the lab a long three hours later, she didn't have any good news for him.

"That bloody arrogant tosser," he said angrily the moment the lab door closed behind him.

Not good. Dutch never cussed in front of her.

"My apologies, Avera, but, really, I've never in my life met a more disagreeable man."

She smiled sympathetically. "Yeah, I know. I didn't like Morrison the instant I met him."

"Morrison?" Dutch's brows shot up. "Oh, no, my dear, I wasn't talking about our resident suck-up, though you'll be glad to know his fawning attitude didn't get him anywhere today. I was speaking of Barrett Chemicals' illustrious owner and CEO, Mr. Cameron. Now there's a man with delusions of god-hood if I ever saw one. I swear he gets worse every time I meet him."

"Mr. Cameron's here?" She couldn't keep the surprise out of her voice. She'd been working at Barrett's for five months and had yet to meet the man. He lived in a veritable mansion further up the mountain and rarely came into the office. She'd been told he traveled a lot. "Well that's lousy timing for you," she muttered. "Guess he was pretty upset with the failed project, huh?"

"Not as much as one would imagine, actually. I think Morrison had him beat in that department. He was quite offensive until Cameron spoke up and told him it didn't matter."

"But that's good, isn't it? If the owner isn't too upset about losing such a promising product, then Morrison can't stick it to us, right?"

"In theory," he acknowledged. "But that isn't what has my knickers in a knot. What I'm upset about is Cameron's decision to purge Serum 23 from our database."

"Purge it?"

"Yes. Lock, stock, and formula, as he so eloquently put it."

"But, Dutch, all that work... And I'd think he'd want to keep files on a failure like this, for research purposes if nothing else."

He sighed and dropped into a chair. "Not this time, I'm afraid."

He suddenly looked tired, his eyes lacking their usual twinkle. Seeing him like this made her angry. They'd both put in a lot of extra hours, staying late, and even coming in on the weekends a few times. Deleting all their data was next to criminal.

"Why, Dutch? Did he give you a reason?"

"He's the owner, Avera, and this is a private company. He doesn't need a reason to deep-six a project. He did, however, spout some nonsense about not wanting such a dangerous formula to fall into the wrong hands." He gave her a wan smile and pushed up from the chair. "Anyway, I have to go through and delete all the files and refresh the database. Would you mind gathering up the printouts and file folders? Morrison is sending someone by later to collect all the hard copy for disposal."

Avera nodded sharply. Keeping her lips clamped shut was hard, but arguing with Dutch wasn't going to change things. They were both just little cogs in a bigger wheel and she knew it. That didn't mean she had to like it, or the big wheel named Cameron who thought nothing of trashing months of hard won knowledge. Even an incorrect hypothesis had value. It kept you from making the same mistakes twice.

She started stacking files, slamming them together in little bursts of anger. Her only solace was in thinking that if Cameron was so used to sweeping mistakes under the rug, she hoped she was around when he tripped over them and fell flat on his face.

Chapter Four

Avalyr, Realm Illian, Devlin's Study

Morning sun streamed through the tall windows of his study, shining on the new white scroll lying in the center of his desk. Devlin frowned. Surely his mother hadn't simply sent him the prophecy? He couldn't see her giving up the spoils of her victory—the chance to be present when he finally read the damned thing.

Movement in one of the window alcoves caught his attention.

Of course she hadn't.

Lady Patria Kel-Tragar had never been considered a great beauty. A thin woman with thick, dark hair, and pale, creamy skin, her facial features were all planes and angles, smooth, sharp, and not easily dismissed or forgotten. A countenance dominated by clear, vibrant blue eyes capable of piercing a person to their very soul.

Those eyes turned to Devlin and he felt the weight of their accusation. Lips twisted into a wry smile, he crossed the room and took the hands she held out to him, leaning in to kiss her cheek.

"It is good to have you home again, Mother." A partial lie. He'd rather she hadn't gone to the Oracle in the first place. "I hope your journey was not too arduous." Full truth this time. So far, he was doing well.

"It was acceptable. The roads between here and the Oracle are dry this time of year." Her expression changed, eyes narrowing, lips compressing in disapproval. "I thought perhaps my message informing you of my return had gone astray. Yet I found it open on your desk and learned from your steward that you spent yesterday afternoon sweating in the courtyard like a common soldier."

"Is there an uncommon way to sweat? I wonder why I wasn't told. Really, Mother, such things should be written down and bound into a handbook for Illian's future rulers. It would save them immeasurable embarrassment. Imagine if one of the ambassadors had caught me sweating commonly." He feigned a shudder.

Her lips gave the slightest twitch, as if they wanted to smile, but were quickly overruled. She pulled her hands from his. "Be serious, Devlin. You know I'm referring to the fact you chose to ignore my message."

"Ah, yes, that." He left her and drifted over to a side table in search of liquid fortification. Things were only going to get worse from here.

"Yes, that. A perfectly reasonable request for my son, who is also First Bloodsworn, to attend me to receive the translation of the Seventh Prophecy from my hand. Your attempt to ignore it, and me, only delays the inevitable."

Devlin sighed. "It wasn't you I was ignoring, Mother, I'm sure you realize that. I would have come to you, eventually. I simply chose not to interrupt my schedule for the sake of a prophecy that is likely to cause me no end of trouble no matter what it says." Possibly another half-lie, since he wasn't sure he'd have gone to her at all. He had to be careful, the nasty little things were addicting.

He poured a glass of dark blue wine, waiting for

his mother's usual biting comeback. Instead, he heard the swish of silk skirts as she glided up behind him. He took his time turning around.

Stopper in the bottle. Bottle on the tray. Glass in his hand. Sip. Swallow.

When he finally turned he got a good look at the scroll of white paper in her outstretched hand. In addition to a sinister black binding ribbon, the scroll was sealed with a wafer of red wax. The round disk resembled nothing so much as a big drop of bright blood against the pale skin of the scroll. Not a very comforting metaphor.

He told himself it was just stubbornness that made him unwilling to concede the battle to her yet, not nerves. He tipped his head. "The First Bloodsworn thanks the Lady Patria for her service to the Prophecies," he said, keeping his voice even. He walked around her without touching the ominous missive. Rude behavior, but the best he could do under the circumstances. He dropped gracelessly into a chair near the empty fireplace, slouched, and hooked a leg over one arm. Usually, such lack of decorum irritated his mother's sense of propriety. Maybe if she had something else to scold him about she'd forget about the damned scroll. A ridiculous hope, since Lady Patria wasn't the type of female easily distracted.

She frowned at him but said nothing. Instead, she moved until she stood in front of him before presenting him with both the message scroll and an admonishment.

"Take it and be done. You cannot hide from your destiny, my son."

"Oh, I don't know, Mother. The universe is a fairly large place. I'm sure there's somewhere out there I could hide if I wanted to." Mentally, he winced. *If I wanted to?* Now why had he tacked on those damning words?

"Ah, but that is the point, isn't it?" his mother crooned. "You don't want to hide. Not from this." She waved the rolled paper back and forth as if tempting him, or taunting him, he wasn't sure which. "This is what you have trained your whole life for. This is what you were born for. I more than anyone know how important this one is to you."

Devlin sighed heavily. He wished Churian was home. His younger brother was a separate thorn in Devlin's side with his determination not to act as heir, but together they were usually a match for their mother's tenacity. Unfortunately, Churian's journey had been delayed, or so his last letter had explained. How long ago had that been? Two months? Three? The fact he couldn't recall for certain had his brows drawing together in a frown.

"Come, Devlin, do not try to tell me differently. Why else would you have put off finding a wife if you were not waiting for the Oracle's Translation?"

"Perhaps I was simply too busy. I do have a realm to run, if you recall, and a hundred and seventeen Blades to provide for." He could almost see her wince at the reminder of the men in his care. Not that she disapproved of him being Bloodsworn. She was too shrewd for that. She didn't mind him being one of the most powerful magic-wielders on the planet. His status ensured the safety of both Clan and Realm. What she minded was the time he spent with his Blades.

"Blades cannot provide you with an heir. This can." Paper crackled as her grip tightened.

Devlin eyed the scroll and reminded himself not to repeat this part of the conversation to Karess and Strum, his Third Blade. There would be no end to his friends' teasing remarks. He could already hear Karess going on about bedding a rolled up piece of paper. The urge to laugh caught him in mid-swallow, and he coughed several times to clear his throat.

"I'm curious," he said when he could speak again. "Why are you so certain I'm to be saddled with a prophecy bride? Why not Churian or, gods forbid, a prophecy groom for Gwenell? For that matter, why must it be any of us? The blasted Prophecy could be about anything or anyone. What makes you so sure it's about me?"

His mother's stern gaze softened. "Because, my son, it is your life force that I see binding the rest of us together. Myself, Churian, Gwenell, even your Blades, I see as single threads in a greater weave. It is the thread of your life that weaves through them all, pulling them into a whole." Her voice grew hard again. "Yours and your bride's. She is close, Devlin. For good or ill, it is time for you to stop running and accept the destiny you were born to."

She shoved the scroll so close to his face he jerked back involuntarily. For the sake of his nose he finally took the rolled paper from her. He held the end pinched between two fingers and scowled as his mother settled with her usual grace into the chair opposite him. She adjusted her skirts then folded her hands demurely in her lap. Of course she expected him to open the message and read it without delay.

Devlin thought about putting the message on the side table and finishing his drink. He thought about tossing it in the cold fireplace along with his drink. He thought about just getting up and leaving and taking his drink and the message with him. In the end, he heaved a sigh and sat his glass on the side table.

His hand produced a slim dagger from his boot. He tugged the ribbon loose then slipped the small sharp blade beneath the wax to break the seal.

Devlin carefully checked his links. With meticulous care he made sure all one hundred seventeen of them were closed from his side. With a flick of his wrist he unrolled the missive. His gaze swept through the formal writing, looking for one word, daring it to be there. It jumped out at him quickly.

Bride...

He read the lines through once, twice, cursed under his breath, and read a third time. He still couldn't believe his eyes. "This is impossible. The Oracle has gone mad."

"What?" His mother demanded. "Devlin, what is it, what does it say?"

Too angry to speak, he rose, snatching his glass up before tossing the scroll onto her lap. Going to the side table, he refilled the glass and took a very long drink. The wine did nothing to settle the sick feeling growing in the pit of his stomach. If the message was real, if the translation true...

She read the damning words aloud.

"Bound by Magic. Linked by Blood. The first chains of restoration shall be forged through misfortune, their maker borne on the breath of death and pain to awaken to destiny. Embraced Daughter, Fated Bride, delivered from the world called Earth unto the First Sworn, Luma's shining Sword wed heart and soul to the Chatelaine of ancient knowledge."

There was more, but she stopped, raising her head. At least there was some compassion mixed with the triumph and firm resolution of her gaze. "I am sorry, my son, but you know you cannot refuse. Not even because of this."

Hands clenched into tight fists. No choice. Of course he had no choice. As First Bloodsworn, he was his own jailer, the instrument of his own compliance. The primary duty of the First Bloodsworn was to see the prophecies fulfilled. It would have been nice, though, to have someone to fight against. Someone else to blame when he finally fell into line and his life fell apart.

"A world called Earth. A planet still in the grip of technology. Did you know that, Mother?"

"Yes. I've read the Book of Worlds."

"Then you know its inhabitants have no idea magic is real much less that other inhabited worlds exist. How am I to convince a female to leave her entire world behind when she doesn't believe even the most basic things about me? The whole idea is preposterous. The damned Seventh Prophecy was set up to fail right from the start. It's impossible."

"Difficult, but not impossible. Securing her will be tricky, but you are Luma's Sword, her First Bloodsworn. She will not allow the Concourse to stand in your way when you go to retrieve your bride. Though it is true you may not be able to convince the Earth female to come with you willingly, she will have no defense against your magic. Once she is here, with time and patience, the two of you should be able to reach an understanding."

Devlin's head snapped around, his mother's hypocritical words slamming into a wall inside him. A wall built long ago on the foundation of a child's pledge. He remembered the night well. A trembling five-year-old crouched behind a door, listening to his parents rip into each other over and over with verbal swords. He met his mother's gaze and very deliberately shook his head. "No. I will not take her by force. Not from her world and not to my bed. She will come to me willingly, or not at all."

Something flashed in his mother's eyes but was quickly gone. Her gaze hardened. "An admirable sentiment, my son, but in this, your honor cannot rule you. Even if she were Feyune and knew of the importance of the prophecies, allowing her to make the choice of whether or not to accept you would not be wise. The prophecy must be fulfilled. You will have to take her—"

"I said, no!"

The magic inside him reacted instinctively to the strength of his denial. The invisible essence bled through his skin, snapping and popping like cold water on hot metal. Every muscle in his body tightened. His mother sank back into her chair, lips pressed firmly together as his violent emotions hit her. Had he not been looking directly at her he would have missed the flash of pain across her face.

Devlin closed his eyes, feeling ashamed. He usually had more control than this. Drawing in a deep breath, he called his magic to order. By the third breath his emotions were once more in check, though his hold on them slippery at best. He needed time to get himself under control. Time to decide how he was going to satisfy all the aspects of his honor and still remain himself.

"Devlin?"

And he needed that time alone.

"Forgive me, Mother. As you see, my control is not what it should be. I'm afraid we'll have to continue this discussion at another time. I'll call a gate for you, shall I?" He started to lift a hand, the order to his magic half-formed.

"Devlin, wait."

The hold on his emotions slipped. He grabbed the frayed edges and settled his face into a cold mask before facing his mother. "Mother, you of all people should understand why I refuse to make the same mistakes my father and grandfather made—"

"Perhaps you won't have to." Her voice sounded strange. Wary, disbelieving. Hopeful? She looked up from the prophecy scroll. Something shown in her eyes that he couldn't at first identify. His mother had never looked awed before.

"You didn't read the whole message," she said. "You didn't read the notation at the bottom of the page."

Devlin felt his skin begin to tingle before his fingers even touched the paper. The Oracle's notations usually referred to specific Houses and Realms important to the prophecy, information gleaned from visions during the translation. His eyes sought the bottom of the page.

He gasped.

For not only was the name of his prophecy bride revealed, but so, too, the one word that changed everything.

Starmate.

Chapter Five

The Planet Avalyr, Somewhere in Realm Hedaud

Camarie greeted the pain of a forced blood-link like an old friend, eagerly embracing the burning flashes and sharp, biting stings. He relished the futile struggles of the young man he forced the link on just as much, though he didn't allow himself to get too distracted by the simple pleasure. This link was different from the others. The visions of the younger man's life generated by the growing link held far more interest for him than pitiful pleas for death.

He concentrated on the brief, flickering images, sifting them for useful information. His frustration built at their vague randomness. When a blood-link was forced, the blending of lives often fell short of complete. Things could be hidden. The bits of information he gleaned now were next to worthless. Not until the visions caught up to the present did something worthwhile catch his mind's eye.

The young man writhing in the grip of the forced bond sensed his interest and immediately began to struggle harder, trying to release the sword hilt in his hand. Camarie tightened his grip, forcing the needed contact. He leaned closer, whispering. "You cannot fight me. You are nothing more than a weak tool I choose to use. Give in. I will have what I want from you regardless. From this day forward your very existence is contingent on my will. If you seek to defy me, I *will* destroy you."

Power surged as the linking neared completion. The sweet essence of Avalyr's magic burned its way though Camarie's mind, down his arm, and into their joined hands. The sword flared bright once, then changed, blackness bleeding down its length like blood. Another brief moment of struggle and the young man slumped forward, moaning as the essence seared its way into his mind, feeding him the magic he craved while at the same time sealing his fate. Camarie now controlled when and how much of the life-giving essence the other man received.

One more servant to his will. One more link to give him access to more of Avalyr's vast Veil of magic. He took possession of the new black sword with a sense of satisfaction and handed it to the head of his guard.

"Secure him in one of the lower cells. No training, no contact with anyone other than yourself." He thought about what he had learned while the half-conscious man was dragged away. "Send Prayon and Falk to the Oracle. They are to obtain the translation of the Seventh Prophecy any way they can."

"The Seventh Prophecy, my lord Bloodsworn? So soon?"

"Apparently. I want to know if the translation mentions anything about a prophecy bride for that fool, Devlin Tragar. If so, I want details. Her name, her location."

His First Blade's eyes narrowed, lips twisting into a smirk. "You wish to find and secure her first."

"Find, yes. Secure?" He chuckled, washing his hands in a waiting bowl and drying them thoroughly before picking up a glass of blue wine. "A tempting prospect, my Blade, but no. As entertaining as it might be to see just how far the fool would go to retrieve his bride, I want the chain of prophecies definitively broken. Do you understand?"

His First Blade's smile turned predatory. "I do, indeed, my Bloodsworn."

"Good, see to it immediately." The warrior bowed and left. Camarie allowed himself to relax, enjoying the fresh spill of magic into his mind. Avalyr's vast Veil of magic recognized his new link with a blade-sick man, granting him access to more of the magical essence. With the death of the prophecies any chance of stopping the illness that struck at random, stripping men of the ability to absorb Avalyr's essence on their own would die as well. He would be free to force as many blood-links as he wanted. Magic meant power, and one day soon, he would have it all.

Chapter Six

Devlin wandered his private garden oblivious to the fragrant blooms and lush foliage lining the walkway.

I have a Starmate.

There could be no mistake or misunderstanding. The Oracle's notation was very specific.

"To Devlin Kel-Tragar, First Bloodsworn, Ruler of Realm Illian: You will find your Starmate, Avera St. John, residing on the world called Earth in the vicinity of Trinity's Gate."

For the first time in his life, Devlin was truly amazed by the foresight of whoever was responsible for the Prophecies. How else could they have known that he would require a special incentive before accepting its decree wholeheartedly? He'd literally been on the verge of rebellion, not sure if he would be able to force himself into the kind of life he'd seen his parents lead even for the sake of his world. Now? Now, he was simply torn between amazement and disbelief. Any thoughts he'd had of trying to avoid a prophecy marriage banished by a simple word.

No one turned his back on a Starmate. A Starmate was a precious gift said to be the other half of one's soul. Rare. Extremely rare in the past century. He could recall only two other males so blessed that he knew of. He would be the biggest fool in Avalyr's long history if he continued to dig his heels in. Not that he was going to. Oh, no, his problem now was not that he'd been ordered to wed, but where he had to go to claim his bride.

His Starmate was from Earth.

Not Feyune, but human!

"Impossible," he murmured. "How in all the hells of the universe can this be true?" He shook his head, still stunned by the revelation.

A muffled chuckle drew him up short. He spun around to confront the men following him. He'd felt Fate, Karess, and Strum through their links but had been too distracted to acknowledge their presence. He pinned the chuckle's owner with a glare. "You find me amusing, my Blade?"

Unfazed, Karess smiled back at him. "As would you, could you but see yourself, my Bloodsworn. Talking to yourself is not something you usually do. Add that to the alternating euphoria and despair we sense in your mind, and I can think of only one thing that might cause such behavior. So, tell us, is your bride someone we know? Is she pretty?"

Devlin let a growl rumble up from his throat and left Karess to wonder if the cause was the eager questions or the sympathy he felt through their link.

"Best not tease the Tiger of Illian, my brother," Strum warned solemnly. "It is a good way to get yourself eaten."

Devlin felt a stirring in his mind, the equivalent of a polite tug on one of his links. He quickly traced the sensation to the mental bridge tying him to his Third Blade. He opened his side of the link and was met by Strum's vision of an actual tiger snapping his teeth a hair's breadth from Karess' terrified face. With a sense of satisfaction, he forwarded the vision to Karess.

Grinning, Karess took a step back and held up his hands in surrender. "Peace, Devlin. I am on your side, remember?"

"Then instead of teasing my anger, make yourself useful. Tell me how something like this could even be possible."

"Something like what?"

Impatience flared before he remembered he hadn't told anyone about the contents of the Prophecy. Nor would his mother have said anything to anyone. Such a pronouncement should come from him as First Bloodsworn. He met the now worried gaze of each warrior.

"My mother was right. The Seventh Prophecy has named my bride. As tradition demands, I'm to wed on the next solstice."

There was a long pause of silence, which Karess finally broke. "I'm sorry, Devlin. I know you didn't want this—"

"Oh, but I do."

A look of shock passed between Karess and Strum. Fate tilted his head to one side, black eyes studying Devlin intently. "You do?"

Devlin nodded. None of his men looked convinced. Three probing questions hit his mind at the same time. Trying to keep from grinning like a fool, he answered them aloud. "My prophecy bride is also my Starmate."

All of their eyes widened an instant before Karess let out a loud whoop, shattering the quiet evening. He grabbed Devlin in a hug and thumped him on the back. "A Starmate! Praise to the gods, brothers, our Bloodsworn has a Starmate." Strum grabbed him next. Devlin winced as his Third Blade added more enthusiastic congratulations to the center of his spine. Fate squeezed his shoulder.

"We should celebrate," Karess said. "We should... Wait." He snatched a handful of Devlin's shirt. "You've known this for hours. Why are you just getting around to telling us now?"

Strum's eyes narrowed. "For that matter, why is

he still here? Why is he wandering around out here in the dark? If someone had just told me I had a Starmate, I'd skip the celebration and be halfway to claiming her."

"Not if she was someone unsuitable," Karess said, his eyes full of worry again.

"I have no idea if she is unsuitable or not. That's the impossible part. My Starmate is literally from the stars."

"An off-worlder," Fate murmured. He was not First Blade by the strength of his link alone. His mind grasped things more quickly than others.

Devlin nodded.

"Vet," Karess and Strum swore together.

There was another long pause as his two friends looked at each other, the ground, anywhere but him. Devlin exchanged a look with Fate who merely quirked one brow as if to say, "So?"

Strum finally cleared his throat. "Are you sure your mother did not bribe the Oracle into naming your bride? She is quite capable of it."

Karess' face brightened. "If she did, perhaps you could double her offer to have the Prophecy changed."

Despite the serious nature of his predicament, Devlin found himself smiling at his friends' irreverent suggestions. He shook his head in mild reproof. "Capable, yes, but one can only assume that if my mother had thought of doing such a thing, she would have tied me to some noble Feyune family instead of sending me off world for my mate. Believe me, she is as stunned as I am." He continued in a disparaging tone. "No, my friends, I am afraid the Oracle holds sole responsibility for this fiasco."

Karess swore again. "Vet, Devlin, an *off-worlder* for your Starmate. Except for that, I would envy you."

"We all would," Strum agreed, his solemn voice

rumbling from his barrel chest. "What Feyune male wouldn't? To have the one female born just for you handed to you instead of spending your life searching for her?" He shook his head. "No, envy isn't nearly descriptive enough."

"You forget," Devlin said. "This female is not Avalyran. She is an Earthling."

Strum shrugged. "How different can they be if you are Starmates?"

"Different enough. Earth is not part of the Concourse."

Made up of representatives from every magic-based planet in the universe, the Concourse had two major roles. Police the use of magic between magic-based worlds and protect the worlds without magic from exploitation. Since Earth wasn't a member, it was safe to assume the planet relied on technology rather than magic.

Karess recovered from his shock first. "Are you sure?"

Devlin began walking again. "I checked the Book of Worlds to make certain. Earth is technology-based. How am I to understand, much less live with, someone who has no concept of magic? I swear it will be my grandfather and grandmother all over again, two complete opposites who could barely coexist on the same planet. The Oracle has to be mistaken."

"Or just plain crazy," Karess said.

Fate spoke up. "Crazy, perhaps, but never has the Oracle misinterpreted a prophecy."

Devlin found himself torn between a laugh and a snarl. His First Blade was correct. The Oracle responsible for translating all of Avalyr's Prophecies had never once been wrong. Which meant Devlin had no choice but to go to Earth and claim this woman, this...Avera St. John, as his Starmate.

"You know," mused Strum, "this has the potential to go very badly. You will not be able to just show up at her door to claim her like you could if she were Feyune. She won't know anything about Starmates. I doubt she will even consent to leave Earth and come back to Avalyr with you."

Karess made a disgusted noise. "Like I said, crazy. Strum is right. The people of this Earth do not even know our world exists. She is bound to refuse you. There is even a chance she may already be wed to another. What then?"

Devlin's hands clenched into fists. Such a possibility had yet to cross his mind. Shock joined the unexpected flood of possessive anger welling up inside him. The mix of violent emotion rolled like a ball into his gut and settled there like ballast in a ship's hold. A stupid metaphor, since he'd never felt more unbalanced in his life. He ground his teeth and spit out words he thought he'd never say. "She will have no choice." No more than he had. The Seventh Prophecy had to be fulfilled. The blade-illness had to come to an end.

He had to claim his Starmate.

Inside him, his magic roiled, anxious to do his bidding. He shook his head and took a deep, calming breath. All the magic of his planet would not solve this problem. Only the determination to do what was needed.

His men had gone quiet, their helpless anger on his behalf lapping at his mind. "And there are some humans who know about us," he said, shifting their focus so he could deal with his own anger.

Karess picked up the conversation again smoothly, snorting and waving a hand in dismissal. "Gate Watchers, and only a few of those. People like your mate are not going to know about us, and if you walk up to her and say 'Hello, I live on another planet and our Oracle sent me here to claim you as my mate', she is going to think you are crazy. In fact, you will be lucky if she doesn't run screaming in the other direction." He stopped in mid-stride and shot Devlin a wicked grin. "Now there's a thought. Don't think I have ever seen a woman run from you before. Can I come to Earth and watch?" he asked with unfeigned eagerness.

Strum chuckled. "I think I would like to be there to see that as well."

"We should all be there," Fate said, his face deadly serious. "If she does not believe him, she will not come willingly. He will have to force her and there may be those who will try to stop him."

Karess' grin turned into a scowl. "Your doom saying gets old, Fate, but you're right. Now I like the Oracle's words even less. There has to be another way to claim her, Devlin. Some way to get her to come with you willingly."

The path they walked opened into a clearing where several boulders stood guard around a large pool. Fish darted through the clear water, flashes of deep blue, vibrant green, and shining yellow. Devlin seated himself on a boulder and regarded his loyal Blades. He'd never needed their friendship more.

"Actually, another way has already been suggested to me."

Karess' head jerked up in interest. "Oh? By whom?"

"By my mother." As he expected, all three men cursed in unison.

"You can't seriously be thinking of listening to anything she has to say," Karess said, his face twisting with dislike. "Your pardon, Tragar, but your lady mother cannot be trusted when it comes to your welfare."

"But she can be trusted when it comes to the Prophecies," Strum said.

"She *is* obsessed with them."

Devlin nodded his agreement to Fate's observation. His First Blade faced away from the pond, eyes scanning the thick bushes and trees of the garden. Even here, the Captain of his guard watched, ensuring the safety of his Bloodsworn.

"What was her suggestion?" Strum asked without turning. He stood on the other side of the pond, a mirror to Fate.

Devlin ignored their overprotective behavior. "She told me I should send the St. John woman a copy of the Prophecies."

Karess let out a bark of derisive laughter. "Oh, she would. She is probably already scheming to get your mate as wrapped up in them as she is."

"Perhaps," agreed Devlin, watching Karess pace back and forth in front of him. His Second Blade's brows were drawn together in a dark frown. "After thinking it over, however, I believe her idea has merit. It will introduce both our world and myself to this woman so that when I do approach her, she will not be totally ignorant of what I speak."

"You should also send her something from Avalyr that Earth doesn't have," Strum said, turning slightly to look at Devlin. "You know, a token. Something that will let her know the Prophecies are legitimate and not someone's idea of a joke. One of your rare flowers maybe?"

Karess stopping in mid-stride, a mischievous grin spreading across his face. "Ah, a touch of romance. Good suggestion, my brother. He sends her one of the Prophecies each day along with a more personal note and a gift. He can explain about Avalyr and the Prophecies, tell her about himself, and romance her at the same time."

Strum grinned. "Females do get emotionally attached to that sort of thing. She will be half in love with our Bloodsworn before he even opens his mouth."

Devlin shoved off the boulder. His friends had no idea what they were talking about. "No one said anything about love. Love is not a requirement when it comes to the Prophecies, or have you forgotten?"

"But she's your Starmate," Strum said, his voice confused. "Doesn't that change things?"

Devlin froze. Prophecy marriages didn't have happy endings. He'd dreaded the possibility of being forced into one of the damned things for as long as he could remember. He didn't want the same life as his grandparents, so bitter they couldn't even live together. Or his parents, who'd lived together, but fought every minute right up until his father's death. In his mind, a prophecy marriage meant just the opposite of love.

Starmates, on the other hand, were always compatible, complementing each other, making each other stronger, better. But did that automatically mean they loved one another?

Mated heart and soul...

Mated heart.

More than anything, Devlin wanted the two words to mean exactly that. Two hearts mated as one, one love shared by two people. With a female beside him who he could love and who loved him in return, the dreary future he'd always feared would never exist.

"Enough," Fate said, the curt word loud enough to draw Devlin's attention from imagining new possibilities. "If you must do this thing then let it be done. Send her your notes and the Prophecies, include an Avalyran gift with each, and see what happens at the end of seven days. In the meantime, have the Gate Watcher find out all he can about her. If I am not mistaken Earth has technology similar to an Oracle's Seeing. Finding out such information should not be too difficult. Then you will know how best to approach this woman. Once your strategy is planned, and you secure the woman's cooperation, we can all come back to Avalyr where we belong."

43

Devlin, along with the other two Blades, could only stare at Fate. The man had just spoken more words than he usually did in a week. When no one said anything, Fate glanced over his shoulder, scowling.

"Should that not be your first priority? Getting her to return here with you? Convincing her she is your mate can come later."

Devlin had to clear his throat to keep from laughing. It wouldn't do to insult his First Blade. "As always, my Blade, you cut straight through the outer husk to the inner kernel with keen precision. It shall be as you say. My mother is having the Prophecies copied. I will travel to the Concourse's Enclave in Moiwie City to request passage through the Outer Gates as soon as possible. Quickest done is soonest ended, is that not so?"

"It is, my Bloodsworn."

Devlin nodded, feeling a strange emotion run through him, warming his blood, stirring his magic. The high before a battle, the thrill before a hunt. He shared the intoxicating feeling with his three Blades. Strum and Karess bared their teeth in approval. Even the stoic Fate allowed himself a tight-lipped smile.

Devlin grinned, eyes already sweeping the verdant garden in search of the perfect token to tempt his bride-to-be.

Chapter Seven

When Devlin stepped into the audience chamber of the Concourse Enclave his good mood vanished. Four people—three female, one male—regarded him from behind a long, ornate table with expressions ranging from boredom to contempt. They were not what soured his mood, however. It was the empty fifth chair in the middle of the line of Avatars that had him seething with irritation.

Where the bloody hell was Luma?

He'd counted on the presence of Avalyr's Avatar to sway the Enclave's decision in his favor. Now he was left with only his diplomatic skills to get what he wanted. The warrior in him did not like the odds.

He looked over the other Concourse representatives, people chosen at birth to be the embodiment of their respective planet's magic. Guardians, protectors. Enforcers when necessary.

Catching his eye, Talimina, Avatar of world Cowetta, winked. Of the three women, she was the only one he recognized. He had been introduced to her shortly after he'd become First Bloodsworn. She often came to Avalyr to visit Luma. He'd never seen the beautiful blonde woman dressed in anything but red, and the gown she wore now was no exception. Deep red and low cut, the garment drew attention to her flawless copper skin. A large crystal pendant in the shape of a teardrop glinted from the valley between her high breasts. Before, Devlin might have let his eyes linger on the rainbow colors, but not today.

The woman seated next to Talimina wore a cape of some type of animal fur and tapped one sharp nail against the tabletop. The third woman of the group sat without moving, hands folded on the table, a bored expression on her face.

The fourth Avatar, Dominic Tane of the planet Veralon, lounged back in his chair, his body half-turned so he faced the women. His vote would definitely not be in Devlin's favor since he and Tane shared a mutual dislike of one another.

The sound of huge, double doors clanging shut behind him echoed in the room's high ceiling. A signal that the audience had begun.

"Greetings, Devlin Tragar," Talimina purred. "What brings you to the Enclave on this fine day?"

He made a formal bow. The Avatars did so enjoy their rituals, and he had no qualms about giving the powerful beings their due respect. "Avatars, I seek permission for free-travel to, and on, the planet called Earth."

Talimina's brows shot up. The blank, bored expression of the female in black altered, brows drawing together lips thinning in extreme displeasure. The woman in fur stopped tapping her finger, her gaze shifting to him with the speed and intensity of a predator sighting prey. Dominic Tane's eyes flashed with power.

Devlin forced himself not to react to the aggression rising in the room. He'd expected as much, if not worse. The Avatars zealously guarded the worlds without magic.

Tane laughed, humor mixed with derision, and waved a dismissing hand. "Not magical, Earth is. Rules, you know."

"Yes, I know the rules. I would not ask if my

need was not great."

Tane sat forward quickly, all traces of humor banished from his face and voice, lips curled into a sneer. "Impossible, your request. Not allowed on Earth are magic-wielders. Our time, you waste."

Devlin ground his teeth. He was used to Dominic Tane's annoying way of speaking, but it still never failed to irritate him. Nor did the man's condescending tone. The urge to wipe the sneer off Tane's face warred with his determination not to loose his temper. Quickly pushing aside the temptation, he said, "It is not my intention to waste your time. If you will listen, I will explain my request. I believe you are aware of the importance of Avalyr's Prophecies. The Seventh Prophecy has been translated—"

Tane vanished, winking out of existence between one heartbeat and the next. Another heartbeat later, the two women Devlin didn't know joined him. Only Talimina remained, her gaze thoughtful as she looked at him.

Devlin's temper flared. Anger shook the walls confining the magic inside him as he stalked to the table. "Talimina," he said, unable to keep the sharp edge of fury out of his voice. "My request is not a whim. If Luma were here she could tell you how important this is."

Her head tilted slightly, a single perfect brow arching up toward her hairline. He caught himself, realizing he was close to alienating the only person left he could appeal to. He forced his body to bow. "Forgive me. I should not take my anger at Tane out on you."

The female Avatar rose and came around the table to stand near him. "Dominic enjoys annoying people. You need to learn to ignore him." She leaned closer, and ran a finger down his chest. "Since Luma isn't here, why don't you tell me why a visit to Earth is so important to you, sweet Devlin? Perhaps if you convince me, I'll intercede with the others on your behalf."

So, she wanted to play with him. She'd done so before, on more than one occasion. Her teasing games usually didn't bother him. Most times, he enjoyed teasing her back, taking pleasure in her light touches and suggestive words while knowing they would lead to nothing. Now all he wanted was to step out of reach of her playful fingers. Hers weren't the hands his body, his very soul, craved.

He held himself in place, feigning an attraction he didn't feel. He needed an ally, and with Luma's absence, Talimina was his only hope. He took her wandering hand and brushed a kiss across her knuckles.

"That dress suits you," he complimented. "But then, I've yet to see you in anything that didn't suit you."

A smile played across her lips. "Yes, it does, doesn't it? You won't win my aid with flattery, though feel free to try."

He smiled back, reminding himself that while Talimina enjoyed compliments, her beautiful face and often vacant look hid a sharp mind. She could be either a wily opponent or a cunning ally, depending on her mood. Devlin conceded the game to her and plunged into his explanation.

"According to the Seventh Prophecy, I have a Starmate."

Her expression changed. Interest flashed into her eyes, almost banishing the sultry temptress. "Congratulations. But what has that to do with you wanting to go to Earth?"

"My Starmate is a human female from Earth."

"That's..." She paused. Her head tilted to one side as her eyes searched his face. "Well, I was going to say that's not possible, but from the look on your face I take it you're serious."

"Believe me, I would not be here otherwise."

Her gaze turned thoughtful, and she tapped a long-nailed finger against her chin. "I wonder...."

"Yes?"

She shook her head. "Oh, nothing. I'm surprised Luma isn't here. She has to know how difficult it would be for you to gain the Concourse's permission to run loose on Earth." Her smile turned sly. "You are a very powerful magic user, sweet Devlin. Just a step or two away from being an Avatar yourself, but don't tell Luma I said so."

If she'd meant to compliment him, she'd failed. He had no aspirations to replace Luma. He'd always had a problem with the Avatars, or Regents, as they were sometimes called. The beings who embodied the magic of their home planets held far too much power. Case in point, they could prevent him from claiming his Starmate. No one traveled between worlds without the use of Outer Gates and those were created and controlled by the Concourse.

Talimina sighed suddenly, her perfect forehead creasing into a frown. "The others won't like this. I doubt I can get more than one of them to vote with me. We'll need Luma to break the tie, assuming she's amicable to her First Bloodsworn going off-world for his mate. This is bound to have repercussions in the bloodline if you breed." She shrugged. "Oh well, a prophecy is a prophecy, I suppose. We'll just have to assume the Greater Power knows what It's doing."

His shoulders relaxed. "You will help me, then?"

"Aye, sweet Devlin, I think I shall." She linked her arm through his and turned toward the double doors. "Come, don't look so grim. I don't have the power to grant you the run of the planet, but I can allow you access to an Outer Gate for a few hours. You won't be able to physically go beyond the magic

49

barrier, but the Gate's Watcher should be able to help you locate your Starmate with his technology. I know, I know, it's not as easy as using magic, but you'll just have to make do. While you're gone, I'll talk to the others and see if I can locate our dear friend. If I know Luma, she won't want to miss this."

She leaned forward and pressed a kiss to his lips. He froze, not wanting to offend his only ally, but at the same time hoping she'd try to go no further. Just the promise of a Starmate had focused both his body and mind to one purpose.

Talimina drew back and patted his cheek, chuckling. "Oh, I can see this is going to be very entertaining. Maybe we won't need Luma after all. Once I explain things to Dominic, he'll no doubt see this as an opportunity to watch you flounder as you try to claim this female of yours."

Devlin frowned. If it helped him to claim his Starmate, he'd gladly become Tane's source of amusement. On the other hand, Veralon's ass of an Avatar was more likely to continue withholding his approval, just to watch Devlin squirm like a worm on a hook. If he did, the situation could turn deadly. Tane had to know Devlin would do everything, anything, in his bid to claim his Starmate. Including challenging the most powerful beings in the universe if need be.

Chapter Eight

Avera glared at the kitchen clock as she grabbed her purse and bag lunch and headed to her front door. Late again. She *could* blame her lack of punctuality on the hot shower she'd lingered under, but that would be a lie. Frustration was the culprit. Her job was no longer the dream position she'd thought it was. She'd assumed working for a private research company would be better than one of the larger, public firms. Give her more freedom to explore possibilities. Recent events had taught her different. If the company's owner, one man, had the power to bury months of research, she wasn't sure she wanted to work there anymore.

She snatched opened the door to her apartment and stopped suddenly in surprise. Her neighbor, Steven Daniel, stood in the hall holding a clear crystal vase. He had a rapt expression, his gaze fixed on a delicate-looking green flower balanced on a long stem sticking out of the vase.

"Steven?"

He jumped, eyes blinking. When he met her gaze, his face flushed.

"Hi, Avera. I wasn't taking it, you know. Just wanted to get a better look at it."

"You weren't taking what?"

"Your flower." He held the vase out to her.

She felt her own cheeks flush. Steven was very

married. "Umm, thanks Steven, that's very nice of you."

He gave her a puzzled look, then his face colored a fiery red. "Hell, Avera, you think I'm that dumb? Claudia would skin me alive if I ever gave another woman one of her flowers." He held the vase out to her again. "This was by your door when I came out a little while ago. I thought maybe it was an orchid Claudia and I didn't have yet. Then I saw it's not an orchid at all. In fact..." He pulled the vase back toward him, holding the bloom up to eye level. "I'm not sure what kind of flower it is."

Avera found that hard to believe. Steven's life revolved around two things, his wife and his exotic flowers. Their apartment was a veritable jungle with orchids and other hothouse beauties sitting on every surface and hanging in dozens of baskets.

With a curious shrug, he held the flower out to her for the third time. She dumped her purse and lunch bag on a table beside the door and took the vase. Long, silvery green leaves nodded over the side and curled up around the stem to the emerald green flower. Broad petals, thin as a whisper, overlapped each other, framing a blood red heart. "It's gorgeous. Are you sure you don't know what it is?"

He sighed wistfully. "I can honestly say, Avera, that I've never seen one like it before in my life." He started to turn away and stopped, bent down, and came up with a small roll of paper tied with a green ribbon that matched the flower. "This was beside the vase. I guess you must have a secret admirer."

"I guess," she said, taking the paper.

"Oh, Vee." Steven paused at the head of the stairs. "Do me a favor, will you? Take a dozen or so pictures of that little beauty. This morning if you have time. I have no idea how long it will last, and I want to have a good shot of it."

"Are you going to try to find out what it is?"

"Damn right I am. I'll use the Internet to track down its creator. Whoever came up with that crossbreed isn't going to keep quiet about it. It's bound to be on the Web somewhere."

She glanced at the clock again. No way was she going to make it to work on time. Might as well snap a few pictures before she left. "All right. Give me a call tonight, and I'll email you the pictures."

"Thanks, Avera." He gave the flower one last, longing look, before hurrying down the stairs.

Avera stepped back into her apartment and kicked the door closed with her heel.

"Now who could have left this," she wondered aloud. She'd gotten several emails and letters of encouragement after she'd been attacked two months ago, mostly from co-workers, but no flowers. Why would someone send her one now?

She examined the green ribbon tied around the paper as she carried the vase to the kitchen. The beautiful red stitching along its length appeared to be writing of some kind, though she didn't recognize any of the symbols. She wasn't a linguist anymore than she was a botanist.

She sat the vase on the table and tugged on one end of the ribbon. It came loose easily and the scroll of paper slipped free. Picking it up, she glanced at the flower again. It was a strange bloom, definitely one she'd never seen before. Wondering if it had a scent, she leaned forward and sniffed. The perfume was faint, very light, and as delicate as the flower. It smelled wonderful. She breathed in deeper.

Warmth bloomed in her face and a flush of heat moved through her, going from her head to her toes and back again. Her skin tingled. She suddenly felt more alert, like she'd just had a double-shot of caffeine or a blast of pure oxygen.

She backed up, giving the strange flower a cautious look of respect. A light and delicate scent all right, but with a very potent kick. Judging from the slight buzz she felt, maybe even narcotic.

Just to be safe, she took another step back before unrolling the paper. Two thin sheets slipped between her fingers instead of one. Each sheet bore a different handwriting. One, a beautiful, old world script, looked very official, the lettering precisely printed. The other writing wandered boldly across the page, bearing the look of a masculine hand, strong and forceful. At least they were both in English instead of whatever language was on the ribbon.

She started reading the less formal of the two. One paragraph into the personal note she stopped, went back to the beginning, and started reading again. She finished the single page of writing and stood in her kitchen shaking her head in disbelief, no more enlightened as to who sent the flower than when she started. She'd traveled a lot with her father growing up, but as far as she knew she'd never met anyone named Tragar. Of course, that could probably be explained because she'd never been to...

She reread the sentence just to be sure. Yes, it said planet. A planet called Avalyr.

"Unbelievable," she muttered, shaking her head again at the nonsense. She didn't have time for this. She grabbed her camera and snapped a few pictures for Steven, then grabbed her things and headed for her car. She merged her Rav-4 into the morning traffic clogging I5 south of the city of Redding, still trying to figure out who might have left her the flower.

Maybe the guy living in the corner apartment one floor below her? Didn't he work at a comic shop, or something? She ran through the list of other people she knew in her building as she zoomed along the interstate, but couldn't come up with any other suspects. Just once, it would be nice to attract someone other than a first class nut. Someone who knew the difference between make-believe and reality, a down-to-earth man with a little dignity and polish. Was that too much to ask? Instead, she got some sci-fi geek with a "Warcraft" fetish who believed in aliens.

The possibility her admirer might be someone outside her building, someone she didn't know but who evidently knew her, worried her. She'd already had to deal with one unknown psycho stalking her. She didn't need another one.

She ran a hand along one arm straightening the long sleeve, feeling the raised scars beneath.

Yeah, once was definitely enough.

****

Devlin's allotted time on Earth neared its end and the mercenaries sent to deliver his first gift to his Starmate still had not returned. He'd spent the last few hours alternating between grinding his teeth and prowling like a restless animal in a cage. Like the tiger he was sometimes called.

"Here."

A hand appeared in front of him, forcing him to stop. It took him a moment to focus on the rectangle of paper held between two fingers. When he did, his breath caught. Captivating green eyes stared back at him from a small picture.

"I got the printer working," the Gate Watcher said. "Thought you might like to have a copy of your lady's DMV picture."

Devlin made himself raise his hand slowly instead of snatching the picture. A priceless gift, even if he had no idea what a DMV was. "My thanks," he said. Feeling slightly bemused, he stared at the image of Avera St. John. His prophecy bride. His Starmate. She smiled as if any moment she might break into a laugh. An answering smile

55

tugged at his lips. *She is beautiful.* He brushed a finger over the slick surface where dark hair framed her face. Someone chuckled.

"Damn, boy, it's only a driver's license photo." The Gate Watcher, an elderly man who'd introduced himself as Saunderson upon their arrival, bent forward, his head blocking Devlin's view. "Not a very good one either, if you ask me. Bet she's a lot prettier in person."

An insult couched in a compliment. The Gate Watcher had obviously missed his calling as a diplomat. Before Devlin could decide whether to be offended, Saunderson tipped his head back to look Devlin in the face. He no longer looked amused.

"You got half an hour left before the Gate opens."

"I am aware of the time," Devlin answered calmly. "Let us hope your mercenaries are aware of it also." He slipped the precious rectangle inside his shirt. The image was two years old according to information provided by the Gate Watcher's Seer, a machine called a computer. Devlin knew of the scientific devices, but hadn't been aware of their capabilities or of the wealth of information they could provide. It had taken only a moment to discern the location of his Starmate.

Whether an aspect of the prophecy or something related to Starmates, he'd felt an immediate and desperate need to go to her. To see her with his own eyes. To feel her actual flesh beneath his hands. Only then would she be real. The one thing keeping him from racing to her side was his promise to Talimina. He'd sworn an oath to abide by the Concourse rule requiring him to remain behind the barrier surrounding the Outer Gate. He would keep his word.

For now.

Sending a pair of human mercenaries,

Saunderson's son and grandson, to deliver his first gift to Avera was a poor alternative, but one he accepted. The sooner his courtship of her began, the sooner he would have her safely in his arms. He waited for their return, wanting confirmation their task was successfully completed. A desire he feared might go unfulfilled.

Saunderson lifted his head suddenly and tipped it to one side as if listening to something. Devlin did the same. His ears caught a faint thumping sound. Saunderson smiled. "That should be them now."

The flying machine called a helicopter landed in a field beside the house. Devlin watched through a window as the two mercenaries he'd met that morning climbed out and approached the house. Except for their hair and the difference in bulk on their similar frames, father and son favored each other remarkably.

"Your mission was successful?" he asked, as soon as the men entered the room.

Everett Saunderson swept the room with a sharp-eyed gaze before answering. "The package was delivered per your instructions." A seasoned warrior, Devlin liked the man immediately upon their first meeting, but the man's son, Jacob, was an arrogant youngster.

"Did she see you?"

"We're not amateurs," Jacob said quickly, his lip curling up in a sneer. "We don't need some alien freak telling us how to do our job."

Devlin raised a brow, but said nothing. He was not there to exchange insults with a young male barely into manhood. Ignoring the impertinence became impossible, however, when a growl rumbled at his shoulder—Fate showing his disapproval of the boy's disrespect. With the two Earth warriors standing almost within arms' reach, Devlin should have known his First Blade would be hovering nearby.

Jacob Saunderson, either lacking brains or having more courage than was good for him, narrowed his eyes at Fate, his wiry body shifting forward.

"You think you can take me? Come on, you alien bas—" The back of his father's hand slapped against his chest.

"That's enough, Jacob. We don't insult clients, and we don't pick fights with them either. Bad for business, son."

The young Saunderson straightened slowly, eyes still locked over Devlin's shoulder. Fate's aggression continued to roll off him in waves.

No eating the natives, Fate, he cautioned. *Not even tender young fools like this one.* The answering mental snort—Fate's version of an evil chuckle— almost made Devlin smile.

Everett pulled something from a pocket. "Here's your proof the lady got the package."

Devlin took the evidence. More pictures, he saw, each an image of a long hallway with two people at the far end, one male, the other female. He looked closer at the top picture, frustration making him grind his teeth as he realized the woman's face was turned, half-hidden by a curtain of hair as black as his own. Only a hint of cheek and the tip of a pert nose were visible. Then he glanced at the other person in the picture and frustration morphed into anger. The strange male held the adeseia flower Devlin had chosen as his first gift and appeared to be presenting the flower to *his* Starmate. His blood heated in a flash of possession.

"Who is this man?" he demanded, feeling his magic stir in response to his rising aggression. He did nothing to stop it. The powerful essence spilled quickly from his mind and rushed beneath his skin. His vision brightened as his eyes began to glow with power. He didn't try to hide the startling reaction. His glowing eyes had intimidated stronger opponents than these.

Both mercenaries took a step back. But while the father was content to eye Devlin warily, the son dropped his hand to the weapon strapped to his hip. Foolish child.

Tension in the room soared as five swords whipped out, three poised at the youngling's throat, two at the father's chest.

The eldest Saunderson sputtered from somewhere behind them. "Now see here—"

"No, it's all right, Pop," Everett Saunderson said, his voice as steady as his gaze. "We've just got a little communication problem is all. Isn't that right, Mr. Tragar?"

"Perhaps," Devlin agreed, noting the tension in the man's shoulders, the way his weight shifted forward to the balls of his feet even though doing so forced his chest against sword tips. Even without a weapon in his hand, the man appeared ready to fight for his life and that of his son despite the skewed odds. The last thing Devlin needed on this trip was bloodshed. A quick, mental command along five links pulled the swords back.

Everett tilted his head slightly in Devlin's direction. "The man's name is Steven Daniel. He and his *wife*," he stressed the word, "live in the apartment next to your woman. He left his apartment before Ms. St. John did. He had just picked up the flower and was looking at it when St. John opened her door. The next picture shows her holding the flower, and Daniel explaining how he found it. The third picture is of her taking it back inside her apartment along with your letter. If you look close enough, you'll see she's smiling."

Devlin examined the indicated picture and felt the tension in his shoulders ease. The man's succinct

59

explanation would have been enough, but the smile on the woman's face was even better. His sight returned to normal as he recalled his magic. Another mental command, and the swords returned to their sheaths, albeit reluctantly.

Saunderson the Eldest harrumphed. "Don't think I won't tell the Concourse about this. Damned fool tourists, always going off half-cocked. No wonder the Regents are so strict."

Devlin bowed humbly to the Gate Watcher, the diplomatic side of him once again in control. "Forgive me, Mr. Saunderson. I should not have allowed my guard to pull weapons in your home. The fault is entirely mine."

"Not entirely," Everett Saunderson disagreed. "Your boys were provoked by my son." He laid a heavy but affectionate hand on the boy's shoulder. "Jacob hasn't had enough experience when it comes to dealing with the unexpected but he's learning."

The younger man's face flushed. Devlin felt a sudden rush of sympathy for the youth. He'd embarrassed himself enough times to know what it felt like. He tipped his head to the father. "Thank you for these." He held up the pictures before tucking them safely away.

"No problem. You said you had more packages?"

"Yes, but I hope to be able to deliver them myself."

The man's lips twitched into a half smile. "Good luck with that. Like my Pop said, the Regents are damned strict when it comes to off-worlders wandering around on their own. Didn't used to be that way."

Curious, Devlin started to ask why, but the Gate Watcher interrupted. "Time's up," he called sharply from the doorway.

The words sent a shock of denial through Devlin. He didn't want to leave, not without *her*.

But, again, he wasn't given a choice. There was no way for him to reach his mate now. The limited access to Earth he'd been granted wasn't enough. Not only did he need to meet his bride in order for his plan to work, but being on the same planet yet forbidden to go to her was like an itch he couldn't scratch. The unfulfilled urge was bound to drive him crazy, and Avalyr already had one crazy Bloodsworn. It didn't need two.

Chapter Nine

Urged on by the querulous Gate Watcher, Devlin led his men back through the Outer Gate. Magic flowed over him as he stepped through the powerful gateway, sending a hum through his body and a teasing jolt to his mind. As soon as both his feet were planted in the familiar gate room of Moiwie City's Enclave, the essence of Avalyr surrounded him, brushing eagerly against his mind. He dropped his mental barriers, sighing in relief when the magic flooded in. Being out of touch with the living essence of his world was decidedly uncomfortable. A small taste, he thought grimly, of what his Blades must suffer.

"I hope your trip was successful?"

He looked toward the gate room door at the familiar voice. A large part of the tension in him easing as he sketched a bow of respect. "Luma."

The short, slender woman nodded her head once, her bow-shaped lips curving into a serene smile. "Hello, Devlin." She lifted a graceful hand and the world shimmered into change around him.

When things once again solidified, Devlin found himself in a cozy parlor. Flames crackled in the fireplace, warding off the chill from the snow falling outside the windows. A shiver ran down his spine, having nothing to do with the temperature of the room. Late spring warmed the hills and valleys surrounding Moiwie City. The closest snow lay thousands of miles away, as did the forests of fir trees he saw through the swirling flakes. Staring out the window he said, "Half a world away in the blink of an eye with not even a gate to get us here. You never cease to amaze me, Luma."

Her very feminine chuckle came from behind him and Devlin turned. She lounged in a chair, feet tucked under her like a child, a glass of blue Talla wine in her hand. "Good. I can't have my First Bloodsworn getting too complacent. Complacency leads to discontent, which leads to rebellion, which leads to all kinds of very unpleasant situations."

Though her lips were still smiling he had the feeling he'd just been reprimanded.

She nodded her head toward an empty chair, long, straight hair falling in rippling dark waves across her shoulder and arm. "Join me." An obvious command despite the warmth in her clear, hazel eyes.

He scanned the rest of the room as he moved to obey. His Blades were conspicuously absent.

As if answering his unspoken question she said, "I sent your warriors home. Fate won't be happy, but that's nothing unusual, is it? I swear the man gets grumpier every year."

She waited until he sat and had picked up his own wine from the table between them before taking a sip of hers. He copied her, taking the time to sort his thoughts and get his temper under control. Shouting at Luma was never a wise move.

"So quiet," she teased. "Don't you have a question or two for me? Or shall we make a game of it? I'll guess at your questions, and you can guess at my answers."

Despite his best intentions, he felt his control slip. His future, the future of his world, depended on her cooperation, and she wanted to play games?

Carefully, he sat his glass on the table before he shattered it in his hand. "I don't have the time or patience for games, my lady, as you are well aware."

She twirled the stem of her glass between her slim fingers, blue wine swirling up to the lip. "My, aren't we proper today. So I'm to be *my lady*, am I? Are you sure that's the way you want it?" Her dark brown eyes glinted, daring him to hold her at arm's length.

Devlin took a deep breath before answering. "No, you're right. We've always been friends, you and I, despite our stations."

"Or because of them," she said quickly. "I don't usually take notice of every Bloodsworn on the planet. Nor have I ever considered my First Bloodsworn my friend."

Not until you came along.

The unspoken statement hung between them. Devlin met the challenging gaze of Avalyr's Avatar with one of his own. Friend, she'd named him, though he wasn't sure she knew what the word meant. She was a being of immense power and mercurial moods who had lived for centuries.

As far as he knew, however, she'd never wielded her magic indiscriminately. Never once had she played goddess or demanded anything from the people of Avalyr. She held herself to a strict code of non-interference, leaving Avalyr's inhabitants alone to live their lives as they chose—except for those affected by the Prophecies.

"A friend doesn't blindside you with your worst nightmare then dangle your fondest dream just out of reach. You could have at least warned me. I asked you about the prophecy often enough."

"I couldn't."

"Luma—"

"No, Devlin, I couldn't. As powerful as I am, I don't control the Oracle." She sat back, a pout on her lips and a frown marring the perfection of her heart-shaped face. "I wish I did. I'd have fixed everything centuries ago."

"Fixed everything?"

She ignored his question and leaned forward, extending her hand. Devlin placed his in hers and felt magic simmering beneath her skin. Suppressing a shudder at the thought of how much magic she held, he gripped her small fingers tighter. Approval flashed into her eyes and she smiled, twin dimples appearing in her smooth cheeks. "If I had known your marriage was the object of the Seventh Prophecy I still wouldn't have told you. But," she said, holding up a finger, "I would have found some way to help you accept your destiny when the time came." She shrugged. "Lucky for you, I didn't need to. I'm not sure I would have thought of a Starmate."

"At least you would have had the sense not to send me off-world for my mate," he said in disgust.

She looked at him from beneath her lashes. "Perhaps, but can you honestly say that makes a difference? Mina told me you were extremely upset when Dom popped out in the middle of your request."

Devlin snorted. "Tane is a pompous ass. I don't know how you can stand him." He felt a subtle wash of magic ripple through the air coupled with the faint scent of evergreens as Luma's laughter filled the small room. Flames danced over the wood in the grate and snowflakes swirled against the glass panes.

"He says the same of you, you know," she said, still chuckling. "You should be honored. He never bothers teasing any of my other friends."

Devlin picked up his glass and sipped the fragrant wine. "I feel truly fortunate." He didn't hide the sarcasm. "You do know he is likely to withhold his approval for me to claim my Starmate simply out of spite."

"Doesn't matter." She waved a delicate hand in the air. "Mina and I have already talked to Cacherie and Trella. They've both agreed to grant you free access to Earth..." She paused and brought her thumb and forefinger together, almost touching. "With just a few little restrictions."

Devlin frowned. Something told him those little restrictions were going to cause him big problems.

Chapter Ten

Avera left work even more depressed than when she'd arrived. After two days spent purging months of work, she needed comfort food, she decided. A hot, deep-dish pizza from Luciano's would be just the thing. Nothing better than a little marinara sauce to sooth the soul.

The rich smell of the spicy sauce teased her nose all the way home, making her mouth water and her stomach growl. Balancing her large soft drink on top of the pizza box, she made it inside her apartment building with no problem. She hurried up the stairs and down the empty hallway to her apartment where she bent down slightly to stick her key in her lock. The box in her other hand tilted. She snatched at the cup to keep it from falling just as a voice behind her said, "Would you like some help?"

The words themselves held no threat, but the unfamiliar deep voice uttering them sent a shot of adrenaline into her veins. Memories crashed through her until all she could see was the hallway outside her old apartment. The hallway where her attacker had waited when she'd come home late one night, tired, not paying attention to her surroundings. Just like tonight.

Without thinking, without even turning around, she flung the pizza box and drink in the direction of the voice. The sound of splashing liquid accompanied a startled oath as her hand dove into the special compartment in her purse for her gun. She spun around, both hands holding the revolver steady.

"Back off," she warned. "I have a permit for this and I know how to use it."

Dark eyebrows rose over the bluest eyes she'd ever seen. Eyes that dipped down to the gun before quickly returning to her face. Their owner took one deliberate step back. Avera didn't relax. Whoever he was, he didn't look like the gun scared him. His expression was wary, not scared. Wary wasn't enough to keep an attacker at bay. Fear was.

With slow movements he shifted the half-open pizza box he held to one arm. Avera tightened her grip on her gun. Since his eyes were still locked with hers she didn't see how he could have noticed the tiny movement, but immediately he froze. Then, slowly, his free hand turned to show her an empty palm.

"I mean you no harm."

She knew it was stupid, but her gaze jumped to his lips. Full but not thick, smooth but not feminine. Masculine. Very masculine, very firm lips. She risked a quick glance over the rest of him before returning to glare into his eyes. Eyes gave away intent, heralded movement. They'd tell her if he was going to try anything.

He should have looked ridiculous with his shirt and pants soaked in cola and pizza sauce. He didn't. Even with slices of pepperoni decorating his shirt she detected no embarrassment at all in his striking blue eyes. No awkwardness, no anger, not the slightest hint of crazy stalker weirdness. A sliver of doubt wedged into her adrenaline-hyped brain. She didn't lower her gun though. She'd met almost every tenant in her new apartment building, knew all the ones on her floor by name. This guy was a stranger. She definitely would have remembered if she'd met him before.

"Who are you?" she demanded.

The man opened his mouth to speak at the same time the door to Steven and Claudia's apartment opened. Mr. Blue-eyes didn't turn his head at the sound and neither did Avera. She wasn't about to take her eyes off him.

"Avera?"

Steven's voice, full of concern. The slight squeak of his sneakers on the tiled floor told her he was hurrying toward them.

"Avera, honey, what's going on? Are you all right? Why are you pointing a gun at our new neighbor?"

New neighbor?

"My fault," the man said. "I believe I made the mistake of startling her."

His deep voice sounded less threatening now that she was looking at him, but her heart still hammered away, spurred on by his intense gaze. She had the wild notion that if he wanted to, he could see right inside her. The possibility terrified her. All the barriers she'd erected around her heart and soul to keep out her personal fears of loneliness and abandonment would crumble into dust under such penetrating examination. She needed those barriers. Now, more than ever. With her father gone, she had no one to lean on, no one to depend on but herself. She had to be strong to survive.

"Avera, it's okay, really," Steven said. "This is Devlin Kel. He moved into the empty apartment across the hall this afternoon."

Her already tight stomach clenched with a sick feeling. She hated making a fool of herself. Cheeks hot with embarrassment, she lowered her gun, glancing at Steven and giving him her best glare. He should have called her at work and warned her.

Steven smiled apologetically, shrugged a little,

and mouthed the word, "Sorry." Then he cleared his throat. "Yes, well, Devlin, may I present Avera St. John, head of our welcoming committee and sole member of our neighborhood watch. The bad guys don't stand a chance with her around."

Avera ground her teeth. She knew he was trying to make light of the situation for her sake, but did he have to make her sound like a one-woman army? Devlin Kel's voice drew her attention back to him.

"It is a pleasure to meet you, Miss St. John." His tone didn't carry a hint of censure. His blue eyes, however, looked pointedly at the gun in her hand before he added, "All things considered."

Her whole face burned with embarrassment. "I'm sorry. Like you said, you startled me. I don't do *startled* very well." She lowered her face as she tucked the weapon back in her purse. Okay, so she'd overreacted. She'd apologize, offer to have the man's clothes cleaned and hide inside her apartment for the next ten years. Could her day get any worse?

Steven wasn't helping matters. He leaned over the pizza box Devlin Kel still held and sniffed. "Was that a deep dish from Luciano's?"

She sighed. "Yeah." *Was* being the operative word.

He made a sympathetic noise. "Too bad."

She shrugged, trying not to show her disappointment. She'd been looking forward to that pizza. Irritation quickly replaced some of her embarrassment as she reached for the box. If Mr. Blue-eyes hadn't surprised her, she'd be teeth-deep in tomato sauce and melted cheese right now. So much for drowning her day's frustrations in comfort food.

"Look, Mr. Kel, I'm really very sorry about your clothes and, um, the gun. You can bring the clothes over after you've changed, and I'll be happy to have them cleaned. Or replaced," she added. That red sauce probably wasn't going to come out of his white shirt.

"Thank you," he said, bending down to pick up her empty drink cup. Her eyes followed his movement, and she noticed the puddle of ice-sprinkled cola surrounding his shoes. His very expensive-looking shoes. She winced inwardly, wondering if those would need to be replaced as well. His next words stopped her from offering. "But there's no need for you to feel obligated. My clothes are not important." He straightened and his eyes locked with hers again. "And as I said before, the fault is mine for startling you. My apologies. And please, call me Devlin." He held out the cup.

"That's...very gracious of you, Devlin, but I..." Her fingers, curling around the cup, brushed his.

For a moment, Avera couldn't speak, couldn't even breathe. Something—not a shock exactly, but definitely something, ran up her arm from her fingertips. Heat bloomed inside her. She began to shake and took a step back, suddenly afraid. Not of him, but of what she felt. She'd never reacted to a man's casual touch before, not like this. His eyes widened slightly, and his nostrils flared. Had he felt something, too?

Neither of them spoke. They might have stood there silently staring at each other for the rest of the night if Steven hadn't cleared his throat. Avera blinked and jerked her gaze away.

"Well, now that you two are on speaking terms," Steven said pointedly, "I'd better get back. Claudia will be wondering where I disappeared to. Oh, Avera, I almost forgot. Did you get those pictures I asked you about this morning?"

Grateful to have something else to focus on, Avera nodded. She'd already made a fool of herself once tonight. If she wasn't careful, she'd be doing it again. "Yes, I did. I'll send them to you in a few minutes."

"Great. Let me know when the flower starts to wilt, will you. There's no way of telling when it first opened, but it might help me identify it if I have some idea of its bloom time."

"All right," she said. She watched him retreat to his apartment and go inside before she turned back to Devlin Kel. She forced herself not to look at his eyes. Instead, she took in the rest of him, noting details this time. His hair was black, wavy, and a little longer than shoulder-length, the dark strands pulled back and tied neatly at his nape. His face was a cross between classically beautiful and ruggedly handsome, as if someone had taken a blueblood and a blue-collar and rolled them into one.

The habit of cataloging her observations in the lab had her creating a mental list of his features. High cheek bones, strong chin, and straight nose that wasn't too long or wide. She forced herself not to dwell too long on the lips. They were almost as dangerous as his eyes.

He was tall, at least a couple of inches over six feet. That pleased her, though she couldn't have said why at the moment, because her gaze wandered, reaching his chest, and her mind suddenly refused to work. The cola-soaked dress shirt plastered to his body left nothing to the imagination. She could see every curve and dip of every muscle, all the way down to his waist. His nipples stood out beneath the wet fabric like dark points of interest.

Avera took a deep breath, her attention snapping back to his face. Were his blue eyes darker? Maybe. Or maybe she was imagining things. It was late, she was tired, and crazier things had happened than a case of mistaken eye color.

There was no mistaking the slight smile of his lips, though. He knew she'd been looking him over and didn't seem bothered. In fact, she got the feeling he'd been checking her out, too. Her cheeks warmed again. She had to be crazy. The man might not be a stalker, but he was still dangerous in a delicious sort of way, even in his ruined clothes.

Delicious? Dangerous? He had her so confused she couldn't think straight. She needed to leave, needed to... The word *escape* popped into her head and she nearly laughed. Why would she need to escape? He disturbed her, yes, but he wasn't a threat. Feeling silly, she smiled and took a step toward her door.

"Well, I guess I better go toss this stuff and grab my mop. These old tiles can be lethal when they're wet. Be careful you don't slip."

He nodded. "I'll be careful."

"Sorry again, especially about pointing a gun at you. And of course," she said, dropping her attention back to his chest, "about your clothes."

"They are only clothes."

Yeah, just clothes. Very wet, very revealing clothes. She stared at the wet shirt one last time, then glanced lower. When she got to the front of his wet slacks she jerked her gaze away. Getting caught admiring his chest was one thing. No matter how tempted, she wasn't about to get caught admiring anything else. She got her door open with one foot across the threshold, before he spoke again.

"Avera St. John..."

"Yes?" With an inward groan she turned back to him. Determined not to ogle him again she kept her eyes focused on his. Maybe not the wisest thing she'd ever done, considering she felt the impact of his intense interest far more than she liked. Was he trying to intimidate her?

"I will see you again."

She suppressed a shiver. Not, "Will I see you again?" but "I *will* see you again." It sounded more like a warning than a statement. Like he'd be watching out for her. He probably didn't want to get buried under mozzarella and tomato sauce, then drenched in cold, sticky cola again, she decided.

Relieved to have an explanation for his intense stare, she smiled. "Yes, I imagine we'll run into each other from time to time since we share the same hallway. Don't worry though, I promise not to throw my dinner at you next time."

His lips twitched and when he took a step back his foot slid out from under him. Luckily, he was close enough to the wall to catch himself easily. He scowled down at the floor and Avera swallowed the giggle bubbling up. She'd done enough to the man for one night and didn't want to embarrass him any further. Without another word she slipped inside her apartment and closed the door.

She leaned against the cool wood and closed her eyes, reliving the whole awkward scene. A small groan slipped past her lips as she finally pushed herself upright and moved into her kitchen. The hottest neighbor she'd ever had, and he probably thought she was crazy. She tossed the pizza box on the table, the cup in the trash, and went in search of her mop and bucket.

When she stepped back into the hall she stopped, confused. She squatted down and eyed the smooth surface from several angles. Not a drop of liquid to be seen. The tiles weren't just clean, they were completely dry.

Frowning, she stood, looking up and down the hall before settling her gaze on the door across from her. Had Devlin Kel cleaned up her mess? If so, he had to be the fastest mopper in the west. Either that or she'd been day dreaming longer than she thought.

She shrugged and headed back inside her apartment. It was very nice of him to clean up her spill. Maybe she'd get another deep dish pizza tomorrow and invite him over for dinner. A welcome-to-the-building type of thing. A little food, a nice neighbor-to-neighbor chat. Nothing personal at all.

Yeah, right. Who was she kidding?

****

Devlin pressed his eye to the convenient spy hole in the door and watched Avera St. John re-enter her rooms.

He'd waited until she'd gone inside the first time before tapping into his very limited supply of magic to clean the slippery tiles. Then he'd waited again on the other side of his door for her to come back out, just to get another look at her.

She was beautiful. Young and beautiful and full of fire. And humor. The thought of the smile on her lips and laughter in her eyes when she'd promised not to soak him again made him grin.

"Do you know you're dripping on the floor?"

Karess' innocently asked question held a wealth of suppressed laughter. Devlin glanced down at himself and grimaced. He'd been so distracted by his first meeting with his Starmate he'd completely forgotten to take care of his clothing when he'd cleaned the floor. He checked his store of magic and decided he had enough to freshen his clothes and remove the small puddle forming around his feet. Any more, though, and he'd risk stranding himself and his Blades miles away from the nearest Outer Gate. Not a pleasant prospect.

One of the Concourse's little restrictions limited his store of magic when on Earth. The small amount they allowed guaranteed both his movements and his actions were kept circumspect. There'd be no indiscriminate opening of gates in public places. No flashy use of magic. Not that he would have done either, he thought in disgust. Trying to impress his mate with something she wasn't prepared to accept was not in his plans.

His clothes cleaned and dried, he turned,

meeting the amused gazes of the five large warriors spread around the room. Sarreth, his Fifth Blade, reached out and punched Karess in the arm. "I told you he didn't realize he was soaked."

Karess chuckled. "I would say he has a good excuse. Not many men have their promised bride attack them on their first meeting."

"Or with such weapons," Strum added, leaning forward and making a show of sniffing. "I can still smell the lethal combination of tomatoes and onions. Can't you, Kiel?" He nudged the young novice Blade, Kiel Na-Turesh, sitting next to him.

Kiel nodded solemnly. "Mmm, yes, and garlic, don't forget the garlic."

Barely twenty summers, Kiel had come to Devlin a year ago, already skilled enough in sword work to shadow his mentor, Strum, on assignments. The last few months had honed the young warrior's skill even more, and apparently his wit as well.

Devlin kept his expression neutral while he called forth the merest wisp of magic. Four plump pillows answered his summons, zipping off the furniture. Three smacked into the heads of Sarreth, Strum, and Karess. Kiel dodged the pillow aimed at him, tipping over the chair he was sitting in, and rolling back to his feet in a cat-like move. Devlin turned his missile in mid-air and sent it after him again. The young warrior grinned, accepting the challenge. He managed to dodge four more passes in quick succession, leaping over furniture and ducking behind his blade-brothers who called out encouragement.

"Look out, Kiel."

"Damn, the kid's fast."

"Duck behind Fate. Devlin won't risk hitting him."

"Right," Kiel said, diving behind a sofa and rolling to his feet in one fluid move. "And if that pillow does manage to hit our Captain, who do you think he's going to blame?"

Devlin shot a glance at Fate and on impulse, sent the pillow in a wide arc close enough to his First Blade that the breeze of its passing stirred the man's hair. The stoic warrior never flinched, but his gaze slid to Devlin, the warning easy to read in his dark eyes. Devlin grinned back. As much as he was enjoying himself, he could feel the wisp of magic he'd called nearing its end. He used the last of the capricious essence to end the game, sending his weapon flying almost faster than the eye could follow. The light green pillow smacked Kiel in the back of the head. Too hard, he realized an instant later as a sudden blizzard of white feathers shot into the air. Karess and the others burst into howls of laughter. He could have resisted joining in if not for the look of disgust on Fate's face as he began plucking stray feathers from his clothing. Amusement avalanched into full belly laughter— something he hadn't done in a very long while.

Devlin's first meeting with his Starmate had not gone as planned—one could hardly expect to impress a female when covered in food and drink. But he'd seen her. Spoken to her. Touched her. He'd felt the connection between them flare to life at that brief brush of fingers and from her reaction, she'd felt it, too. She could have no way of knowing what the strange feeling was that rushed through her body, but he'd sensed her awareness—shared it. The awakening of Starmates to one another's existence. A good beginning to his courtship.

He welcomed the lighter mood flooding his soul with a sense of relief. Having gotten past his first meeting with his Starmate he could afford to relax a bit.

His laughter trailed off to a rusty chuckle. Only one thing marred the joy of their first meeting. The memory of the gun in her hand. He knew about the weapons of this world from his recent studies, knew the kind of injury a gun was capable of inflicting. The dangerous metal object in his mate's small hand had filled him with fear. Not fear for himself—his magic would have jumped to his protection if needed—but for her. He knew of several instances where the backlash of violence actually killed the female placed in such a situation. And in those cases, death had been considered a blessing. The thought of Avera St. John pulling the trigger of her gun and shooting someone, either on purpose or by accident, made him sick with worry.

Perhaps he needed to revise his plan to woo his mate slowly. The longer she was left on Earth without his protection, the greater the chance for something to go wrong.

Chapter Eleven

"This is getting to be a habit," Avera muttered, reaching for her doorknob. Just like yesterday, she was running late, and, just like yesterday, she came to a stumbling halt when she snatched her door open. One glance at the couple standing in the hall and she groaned. "Not again."

"Sorry, Vee," Steven said, handing her a rolled up piece of paper tied with an orange ribbon this time. His grin said he wasn't sorry at all, just amused at her expense. What a good friend.

His wife, Claudia, gave Avera a wide, teasing smile. "Oh, come on, Avera, don't you think this is romantic? Look at the detail. Someone went to a lot of trouble here." Claudia held up the dark green bowl she held in two hands.

Steven snorted. "Trouble nothing, it's a dish garden, love. He probably bought it off eBay."

"So what if he did," Claudia said. "Something like this doesn't go for peanuts, even on eBay. I swear, the glass bowl alone is worth fifty bucks, easy. Look at the color. It reminds me of an emerald." She held the dish garden up. The smooth, dark green surface of the bowl glinted, catching the subdued overhead light and bouncing it back like a magnifier.

"Yeah, pretty fancy," Avera admitted. "Especially for your average dish garden."

"Average?"

The note in Claudia's voice almost made Avera cringe. She'd forgotten how touchy her friend was when it came to plants. From the look on her face you'd think she'd just been insulted. "Have you really looked at this, Avera? Here, take a good look and tell me again if you think this is just some run-of-the-mill dish garden."

Avera had to take a step back to keep from getting a face full of plants. Frowning, she placed a couple of fingers against the bowl and pushed back a little intending to give it a quick look before saying something suitably soothing. One glance told her a quick look wasn't going to be enough.

Man, this guy must really want to impress her.

A palm-sized pond of actual water sat in the middle of the dish. Around the pond lay a border of gray pebbles and sand interspersed with wire thin plants that looked like water rushes. Tiny round things floated on the water's surface. Lily pads? How could they be so small?

Claudia shifted impatiently. Her movement caused the water to ripple. The lily pads jiggled in place and the feathery tops of the water rushes swayed. Despite herself, Avera felt a delighted smile tug at her lips.

More vegetation sprouted further back from the pond. Grasses. Bushes. Trees. One could easily imagine birds flitting through the branches.

Diminutive spots of color were scattered through the green landscape like candy sprinkles on a cake. Bending closer, Avera could see that some of the colorful spots were tiny flowers while others were petite orange and red pearls nestled among the sheltering green. She tapped an orange *fruit* with the tip of a finger. "These can't be real. Nothing grows this small."

Steven shrugged. "We didn't think so at first,

either, but they're doing a lot with bonsai's nowadays. If you want to know for sure, we could pull one of these out to see if it has a root system." He reached toward the miniature garden.

"Wait..." Her hand came up to stop him but Claudia was faster.

"Steven Daniel, don't you dare!" She moved the dish out of his reach and Avera felt herself relax.

She didn't plan on keeping this gift any more than she did the flower, but didn't want it damaged either. She glanced at her watch. "Look, I'm running late. Could you guys just put everything on the kitchen table and lock up for me, please?" She shoved the rolled letter back at Steven.

"Sure, Vee. Claudia wanted to see your flower anyway. Has it wilted yet?"

"Nope, still pretty as a picture." She waved and headed down the hall.

****

The day passed too slowly. Avera and Dutch spent the day calibrating every machine in the lab in preparation for their next project. The routine work left her mind plenty of time to wander and it frequently wandered to the memory of Devlin Kel. Twice she caught herself fanning the heat from her face after dwelling too long on those sinful lips of his, wondering how they would feel against her skin.

The phone in her office rang.

She left the liquid analyzer she was working on and hurried to her desk. Picking up the receiver, she said, "R&D."

"Hey, Vee."

She recognized Steven's voice immediately. "Hi Steven, what's up?"

"Just wanted to make sure you didn't forget about Claudia's birthday party tonight."

Avera slapped a hand to her forehead. She *had* forgotten. So much for her tentative plans to be neighborly.

"Don't worry, Steven, I'll be there." She recalled promising to help with the food and added, "Did you need me to pick up anything?"

"No, I've got it covered, thanks. Sorry to bother you at work, but you know me, I'm always double checking things." His apologetic tone shifted to one of light teasing. "Uh, by the way, I invited our new neighbor to the party so he can meet some of the other tenants. Thought I should give you a heads up so you don't, you know, get startled again. Don't think Devlin would look any better in green cake frosting than he did in red pizza sauce."

"Very funny," she said, ignoring his chuckle along with the funny feeling in the pit of her stomach. Guess she'd be seeing Devlin Kel tonight after all. "If you don't cut out the teasing, I'm not going to let you visit my flower," she warned.

He cleared his throat. "Yes, ma'am," he said smartly, a salute in his voice this time. She heard him chuckle again before he hung up.

****

Helping with the food at the party turned out to be a good thing. It kept her busy, smiling and talking to the guests as she refilled the buffet table. Too busy to check the door every time it opened. Well, most of the time, anyway. She wasn't always able to resist temptation.

She was in the middle of slipping a fresh platter of cocktail shrimp between the cheese tray and Swedish meatballs, when she heard the door open and glanced up. The sight of Devlin Kel standing in the open doorway, shaking hands with Steven, sent a funny feeling zinging through her. Dressed in dark pants, dark, long-sleeved shirt, his long hair tied back neatly, he looked even better than he had last night.

What would he look like with all that black hair

82

hanging loose around his shoulders, she wondered. Probably like a barbarian prince. She'd seen a couple of those in her travels with her father. Macho men, totally sure of themselves and their place in the world. Men capable of bringing small countries and swooning women to their knees...

"Hey, look out!"

Avera jerked her attention back to what she was doing, dismayed to find the full shrimp platter tilting off her hand. She tried to catch it by shoving her hand further underneath the tray. The sharp move only succeeded in bumping the edge of the platter harder against the table. Pink shrimp cascaded off in a wave and tumbled across the spring-green tablecloth. Some landed in a bowl of nuts, others slipped completely off the table and onto the floor.

"Sorry, sorry," she mumbled to no one in particular. Her face burned and she knew it had to be as pink as the shrimp. She didn't look over at the door as she gathered the wayward seafood.

Claudia appeared on the other side of the table. "Don't worry about it. Stephen always buys too many." Her voice was full of humor as she bent down to gather up whatever shrimp made it to the floor. "He'd eat shrimp every day if I let him. And when I call him on it, he gets mad. I keep telling him he's going to turn into one, one of these days."

Her friend's banter made Avera feel a little less self-conscious as she scooped up headless crustaceans wondering if Devlin Kel saw her tossing the shrimp around. He'd think she was a total klutz. Well, at least she hadn't pulled her gun and waved it at anyone this time.

"Yo, Claudia, you got a present here, babe."

Claudia's head popped up at Stephen's call. Her eyes widened. Avera thought it was in anticipation of another gift, but when her friend stood and leaned over the table toward Avera, she plopped a handful of shrimp on the platter and whispered, "Don't look now, but your knight in shining pizza sauce is here." With a wink, she wiped her hands on a napkin.

"He's not mine," Avera hissed.

"Maybe not, but he's looking at you right now like you were the one drenched in tomato sauce and he hadn't eaten in days."

Not fair. Avera couldn't stop herself from looking in the direction of the door again. Thankfully, Claudia was only partly right. Devlin Kel *was* staring at her. His blue eyes met her curious gaze with a look that reminded her more of a Cheshire cat than hungry man. She dropped her eyes quickly.

"Don't worry," Claudia said, leaning over the table. "My little geek husband did a background check on him. Steven says the man's a saint, not even a parking ticket to his name. And he's single." Her eyebrows waggled meaningfully.

Avera groaned quietly. "Claudia, please don't get any ideas, okay?"

She snuck a glance at the door again to make sure the object of their conversation was still far enough away not to overhear. Devlin Kel looked her way at the same time, and his eyes immediately locked with hers. The expression in them changed. He was suddenly looking far too pleased about something.

Infuriating man. Who cared what went on behind those lovely blue eyes of his? Certainly not her.

Just to show him how little she cared, she casually picked up a peeled shrimp and dipped it into some cocktail sauce. Placing it in her mouth she bit down to separate the meat from the tail. When she glanced back at Devlin, she almost choked on the spicy sauce. That cool Cheshire cat look was gone. If she didn't know better, she'd say the man looked absolutely ravenous.

A shaft of...something, shot through her and it felt like the temperature in the room jumped up several degrees. Then thankfully Claudia walked up to claim Devlin's attention. As soon as he looked away Avera grabbed the shrimp trays and made her escape to the kitchen, lecturing herself all the while to calm down. So what if Devlin Kel had just looked at her like she was his next meal. Damn it, the man was barely an acquaintance. He shouldn't be drooling over her, and she certainly had no business drooling over him.

If only he didn't look so delicious.

The kitchen turned out to be the last place she should have gone.

"I've got a vase for these somewhere." Claudia's voice was partially muffled as she entered the room with Devlin, her face buried in a bouquet of fresh flowers.

"I'm glad you like them."

"Are you kidding? I love freesia. There must be at least half a dozen varieties in this bunch. Where on earth did you find a local florist who carried freesia? Look, Avera, aren't these gorgeous?"

Standing at the sink where she was rinsing the empty platters, Avera glanced over her shoulder, determined to keep her gaze on the flowers. It shouldn't be that hard. The bouquet was a beautiful mixture of several different species, with clusters of fragrant freesia blooms dominating the assortment. "Wow, those are beautiful," she agreed.

Don't look at him, don't look at him.

Her traitorous eyes ignored her and shifted of their own accord. It was almost as if he'd been waiting for her to look at him. His smile transformed right before her eyes, changing from coolly polite to warmly pleased, as if just seeing her brought him pleasure. She flashed him a quick, hopefully generic, smile in return and went back to scrubbing platters. It was the hot water making her face warm, not his eyes, and certainly not the thought of his lips.

"The flowers aren't from a florist," she heard him inform Claudia in that deep voice of his. "I happen to know someone with a greenhouse. Here, why don't you let me take care of these for you? I'm sure your guests would appreciate your presence."

Say no, Claudia, say no.

"Why, thank you, Devlin. I have to say, it's a pleasure to have another gentleman in the building."

Avera groaned silently. The last thing she needed was to be alone with Devlin Kel. She might do something really out of character, like imagine him as that barbarian prince again. God, she so had to get her mind out of the fairy-tale-gutter and back in the real world.

"...Isn't it, Avera?"

"What? Oh, *gentleman*, yes. Yes, I suppose it is."

Claudia laughed. "Don't take Avera's distraction personally, Devlin. It didn't take Stephen and me long to realize her mind is usually somewhere off plotting formulas and dissecting exotic chemical compounds. I'm surprised she tears herself away from that lab of hers much less finds her way home at night."

She was used to Claudia's gentle teasing, but for some reason her words tonight bothered Avera more than they should have. She hid her reaction behind an accusing smile as she reached up and tapped the thick leaf of an orchid plant hanging over the sink. "Right, like you don't have your own obsessions. Don't let this sparkling façade of hers fool you, Mr. Kel. Given a choice, our Claudia would much rather be researching hybrids and planning her next cross-pollination."

Claudia laughed again. "You are so right. But

since it's my party, I better go back out and do some more *sparkling*." Her friend's warm arms wrapped around Avera and a swift kiss hit her cheek. "Don't work too hard, girlfriend. I still haven't introduced you to Dave and he's dying to meet you."

Oh, joy, another blind date. "Right. Did you warn him about my disability?" From the corner of her eye she noticed Devlin pause in the act of unwrapping the florist paper from the flowers, and wished she'd bitten her tongue.

A finger shook in her face, its perfectly polished nail a strange contrast to the pad stained by hours of digging in potting soil. "Don't you dare start. I've told you, your intelligence isn't a disability. You just haven't met the right guy yet. Dave graduated from MIT. You and he should have loads in common, even if his field is robotics instead of chemistry."

"Uh-huh." Avera wasn't nearly as optimistic.

Claudia shook her head. "Drag her out with you when you come, won't you Devlin? I hear Stephen calling me again. He's probably wondering what happened to the shrimp. I'd better take out the other tray." She snagged the full platter from the fridge, balanced it on her hand like a pro, and disappeared through the door.

The kitchen suddenly felt much smaller.

Chapter Twelve

Avera couldn't keep from glancing around, checking on Devlin. He stood right behind her, waiting patiently. She shifted to the side as soon as she rinsed the last platter. "All yours."

"Yes," he said, his voice giving the word a lot more weight than it should have. "Thank you." She stepped back and leaned against the counter, drying her hands on a towel as she watched him fill the vase. When he unwrapped the bouquet she expected him to just stuff the flowers in like most men would have. Instead, he leaned toward her, reaching for the dishes drying in the rack beside the sink.

She should have moved out of his way, but for the life of her she couldn't seem to make her muscles obey. He leaned closer, eyes locked on her face, until his arm brushed her shoulder. It was a good thing she was holding onto the counter. The nice, strong, marble counter made of fine-grained metamorphosed rocks chemically composed of calcite, dolomite, lime, silica...

"Who is Dave?"

It took her a moment to pull her thoughts together. "I'm sorry, who?"

He leaned away, taking a knife from the rack with him. "The man Claudia said is dying to meet you."

Was it her imagination again or did he just put

an emphasis on the word dying?

"Oh, him. That would be her cousin." She shook her head and gave him a solemn look. "I should probably warn you, Mr. Kel—"

"Devlin, remember?"

"Right, sorry, I forgot. You can call me Avera, by the way. Don't think we got that far in the introductions last night." She hoped he didn't remember how tongue-tied she'd been. She wasn't usually so inarticulate.

Deep blue eyes glanced at her from beneath thick lashes. "It will be my pleasure, Avera."

She ignored the husky way he said her name and cleared her throat. "So, as I was saying, Claudia and Stephen are great as friends go, but they have one little annoying idiosyncrasy. They assume anyone who's single is miserable."

His lips twitched into a smile. "An assumption no doubt based on the happiness they have found in each other, wouldn't you say? After all, discovering and winning one's perfect mate is said to be the ultimate joy."

She laughed until she realized he wasn't smiling any more. Did he really believe what he'd just said? "Sorry, but that sounded exactly like something Claudia would say. Are you sure you only met her yesterday?"

"You don't believe happiness can be found in marriage?" Damn if he didn't sound as if the possibility offended him. Looked like it, too, judging by the frown pulling his brows together.

She crossed her arms and shrugged. "Do you?" she countered.

His nod came quick and emphatic. "If the marriage is between two people who are both willing to commit themselves to one another without reservation, yes."

"That's a very clinical way of looking at it." And

89

very male. The men she knew were notorious for sidestepping the emotional issue in everything leaving her to hypothesize that all men were that way.

Devlin wielded the knife, carefully cutting off about a half inch from the end of each stem before placing it in the vase. He paused and looked at her, his head tilting slightly to one side as if studying her. "Ah, I see my error."

She just bet he did.

"I neglected to mention that said commitment includes one of the heart as well as the mind." He went back to cutting. "I would guess Stephen and Claudia might say the same if asked."

Was he talking about love? How shocking. So maybe all the men she knew weren't a typical representation of their gender. Either that, or Devlin Kel was one of those rare scientific anomalies, a man not afraid of the L-word. She shrugged off the fanciful notion.

"They might. It would certainly explain why they made me their pet project the moment they found out I was sans significant other. Their new mission in life appears to be finding me a husband. I think Dave's the fourth, no, the fifth guy they've tried to fix me up with."

"You should tell them you're not interested," he said, his forehead furrowed in a tight frown. She put his expression down to intense concentration since he was brandishing that knife pretty fast. Any minute she expected to see blood spurt.

"I could, but I don't want to hurt their feelings. They're good people. Besides, one blind date isn't going to kill me." It wasn't like any of them ever bothered with a second date. She ignored how pitiful that sounded and watched Devlin cutting and arranging the flowers in the vase. He appeared to treat each stem as if it was a piece of a puzzle he was putting together. She found the process fascinating, both for the sake of the process itself and for the fact he looked like he knew exactly what he was doing. Where did a man who wasn't a florist learn to arrange flowers?

"If this Dave invites you to dine with him, you could tell him you already have plans."

The laugh that bubbled up caught her off guard. "You think I should lie?"

"Of course not," he said. He picked up the finished arrangement and held it out to her, his face solemn. Bemused, she took the vase without thinking. When he released his grip, the tips of his fingers brushed up and over the back of her hands. Her fingers tightened spasmodically against the smooth glass as her breath caught. His lips twitched into another Cheshire cat smile. "How could it be a lie if you have already accepted an invitation from me?"

"But...I haven't...you haven't..." God help her, she was actually stuttering.

He took a step back and swept her an elegant bow. "Miss St. John, would you do me the honor of accepting my invitation to dinner, the time to be determined at your discretion?"

It took her only a moment to process his wording. She smiled in appreciation. "What are you, a lawyer? That's positively devious. And I'm not at all sure it's ethical."

He chuckled. "I assure you, it's perfectly acceptable. I have it on the highest authority."

"Oh, yeah, and whose authority would that be?"

He took the vase from her in one hand and held his other arm out to her just like some gallant from an old movie. "Mine, of course." His smile was warm, inviting, with a touch of mystery. Avera liked mysteries. Or rather, she liked to solve mysteries.

Like an unknown compound, a mystery

presented a challenge to her scientific mind, one she couldn't resist. She would filter it, poke it, prod it, and analyze it until she'd learned all its secrets.

Slipping her hand through his arm, she wondered what it would be like to discover all the secrets behind Devlin Kel's smile.

Chapter Thirteen

Lights cut through the darkness, flashing across the back of the apartment building. The blinding glare slid over several innocent looking bushes before zeroing in on a patch of bare wall. The vehicle stopped. The engine's roar died. One of the doors opened and a female emerged.

The two men hidden behind the bushes studied her black hair and pale features only for a moment before turning to one another and nodding in agreement. Sarreth Te-Allian sent the message to his Bloodsworn through their mental link.

She has arrived, my lord.

In the apartment upstairs, Devlin breathed a sigh of relief at Sarreth's report. Not being able to keep watch over his mate during the day was bad enough. If he'd had to leave Earth without knowing she was safe inside her home... Well, suffice to say, he was extremely glad he would not have to find out how he would handle such a situation.

Wooing Avera was turning out to be a kind of slow torture. Especially when he wasn't allowed to watch over her like he wanted to. Damn the Concourse and its time restrictions.

Thank you, Sarreth. Watch over her well, my Blades. He included Kiel in the mental message since the young warrior would be staying behind with Sarreth. *I leave her in your care.* But not before he saw her once more with his own eyes, he vowed. He moved to the door with its convenient if thoroughly inadequate spy hole.

"Is she here?" Strum said, an unaccustomed edge of anxiety in his voice.

Relief flowing through him, Devlin could afford to tease his Third Blade a bit. "Still worried about leaving Kiel behind, old friend? You know I had no choice but to accept his offer to stay." It had taken Kiel, not yet a full-fledged Blade, to hit upon the idea of two men remaining behind when he was forced to return to Avalyr. Blades wielded no magic, and as long as they kept their presence circumspect the Concourse had no problem with the arrangement. Leaving his trusted warriors to patrol around the building in which Avera slept gave him some small measure of peace. Maybe it would even be enough for him to get through the rest of this wooing without losing his mind.

Strum grunted. "I still say he's too young to be left on some strange planet. He doesn't have enough experience."

Karess laughed. "Don't let Kiel hear you say that. Not even you would be safe from his challenge."

"I'm his mentor, he knows better than to challenge me."

"Your days of hovering over him like a mother hen are fast coming to an end. Kiel is close to taking his place in our Bloodsworn's Outer Decca," Karess pointed out, grinning. "He won't appreciate you still worrying over him any more than I would."

"I wouldn't waste my time worrying over you, Karess. You're too pretty with that pale hair of yours for anyone to mistake you for a threat."

Karess' grin vanished.

"Peace, my Blades," Devlin murmured, before pressing his eye to the spy hole. "No need to worry about your young protégé, Strum. I have full confidence in his abilities. He and Sarreth will be fine."

Just as Avera came into view, Devlin felt an uncomfortable push against his mind, a reminder, courtesy of the Outer Gate magic, that he needed to return. He swore softly and ignored the unpleasant sensation. It wasn't yet painful, but soon would be. The precious time allowed him on Earth had been wasted this day in futile waiting. Avera had not arrived home at the expected time. Devlin had grown positively frantic as the minutes dragged by with no sign of her. He'd been on the verge of using forbidden magic to search for her when his pragmatic First Blade had suggested he ask Steven and Claudia if they knew of Avera's whereabouts.

"Oh, she's probably just working over." Steven had informed him after answering Devlin's insistent knock on his door, clearly unconcerned. "Sometimes she gets caught up on one of her lab projects and doesn't get home until pretty late."

"I have her number if you want to call her," Claudia offered, her face a picture of studied innocence.

Devlin had thanked her and taken the series of numbers because it seemed expected of him. He'd returned to his rooms, feeling somewhat calmer though no less frustrated. The wait for his Starmate to appear had seemed interminable.

Tonight, he would have to settle for a brief, stolen glimpse of his lady mate. Tomorrow, he would prepare a better plan.

Avera moved slowly up the hall, fatigue apparent in her every step. Despite her visible weariness, he saw her scan the empty hallway several times, one hand tucked into a pocket of her shoulder bag. No doubt she clutched that weapon of hers, Devlin thought, teeth grinding in frustration. She shouldn't have to live in fear. Not when he could keep her safe.

The urge to go to her, comfort her, almost overwhelmed him. He had to make an effort to hold himself in place. He had no time left to offer her this night.

She paused outside her rooms, her gaze resting on his door. For a moment, it was as if she was staring right at him. Did she know he was watching her? Could she feel the weight of his gaze?

He held his breath as her wary expression shifted to one of thoughtful curiosity. White teeth caught her full bottom lip in a nibbling bite. His body reacted with a physical tightening and the urge to fling open the door, or worse, make it disappear entirely with a burst of magic.

He watched, spellbound, while curiosity turned to wistfulness a moment before she turned away. Warm satisfaction shot through him, making him smile.

First, awareness.

Second, desire.

Even if she didn't yet know exactly what, or rather who it was she wanted.

Chapter Fourteen

Avera leaned against her kitchen counter, sipping her morning coffee while she contemplated her *four* strange gifts.

The green flower, the miniature dish garden, the gift she'd received yesterday...

She hadn't quite decided if yesterday's gift was vegetable or mineral. While the purplish-green stem and rose-colored flowers looked and felt like they were made of glass, the vase contained water. The flowers even carried a light fragrance, though, thankfully one not nearly as potent as the green exotic she'd received first.

And the fourth gift?

She sighed.

Getting up two hours earlier than usual hadn't helped her catch her secret admirer. When she'd opened her door, there they were, gift and scroll number four.

She'd thought seriously about leaving the strange thing in the hall knowing Steven or Claudia would pick it up and keep it for her until she got home. She'd finally given in and brought the foot high sculpture—definitely mineral this time—inside, and set it on the counter next to the others. Just a fantastic piece of worked glass she'd thought at first. One hot shower and half a cup of coffee later, she wasn't so sure. Leaning closer, she could see tiny prisms flashing off the uneven surface, their internal structure easily discernible. Crystals? Surely not. It would take decades to get crystals to grow like this.

Two thick strands, one a bright green, the other cerulean blue, grew out of an almost black base. The strands twisted sinuously around one another like a pair of snakes. Near the top, somehow embedded in the twining crystal strands, was a creamy sphere the size of a large apple. The whole thing managed to look strong and fragile all at the same time.

She bent down to peer into the sphere. It wasn't solid, that much was apparent. Something swirled inside, the movement lazy and slow. Fluid or smoke? She couldn't tell. Coupled with the unanswered questions generated by the other gifts, she was beginning to get aggravated with her little WarCraft nerd. She didn't like unanswered questions and the four intriguing little enigmas seemed designed to drive her to distraction. If she didn't find their owner soon, she wasn't going to be able to resist trying to figure out some of the answers.

She propped an elbow on the counter, rested her chin in her hand, and sighed in frustration.

As soon as her warm breath washed over the cool glass sculpture, the sphere began to glow.

Avera jerked back.

The light grew stronger until it steadied at a comfortable reading level. After a long, wary minute, in which nothing else strange happened, Avera leaned forward, pursed her lips, and blew out another short puff of air. The swirling light dimmed to a faint glow. She blew again, and the light winked out entirely.

"Huh," she said, smiling and reaching for her coffee cup. She took a warm sip and then leaned over and blew on the sphere again. The dark cream swirl inside the sphere blazed to life. If she hadn't seen those fake candles last Christmas that came on and switched off by blowing on them, she might have been a little more impressed.

After blowing out the fancy nightlight, she moved to the bedroom to get dressed without her usual enthusiasm for her job. Not only did they *not* have a new project set up yet, but the spot inventory check Morrison had ordered yesterday dragged on. Today promised to be a repeat of yesterday—long and boring.

At least she had something to think about while cataloging chemicals all day. Something besides her secret admirer.

Her date on Friday.

Excitement stirred inside her at the memory of Devlin's conspiratorial wink when she'd looked at him after turning down Claudia's cousin. Dave hadn't been easy to turn down either. A man who didn't seem to mind a woman admitting she knew nothing about sports was a rare beast. Last week, she would have accepted Dave's invitation to dinner without a second thought. This week?

All she could think about was the charming man she'd only met twice, yet whose image she couldn't get out of her head. One day and she already missed seeing Devlin's indigo eyes and mischievous smile. How high school was that?

****

Avera called up several memories of Devlin during the long day, welcoming every little breathless rush, every tingle of anticipation. She couldn't wait till Friday to see him again. Maybe she'd knock on his door and invite him over for that welcome-neighbor dinner when she got home.

Unfortunately, the inventory Morrison had ordered didn't cooperate with her plans. Even without stopping to pick up something to eat on the way home, the clock in her car read after midnight when she finally pulled into her apartment building's parking lot.

"Stupid inventory," she grumbled, slamming the gearshift into park. She got out and slammed the door for good measure. The loud sound echoed in the quiet darkness, setting off two dogs somewhere down the block. Their barks punctuated the night and made Avera wish she could bark back without looking like a complete idiot.

Her plan to invite Devlin over was, again, completely ruined. Luciano's closed at ten on weekdays. A microwaved frozen dinner might be okay for her, but definitely wouldn't impress a potential boyfriend.

The B-word brought a little smile to her lips and warmed her cheeks. She'd only met Devlin all of two times and here she was plotting "boyfriend" strategy.

"It's ten minutes after midnight, stupid," she reminded herself. "He's probably already asleep by now." Everyone else seemed to be. Her usually quiet neighborhood felt especially deserted tonight. Little traffic flowed on the adjacent street, silence stretching long between the hum of tires. Even the dogs had settled down. The night was eerily quiet.

Avera glanced around, feeling a sudden case of nerves. The parking lot, though lit by several amber streetlights, held pockets full of shadows. Deep, black holes that could hide anything, or anyone.

A shiver slithered down her back, making her frown. "Fear is not an option." She recited the line from one of her favorite movies. Before her attack, she'd never been skittish about being alone in the dark. She hated feeling vulnerable, as if she was some unseen predator's prey.

She slipped a hand inside her purse, closing on the smooth handle of her gun. There, that was much better. Straightening her shoulders, she marched toward the glow of light shining through the glass door to her apartment building. As she neared the entrance, a strange feeling grabbed her, making her stumble.

I'm being watched!

Her heart started pounding, making her lightheaded. She desperately wanted to turn around, but made herself keep walking. Her ears strained to catch the fall of a shoe, the quiet tread of sneakers. Heavy breathing. Anything.

Nothing but the sound of a distant car engine and her own footsteps disturbed the night. The car drew closer in a hurry, speeding down the empty street. As the vehicle passed in front of the building, its loud engine drowned out everything else.

Avera swung around.

No one was there. Nothing moved.

Her shoulders sagged and she gave a shaky laugh. "You've really got to get it together, girl. You're starting to jump at shadows." Her gaze swept the parking lot a final time. She started toward the door to her building again only to freeze the next instant.

Down the sidewalk, near the corner of the building, shadows moved.

Chapter Fifteen

One, two, three... Avera stopped counting the dim outlines of tall, dangerous-looking men when one of the shadows separated and started moving toward her at a brisk pace. The others faded back, one by one, their forms blending with the night. Her breath caught and her grip tightened on her gun.

The sound of shoes on cement grew louder as the dark shape came closer. Hand still on her small revolver, she headed for the door, trying not to break into a run as she pulled her card key from her purse. She could see his outline clearer now. Definitely male. Tall, broad shoulders, slim waist and hips, muscled thighs. His walk was very masculine, very confident and assured. A sense of awareness buzzed through her an instant before Devlin stepped into the glow of one of the lights.

"Good evening," he said. His sexy voice blended with the night, deep and dark like the shadows.

Avera shook her head, sucking in a deep breath that did nothing to calm her quivering stomach. The relief from fear made her voice sharp. "You know, you really should stop sneaking up on people. Sooner or later you're going to get yourself shot." He was close enough she had no trouble seeing his eyes widen in innocence.

"But I wasn't sneaking. I was merely taking a walk."

"Do you always take your walks at midnight?" She turned to unlock the door, but he was suddenly there ahead of her, his card key in the lock. He pushed the door open and stood aside.

"Thanks." She walked past him, ignoring the sudden urge to lean into him when her shoulder brushed against his chest.

"You are very welcome. And yes, I often take walks late at night. It helps to calm me when I'm...restless."

"Oh, do you have trouble sleeping?" She wanted to keep him talking. His presence by her side made her body tingle, little flashes of awareness shooting through her every time they came close to touching. She could even feel his arm hovering near her back, ready to catch her if she so much as stumbled on the stairs. A tiny voice whispered in her head, daring her to stumble on purpose. She ignored the temptation.

"Sometimes," he said. "Do you usually arrive home so late?"

His voice sounded disapproving. She glanced at him, but his face was smooth, only polite interest showing in his blue eyes. "Sometimes." She mimicked his one word response, but spoiled it with a follow up. She wasn't used to delivering vague answers. "Depends on what stage a project is in. Things usually get pretty hectic when we're closing on a deadline."

"You are close to one of your deadlines now?"

She couldn't keep the small grimace off her face as she unlocked her door. "Unfortunately, no. My boss thought some chemicals were missing, so we've been taking inventory the last two days." Of course, they hadn't found anything missing. It wasn't the first time Morrison had exploded for no reason. How he got to be supervisor of even a small private lab like Barrett's she'd never understand. Maybe he and

Cameron were related somehow. Wouldn't be the first time good old nepotism put a jerk in power. She could only hope that when Cameron tripped up he'd take Morrison down with him.

An image of the two men literally tangled in a heap on the ground made her chuckle softly. Still smiling, she turned to Devlin to tell him goodnight. The words caught in her throat. Were his eyes glowing? She blinked and the effect was gone. The eyes regarding her remained a deep, vivid, but very natural blue.

"Is something wrong?"

"No, I..." She glanced up at the ceiling. "I guess the lights flashed or something. Did you notice anything?" In the quiet before he spoke, her stomach growled. Loudly. She threw a hand across it. "Sorry," she said, embarrassment making her cheeks burn.

"You are hungry," he said, the words sounding like an accusation.

Her defenses shot up. "Yes, well, you'd be hungry, too, if you worked through lunch and dinner. I was going to stop on the way home, but—"

"Wait here." He spun around, took three long steps, opened his door, and disappeared inside.

Avera stared in disbelief at his closed door. After only a few seconds of standing there, the feeling of being watched swept over her again. She glanced uneasily up and down the empty hall. Great, now she was getting paranoid *inside* her building. Shaking her head, she entered her apartment and shut the door. Surely Devlin would knock when he came back out and didn't find her waiting. *If* he came back out.

Sighing, she tossed her purse on the couch and kicked off her shoes. The three knocks on her door came in a staccato burst.

"Avera?"

Even hearing his voice, habit had her checking

the peephole. Devlin glared straight at her, displeasure tightening his handsome features, making him look less like a businessman and more like the barbarian prince she'd imagined. Her breath caught before speeding up again. Could he really be angry because she hadn't stayed where he told her to?

I'm not a trained dog, for Pete's sake.

She might have left him standing there on general principle if she hadn't noticed the logo on the two plastic cups balanced on the large flat box in his hands. She snatched the door open. The movement pulled in the air from the hall, bathing her in the heavenly scent of tomato sauce.

"You went to Luciano's? How? When? Oh, never mind." She grabbed the two cups of soda and noticed immediately how cold they were. Ice sloshed inside. He must have put them in the fridge, the dear, sweet man.

"I wanted to make up for ruining your dinner at our first meeting."

She ignored the amused look rapidly replacing his scowl and headed for the kitchen. He could scowl or look amused all he wanted as long as he shared his pizza. When he set the box on the table and lifted the lid, steam wafted up. She almost whimpered. "How did you keep it hot so long?"

He gave her an enigmatic look as he took the pizza cutter from her. "I have my ways. You would have had the pizza yesterday if I had planned better. It worried me when you didn't come home at your usual time."

She set plates and silverware on the table, feeling flattered and a little worried at the same time. He'd been living across the hall less than week. How did he know what time she usually came home? "Why would you be worried about me? We barely know each other."

His gaze shot to her face. "We know each other well enough." He laid the pizza cutter down and reached for her hand. "Peace, Avera, I mean you no harm. I asked Claudia to help me order your favorite meal and find out when you would be home this evening. I wanted the food to be as fresh as possible when you arrived."

She blushed a little. So that had been the reason for Claudia's call earlier. She'd thought her friend sounded strange, her voice a bit too nonchalant when she asked what time Avera would be getting off work. Now she knew why, the little matchmaker.

Her stomach growled again.

"You should eat," he said softly. He stepped over and pulled her chair out, moving slow and careful, as if he didn't want to startle her. When he pushed her chair in, his hands brushed her shoulders. Even through the material of her blouse she felt their heat.

"Thank you," she said.

"You are very welcome."

The pizza tasted wonderful and all the while, Avera tried not to stare at Devlin. As they ate, she found she couldn't keep her eyes off him entirely. No question about it, he confused her. While his English was flawless, he spoke with a slight accent, one she couldn't place. And he sometimes used strange, proper-sounding phrases like "peace, I will not harm you" and "you are very welcome." Phrases like those would have made her snicker if anyone else had used them on her, but with him the words seemed...natural.

"You're not from around here, are you?" she asked wanting to understand him better. Maybe when she knew more about him she wouldn't be so afraid of getting close.

"No. I'm from quite far away in fact. I'm only in the area temporarily."

"Oh." Disappointment flashed through her. She ignored the uncomfortable feeling while at the same time wondering how long "temporary" was. That still didn't explain what he was doing leasing an apartment in her modest little building. From the way they fit, his clothes had to be tailor-made. That meant money.

Sitting across from her in his crisp, dark blue, button down shirt, a color perfectly matched to his eyes, Devlin Kel looked like some high-powered executive. Or a runway model. That thick, black hair of his was incredibly sexy.

Avera stifled a groan in another bite of pizza. Lately her imagination had no concept of propriety.

He slid another slice of pizza onto his plate. "This food is delicious."

"I'm glad you like it. Luciano's makes the best Chicago-style deep dish in California."

He smiled at her over a fork dripping with cheese and tomato sauce. "A reputation well deserved."

Avera watched the way his lips closed over the fork before jerking her eyes away and reaching for her soda. She swallowed the cold liquid, hoping for a brain freeze to prevent her from indulging in any more fantasies. Maybe a change of topic would help.

"So," she said, setting the cup down. "What brings you to our little slice of the Golden State anyway, business or pleasure?"

"Both." The quick, non-committal answer came with a smile that sent butterflies fluttering through her stomach. She waited, but he didn't offer to elaborate, giving her the impression he didn't want to talk about himself. Too bad. The man was sitting at her table in the middle of the night. Pizza and soda aside, he owed her a little insight into what kind of man he was. She trusted Steven's assessment of Devlin Kel, but that only went so far.

She wanted to know more.

"Really? What kind of business are you in?" An innocuous enough question, certainly nothing to cause the man across from her to go suddenly still, though that's what he did.

"I...manage things," he finally said.

She wasn't giving up that easily. "What kind of things?"

"People, mostly."

People, huh? Again, not very informative. Avera frowned and decided to take the bull by the horns. "Are you deliberately being vague or is this your normal way of handling questions?"

"Yes and no."

Oh, hell, he wasn't a lawyer, he was a politician.

She threw her napkin on her empty plate. "You know, for a guy who wants to get to know his neighbors, you're sure going about it the hard way. Don't you know you have to give a little to get a little?"

His brows rose and his gorgeous eyes developed a glint. Avera replayed what she'd just said in her mind. Nothing worth creating that interested look in his eyes, except... Well, surely he didn't think she was talking about *that*?

"Show me."

Her heart shifted into high gear. Her mouth went dry and she took a sip of cola before answering. "Show you what?"

The ticking of the kitchen clock sounded overly loud in the lengthy pause. The disturbing man sat back in his chair and gave her one of those seductive smiles of his. To hell with butterflies, the wings in her stomach felt like they belonged to a flock of agitated geese.

"Show me what you mean," he said slowly. "Tell me about yourself."

The sudden mix of relief and disappointment

had her stammering. "Oh, well, um, what would you like to know?"

"How long have you been a...scientist?"

That was a surprise. She thought for sure he'd been about to ask something a lot more personal. She laughed a little. "I've always been interested in science. However, if you're asking how long I've actually been working as one, the answer's three years full time. Part time for two years before that while I finished my degree in chemistry."

"The question amuses you?"

"Just the way you said the word scientist. You made it sound like I was engaged in something disreputable."

Forehead creasing, he shifted in his chair. "Did I? That was not my intention. Forgive me."

She started clearing the table. He sounded sincere, but... "Don't worry about it. I'm used to men being put off by my profession." It wouldn't be the first time a man had walked away because he'd been intimidated by her intelligence.

He chuckled, a deep, throaty sound more suited to a dimly lit bedroom than a bright kitchen, and laid a hand over hers when she reached for his empty plate. "Trust me, your profession does not put me off in the slightest. I admire a female with a strong mind."

"That's...um, nice." There went her grasp on her vocabulary again.

She slipped her hand from beneath his and finished gathering the dishes. After loading the dishwasher, she turned back around, to find Devlin folding the empty pizza box into a compact square. She watched, impressed by his obvious strength. When she folded them, she had to stand on those boxes to get them to cooperate. He simply grabbed two sides and forced them together, no problem. The way his shirt tightened over his arms and shoulders, outlining the smooth play of muscles made her bite back a sigh. It would be nice if those muscles moved beneath her hands, flexing and straining. He'd be gone in a moment, and she wasn't ready for him to leave.

"There's chocolate cream pie in the fridge if you'd like some dessert." She reached for the refrigerator door just as a vision of Devlin, chocolate cream, and a long night of slow licks jumped into her brain, almost making her eyes cross. "I can have coffee ready in a couple of minutes," she said, proud of herself when the words didn't come out strangled.

His fingers closed over her hand, pulling it away from the door handle. When she turned to face him, she couldn't keep her pulse from speeding up. She wished her fingers didn't feel like the middle of winter, cold with a sudden case of nerves. His felt hot, strong, and slightly rough in places. Funny, she hadn't expected him to have calluses of any kind.

"Thank you for the offer, but I'm afraid the hours have slipped away from me. I have time for only one kind of dessert," he said, both hands reaching for her face.

She couldn't move as fingers brushed her skin and slid slowly into her hair. His thumbs stroked back and forth over her cheeks. The slight friction of the duel caress coupled with the growing fire in his eyes caused her whole body to flush with heat. Air sped between her parted lips.

"What...what kind of dessert do you have in mind?" she whispered.

"This." He lowered his head, his lips pressing a soft caress to her mouth.

She thought she'd been hot before, but at the touch of his lips, her body burst into flames. Pleasure flowed from her mouth, making its way to the very center of her. Her stomach quivered. The place between her legs throbbed and grew unbearably wet as she waited for the touch of his tongue. It didn't come. A frustrated groan built in her throat when he did nothing but move his lips slowly back and forth across hers. She wanted more than a teasing pressure of lips against one another. For the first time in her life, she wanted it all.

Her hands came up, palms rubbing, fingers flexing into the hardness of his chest. His movement stilled and he started to draw back. She rose on her toes and sent her tongue into his retreating mouth, needing a full taste of him more than she needed her next breath. He froze for the briefest moment, and then his arms shifted, wrapping around her, pulling her closer, tighter. His mouth took possession of hers. Satisfaction filled her as his tongue swept between her lips in a long, dominating lick. She moaned, letting him invade every crevice, explore every surface, while sliding her tongue against his every chance she got.

So good. He tasted so good she didn't think she'd ever get enough. Her hands, trapped between their bodies, curled into demanding fists. She still wanted more.

She slipped her hands free and wound her arms around him. Their bodies touched and the world shifted. He pressed her back against the cold surface of the refrigerator door. Goose bumps sprang up all along her arms only to be wiped out by a brush of his hot hands. Every inch of skin he touched burned with heat and desire. When the part of him nestled so tight against her lower belly pulsed against her, her body jerked in response.

The analytical side of her brain shouted a warning that things were fast getting out of hand. The rest of her brain along with her whole body shouted back that she didn't care. She wanted this, him. Wanted him with a passion that surprised her and made her heart pound with anticipation.

She lifted her leg and curled it around his thigh to pull him closer, tighter. Her hips began to push against him in sync with the motion of his tongue thrusting rhythmically inside her mouth. Her hands moved restlessly up and down his back. Frustrated with the cloth keeping her from touching his skin, she began to pull his shirt from his pants.

As soon as her fingers found his hot flesh, he broke the kiss. The next thing she knew he'd captured her wrists, pulled her arms around, and pinned them to her sides. His groan sent a shaft of need through her as his forehead dropped against the fridge door. Their bodies weren't touching anymore, but she still felt surrounded by him, the air between them saturated with the luscious scent of his warm body. She breathed in deeply, drawing the aroma, spicy and essentially male, deep into her lungs. Her thighs clenched together. She ached to touch him, to have him touch her far more intimately. When he wouldn't let go of her wrists no matter how much she wiggled and pulled, she turned her head intending to press her lips to his neck. Just before she touched him his body jerked. He released her and stepped back. He looked away quickly, but not before she glimpsed something in his eyes. Was he in pain? She glanced down to the bulge at his crotch. Yeah, that looked like it might be painful.

Holding out a hand she took a step toward him, confusion and concern dampening the fire inside her. Why had he stepped away? "What is it? What's wrong?"

"I'm sorry. We can't." He backed away until he was on the other side of the room. Between his words and the kitchen table separating them, she couldn't mistake his meaning.

Hurt and humiliation washed away the wonderful hot passion of a moment ago, leaving her cold and shaken. Heartbroken. The first man she'd ever really wanted, and he was rejecting her. How could she have misread him so completely? *How could I have been so stupid?*

And how dare he make her want him and then walk away, leaving her aching?

A little anger mixed with the hurt, unfreezing her cold body. She tried to smile, though her lips wobbled, and waved a hand dismissively. "That's okay. No need to apologize. No harm done, right?" She started for the archway leading to the living-room and the front door, certain that he'd be as anxious to leave as she was to have him gone. She needed privacy to get her head on straight, to figure out where and when she'd made such a colossal mistake. And maybe to cry a little. His rejection hurt more than she would have imagined possible. "Thanks again for the pizza."

"Avera—"

"No, no, it's okay, really. I need to turn in, anyway. It's been a long day." She hurried to the door. Two hands settled on her shoulders, pulling her to a stop. She resisted when he tried to turn her around. She didn't want to face him. It was late, she was tired, and her emotions simmered too close to the surface. If she saw pity in his eyes she'd either burst into tears or look for another cup of soda to pour over his head. Maybe both.

"You need to leave," she said, trying to put as much firmness in the words as possible.

The fingers on her shoulders squeezed once. His voice, husky with desire, poured over her like liquid gold straight from a blast furnace. "Yes, but not before you understand why I must leave you. Why we can't finish what we started. Why, right now, we can't have what we both want."

What we both want? Did he mean that?

Before she could think better of it, she turned

around. Emotion filled his dark blue eyes. Not pity, thank God, but desire. Definitely desire. The sight soothed her wounded soul. Still, she was cautious. "Are you saying you want me?"

She'd swear his eyes brightened. "Want you? Gods above, yes! How can you doubt that? I want nothing else more."

"Then…"

"Avera, forgive me for being such a greedy fool. I never meant to hurt you." His finger brushed across her lips. "I only wanted a taste, something to see me through the long hours until I see you again. Believe me, I would not be leaving you at all if my presence was not required elsewhere."

The cold around her heart melted. "So you really have to go?"

"Yes, very far away actually. That is why I must leave now. But I'll return soon." He captured her hand and brought it to his chest, right over his heart. "You accepted my invitation to dinner for tomorrow, remember? Will you be late returning home again?"

"I don't think so. What about you? Managing people doesn't keep you late at the office?"

A rueful smile tugged his lips, making her want to kiss them again. "Indeed it does, on occasion, but not tomorrow. Tomorrow evening I reserve solely for you." He brought her hand up and brushed those smiling lips against her skin, watching her with eyes the color of a stormy sky.

Avera fought to keep breathing and to keep Devlin from seeing just how hard that fight was. He didn't need to know how much, how deeply, he affected her. Not if he wasn't going to be around for long. He'd said he would only be in the area temporarily. When he left, it was going to hurt, but she already decided she'd handle that pain when the time came. Better to have loved and lost, right? She raised a brow and gave him an easy smile, one she kept firmly in place until he was in the hall and her door closed between them.

Only then did she let her face dissolve into a worried frown. Devlin Kel was just too good to be true. He had a voice as smooth as satin, and eyes that made her hotter than a Bunsen burner. Not to mention his sexy body and wicked mouth. On top of everything else, he appeared to have no security issues, intellectual or financial. As her father used to say, if something sounded too good to be true, it usually was.

What then, did that make Devlin Kel?

She took a step away from the door, realizing as she did so that she held the hand he'd kissed curled up and pressed against her chest, right over her heart.

Oh, yeah, she was in so much trouble.

****

Hours later, Avera rolled over in bed for what felt like the millionth time. It was no use. Her covers lay in a tangled mess, and she'd pummeled her pillow into submission long ago. Nothing helped. She just wasn't going to be able to sleep. Not with visions of Devlin running through her head.

Visions, hell, more like full-blown fantasies.

Where was her practical, scientific brain when she needed it?

She groaned and pushed herself up, fighting with the tangled covers until she could sit on the edge of the bed. Pushing back her hair, she read the red numbers on her clock and grimaced. Only a couple of hours before the alarm went off. She really needed some sleep, or dealing with Morrison again was going to be next to impossible. Somehow, she had to find something to take her mind off her sexy neighbor. Preferably something so ridiculously boring she'd fall asleep fast.

Or just plain ridiculous maybe?

Avera got up and headed for the kitchen. Faint moonlight seeped through the top of the window, guiding her to the far counter. A quick puff of air, and her new nightlight burst to life, forcing her to shield her eyes. Once accustomed to the glow, she retrieved the four scrolls from the kitchen drawer and took the scrolls and her nightlight back to her bedroom, determined to read herself to sleep.

Chapter Sixteen

Settling into bed, Avera made sure she was completely comfortable before picking up the first scroll. Might as well start at the beginning.

She smoothed out the formal letter and read the bold words in the fancy script swirled across the top.

The First Prophecy of Avalyr.

In the pain of a precipitate birth was the Veil born.

Overwhelming all, transcending purpose.

Consciousness became awareness, became need;

A violation wrought by the hand of an impetuous child.

Striking without thought, without regard.

The Sickness shall manifest an all-consuming Hunger.

Pain devouring the body, Madness consuming the soul.

And death shall grace their banquet.

Everlasting sorrows bloom like Wildflowers across the land,

Until the Joining of Clans shall bear the Blood,

The sworn Salvation for those who Hunger.

By their Blood shall Pain be replaced by Solace.

By their Blade shall Madness be given Purpose.

By their Magic shall Death be Banished.

Only when the Ten successfully stand as One will the Essence of Magic return to its rightful

117

purpose.

There were a few more lines, strange names linked together by even stranger symbols. She tried to force them to make sense but gave up the exercise quickly. She'd save that puzzle for another day. She wanted to sleep, not get caught up figuring out a brainteaser.

She moved on to the less formal letter. It was so short, she almost had it memorized from the first time she'd read it.

Greetings, Lady Avera St. John.

Formal. And he didn't even get her title right. Someone should tell him Ms. was the politically correct term now.

I beg you to accept this small token, a tribute to the timeless beauty of your soul.

She squelched the warm feeling growing in her chest. Now wasn't the time to get caught by such calculated compliments.

Your questions are no doubt many and will probably grow in number as the days pass.

You got that right, buster.

The Prophecy scrolls may hold some answers for you, though, being prophecies, they are notoriously vague in places.

Of course, weren't all prophecies?

As the first Six prophecies have already been fulfilled, I would be honored to explain them to you later if you so desire.

I assure you, all of your answers await your arrival. Be patient, my lady.

Easy for him to say.

Read the scrolls, enjoy the gifts from my world, and know that I will see you soon. I count the hours until we may meet.

Your Humble Servant,

The Tragar, Ruler of Realm Illian and First Bloodsworn of the Planet Avalyr

Yeah, it still sounded hokey.

Avera carefully rolled up the two sheets into one scroll and re-tied the green ribbon. Then she picked up the second scroll, tied with an orange ribbon the same shade as the tiny fruit on the miniature trees. Predictably, the formal scroll was labeled, The Second Prophecy of Avalyr.

This one was even more ominous than the first.

Rebellion shall hold the world in thrall

Giving rise to a division of totality;

Realms, Clans, Houses, the blood of all shall flow.

The embodiment of life shall not be spared.

Death's embrace slips the guard of restful Slumber,

Claiming the bride before the Heir takes his first breath,

Sending her mate deep into the heart of darkness.

Fleeting time dwells for a brace of Deccas in a place

Where men of abject despair are driven mad by measures.

Where Screams ring like dissonant Hymns as the tortured

Open their own skulls to let the madness out.

Where blades rend the flesh from their bones

To feed the craving only sworn blood can sate.

Heeding their summons, the Heir divines

The Path to Freedom; redeeming his Soul

And setting free the Author of his body.

The list of strange names was there again; Mystia, Illian, Peregrine, Turesh, Hedaud... Some of the symbols were the same, but a few were different. She didn't have to be a genius to guess what the black mark that looked like a skull meant. Halfway down the list she found the name Tragar followed by one of the black skulls and two red slashes.

Apparently her admirer's family had not escaped such tragedy unscathed. She finished the page, visions of a bloody civil war slipping like ghosts through her mind, and shuddered.

Not real, she reminded herself. These were words of fiction, a made up war for a made up world. Still, she couldn't quite shake off the weight that pressed down on her in the shadow-filled room. She suddenly felt cold, alone. Insomnia or not, she wasn't sure she wanted to read anymore. She didn't need a case of depression on top of everything else.

She picked up the less formal page, intending to put it away, and noticed that her hand shook. She frowned, clenching her fingers around the paper, the letter from her supposed admirer.

Yeah, right. What kind of a sick minded person would send such disturbing prophecies to a woman he wants to impress?

Her eyes skimmed over the first line of the letter. Now this was interesting. She uncurled the rest of the page. How had he known how she would feel after reading the Second Prophecy or what to say to make her feel better? For that matter, how had he known she would read the prophecy first and need the comfort of such words?

Lady St. John,

Forgive me. I know how the words of the Second Prophecy must affect you. I would never willingly cause you pain, but neither would I seek to hide the darker parts of my world from you. I could tell you that Avalyr is a bright planet full of light and magic, shining cities, and calm peaceful gardens much like the small one accompanying this letter. Such words would be true. That is not to say all of Avalyr is at peace. Like your own world, our history is dusted with episodes of blood and pain. Ah, but I must be completely honest. The blood and pain is not relegated just to the past. We still strive with the darker elements of life. Realms and clans still disagree despite the best efforts of our peacemakers. You see, no one race, one world, can truthfully say they are exempt from the foibles of man. There are good and bad in us all, myself included. Though I would like to think you will find nothing in me that you cannot accept and hope there is much you will come to admire.

I Remain Your Loyal Servant,
The Tragar

Avera wrinkled her nose. 'I Remain your loyal servant' was so...Victorian. So proper. The only one she knew who came anywhere close to using phrases like that was Devlin, and she'd already dismissed him as her crazy admirer. He didn't seem the type who'd resort to a gimmick to attract a woman. He was too self-confident and direct. Strictly a down-to-earth kind of guy. Besides, her first gift had arrived at her door *before* she and Devlin had even met. No, this Tragar had to be someone else. Someone who was good at making up fiction, she reminded herself. This whole prophecy thing was just a joke.

But what if it wasn't, whispered a rebellious little voice in her head—the one that still believed in hopeless things. Things like her father being alive somewhere and not dead like the military claimed. Sure, he'd been missing for over a year now, but until she saw his body a stubborn little voice inside her refused to accept his death as real. The death certificate in the drawer was just another piece of fiction. Something else that seemed too impossible to be true.

Just like these letters.

Avera caught herself yawning and smiled. Her plan appeared to be working.

A violet ribbon stitched with mauve-colored symbols secured the third scroll. Something made her toss the formal sheet aside this time and skip right to the letter. Not fear. She wouldn't admit to that. Curiosity was an easier word.

My dear Avera,

Moved on to first names, have we?

As I sit down to write, I must remind myself of the reason for these letters. There is so much I wish to tell you. I would answer every question you have, but doubt these few pitiful lines would suffice. Nor would asking my own questions be of any use. What questions might I have, you may wonder? Many, I assure you. I know so little about you. At present, I know only that you are a woman of courage, of strength, and, thankfully, a woman with a sense of humor. Laughter can bridge many gaps, and the gap between science and magic is a chasm indeed. Don't, I pray you, allow such an abyss to stifle the birth of the possibility I hope is growing in your heart and mind. Be curious, my lady. Question as you have never questioned before. The impossible is not always what it seems.

Both our answers await our meeting. It will be soon, my destined lady mate, that I promise.

Your Devoted Servant,

The Tragar

Avera felt a warm tear trickle down her cheek and wiped it away roughly. Okay, this was so not funny anymore.

The impossible is not always what it seems.

Wasn't that just what she'd been thinking?

The possibility that her admirer was someone who knew her, knew how she felt about her father being declared dead, had her skin ruffling with goose bumps. No one she knew would do something like this, would they? A friend wouldn't play with her this way.

But if it wasn't a friend, that made the things he said even more scary because they seemed so personal. They touched her.

Avera swept the scrolls off the bed and flopped down, punching her pillow for good measure. This had to stop. She had to find out who was leaving these freaking strange gifts and she had to do it now. It was time for some answers.

With that thought, she took a deep breath, leaned over, and blew hard at the glowing orb entwined in green and blue crystal strands. Obligingly, the light winked out.

Chapter Seventeen

Avera walked into the lobby of Barrett Chemicals juggling her purse, her lunch, and the box holding two items she hoped would give her a few answers.

The green flower she'd received Monday morning still looked fresh and beautiful. The stubborn blossom simply would not wilt and Avera found herself getting a little peeved because it refused to conform to normal plant standards. If it was a plant, it should certainly act like one, shouldn't it? No flower bloomed forever.

She'd found the second item outside her door that morning. Gift number five, another flower, came planted in a box made of wood so smooth it felt like satin. Small, dark green leaves grew close together and crowded over the edge of the box. Here and there, a stem rose, presenting a flower with multiple bright orange petals. Beautiful on their own, but the inside of each bloom simply took her breath away. Mellow shades of pink, rose, and yellow swirled and blended into a miniature sunset. Even its fragrance brought to mind the end of a warm spring day, the sun low in the sky, shadows stretched out long and lazy on the ground. A gentle breeze hinting at rain in the distance. Two lovers walking hand in hand, pausing to kiss as the pink and rose sky faded to shades of violet and purple.

For a moment, the vision of her and Devlin had seemed very real. So real, she could feel him beneath her hands, taste him on her lips, and hear his ragged breathing.

Then the microwave had dinged.

She shook her head and shifted the box of flowers further away from her face. Enough was enough. The Tragar, whoever he was, had told her in his letter that he wanted her to be curious, to question. She wondered if he had any idea what he was asking for. No one hated unanswered questions more than her. So she wasn't waiting around for answers. Not when a few chemical tests might shed some light on the subject of where such strange things as un-wilting flowers and vision-inducing scents came from.

"Morning, Avera."

"Hi, Michelle." Avera smiled at the petite blond sitting at the reception desk.

"Oh," Michelle exclaimed, "those are beautiful flowers. Where did you get them?"

"Er, I have a neighbor who raises exotic flowers." She hoped Michelle wouldn't push the issue. She really didn't want anyone else at work to know she was getting daily gifts along with some pretty crazy notes from some nut case.

Michelle made a face. "You lucky girl. My neighbors are all either jerks or potheads."

Avera gave her a sympathetic look as she walked by the desk. "Moving to a new apartment building might help with that. I've heard you talk about that neighborhood you live in."

Michelle laughed and called down the hall. "Yeah, but the price is right. For that, I'll put up with a few jerks."

Laughing, Avera turned a corner and bumped into a tall thin man in a gray suit. Her boss, Taylor Morrison, stood beside the man and reached out to steady Avera as she stumbled back.

"Well, for—" She cut off as Morrison gave her arm a warning squeeze. She frowned at him, saw him widen his eyes and nod meaningfully toward the man in the gray suit.

"Avera, this is Mr. Cameron, the owner and CEO of our little company." His tone said she'd better be appropriately apologetic.

Avera clamped her lips together. An apology was the last thing she wanted to offer the high and mighty Mr. Cameron. His total lack of scientific acumen in regards to Serum 23 was unforgivable, and she would have loved to let him know it. Dutch's sweet face flashed through her mind and she winced mentally. Okay, so maybe reaming out the uber-boss wasn't the best idea. She didn't want Dutch to get caught in any repercussions.

She pasted a false smile of apology on her face and turned to the object of her disdain. Strange, he didn't look like a total idiot. He looked smart, even attractive, in a mature, GQ sort of way. His gray suit fit him perfectly. His hair, a rich dark brown, matched his neatly trimmed mustache and goatee, the warm color contrasting sharply with his pale skin. A bit too pale for someone living in sunny California. Maybe he was part Scandinavian despite the dark hair.

He didn't appear to be a young man, but beyond that, she had trouble pinpointing his age. He could have been in his thirties as easily as his fifties. Overall, he looked more like a college professor than someone who ran a lucrative chemical research company. Until you looked into his eyes.

Whoa. This guy definitely has power issues.

Avera fumbled her box into the crook of her arm and held out her hand. "Mr. Cameron, it's a pleasure to finally meet you." He didn't take her hand, nor did he acknowledge her. He appeared to be staring at her new flower. Feeling self-conscious, she let her hand drop. "Do you like exotic flowers, Mr. Cameron?"

He finally stopped looking at the flower and turned to her. His piercing, dark-brown eyes had a strange look in them as he focused on her face. He blinked, and the look was gone, replaced by one of keen interest. "Yes, as a matter of fact, I do, Miss..."

"This is one of our research chemists, Avera St. John."

Mr. Cameron reached for her hand. Instead of shaking it, he brushed his lips against her skin. When he spoke, his voice purred. "Miss St. John. I cannot tell you what a pleasure it is to finally meet you. Mr. Morrison has mentioned to me several times about what an excellent employee you are."

The kiss seemed an odd gesture for an employer. Maybe he did come from some Scandinavian country. He had that prim and proper European air about him with just a trace of accent to his speech. Something she couldn't place, but was sure she'd heard recently. Any other time she might have found the puzzle intriguing, but to her surprise she found herself hiding a grimace of distaste. The man's lips were as cold as his hands.

Steady, she told herself. It wouldn't do to alienate the head of the company, especially in front of her boss. She smiled and nodded politely. "Thank you. I have to say I feel very fortunate to be able to work here." She eased her hand away as gently but firmly as she could. He smiled at her, his eyes watching her in a way that made her uncomfortable without knowing exactly why. She lowered the wattage on her smile.

"Indeed." He gestured to her flower. "And may I ask where you came by such rare specimens?"

She opened her mouth to mention Steven again, but Morrison jumped in.

"Oh, Avera's got some wacko leaving her presents outside her apartment. How many does this make, Avera?"

"Five," she said through a smile of clenched teeth. She would have socked him a good one if she could have gotten away with it. When she'd talked to him yesterday about the possibility of using the lab equipment to run a few non-work-related tests, he'd insisted on knowing why, and she'd been forced to tell him about her secret admirer. He'd been studying some kind of report at the time, and she wasn't sure she even had his attention. He'd finally waved her away with a quick, "Sure, go ahead." Apparently, he'd heard every word she'd said except for the "I'd like to keep this confidential" part.

"Right. Anyway, I told her she needs to hire a bodyguard for a while. Especially after—"

"Mr. Morrison, please. I'm sorry, but I'm afraid you'll have to excuse me." She would not stand idly by while Morrison let slip more of her personal business to creepy Mr. Cameron. "The analyses on those new samples you were asking about yesterday are scheduled for completion at eight-thirty. I really need to get to the lab if you want the results by the nine o'clock meeting."

"Oh, yes, of course, the new samples. Business first, right? Good job, Ms. St. John."

"Thank you," she said, trying to keep her sarcasm from showing. "Mr. Cameron, it's been a pleasure." She nodded to them both and slipped past Morrison who, thankfully, was already off on another tangent, regaling Mr. Cameron with tales about the newest compound.

Chapter Eighteen

The sun made its appearance over the distant mountains just as Devlin and his Blades reached the front steps of the Concourse building in Moiwie City. He hadn't slept at all during the night, had trouble even breathing evenly. That soul-searing kiss in Avera's kitchen had done something to him. Words like want, desire, and need were too mild for what he felt. Obsession, fixation, addiction, those fit better.

Despite Sarreth and Kiel staying to watch over her once again, leaving Avera St. John on her world last night had been almost impossible for Devlin. There was no apparent reason for the uneasiness that wrapped itself around his heart when he'd told her good night and watched the door close between them. He'd had to force himself not to will the door open again so he could sweep her up in his arms and run back to Avalyr with her.

The unease only grew stronger during the long dark hours spent imagining darker scenarios where Avera had to defend herself with her weapon. If human females were anything like their Feyune sisters, the consequences of such an action alone could be deadly. The mere thought of her hurt or injured caused a crushing weight to press against his chest. He couldn't take another night of such torment. He had to tell her today, now. Reveal to her who he was and where he came from. If it took a show of magic to convince her he was telling the truth, then so be it. One way or another, she was coming home with him.

He strode through the Enclave doors with purpose, waving aside the usual escort of footmen. He knew his way and had no patience for their slow, measured tread. Fate, Karess, and the rest of his half-decca of Blades followed close behind. He knew all of the warriors could feel his disquiet, even with the links closed. It was no wonder they walked as if entering an enemy camp, eyes alert and wary, hands hovering near sword hilts, faces grim.

Luma usually awaited his arrival in the Gate room. As Avalyr's Avatar, she monitored his journeys to and from Earth. A task she seemed to enjoy. This morning, however, she emerged from one of the receiving rooms just off the main doors, her expression full of irritation. And she wasn't alone.

"Jerran." Devlin acknowledge his friend and fellow Bloodsworn with a nod. "What brings you to the Enclave?" Nothing good, judging by the look on his face. The unease increased tenfold.

"I was hoping to catch you before you left, Devlin. Caveon received a strange message a short while ago from Camarie."

"Did he now?" The name took Devlin by surprise. He hadn't thought of his uncle for several moon changes. Known to all as the Dark Bloodsworn, Camarie usually kept himself well hidden unless he was forcing links with blade-sick men. Only one of the many reasons he was wanted by the Bloodsworn High Council.

"Yes, he claims he's willing to sit down and answer the charges the Council has levied against him. He even intimated he might be willing to give up some of his links."

That didn't sound like the Camarie Devlin knew. He couldn't see his power-mad uncle giving up access to one wisp of magical essence. "What does Caveon think?"

Jerran shrugged. "Same as the rest of us, that the Dark Bloodsworn is planning something. A man doesn't do the things Camarie has for years and decide to change overnight."

"I agree. When does Camarie want to meet?"

"That's why I'm here. He wants to meet now, and he insists that you be present. He wouldn't say why. Caveon thinks it's either because of your status as clan leader or because you're family."

Devlin snorted. Neither reason was likely. "Camarie has never sworn loyalty to me as the Tragar. I doubt he's ever thought of me as leader of anything." Of course, he was only guessing, since he couldn't remember the last time they'd even spoken. Assuming he chose to attend this farce of a meeting, Camarie was in for a surprise if he thought to appeal to Devlin based on a familial connection.

"Is Caveon expecting me?"

Jerran nodded. "He knows the timing is bad, Devlin. And he knows Camarie. Despite his age, my grandfather's mind is still sharper than a Blade's sword. He wants you there to make sure Camarie doesn't use your absence as an excuse to cry foul."

"Vet!" Although Devlin doubted very seriously his uncle would show, he knew he had no choice but to comply with the demand. He wanted Camarie stopped as much as anyone. Maybe more than anyone. "Fate?" The Blade was at his side in an instant. "I want you to go ahead to Earth."

A hiss passed through Fate's lips as his head jerked once in denial. Devlin felt a sharp tug on their link—one he didn't answer. He already knew his First Blade didn't like the idea of the meeting with Camarie. Fate wanted to be there in case of trouble.

He put a calming hand on his Blade's shoulder.

"Fate, I need you to do this. Camarie will not

attack me in the Bloodsworn Hall. He values his life too highly. I doubt you will miss anything here. Sarreth and Kiel, on the other hand, will be expecting us. Have the mercenaries take you to them. Make sure your blade-brothers and my mate are safe. If she... If there is the slightest problem, have the mercenaries send word back to the Gate Watcher." He turned to Luma. "Can the Gate Watcher get a message to me through you if need be?"

"Messages from a Watcher usually take a little time to reach us because they're using borrowed magic. But, yes. If he sends one, I'll see that you get it."

"Thank you." He turned back to Fate. "I'm trusting you with the other half of my soul, my old friend. Don't fail me."

The First blade straightened his shoulders before bowing. "As you command, my Bloodsworn. I will see to the safety of your mate until you arrive."

Chapter Nineteen

Fate knew he faced trouble before the Outer Gate even closed behind him. Not because of the hostile look on the Gate Watcher's face and not because of Jacob Saunderson standing off to one side, out of sight of anyone looking through the Gate from Avalyr. Not even because the young mercenary held one of the weapons called a gun pointed in Fate's direction. Not that those weren't obvious signs themselves.

No, it was the heavy scent of blood in the air tensing his muscles and making him want to reach for his sword. Only years of self-discipline allowed him to stand at ease instead of answering the challenge of the apparent ambush.

Fate focused his attention on the Gate Watcher, while remaining conscious of every move the younger Saunderson made. As a warrior, he respected the weapons of this world, and he already knew from their first meeting the young male lacked self-control. The eldest Saunderson looked away quickly, wetting his lips and rubbing the palm of one hand against his thigh. Angry, but nervous, the old man was a fair target for answers. "Explain," Fate snapped.

The gray-haired head whipped up. "Don't you take that tone with me. I ain't the one breaking the rules here."

"Neither am I."

"Liar." Jacob Saunderson edged into the room, still holding the gun steady. "I've yet to meet one of you aliens who didn't lie through his teeth. You know, leaving some of your buddies behind without telling us wasn't a very smart move. Now we've got two dead bodies and a lot of unanswered questions. You can see how that might make us a little nervous about letting you run loose on your own any more. By the way, where are the rest of your friends? Your boss too scared to show his face?"

Fate barely registered the insult to his Bloodsworn.

Two dead bodies? His *buddies*?

The word was strange but he had no trouble deciphering the meaning. Sarreth and Kiel, his blade-brothers, were dead.

Hot rage blazed through him, burning out his control. He welcomed the heat, letting it flood his body, tighten his muscles, until his entire being vibrated with fine tremors. His vision narrowed on the one who so callously informed him of the murder of two men he considered family.

He unsheathed a silver knife and sent it flying through the air in the next instant. The speed of the throw took the young, inexperienced mercenary completely by surprise. The knife sank into the back of his hand, drawing a pained curse along with the blood. Not waiting to see if Jacob dropped the gun or not, Fate followed immediately after his thrown blade. He knocked hand and weapon aside and grabbed the young whelp by the throat. With a powerful lunge, he slammed the human into a wall. The plaster surface cracked, showering them both with dust.

Fate no longer cared that his control was gone. Even the boy's grunt of pain wasn't enough to quell the rage boiling his blood. Falling in honest battle in the defense of their Bloodsworn and brothers was a death all Blades expected. There was honor in such a death, a purpose. There was no purpose in Sarreth's and Kiel's murder at the hands of these supposed allies. All he wanted now was vengeance, and beating this pitiful male senseless would make a good beginning.

He lifted his fist.

Ten fast beats of his heart later, his fist still hung in the air, held there by what he read in Jacob Saunderson's eyes. Stubborn pride, youthful arrogance. But it was the kernel of fear wrapped in shreds of courage that stayed his hand. These were not the cold eyes of a murderer.

"I can understand you being upset about your friends, but the boy you're holding is my family. I'd appreciate it if you let him go."

The Gate Watcher's words accompanied the sharp nudge of a metal barrel against his back. Foolish of him to have dismissed the elderly man so completely. But then, that's what he deserved for letting emotions have free rein.

Fate pulled back slowly. He acknowledged the gun in the Gate Watcher's hand with a solemn nod as the man's grandson slumped to his knees, coughing and cradling his wounded hand. A new voice heralded the arrival of the boy's father.

"Damn it, Jacob, I told you to bring the Avalyrans to me when they arrived, not piss them off until they killed you. You're lucky there's only one of them." Everett Saunderson directed his black scowl first at his son, then at Fate. "And you're lucky you aimed for his hand and not his heart. I'd hate to have to kill you, warrior."

The Gate Watcher stepped back, the weapon still leveled at Fate. A gruff chuckle passed his lips. "You can't blame it all on our guest here, Everett. Boy's got a mouth on him just like you had at his age. You could piss off the priest just by saying amen."

"Don't encourage him, Pop."

Fate stepped away from the three humans and watched Everett Saunderson examine his son's hand. "Good throw, right between the bones." He jerked the knife free without warning.

"Shit! Son of a..."

"Go ahead, get it out of your system, son."

"Bitch, Dad, couldn't you have counted to three or something?"

The father pulled a cloth from one of the many pockets on his pants and wrapped it around his son's hand. "Why? It still would have hurt. You might as well get used to the pain now. It's not like it's going to get better any time soon."

"It'll heal," the young mercenary said through clenched teeth.

His father snorted. "Healing is just the first step. You'll have to work the stiffness out of it if you want the full use of that hand. That's not going to be a picnic. At least you're walking away from this alive. Again."

"That's more than can be said for those two down the hall." Both men grinned.

Fate's anger spiked once more. Did these men care so little for life?

Not until the Gate Watcher spoke did he realize he'd started forward, hand on his sword hilt.

"Now, now, you just stay right where you are, Mr. Fate. Jake, boy, I swear you've got a death wish today. You need to be a bit more respectful of the dead."

"Sorry, G-Pop, but when two men try to stab me in the back, I lose all respect for them, alive or dead."

"Now who lies?" Fate demanded. He faced Everett Saunderson, holding him responsible for his son's actions. "Sarreth and Kiel would not have attacked your son from behind. There would be no need for them to attack at all unless they were defending themselves or our Bloodsworn's bride." The possibility left a cold lump in his chest. To have lost two blade-brothers was bad enough. To lose his Bloodsworn's mate would be far worse. He had spent enough time studying the Prophecies to know if anything happened to Avera St. John, it could be devastating to his world.

Everett Saunderson's brows drew together. "Sarreth and Kiel? Those are the two men you left at St. John's apartment building, right?" Fate nodded sharply and saw a look of understanding slide into the mercenary's eyes. "Well, that explains this little mix-up at least. Those aren't the two men Jacob killed last night."

"Sarreth and Kiel live?"

A shrug. "As far as I know. I haven't heard anything different from the man I've got watching St. John's building. I can have him check on them if you need confirmation. Course, that still means you've got two other bodies you need to identify."

Two others. But not two blade-brothers. His Bloodsworn would not have secreted more Blades on Earth without telling his First Blade. Were they even warriors from his world? "Where are they?"

Instead of answering, the mercenary held up a hand and beckoned with one finger. "Come with me. Shouldn't take long to sort this out."

He followed the man into the hall, aware of son and father falling into step behind him. As they approached another room the smell of blood grew stronger; a sickly sweet, metallic odor hanging thick in the air. He saw why when the older mercenary stopped and waved him inside.

Two bodies lay in the center of a ground cloth placed on the floor, their clothes soaked in blood.

Jacob slipped past him and went to stand on the other side of the bodies. His stance was purely aggressive, feet planted wide, arms crossed with the injured hand tucked out of sight. A harsh frown dug furrows into his young brow. When he spoke, he practically spat the words out.

"If you want to take your dead friends back to your planet you better have a damn good explanation for why they tried to kill me last night."

Fate moved further into the room, slipping to the side so he wouldn't have the other men coming through the door at his back. He studied the bodies, noting the killing wounds; a slit throat for one and a stab to the heart for the other. The body with the heart wound also had a long gash across the stomach deep enough that a loop of glistening intestine had slipped through.

"These are Feyune warriors, but not ones I recognize."

"I think you're lying. Your bunch are the only aliens who have been through here in the past six months. These have to be friends of yours."

Fate allowed himself a small sigh. He was getting tired of the younger Saunderson's accusations. The pup had done nothing but snap and snarl ever since their first encounter. Despite the presence of father and grandfather, Fate was tempted to instruct the boy in a much-needed lesson in manners. "Believe me," he said, keeping the impatience from his voice, face, and body with effort. His perfect control had not returned completely, and the condition made him uncomfortable. Emotions gave too much away. "I would know if I had lost a blade-brother. These men do not belong to my Bloodsworn."

Jacob started to speak again, but this time his father stopped him. "Go have Billy bandage your hand, Jacob, and help him get the chopper ready.

Unless I miss my guess, we'll be leaving soon."

Still angry, the young mercenary nodded sharply, and stalked from the room. The tension in the room dropped noticeably, allowing Fate to take a calming breath. Despite his attack earlier, he wasn't in the habit of fighting with children, and Jacob Saunderson was indeed a child despite his age and physical size. The boy was far from disciplined.

Fate didn't envy the father having to train such a volatile youth. But then, he'd had the responsibility of training more than one emotion-ridden youth himself in his nearly thirty years as a warrior. His current Bloodsworn included.

The nostalgic smile stayed hidden inside as he met Everett Saunderson's gaze. The man's eyes hadn't left him even when he'd been dismissing his son. A shrewd warrior, this one. One worthy of respect.

"Where did you find these men?" Fate asked.

"We came across them while doing a standard recon around Barrett Chemicals, the place where your boss' lady works. He'd mentioned he might have to go there at some point, and we didn't want any surprises." His voice lowered with meaning. "It's our job to make sure all of you *visitors* maintain a low profile.

"We didn't go in expecting problems. Barrett is privately owned and located in an isolated area surrounded by forest. I was on one side of the facility, Jacob on the other. He ran into the tall guy and had barely taken him down when the second one showed up. By the time I got there, number two had a slit throat and bled out a minute later." He glanced down at the bodies and made a disgusted noise. Shaking his head, he said, "That boy knows better than to go for a kill in these situations. If I've told him once, I've told him a hundred times, you can't get quick answers from the dead."

Fate sank to his haunches to study the two swords lying next to the bodies. At the time of linking, a Blade's sword became stamped by the spirit of his Bloodsworn, taking on certain characteristics unique to that man. These two swords retained no hint of the men's former Bloodsworn. When their owners had died, the links to the Bloodsworn were severed. Deprived of the connection, the swords returned to being the simple weapons they were. Sharp, useful, efficient, but nothing more than cold, gray steel.

Standing again, he felt compelled to point out the obvious. "Blades are highly trained warriors. I doubt either would have presented your son with an opportunity to take them alive. It is impressive that he managed to kill both without sustaining an injury."

A smile of pride stretched Everett Saunderson's lips. He leaned a little toward Fate. "Don't tell him I told you, but he didn't get away without a scratch. And if someone like you didn't notice, that means he's learned at least one lesson I've been trying to pound into him."

The pup had been injured? Thinking back, Fate could not recall a single sign of weakness. A lesson well learned indeed. Lips twitching up slightly, he inclined his head to the mercenary, one teacher to another.

"These two may not be friends of yours," Saunderson continued, "but you can't deny they look the part. Same clothes, same equipment." He nudged the collection knives piled next to the swords. "How do you explain that?"

"The only way possible." No need to elaborate. From the look in the mercenary's eyes he'd already guessed the truth. Another Bloodsworn, someone who hadn't come through this particular Outer Gate, was stalking Avera St. John.

Fate felt a cold rush of outrage sweep through him. He let the strong emotion come, knowing this time there would not be a single outward sign to betray him to the careful eyes of the man watching him. His Bloodsworn had assigned him a task, one that appeared threatened with failure. An outcome he was not in the habit of allowing.

The sound of heavy thumping came from outside, growing faster, louder.

The mercenary straightened. "So, are we taking off now to pick up your friends and go get St. John, or do you have to wait for your boss to get here so he can make that decision?"

Fate kept his expression smooth and nodded once. "We leave now. Please have your elder send word back through the Gate to my Bloodsworn."

"Consider it done."

Chapter Twenty

Avera sat alone at one of the tables on the outdoor lunch patio, wishing she could have worn one of her sleeveless blouses instead of the long-sleeved knit shirt she'd put on that morning. The day felt almost too warm. Only the shade of the patio umbrella and the slight breeze lifting her hair made it bearable. She thought about pushing her sleeves up, but while they were hot, they were also necessary. The scars on her arms still looked too raw, too prominent. They embarrassed her, made people look at her with pity in their eyes, and she hated pity.

With a sigh, she turned her mind to the more immediate problem—making sense of the morning's test results. She'd checked the machinery three times, but all the analyzers were working properly. It was the resulting data from the tests she'd run that was a problem.

The organic chemical properties of the two plants she'd tested had proven very similar to Earth's standard. Similar, but not an exact match. She hadn't even told Dutch about the two strange, unidentified elements she'd found. She wanted to run the tests again to make sure she wasn't imagining things.

Right. Don't lie to yourself, Avera. You're just starting to believe all that silly propaganda you've been reading.

She'd brought all of the scrolls to work with her and finished reading the pages while the analyzers ran the first tests. The two letters from her admirer had been lovely. The world he described sounded a lot like Earth except for the magic part.

Yeah, "magic." Apparently the author of those letters thought magic was real, with properties similar to that of a living organism. It came when he *called* it, went wherever he told it to go. She wondered if it sat up and begged, too, and stifled a laugh by clearing her throat. She was getting as silly as those scrolls.

No, she took that back. Nothing was as ridiculous as the scrolls. On top of all the magic and prophecy stuff, her secret admirer had called her his *mate*. What man now days would even dare use that archaic word?

She thought of her love-bird neighbors and grinned. Steven could probably get away with using the word mate. Claudia would love it. She could just see her friend melting on the spot. Avera hadn't believed melting for a man was possible until last night. Devlin had certainly proved that conjecture wrong. But he was a flesh and blood man, real, not make-believe. Magic, a planet called Avalyr with a race of people living on it called Feyune, now those were fiction. Problem was, she couldn't argue with science. If she ran the tests again and they told her the same thing, was it enough to turn fiction into reality?

Avera frowned. No, damn it, there had to be another explanation. There was no way some alien Prince Charming from another world was going to knock on her door and ask her to marry him. It was just too farfetched. Whoever this secret admirer was, when he played out his part and showed up to claim her as his *mate* like the scroll said, she'd have to make sure he knew she wasn't interested in participating in his little game.

Satisfied with her plan, she turned her attention back to her lunch. Several of her co-workers were enjoying the warm day as well, munching on salads and sandwiches while discussing weekend plans. Avera nibbled on a cheese cracker, taking her time as she went over her own plans for the weekend. She smiled, not surprised to feel a small burst of pleasure at the thought of seeing Devlin again. Just the memory of his scorching lips and wicked tongue made her insides quiver.

A loud, droning roar interrupted her day-dreaming. She looked up, surprised to see a black helicopter skimming just above the trees to the north. The sleek craft dipped lower as it passed over the cluster of buildings making up Barrett Chemicals. The down-wash from the spinning rotors swept across the lunch patio, scattering napkins and lunch bags, and making the umbrellas sway wildly.

Avera rescued her tottering, half-empty bottle of soda and eyed the ominous looking craft. A Sikorsky, if her memory served, business class, though, definitely not military. She'd seen enough of those on various military bases where she'd lived as a child to be sure. Probably some expensive service flying in to pick up Mr. Creepy.

Stop it, Avera, she scolded herself. *You start calling him that in your mind and you'll Freudian slip one day and do it out loud.* Wouldn't do for something like that to get back to him. She probably already had one black mark against her for leaving him and Morrison so abruptly this morning.

She was surprised when the helicopter suddenly scooted east over the main office building. It should have turned north, toward the clearing on the other side of the employee parking lot that served as a landing pad. Instead, it dropped lower, until it disappeared on the far side of the building. Surely it wasn't landing there?

Her curiosity growing, she joined several people who'd already gone inside and were heading for the front lobby. She ran into Dutch at the intersection of the hallway leading to the main lab.

"What's going on?" she asked.

"I don't know, but OSHA and the FFA are going to have a fit if they find out that pilot didn't land where he's supposed to."

By the time they reached the front door, it looked like everyone in the building had stopped working. She spilled out the doors with the others.

The chopper had indeed landed where it wasn't supposed to, occupying a wide swath of open grass between the building and visitor parking lot. The rotors still whirled, sending out waves of wind. The flag on the pole in front of the building lashed back and forth, popping like a whip, the ropes banging against the metal. Some of the women in skirts hurried back inside where they watched through the big plate-glass windows.

The chopper's door slid open and several men exited. The first six wore military fatigues and carried guns—pistols snapped into tactical holsters strapped around the thigh. Then, three more men emerged. The growing tension Avera felt from those around her suddenly evaporated. This had to be some sort of movie stunt. Why else would there be three barbarian-type warriors with swords mixed in with modern soldiers?

The three warriors stopped to speak with one of the soldiers, giving Avera and the others a chance to look them over. Two had pale, light skin while the third, the tallest of the three, was very much darker in comparison. Not black, but a warm mocha cream.

Despite the sword and knife hanging from his belt, the dark-skinned man looked too pretty to play

145

the part of a barbarian, too GQ. The man standing next to him, however, was a different story. Neatly trimmed beard and mustache, two small gold hoops in each ear, bare arms, thick with muscle, sword hilt peeking over his shoulder. Oh, yeah, the quintessential barbarian. The last of the trio stood apart from the others, his long, bronze colored hair hanging loose around his shoulders like some freshman college kid. His body vibrated with restless energy—eyes roving, feet shifting, hand constantly caressing the hilt of his sword.

Speculation soon began to fly as to what was going on and who the person responsible could be. "This has to be some kind of movie stunt," a man said. One of the women murmured something about "eye candy" and another woman piped up, "Joke or not, if one of those three decides to try and throw me over his shoulder, I just might let him."

Everyone laughed.

Avera would have laughed with them but for a nagging little voice in the back of her mind warning her something was wrong, that this wasn't a joke at all. The men with the swords bothered her. Their appearance tugged at her memory. Something she'd heard, or seen recently. Or read.

"Shoot!" she muttered under her breath. Those crazy little scrolls. There'd been something in one of them about guys with swords. Something about warriors with blades. No, warriors *called* Blades.

Unease settled between her shoulders. She slowly stepped back into the crowd as all of the men began moving toward the building. "Now we'll find out what's going on," someone in the crowd said.

One of the men dressed in military green pulled something from a pocket as he walked. He looked at it closely then scanned the crowd with sharp eyes. Avera felt a cold sweat pop out on her skin when his gaze jumped back to her at once, lingering before he glanced down again at what he held in his hand. He said something she couldn't hear. The three men with swords looked at him sharply. Her feeling of unease increased. She slipped behind a tall, broad-shouldered man from HR.

If anyone were to ask her why she'd felt the need to hide, she couldn't have told them. Nor, she found, could she stay hidden. She had to know if the three sword-carrying warriors really were looking for her or if it was just her imagination. This couldn't really have anything to do with all of those stupid little scrolls, could it?

Just as she peeked around her shield's shoulder, a loud voice shouted over the whirr of the helicopter's slowly spinning rotors. At first she thought the bronze-haired warrior pointed at her, but then another shout came from behind Avera and her co-workers. Looking around, she saw several men pouring out of a side door of the adjacent warehouse. They were dressed similarly to the three action studs, except these guys didn't look the least bit friendly and already had their swords drawn. Long, black, deadly looking swords.

A hand closed on her shoulder, making her jump. "I don't like this," Dutch said. "Let's watch the show from inside, shall we?" Others around them murmured in agreement. Everyone started moving back toward the building.

A moment later all hell broke loose on the front lawn. Bullets whined, accompanied by shouts and yells that sounded like battle cries. One of the front windows shattered. People screamed.

Avera bent over, staying low. She avoided the sudden logjam at the doors and ducked through the open space where the window had been. Glass crunched under her feet. She gave a fleeting thought to being grateful for thick-soled sneakers before the whine of a bullet sent her ducking into an empty hallway.

More screams. The sound of running. Someone shoved her in the back. She hit the hallway wall, nearly going down. A hand grabbed her arm as several other frantic people rushed past her.

"What in the bloody blazes is going on?" Dutch yelled, pulling her against him long enough for her to gain her feet. "Dear God!"

She heard the horror in his voice, glanced over her shoulder, and immediately wished she hadn't. This was no show, no movie production. Men were dying just a few dozen feet from her. No way those wounds, that amount of blood, could be fake.

Dutch tugged on her arm. "The lab. The fire door can be locked from the inside." She could only nod, eyes glued to the horrific scene in disbelief. "Go on," he told her, giving her a little shove before turning down an adjacent hall. "I'll meet you there." She nodded again, but didn't turn to watch him leave. A moment later she heard him yelling orders, sending others to the lab.

This is crazy, just crazy, Avera thought as she clung to the wall. Most of the gunfire had stopped, but the men were still trying to kill each other using long knives and swords.

Swords, for pity's sake!

A few of the men broke away from the fighting and started for the building. Avera slid back along the wall several steps before turning and running.

Footsteps pounded the floor behind her. "There she is! Miss St. John!"

She darted a glance over her shoulder to see who had called her and stumbled to a stop in shock. Two men dressed as soldiers raced after her. Both of them had pistols in their hands. She was trying to decide whether to wait or run when a sword-wielding barbarian jumped out of a side hall and cut down one of the men. Blood splattered the walls. The whine of a ricocheted bullet sent her cringing to the floor. When she looked up, barbarian and soldier grappled in the narrow hall, slamming each other against the walls. Finally they went down. A strangled cry of disbelief left her as she saw a knife cut into the soldier's neck. She slapped a hand over her mouth, her lunch churning in her stomach.

Then she heard another shot, muffled this time. The barbarian's body stiffened before going limp.

Her heart pounding, Avera glanced up and down the hall, but saw no one else. Making her decision, she moved toward the men as silently and as quickly as she could. She froze when the barbarian's body rocked once, and then again, as the man beneath shoved the dead body aside. He held on to his gun with one hand, the other he held clamped to the side of his neck. Blood leaked between his fingers in steady streams.

Seeing her, he motioned her closer with his gun. "You're St. John..." he gasped.

She inched closer, trying to keep her eyes on the dead barbarian, the hallways, and the gun, all at the same time. "Yes," she said finally. "How do you know me? What do you want? What's...what's going on?" Despite her best efforts, she heard her voice rising. She was close to hysteria. That couldn't happen. She didn't know what was going on, but she knew she had to keep her head, or she just might lose it. Literally.

The man groaned in pain, squeezing his eyes shut. Avera stepped over his legs and knelt at his side. She was too compassionate a person to wish anyone this kind of pain. She laid a hand lightly on his chest. "I'm sorry. I'm so sorry you're hurt, but please, I need to know what's going on."

His eyelids rose slowly. Avera could hardly bare to look into his eyes. He was already beginning to drift away. "We were...h-hired to find you," he murmured, his voice a breathy whisper.

"Who hired you?"

"Don't know. S-someone, from a-another...pla..."

He stopped talking. A moment later, he stopped breathing. Beneath her shaking hand, Avera could feel his heartbeat slow, grow fainter, and finally stop altogether. Sympathy stung her eyes with tears. Tears she didn't have time for, she reminded herself, hearing raised voices from somewhere up ahead. They weren't coming from the direction of the lab, but through the door down the hall leading to the warehouse.

She couldn't imagine anyone going to such lengths as to send a helicopter full of men after her. The wild possibility that whoever it was, was responsible for her strange gifts with their accompanying fairytale and prophetic messages, seemed preposterous. If that was true, then how the hell did the military guys fit into this, and why all the fighting? Why were they killing each other?

She glanced back down at the soldier. His eyes had closed, thank God. She didn't relish closing them like she'd seen people do in movies. Taking his gun, however, was another thing entirely. A simple matter of self-preservation. A means of keeping a promise she'd made to herself after she'd been attacked.

"I'm so sorry," she whispered, blinking back tears and slipping the Glock from his lax fingers. The pistol was just like her father's, the one in the spare closet along with all his other things. She checked the clip. It was half-full so she shoved it back in place. Grimacing a little, she gave his pockets a quick pat. She took the first two clips she found, stuffed one in her jeans pocket, the other in her bra. Then she headed toward the door to the warehouse, trying to keep her sneakers from squeaking on the tile floor.

She didn't like thinking someone was after her, or that men had died because of it. She wanted this over. No, more than that. After what the dead man said, she wanted answers.

Someone owed her a boatload of answers. And they better be damn good ones.

Chapter Twenty-One

Crouching, Avera eased the door to the warehouse open, just wide enough to slip inside. Loud voices—angry and arguing—echoed in the large building. She tiptoed quietly past stacked boxes and bins full of beakers, test tubes, and supplies, until she could see who was talking. The three swordsmen from the chopper faced off against four of the other barbarians. She noticed immediately how the chopper warriors' silver swords gave off a faint glow in the dimness of the warehouse. The other men held swords of plain black. Or maybe not so plain. She had to blink a time or two to make sure, but yeah, those were glowing, too, with some kind of dark, freaky-looking aura.

The tall, dark-skinned warrior spoke, his voice calm, as if he carried on an everyday conversation. She listened avidly, hoping to get some of the answers she was looking for.

"Leave now and the Tragar may not order your deaths."

A cold-eyed warrior standing in front of the others shook his head. "You know we cannot. Our Bloodsworn has demanded her death. He will not allow the Tragar his bride." The men behind him stepped away from each other, spreading out to fill the wide aisle.

"The dark Bloodsworn cannot prevent the Prophecy by killing the Tragar's bride. The Oracle will only find another."

"You lie. She is his Starmate. Without this one, the Tragar's house will fall—"

"And plunge Illian into civil war," one of the other silver-sword warriors said. "If that happens, it will take half the realms with it. Is that what your damned Bloodsworn wants? Is that what *you* want?"

The black-sword warrior shrugged. "I am not responsible for what happens after. My orders are to find the woman called Avera St. John and kill her. You will not stop me."

Avera jerked back into hiding, trying to keep from crying out. Kill her? *Now they wanted to kill her?* The word "NO" resounded in her head.

Swift anger burned its way through her veins, her limbs. It flooded her stomach, wiping out the queasy feeling and replacing it with a cold, hard lump of resolve. She glanced down at her arms, thinking of the scars hidden by the long sleeves. She would not be someone's victim again. She wouldn't sit back and let someone take her life by cutting her head off with a damn sword. Not now, not ever, and especially not when she had a perfectly good gun in her hand.

She would try to slip away first, but if they wouldn't let her...

Avera turned to leave and found her way blocked by two men.

"That is her," one said, pointing at her with his sword. "Camarie will be pleased."

"Hurry, before someone else takes the glory of her death for himself," the other said.

They stepped toward her.

The gun in her hand went off, the loud noise echoing in the huge building. The first man fell, his mouth and eyes round with shock. The other growled and lunged. Avera stumbled back, pulling the trigger a second time. A shout came from her left as he, too, dropped to the floor. The queasiness returned to her stomach with a vengeance.

The sound of swords clashing jerked her gaze away from the still bodies. The men who'd been arguing fought in a battle that looked all too real. The warrior who'd calmly declared his intention to kill her dodged between two other fighters, his cold eyes locked on her. She brought the pistol up and aimed, forcing herself not to think about what she was doing. If she thought about it, she probably wouldn't be able to pull the trigger despite her resolve. She fired. The warrior just grinned and kept coming. She clenched her teeth and fired again, making sure the barrel pointed in the center of his chest. The bullet ricocheted wildly. It was then she noticed the air in front of the man appeared thick and hazy, as if he had some kind of invisible shield.

She gulped, fear gripping her muscles when all she wanted to do was run for her life.

The dark-skinned warrior from the helicopter appeared beside her. Air rushed out of her as his arm wrapped around her waist like a steel band and spun her around. The released breath freed her limbs and she started to struggle.

"Stay back," he said, pushing her behind him. He put himself between her and the man with the black sword. She staggered back, eyes wide, as steel rang against steel. The swing of a sword sent blood splattering across the floor, a single drop hitting her white sneaker. She stared down at it in disbelief.

Oh, God, this can't be happening.

Except, it was.

The other two men from the helicopter suddenly flanked her, making it impossible for her to run. Her heart pounding a frantic beat, she watched the fight in front of her, wishing it was over. Wishing the whole day was over and she was safe with Devlin on their date.

Then the fight *was* over, leaving her facing three men, bloody silver swords in their hands. Her grip tightened on the gun. Would pulling the trigger do any good this time, or would the bullets bounce off them as well?

"Are you here to kill me too?"

Even with the poor lighting in the warehouse, it was easy to read the surprise on their faces.

"Vet, no!" the youngest man sputtered.

She didn't know what "vet" was but it had the tone of a swear word. She buried the urge to laugh and waited for them to say something else. They continued to look at her, surprise giving way to a curious regard, as if they didn't know what to make of her. Their eyes kept darting between her and the two men she'd shot.

She didn't want to look at the men on the floor. The smell of blood thickened in the air by the minute. God help her, she was in so much trouble. She'd just killed two people! The man who'd attacked her months ago had been lucky. She'd missed his heart by a few inches. But these two—she glanced at the bodies and, stomach lurching, looked quickly away. Her conscience argued self-defense, plain and simple.

Well, maybe not so simple, all things considered, but they had intended to kill her. They'd said so right in front of her. Right now, though, she wasn't sure if she could pull the trigger again, take another life. God, she hoped she wouldn't have to find out.

"Look, if you don't mind, I need to get out of here." She needed to find Dutch and the others. She also needed to know what these three wanted, and whether or not they were going to stick around. There would be a lot of explaining to do to the police later, and she had a feeling that without this strange trio to back her up, she was going to be in a lot of trouble.

"You killed them." This close, she could see the tall warrior's dark eyes, and felt a little comforted that they didn't look quite as cold as he sounded.

Avera motioned the barrel of her gun in the direction of the bodies. "Since he'd just said he and his friends were going to kill me, I thought maybe it was a good idea at the time. Besides," she added defensively, "I only killed two. You guys took out the rest."

The young, bronze-haired warrior shook his head as if confused. "But, you killed them, and yet you stand here speaking to us."

"And your point would be?"

The one with a wrestler's body tilted his head, the look on his face reminding her of how Dutch looked when trying to decipher a new chemical formula. "Our females cannot kill. The taking of life snaps back on them and renders them unconscious, sometimes even killing them. Those that live usually go mad."

He said the three sentences quite matter-of-factly. From the "our females" part right through to the "go mad" part, it sounded like he believed every word. Just who were these guys anyway? The idea that they were actors had died the instant the first bullets spat across the front lawn, and she'd yet to come up with another theory. At least, not one she was ready to look at too closely.

"Yeah, well, it might snap back on me too, later, but I guarantee I won't die from it. And you really don't want me any 'madder' than I already am, so I suggest you start talking. If you're not here to kill me, why are you here?"

Mr. Model stepped a little in front of the other two and bowed slightly. "We are here to protect you and to escort you to our Bloodsworn."

Bloodsworn? Wasn't Bloodsworn the name of the guy who wanted her dead? And they wanted to take her to him? She took a wary step back and leveled the barrel of her gun at the three men. "Sorry, but until I know what's going on, I'm not going anywhere with anyone. None of this is making any sense at all. In case no one's told you, this is the twenty-first century. People don't go around killing other people with swords!"

"Be calm, Lady St. John, we mean you no harm. All will be explained. Rest assured everything is as it should be, just as it was foretold."

"Everything is as it should be." She repeated his words quietly, calmly, waited for maybe a heartbeat, and then let her anger loose. "Are you kidding me?" she hissed. Self-preservation kept her voice low. She didn't want to take the chance of attracting more sword-wielding barbarians looking to take her head. "I just killed two men. I watched you kill those others. There are three more back in the hall, and I don't know how many more out front. How in the world do you see this as being as it should be? And what do you mean it was foretold?"

She thought she saw emotion flash across his face, but it was gone so quickly she wasn't sure. His voice held a note of exaggerated calm, as if explaining something to a child. "As foretold by the Oracle."

Avera stifled a growl. He still wasn't making sense. She had no idea what he meant by an Oracle.

Then a feeling of cold fingers crawled down her back as something in the back of her mind clicked.

Oracle? Some of the pages from the little scrolls were supposed to be prophecies translated by an Oracle. Prophecies accompanied by letters describing a world of magic populated by a race of people called Feyune. A warrior race, some of whom were called Blades, and others...Bloodsworn.

157

She shook her head slightly, looking around her. This was taking a joke too far. Only it wasn't a joke. The blood was real. The men lying dead on the cold warehouse floor were real.

Another race? Another world? Could things get any crazier? She tried to steady her shaking hands and stared hard at the three men with their silver swords.

"Are you...are you Blades?" If they didn't know what she was talking about, she figured she could at least dismiss the whole race from another planet premise and move on to more logical explanations.

As if anything about this day was logical.

Unfortunately, Mr. Model nodded immediately and held up his sword as if saluting. "We are Silver Blades sworn to the Tragar, ruler of realm Illian, and First Bloodsworn of Avalyr."

Avera closed her eyes for a moment and pinched the bridge of her nose. She didn't want to believe him. If those tests had come back normal this morning, she would have been able dismiss his words without a second thought. But they weren't normal. Those two flowers weren't *Earth* normal. Which meant they were something else. From somewhere else. She looked up and caught a hint of impatience in his expression before his face went blank. Talk about a poker face. "So, let me get this straight. You're telling me everything in those silly little scrolls I've been getting is true."

A nod.

"There's another world out there in space somewhere called Avalyr."

A sharper nod, accompanied by a verbal assent. "Yes."

"A world based on magic, not science."

"Yes." Snappy and emphatic. Interesting.

"And you're from this world."

"Yes." Down an octave this time, his face

158

tightening just a bit around the eyes. He was starting to get a little frustrated with her. If her head didn't hurt so bad trying to catalogue, compile, and transfer fantasy into fact, she would have smiled. Instead, she closed her eyes again and massaged her temple. "Can you just tell me why someone is trying to kill me?"

"Forgive me, Lady St. John, but there is little time. We must get you to safety. The Tragar will tell you all you need to know."

She opened her eyes. She had a lot of questions and not much in the way of answers. Apparently, she wasn't going to get them from anyone but this Tragar, the man who'd delighted her senses with his gifts and teased her mind with a bunch of enigmatic prophecies. The man who'd messed with her emotions with those damn letters, telling her things she'd been able to pass off as nonsense. Until now.

Chapter Twenty-Two

The more Avera thought about the whole mess—guns, swords, dead men in the halls, more on the warehouse floor—the angrier she got. Nothing was going to keep her from meeting this Tragar person and giving him a piece of her mind. Whoever he was, he had a lot of explaining to do.

"All right, let's go find this Tragar of yours. Lead on, McDuff."

His forehead creased slightly, but he motioned to the others and began moving toward an exit. "I am not McDuff. I am Fate An-Derrith, First Blade to the Tragar."

She followed him, glancing warily over her shoulder when the other two dropped in behind her. "First Blade. Is that supposed to be some kind of title?" He nodded. She looked over her shoulder again. "What about you guys?"

"Sarreth, Fifth Blade," the big, quiet warrior said.

"I am Kiel. My status, at present, is Novice, but I hope to change that soon." The younger man went so far as to smile a little at her, though his warm, brown eyes still looked wary, as if he expected her to fall apart any minute. Avera turned back around and despite the seriousness of the situation, she grinned. She'd have a hell of a story to tell Devlin tonight.

Assuming she made it to tonight.

Before they'd gone ten steps, more black-sword warriors flowed out of a side aisle and blocked their exit from the warehouse.

"Protect her."

Fate An-Derrith snapped out the order to the warrior named Kiel as he and the burly Sarreth ran forward, blades swinging. Avera watched Kiel bring his own sword up as two of the bad guys fought their way past Fate and Sarreth, their eyes locked on her.

One of the two charged in, yelling, engaging Kiel in a rapid exchange of blows that left her in awe. The other warrior stalked toward her silently, his dark-eyed gaze emotionless and cold, like he'd seen more than his share of death, and hers was about to be just one more. She swallowed hard and brought her gun up.

Pull the trigger, pull the trigger. Oh, man, did she want to pull the trigger. But something stopped her. Biting her lip, she looked at his eyes and tried again. Nothing. She simply couldn't kill him. And before she could figure out why, he flicked his sword toward her so fast she never saw it coming.

Avera gasped as the gun flew out of her hand, leaving her weaponless. She took a couple steps back.

Stupid, stupid. She'd never done anything so stupid in her life. She'd never frozen with indecision before. Why the hell did she have to pick now?

She should run. Any sane person would. But then, she wasn't sure if she was sane any more. And she really didn't want to die with a sword in her back. If he was going to kill her, he was going to have to take her out face-to-face. Scared as she was, she planted her feet and put her hands on her hips, more to try to hide how bad her hands were shaking than a show of defiance.

He'd probably been expecting her to run because

161

when she didn't, he stopped cold. They stared at each other for a handful of heartbeats before Avera snapped out, "Well, if you're going to do it, get on with it. I don't have all day, you know." Her body trembled, adrenaline making her heart pound so fast and hard she was amazed it didn't burst through her chest. She tightened her muscles and stared into his dark eyes hoping to catch a warning of when he was about to strike. Not having a gun in her hand didn't make her completely helpless. She knew a few tricks from the years of lessons her father had drilled into her. She might have a chance if she could just get inside the reach of that sword.

The man's brows rose sharply at her words. She'd definitely surprised him. Then his dark brows drew together, and he regarded her with a look of wary confusion. His eyes darted from her to his black sword and back again. His jaw tightened. If she didn't know better, she would swear he was waging a war with himself in his mind.

Kill her, don't kill her, kill her, don't kill her...

Damn, she wished he'd make up his mind.

Then Kiel was there, having dispatched his other opponent. The black sword warrior turned away from her, a clear look of relief on his face as he caught Kiel's descending blade. The two began to fight.

Avera dragged in a few breaths, something she hadn't been sure she'd be doing a few seconds before. She glanced around and located the Glock, snatched up the weapon and stood back out of the way of flying swords. Kiel fought hard, full of the strength of youth and, if she read him correctly, righteous anger. The other warrior was older, his style deadly calm in comparison.

She knew more about guns than she did about swords, but from what she could tell, the silent warrior could have taken Kiel's life more than once.

He was defending, not attacking, and she suddenly had a burning desire to know why. Why would every warrior carrying a black sword want her dead but this one?

A quick glance at Fate and Sarreth showed they were still fighting their own battles. When they finished, they would come to Kiel's aid. The mysterious warrior wouldn't have a chance against three. He'd be just another dead body on the floor.

She didn't want that to happen, but she didn't know what to do about it either. Her gun certainly wasn't going to help. These guys moved so fast she couldn't be sure of her aim. She'd be more likely to kill someone than merely wound them, and she didn't want to kill anyone else if she could help it. She tucked the gun in her waistband at her back and looked around for an alternative.

The sword belonging to the first man Kiel faced lay on the warehouse floor. At least she thought it was his. This sword wasn't black, but flat gray. It looked dull, unpolished. Dead. Suppressing a shudder, Avera hurried over to it, hesitated, then snatched it up.

No jolt, quiver, or flash of heat met her palm. Nothing magical. Just reassuringly cool leather wrapped around colder metal.

A grunt and a clatter of steel behind her had her turning in time to see Kiel go down.

"No!" she yelled. She started running toward them, but knew she wouldn't make it in time. The black sword pressed against Kiel's throat. The man holding that sword glanced up at her shout. His dark eyes widened. She didn't see him reach for the dagger, but she saw him throw it. Before she could even think to duck or take cover, the knife skimmed over her left shoulder. Thank God his aim was off. Then she heard a gurgling sound coming from behind her. Spinning around, she gasped.

Not three feet away stood a man holding a raised black sword. Avera cringed back and swung her scavenged sword up in a clumsy block. The two weapons clanged together. She could hardly believe it when the black sword went flying off to the side. She blinked and focused on the man, then wished she hadn't.

No wonder she'd been able to knock his sword away.

Blood gushed from around the knife buried in the man's throat. Weak fingers plucked at the hilt. His eyes fixed on her, filled with a mixture of hatred and fear. All the while his throat worked, spilling out horrible gurgling noises. He finally dropped to his knees and fell over on his side. Even then, she couldn't tear her eyes away from the red liquid quickly pooling on the floor.

It had to be a mistake. The man fighting Kiel didn't just kill one of his own men to protect her. He'd been aiming at her and missed, that's all. Lucky her.

Kiel's angry bellow jerked her around again. He'd rolled away and recovered his sword while his opponent had been inadvertently saving her life. The strange man met her eyes for only an instant before turning to defend himself against Kiel's attack, but it was enough to shake Avera out of her stunned disbelief.

Okay, so his throw hadn't been off. He'd known exactly what he was doing. The question now was, why.

Fate and Sarreth passed her at the same time, their intent clear. If she didn't stop them, she would never know the answer to this new question, and she was getting tired of not knowing what was going on. She ran after the two men.

"Wait! Wait!"

They stopped a few feet from the fight. Fate held

an arm out. "Stay behind us," he ordered.

"No, listen to me. Don't kill him."

They paid her no attention, eyes focused on the fight before them. The mystery warrior continued defending himself, only defending. That would have to change soon. As fast as Kiel was, he was bound to slip inside the other man's guard at some point. On the other hand, she knew if the warrior incapacitated Kiel, he'd probably be dead in the next instant anyway. Sarreth and Fate wouldn't give him time to catch his breath.

Stupid men. She'd had enough of people dying today. If they would just stop fighting long enough to listen to her!

Her hand went to her back and fingered the gun stuck in her waistband, a half-formed plan in her mind. But at that moment, the fighters shifted and the other man's dark eyes met hers.

"Stop fighting. Please," she whispered.

He couldn't have heard her, but something in his eyes flickered. Acknowledgement?

She watched his whole posture change as he took a step back from Kiel. A clear sign he was willing to stop. Avera let out a breath in relief only to suck it in again in dismay. Kiel must have seen the other man's retreat as a sign of weakness. He leapt forward, sword flashing snake quick.

Avera cried out and tried to push between Fate and Sarreth. Their broad shoulders kept her from seeing exactly what happened next. All she saw was Kiel's silver sword suddenly flying up into the air, spinning off to the side. Both warriors jumped forward, only to have their hands full as Kiel's body came crashing into them. Fate and Sarreth caught him awkwardly, and Avera took advantage of their entanglement to dodge around the three men.

"No!"

"Lady St. John!"

She slowed as she approached the strange warrior, her gaze shifting between his stern face and the sharp weapon in his hand. Dear God, please don't let her be making the biggest mistake of her life, she thought. The sword tip wavered, then dropped until it rested on the floor. She took a relieved breath. Meeting his dark-eyed gaze, she held a hand up, palm out.

"Don't move," she said. His gaze darted to the warriors behind her but he nodded once. Despite his actions, she still found it difficult to turn her back on him. The hairs on her neck stood straight up as she put herself in front of him and faced the Silver Blades.

Kiel's stiff body radiated fury, chest heaving, fists clenched. Sarreth's wary gaze flickered back and forth between her and the man behind her. Both men appeared poised to attack. Fate held his sword up to stop them. As his eyes focused on the man at her back, he held out a hand to her. "My lady, you do not know what you are doing. Please, come here, now." His fingers flicked urgently.

If the moment had been less tense, Avera would have rolled her eyes. "No, listen to me. I tried to tell you before. He's not like the others."

Sarreth's low voice rumbled. "He is a Black Blade, a bloodthirsty killer sent to murder you. He deserves death."

"If he wanted to kill me, I'd be dead already. Twice." She held up two fingers for emphasis, and then pointed one at the man lying dead behind them. "The dagger in that man's throat is not mine." She looked straight at each warrior, saving their tall leader for last. His eyes left the man behind her for the first time and met hers with the force of a blow. Fate An-Derrith was not happy with her.

But at least he was listening.

He glanced over his shoulder, and then back at

her. "Kiel, get your sword." He waited until Kiel returned. "Watch him," Fate ordered. He quickly stepped back to the dead man. Avera had to swallow hard when he reached down and jerked the knife free to examine it more closely. He wiped it on the dead man's shirt, stood, and met her eyes again before his gaze slid once more over her shoulder. He held the dagger up. "This is yours?"

A pause. The man behind her must have nodded, because Fate grunted before shoving the dagger through his belt.

"He is lying," Kiel said.

Avera raised her brows. "That would mean I'm lying too, wouldn't it? What possible reason would I have for doing such a stupid thing? I'm trying to stay alive here."

The young man met her steady gaze for only an instant before dropping his eyes. It looked like his face pinked a bit in embarrassment, but it could as easily have been temper.

Avera sighed. Trust her to make enemies of her only allies. Her diplomacy skills sucked. She turned around, and got her first unhurried look at the warrior who had not only spared her life, but saved it.

The term "ruggedly handsome" popped into her mind. He had a no-nonsense face with strong cheekbones, firm lips, and a square jaw darkened by a light growth of beard. The rest of his face was smooth skin right up to the corners of his eyes where a few creases only served to emphasize his piercing gaze. Age-wise, she didn't think he was much over thirty. No gray showed in the dark brown hair hanging past his shoulders. A small hoop of gold glinted from one ear, making him look as much of a pirate as Sarreth.

She tried to catch his eyes, wanting to see if they still held that cold look of death, but he refused to meet her gaze. He stared determinedly at some boxes stacked on a shelf behind Sarreth. She turned back to Fate. "He could have killed me just now and didn't. Instead, he saved my life. He could have killed Kiel too." She ignored Kiel's hiss of denial. "I think we need to think about this for just a minute."

Fate's voice held more than a little impatience. "Lady, we do not have time."

The dark eyed warrior shifted his eyes, but he still did not look at any of them directly. "He is right, my lady. Even now more of Camarie's Blades could be gating here."

Fate swore. "He is creating outer gates?"

"My Bloodsworn is not one to play by the Concourse's rules." He turned his head, his gaze locking somewhere over her head. "The Tragar cannot let me live. I am still tied to Camarie by the blood-bond. It would be best if these warriors took my head."

"Vet, yes," muttered Kiel as he stepped forward, raising his sword.

"Don't you dare," Avera snapped, holding out her arms.

"Lady St. John..."

"No, I won't let you kill him. And I've decided I'm not going anywhere with anyone until I know more of what's going on. I don't like making decisions without all the facts." She turned and pinned a determined glare on the man she'd begun to think of as her warrior. "Just who is this Camarie? Is he the one who wants me dead? If so, why? And what do you mean you're tied to him by a blood-bond?"

She was just beginning to get a handle on the whole other-world-swords-and-magic business. Now they wanted to add *blood ties* into the mix? So help her, if he said one word about vampires, she was going to scream.

Chapter Twenty-Three

Bracca shifted his eyes to the feisty female before quickly looking away. So many questions. He chose to answer her first and last ones.

"Camarie is my Bloodsworn. He and I are tied together through this." Bracca raised his own dark sword slowly, aware any quick move on his part would send three silver swords slashing at his throat. While it was true that would be best for several reasons, he found part of him wasn't quite ready for death. Not anymore.

The woman intrigued him. He felt pulled to her, drawn by an invisible thread. Just as the old tales claimed Blades were once drawn to the Bloodsworn they were destined to serve. Yet, this feeling could not possibly be the same. No female had ever been Bloodsworn. Women could not handle the violence of a linking, much less the brutal emotions they would experience through the link with their Blade. Why then had he felt *it* the moment he'd set foot on this planet's soil? The subtle Calling, the persistent tugging at his mind he could not ignore. Somehow, near to the place where he'd arrived on this world, was the Bloodsworn he had been destined to serve. The possibility that Bloodsworn was the Tragar would have been difficult enough to handle. He had served Camarie for more years than he wished to count, given no choice but to obey his Bloodsworn.

Even if his black deeds were not laid at his door, he still doubted the Tragar would ever trust him enough to establish a blood-link.

But this woman...

Every moment he was in her presence, he became more convinced she was his destiny, no matter how impossible the idea might seem.

"I don't understand," she said, pointing to the black weapon in his hand. "How can you be tied to someone through a sword?"

His glance flickered to the Silver Blade leader, a man described to him many times. Fate An-Derrith, First Blade to the Tragar. The one called The Stone Warrior by those who'd seen him fight. Impatience bled from the Stone now. Not overtly, but in his stance, in minute flex and twitch of muscle. Impatience barely held in check.

He expected to hear the warrior issue the order to relieve him of his miserable life.

Or leap in and take it himself.

When Fate hesitated, Bracca mentally berated him. Were he in charge, he would toss Avera St. John over his shoulder and take her back to the Tragar with all speed. He never once expected the Tragar's First Blade to prod him with his sword and say, "Tell her what she wants to know. You have two minutes. Sarreth, Kiel, watch the doors."

Two minutes to explain a lifetime of tradition and magic? Impossible.

Apparently, Lady St. John was not so skeptical. "All right, talk fast," she said looking up at him expectantly.

Without looking directly at her, Bracca obeyed. "To form a blood-bond, a Bloodsworn first feeds a sword his own blood. He then adds the blood of the man petitioning his aid. The sword transforms, becoming a manifestation of the link between Bloodsworn and Blade. It is part of what ties them together until one of them dies. Through the sword, a Bloodsworn knows where all his Blades are. He can pick up emotions from them, images and impressions. The power of a Bloodsworn's link varies from Blade to Blade, but the stronger the link, the more information he can gather." Her brow furrowed and he stopped, assuming he'd lost her several sentences ago. She surprised him.

"So this Camarie knows you're here, now, with me?"

"Yes."

"Can he hear our conversation?"

"I do not know. Unless told, a Blade never knows how much his Bloodsworn receives through their link. Camarie is not one to tell his secrets." He had closed his side of the link the instant he made the decision not to kill her. Still, he couldn't be sure just how much control Camarie had over their blood-link, how much information he could glean, even with it closed. Bracca did not want to be the instrument of her death, even indirectly.

"Can this link be broken?"

Sweat popped out on his forehead. He had seen a link broken several times in his life. "Yes, a Bloodsworn can sunder the link either mentally, or by physically breaking the sword." He had seen both. Once a year, Camarie gathered his Blades and proceeded to demonstrate the extent of his power with very graphic details. Breaking a link was the ultimate punishment, a death sentence. The men he'd seen go through the painful process had not survived.

She frowned, as if furiously turning over the information he had given her. By the Veil, she continued to surprise him, stirring up feelings he thought never to see again. Humility, awe, concern, and even more remarkably, pride. She'd chosen to face down three angry Feyune warriors for him, someone she knew had been sent to kill her. Her courage seemed to know no bounds. Nor did her thirst for information.

"What if someone else breaks the sword? What if it's broken while you're fighting?"

"I do not know. I have never heard of a sword breaking in battle."

"The Blade usually dies no matter how his sword is broken," Fate said.

Lady St. John's eyes widened in shock. Her surprise quickly changed to a stern frown as she turned to Bracca. She stabbed a finger at him. "You didn't tell me that. Don't you think dying is an important variable?" She sighed loudly and raised both hands to rub her temples.

Bracca dared a full glance at her, concern filling him at the pain in her eyes. She looked flushed, her skin too warm. Was she ill?

"There has to be a way around it," she murmured

"My lady, we do not have time for this," Fate growled. "We must leave here if you wish to live."

She winced, the slight motion, whether from pain or chagrin, made Bracca want to slam a fist into Fate's expressionless face.

"Okay, okay," she said quickly. "Just one more question. Well, two actually. If a Blade's sword is broken, can he be linked with another Bloodsworn? Will that save him?"

"Yes, I've seen it happen," one of the other two Silver Blades said as he rushed up to them. He turned to Fate. "Black Blades are in the corridor. They are headed this way."

"How many?"

"Too many."

"Some coming from this side, too." The third Blade, the one who'd faced Bracca, came running up on light feet. Barely an adult, the boy had fought well. Considering the reputation of the Tragar's Blades, he'd expected nothing less.

"We leave now." Fate stepped toward Bracca, his sword rising.

He waited for the bite of the shining blade without flinching. Nor did he bother to raise his own sword in defense. The only way he could return to his Bloodsworn and expect to live was if he killed Avera St. John, an act he could never bring himself to do. He considered execution by a man with An-Derrith's reputation a more than acceptable alternative.

"No!"

Once again, Lady St. John placed herself between him and certain death. Instinct told him to move her aside, out of the path of harm. He should be the one standing between her and death, not the other way around. From the look on An-Derrith's face, however, Bracca knew he dared not touch her. Nor did An-Derrith or the other Silver Blades touch her, as she continued her tirade.

"You guys just stop it, now, I mean it. Damn, you warrior types are bloodthirsty. Just back off, all right? He's coming with us."

Her words froze Bracca, but they had the opposite effect on Fate. With a wordless snarl, he stepped forward, a move intended to force Lady St. John into retreat. Bracca felt an odd tug at the corners of his lips when she responded by placing her hands on her hips and tilting her head back to meet Fate's black gaze.

He glared down at her. "I will not bring a Blade of Camarie's into my Bloodsworn's presence," he declared. "To do so would not only place my Bloodsworn's life in danger, but would mean my death as well. The Tragar does not suffer stupidity lightly."

She threw her hands in the air. "Give me a

break, will you? I didn't even know Blades and Bloodsworns existed until five minutes ago."

To Bracca's astonishment and pleasure, she turned her back on the intimidating Silver Blade and held her hand out to him. He hardly dared to breathe as he slowly raised his hand and carefully closed it around her much smaller one. Gods, she was magnificent! When she started walking, all he could do was follow.

"I just need a little more time to work on figuring things out. We'll just have to fix things before we reach this Tragar of yours," she said as they passed the Silver Blades.

By their faces, Bracca wasn't sure which of the three men was more shocked by her bold behavior. He expected to feel cold steel against his neck or buried in his back as the warriors closed in behind him. When it came, the flat of a blade merely tapped his sword arm. Low words laced with irritation, spoke into his ear.

"Sheath your sword, *tu-kai*, and pray my patience with the Tragar's Starmate does not run out."

Releasing the breath he held, Bracca watched Fate take over the lead with long strides. The First Blade's implacable visage had probably reduced new Blades to quivering infants on the training field, but seemed to have no effect on Bracca's lady champion. His admiration for her increased when she did nothing more than wave An-Derrith on impatiently.

Bracca decided he could afford to pity the Silver Blade. The warrior truly faced a dilemma. Duty demanded Fate protect his Bloodsworn's chosen bride at all costs. As the Tragar's Starmate, a position of high status, honor demanded Fate defer to her wishes. Between duty and honor lay a very narrow and slippery road, one not easily trod. Bracca should know, since he'd traveled that same road from the moment he became a Black Blade.

He glanced down at his sword, a weapon he'd grown to hate, before sliding it into its sheath. The hilt clicked against the scabbard with a sense of finality. He would not draw the dark Bloodsworn's black sword again.

They neared the exit when a subtle shift of air warned him. He jerked his arm back sharply, pulling Lady St. John completely off her feet and into his arms. Her yelp had Fate An-Derrith whirling around with an angry hiss and the thirst for Bracca's blood in his eyes. Those eyes widened in surprise as a long black sword snaked out from between two tall crates, slicing the air where Lady St. John had stood an instant before. The sword's owner stumbled out from his hiding place as Bracca swung the Lady around, passing her to the two Silver Blades behind him. He dodged the next attack, darted in close, and delivered a crushing blow to the man's throat. Immediately, the man bent over, choking, giving Bracca full access to his head. A quick twist of hands and the black-sword warrior lay dead on the floor.

Bracca met An-Derrith's furious gaze before turning his back on him to check on the woman he'd chosen to protect. "You are unharmed, my lady?"

She stared at the dead warrior, one hand cupping her throat, her green eyes wide, lips pressed tight together. At the sound of his voice, she lifted her stunned gaze to him. He could see her visibly pull herself together, the slight, fearful hunch of her shoulders lifting as she took a deep breath. Leaving the safety of the Silver Blades, she walked up to him and placed her palm on his chest. Something inside him shifted, almost falling into place, but not quite.

"Thank you. I...thank you." Her eyes shimmered, as if holding back tears. She patted his chest twice before taking his hand again and turning to An-Derrith. "I would really, *really* like to leave now."

Instead of following her, Bracca walked close beside her, eyes alert, as Fate led them through a door to the outside. They made their way down the side of the building without incident and crossed the lawn to a large machine topped with long, whirling blades. Two men, dressed in dark green clothing and armed with long knives, met them near the machine's open door. One of the men stepped in front of Bracca. "Who's this?"

"He's with me," Lady St. John said.

The man looked at Fate. "You okay with this?"

Bracca met the eyes of the Silver Blade and waited for him to say no. He should have known his little champion would not stand idly by. Black hair whipping around her face, she shouted over the noise of the spinning blades. "If he stays, I stay." Her chin tilted up stubbornly. The dark skin over An-Derrith's jaw paled as teeth ground and muscles clenched. Then the warrior nodded sharply and motioned for them to climb into the machine. The whirling blades picked up speed.

Bracca settled into a seat next to Lady St. John, ignoring the warning looks from the Tragar's three Blades. She leaned close to him, one arm reaching across his body. He sat back in surprise, hands raised and open, as she tightened a wide belt across his lap. He thought it a restraint of some kind, because she didn't trust him, and felt a twinge of regret. Then he saw Fate and the others fasten belts around themselves. He finally understood why when the flying machine lifted off the ground and spun around, tilting dangerously. He grabbed the edge of his seat, feeling as if his stomach was still on the ground and might never catch up. By the satisfied smirks on the faces of two of the Silver Blades, this experience was not new to them. They appeared to be enjoying his initiation.

The machine tilted again, throwing Lady St.

John against him. He wrapped his arms around her to hold her steady, his own discomfort forgotten. He would have released her after their conveyance leveled out, but seeing the displeased frowns on the faces of the other warriors changed his mind.

A minor defiance perhaps, but extremely satisfying nonetheless. He may not be hers by blood, but the possibility existed that he could be, *should be*. True, women were not Bloodsworn, had never been Bloodsworn. But he had lived too long not to believe in change. Had Avera St. John been born on Avalyr where he could have sensed her, he had no doubt the past hellish decade of his life would have been quite different. Even now the *Calling* pulled so strong inside him he wondered why she could not feel it, too. Then again, perhaps she did. Perhaps that was why she kept the others from killing him.

Hope stirred inside him while logic told him he was a fool. Assuming she would even agree to try forming a blood-link with him, there was no guarantee she would be able to convert Avalyr's magic into the essence that would keep him alive.

Still, it would have pleased him greatly to see the stunned and envious looks on the faces of the Tragar's Blades. They belonged to Avalyr's First Bloodsworn, but he would have belonged to a living legend...the first female Bloodsworn in Avalyr's long history.

Chapter Twenty-Four

Avera took in the tense expressions on the faces of the three warriors across from her and leaned away from the one beside her. No sense causing more trouble until she had to. He let her go, his arms slipping from around her slowly, as if reluctant to do so. Then he crossed his well-muscled arms over his chest and tipped his head back against the padded headrest. His eyelids lowered until they almost closed. He looked completely relaxed, without a care in the world. Avera felt the complete opposite.

Part of her had been silently screaming ever since she'd witnessed the bloody fighting on Barrett Chemical's front lawn. Things had happened so fast. Too fast. She'd had to concentrate on just staying alive and that had kept fear and panic from getting the upper hand. Now that she was sitting down with nowhere to run, no bullets or swords to dodge, she could feel herself starting to shake inside.

God, what had she been thinking? If her father could somehow see her now, he'd be throwing one of his famous Marine fits.

A pang of longing pierced her heart, and she choked back a sudden sob. Oh, how she missed him. After her mother's suicide, it had been just him and her. Despite the demands of his career, Raphael St. John had been her father, mother, and best friend, watching over her like a hawk. His protective nature had made for a strange childhood and adolescence. Firearms courses and self-defense training marched side-by-side with tea parties and dance classes. She remembered a few rebellious moments, but not many. Looking back now, she could only thank God for her father's perseverance. Something told her she was going to need everything she'd ever learned from him.

One thing he taught her was that in a life and death situation she had to do what she needed to do to stay alive and save the consequences for later. Right now she couldn't afford to think about the fact she'd killed two men. Processing something like that, getting past the consequences, would take time she didn't have. Not when she might have to kill again. Maybe that was why she felt so determined to keep the man beside her alive.

Of course, she still wasn't sure she believed everything. Sure, she was in a big black helicopter, but that's where reality ended, right? Sword-wielding warriors? Bloodsworn, Blades, and mental links? Prophecies and Oracles? They all had to be crazy.

Or she was.

Now, there was a depressing thought.

Fierce denial rose up inside her. *No, I am not going down that road.*

She wasn't her mother. Dealing with the real world, no matter how unbelievable things got, didn't scare her. She refused to let whatever situation this Tragar was pulling her into get the best of her. Life was not a stagnant pool. Things changed. Maybe not always for the better, but not always for the worse, either.

She thought of the most recent "good" change in her life with a surge of longing. If Devlin were with her, she knew she wouldn't be afraid. Then she opened her eyes a little and changed her mind. If he *were* here, he would definitely want to protect her, and she didn't like the idea of him facing off against the three men sitting across from her. Yes, they were three of the most incredibly good-looking men she'd ever laid eyes on barring Devlin, but these were true barbarians. Her handsome business executive wouldn't stand a chance against those deadly silver swords. Swords none of them had put away because of the tall, dark, and menacing man sitting beside her. Even with his sword safely in its scabbard, they remained on guard.

She wondered why Fate had only told him to put the weapon away instead of taking it from him. Then logic told her it probably had something to do with that link thing he'd told her about. Maybe this Camarie knew when one of his Blades lost his sword to an enemy.

She leaned toward the man beside her, noting with wry amusement how all three silver swords jerked in reaction. "I think if someone saves my life, I should at least know his name, don't you? I'm sorry I didn't ask before."

He glanced at her, and she saw surprise in his eyes before he quickly turned away. Why wouldn't he look at her for more than a couple of seconds? She didn't think it was a warrior thing, since Fate glared straight at her all the time. His eyelids drifted down again, but didn't close completely. She could see his dark eyes staring straight ahead though his lashes.

"My name is Bracca Cu-Laurian."

Strange, sharply muttered words that sounded like swearing came from the other side of the helicopter. Fate unbuckled his seatbelt and sheathed his sword. He pulled the thin-bladed dagger he'd taken from the dead man's throat in the warehouse, his eyes so cold she felt chilled.

"What?" she asked, alarm shooting through her like sparks.

"Bracca Cu-Laurian is one of Camarie's deadliest Blades. Part of his Outer Decca, if the rumors are true," Kiel said, his lips lifting into a snarl. "I knew I should have taken his head when I had the chance."

Avera grabbed at her seatbelt buckle. "No. Stop."

Fate didn't acknowledge her. He braced a hand against Bracca's shoulder and slashed down with the knife. She cried out, gave up on the seatbelt buckle, and lunged, snatching at Fate's knife-hand. He jerked out of her reach, looking at her as if she'd lost her mind. She felt like she had. Desperation held her in a tight grip while angry tears stung her eyes. She couldn't just sit there and let them kill him. "Leave him alone." Someone wrapped an arm around her waist and pulled her back. Bracca's deep voice murmured in her ear.

"Peace, my lady, I am unharmed. The Tragar's First Blade only does what is necessary for your protection."

"You're not hurt?" Confused, she looked at his shoulder, expecting to see a bloody wound. The sleeve of his shirt hung half off his shoulder but the skin beneath was still in one piece. She touched a finger to the cut cloth, relief making her angry. She glared up at Fate. "And just how is ruining his clothes supposed to protect me?"

Bracca's body shook. She leaned away and looked at him anxiously. No emotion showed on his face, and she couldn't tell anything from his shuttered eyes. Movement at his mouth drew her gaze. His lips twitch as he wordlessly held his arm out. Did he think this was funny?

The dark-skinned warrior looming over them gave her a warning look before he finished removing the sleeve. Avera felt a flush of embarrassment when he started tying the cloth around Bracca's head like a blindfold. So maybe he'd had a right to laugh. She'd over-reacted. Again.

She took a deep breath and straightened her own sleeves. Too many knives today, that was the problem. Tilting her head, she caught Fate's attention. "Was that really necessary?" she grumbled, not bothering to hide her disapproval.

"If you insist on keeping him alive, yes. And I warn you again, he will not go alive into the Tragar's presence. Not as long as he is still linked to Camarie." He returned to his seat the dagger clenched tight in his hand. It looked like he wanted nothing more than to flip the blade across and into Bracca's heart. From the hard, angry expressions on their faces, Sarreth and Kiel would probably have cheered him on.

Didn't they have any concept of gratitude on their stupid planet? The man had saved her life, for goodness sake.

She settled back in her seat, crossed her arms, and frowned at the three men. The only one who seemed at all affected by her bad mood was Kiel. When he noticed her frown, he at least stopped staring daggers at Bracca and looked away.

Bracca sat beside her like a blind statue, hands resting lightly on his knees. As she studied him, she recognized everything she felt wasn't just about gratitude. Curiosity. Compassion. A sense that he was somehow important to her, which, yeah, was crazy, but so was everything else that had happened to her today. Her eyes went to the sword at his waist. She reached out and touched the hilt with one finger.

"Please don't."

She jerked her hand back. How had he known what she was doing? "Sorry, just curious."

"You should change seats, Lady St. John." Fate had his poker face back on but she'd have to be blind not to see how unhappy he was with her at the moment.

"I'm fine where I am, thanks anyway for the suggestion." She turned back to Bracca. "Why did they let you keep your sword?"

"A Bloodsworn can feel when one of his swords is no longer in the possession of his Blade."

She nodded, pleased to have worked out part of the puzzle on her own. "I figured as much. So what happens then?"

"If a Blade is confronting the enemy and loses his sword, his Bloodsworn can only assume he is either dead, injured, or captured."

"Go on," she prodded. She had a feeling she wasn't going to like where this was going.

"Unless the Bloodsworn senses the return of the sword to his Blade, he will sunder the link."

"But I thought you said breaking the link kills the Blade."

"In most cases, it does."

Her head was starting to really pound so she tried to hold her temper, but it wasn't easy. She believed such things as loyalty went both ways. "I don't understand. Are you saying that if Fate took your sword your Bloodsworn would break this linking thing with you without bothering to find out what happened to you? He doesn't care if he kills you? Are all Bloodsworn so coldhearted?"

"Bloodsworn are like other men in that they can be either good or bad. Many Bloodsworn consider sundering the link at such times both a mercy and a necessity. Enemies torture captured Blades either for information or in the hope he is tied closely enough to his Bloodsworn that the Blade's pain will incapacitate his master."

Across from them, Kiel swore, his voice snapping. "You never heard that being done by a Silver Blade."

183

"No," Bracca agreed. "Not by a Silver. The honor of your Bloodsworn, the Tragar of Illian, is renowned. But I assure you the practice is not limited to only one Bloodsworn." His head turned in Kiel's direction, as if he was looking right at him. "You are a young Blade, no more than two years into service to your Bloodsworn I would guess. It would surprise you, *malimes*, if you knew of the things I have seen."

Kiel's body jerked, as if he wanted to throw himself across the width of the helicopter. She saw his knuckles go white around his sword hilt. Sarreth raised his sword, swinging it slowly up and down between Kiel and Bracca in a lazy gesture. The smile on his face didn't look very pleasant.

"It is true Kiel is young," Sarreth said. "But he is no *small knife* to be ignored. He stands to gain our Bloodsworn's Outer Decca soon, the youngest Blade to do so. I, on the other hand, have been a Blade for many years. As many as you, I would guess. I have seen some of the atrocities visited on others by those of the black sword, Cu-Laurian. I doubt anything you have seen would surprise *me*."

Bracca shrugged one shoulder. "Perhaps. It is possible you have even seen the results of a sundered link. But have you watched a man die whose only fault was in doing the bidding of his heart instead of that of his Bloodsworn?"

His words made Avera feel sick to her stomach. "These Bloodsworn really do that? They just cut off anyone who doesn't obey them? Anyone who loses his sword? Without even trying to find out why? That's just wrong."

"Breaking a link to a captured Blade is a common practice."

She sat back, waving a hand in a sharp gesture even though he couldn't see her. "Well I for one think it stinks. I don't believe in leaving someone to die who has risked their life for you." That wasn't how she was raised. Marines didn't abandon their own.

Bracca's lips twitched again, the ends turning up into a faint smile. When he spoke, his voice sounded wistful. "You are different from other Bloodsworn in so many ways."

"*Other* Bloodsworn? What do you mean by other?"

Fate's voice broke in, as firm and implacable as a rock. "Do not let him confuse you, Lady St. John. Females are not capable of being Bloodsworn."

Outrage poured through Avera. She'd had just about enough of Fate's superior attitude. She may not understand exactly what a Bloodsworn was, but his assumption that she wasn't capable just because she was a woman offended her deeply. He'd seen her kill someone to defend herself, yet he didn't hesitate to lump her in with whatever group of helpless females he was used to. It was thoroughly irritating. "I suppose that statement goes right along with females not being capable of killing someone. Strange isn't it, how that rule doesn't seem to apply to me? Sounds like the women you know are just a bunch of wimps."

The Silver Blade met her innocent stare but instead of sniping back as she expected, he turned his ire on Bracca. "She is not Bloodsworn, Cu-Laurian, she cannot save you. Your only hope of staying alive is the Tragar."

"But I would not get my hopes up were I you," Kiel added. "The Tragar does not need Camarie's cast-offs."

The man beside her stiffened slightly. Avera gathered quickly that being cast-off by a Bloodsworn was a very bad thing. Thinking about it, she could understand why. A Blade considered unfit enough to be let go by his, what?...employer, master, whatever a Bloodsworn was supposed to be, might be considered a risk not worth taking by anyone else. What happened to warriors who were jobless, she wondered.

Bracca's body relaxed and his lips curved up again. The motion smoother this time, looking more natural. His smile had a secretiveness about it, as if he'd just gotten the punch line of a good joke no one else had. "If you are too mind-blind to see what is before you, that is your loss. I am beginning to doubt the Tragar's wisdom in sending three such un-schooled warriors to protect his mate."

"Fate and Sarreth are part of the Tragar's Inner Decca, as is my mentor," Kiel said, pride and anger snapping in his words. "We know our place as well as our worth and do not require your approval."

"What's an Inner Decca?" Avera asked.

Bracca turned his head slightly in her direction. "An Inner Decca is made up of a Bloodsworn's ten most trusted Blades. They are usually the most skilled and have the strongest links."

"And an Outer Decca? Kiel said earlier he thought you were part of that."

He wasn't smiling now. His mouth lay in a flat line and his hands clamped around his knees. He inclined his head. "Yes, I hold the position of Eighteenth Blade, the eighth warrior in my Bloodsworn's second decca of warriors, though it is not a position I sought."

"You lie smoothly, Cu-Laurian," Sarreth said. "All Blades seek the status of serving their Bloodsworn in one of his deccas."

Bracca snorted. "Your Bloodsworn and Camarie are worlds apart. You have no idea how fortunate you are."

"That is where you are wrong, Black Blade. We are well aware of our Bloodsworn's honor. Our links with the Tragar are clear and strong." Sarreth's voice lowered to a menacing growl. "He sees you, *tu-kai*."

Bracca didn't seem bothered by the warning, but then, he couldn't see the way Sarreth's lips pulled back from his teeth. The hungry-looking smile made her wonder what *tu-kai* meant. She started to ask, but one of the men on the other side of Bracca leaned forward, addressing Fate.

"We'll be landing to refuel in another ten minutes. Should take us about half an hour." He glanced at Avera and Bracca, then back at Fate. "You guys going to be able to keep things together?"

"We will do our job, mercenary, as you do yours."

The man shrugged, nodded. "Good enough."

Chapter Twenty-Five

Restless magic pushed at the barriers in Devlin's mind, searching for a weakness, a way out. He did not understand why. There were no enemies here, only impatient Bloodsworn and their Blades. Camarie had yet to arrive.

"Devlin?"

He spun around at the touch on his arm. Several strands of magic slipped free, rushing through his body. He pulled them back in time to keep them from erupting into small, mindless tornados of power, which, considering the magic users in the room would have been more embarrassing than dangerous. As First Bloodsworn, his control was supposed to be unmatched. Right now, he did not feel in control of anything.

Jerran Ti-Peregrine's eyes narrowed, as if he'd sensed the brief spill of magic. "Are you all right, my friend?"

Devlin blew out a breath, running a hand through his hair. Frustration added to the chaotic mix of emotions churning in his stomach as he leaned closer to his friend, speaking low. "I wish I knew. The essence refuses to settle in my mind. I expected to be on edge for this confrontation, but, gods, Jerran, I feel as if I am being torn in two."

Jerran frowned. "That doesn't sound right. I feel uneasy and on edge as well, but my own magic is

188

calm. Nothing like you're describing. Are you sure what you're feeling has to do with Camarie?"

He thought about his sleepless night, the anxiety he felt at having to leave Avera on Earth. His fists clenched as magic thrust against his mental barriers. "No, I am not."

Understanding widened Jerran's eyes. "Ah, I see." He clapped a hand on Devlin's shoulder. "I have heard claiming a Starmate can be a disquieting experience under the best of circumstances. You have my sympathy, my friend. I'll try to see you're excused as soon after Camarie gets here as possible."

"He's not coming, Jerran. I know my uncle. If he had entertained the idea of a meeting such as this it wouldn't be here, and it wouldn't be with the entire Council in attendance. He would choose a place that gave him all the advantages, one with plenty of exits for when he changed his mind."

"Your uncle is the one who suggested this meeting, Prince Devlin." Kapatree Du-Farishi said as he joined them, his thin face pulled into a censoring frown. "He is also the one who suggested it be held here."

"He is also the only one who decided not to attend," Devlin pointed out. He wasn't surprised Kapatree chose to speak up in favor of Camarie. Anytime Devlin took a stand on a subject, Kapatree tended to stand on the opposite side.

"I'll admit he is a bit late—"

"Two hours is not a bit late, Kapatree, it is a slap in the face. Camarie has no intention of submitting himself to the Council's discipline."

Those Bloodsworn not already seated in their chairs drifted closer, most scowling and nodding in agreement.

"I agree with Devlin," Jerran said. "The dark Bloodsworn is probably safe in one of his secret hideouts chuckling over how he manipulated us all into wasting our time."

Kapatree laughed derisively. "Camarie is not the type of man to play tricks just for the sake of amusement. That is more your domain, is it not young Peregrine?"

Devlin felt Jerran tense beside him. "What do you mean by that?"

"Simply that I have heard it rumored you often display your magic for the amusement of others in exchange for certain *female* favors."

Jerran took a step forward at the insult aimed at both his masculinity and his honor. Devlin reached out a restraining hand, grateful to have something other than his uncomfortable magic to concentrate on. While a Bloodsworn duel between Jerran and the annoying Kapatree might be satisfying, now was not the time.

Caveon suddenly appeared at Jerran's side as if he'd gated there. "Are you trying to disrupt this meeting before it begins, Kapatree?"

The thin Bloodsworn held up both hands, his expression one of innocence. "Of course not, Caveon, that was never my intention." He bowed to Jerran. "Rumors can be so very distressing, and persistent. If these particular rumors come to my ears again, I assure you I will do everything in my power to quell them."

Jerran didn't answer. Turning, he walked away stiffly, his Blades falling into step with him. Kapatree moved away as well, dipping his head to hide his pleased smirk from Caveon, but failing to hide it from Devlin. The bastard.

"A diversion," Devlin murmured, careful to keep his voice low, "meant to buy Camarie time."

"Probably," agreed Caveon. "But we have no proof. And no choice."

"He is playing us for fools, Caveon."

"Who? Kapatree, or Camarie?"

"Does it matter?"

Caveon heaved a deep sigh. "Yes, and no. Camarie is a known enemy, whereas I would like to believe Kapatree is still loyal to our ideals. However, the possibility of a traitor in our midst is not a new concept. There are eyes other than mine and yours monitoring the health of this Council, First Bloodsworn."

"Sharp eyes, I hope," Devlin said. Inside his mind, the restless magic surged again. "How much longer do you intend to hold us here?"

"The other elders and I agreed to wait an additional two hours."

Devlin snorted.

"Perhaps," Caveon said, evidently needing no words to understand Devlin's opinion. "But you must agree that if there is the slightest chance of Camarie appearing, we must take it. You, more than any other, realize how important it is for us to bring the dark Bloodsworn under our wing."

"No one will ever control my uncle, Caveon, least of all the Council. Camarie will die before he grants anyone power over him."

"For the sake of the men he is linked to, I hope you are wrong, Tragar. I sincerely do."

Chapter Twenty-Six

The helicopter landed at a tiny airstrip located on the outskirts of a small town. The facility had seen better days. Two rundown buildings bordered the cracked asphalt pad, one a large metal hangar, and the other a much smaller wooden building with a faded sign over the door that read Office/Lounge. The whole place had a deserted feel to it despite the few vehicles parked here and there.

"You can wait in the lounge there," the man who'd spoken earlier told them, pointing to the smaller building not far away. "We'll come get you when we're ready to go."

Fate nodded. He took her arm as she climbed out. He didn't let go as they walked toward the building. She twitched her arm once just to see how serious he was about holding on to her. His grip tightened a little. Very serious, she decided. Maybe his patience had run out. She glanced at his stern profile. Years of self-defense classes with her father tutoring her on the side had left her more than capable of taking down someone of his size. Whether she could handle someone of his skill was another matter, one she wasn't quite ready to put to the test.

Hurrying to keep up with his long strides, she glanced over her shoulder to make sure Bracca was all right. She ground her teeth, watching as Sarreth and Kiel pushed him out of the helicopter without removing his blindfold. He hit the ground hard, stumbling a little, before he caught his balance. He straightened and, without pausing, started walking in her direction, his steps quick and sure, as if the blindfold wasn't there. The other two warriors had to hurry to catch up to him.

The main room of the office/lounge sported a couple of worn couches along with several uncomfortable looking chairs. To one side a young girl perched on a stool behind a counter, popping gum and reading a magazine. Her mouth dropped open at the sight of the four warriors, three with naked swords in their hands and a fourth blindfolded.

"It's okay," Avera hurried to assure her. "We're, uh, on our way to a movie shoot. The guys here are just trying to get into character."

The girl's eyes widened. "Really? Cool. What's the name of the movie?"

"The Silver Blades," she said, picking the first thing that came to mind. "Uh, can you point us to the restrooms?"

"Sure, down the hall on the left."

Avera nodded. "Thanks." She looked at Fate who still had her by the arm. "Listen, you're going to have to let go for a minute. I need to go to the little girl's room." His frowning look told her he didn't understand. She sighed. "The restroom, bathroom, toilet, lavatory..."

His grip loosened. "Where?"

"Down there." She jabbed a finger at the hall.

He let go of her arm entirely and motioned her ahead of him. She found the door marked Ladies and pushed inside, half-expecting Fate to try and follow. Thankfully, he merely took up a station in the hall opposite the door. She closed it on his glowering look and gratefully turned around to take care of a few necessities.

After washing her hands, she splashed some cool water on her face. She still felt hot and she still had a blasted headache. Maybe that's why she felt so grouchy. Couldn't have anything to do with her life getting turned upside down, now, could it. Patting her face dry, she looked at herself in the mirror. Her green eyes looked too bright and her face too pale except for her flushed cheeks. She touched the bright splotches of color and winced at the heat.

Great. Either I have permanent embarrassment or a fever. Neither option sounded good at the moment. Not when she had testosterone-laden, six-foot something, men to deal with. She needed her wits and every ounce of self-respect she could muster just to keep up.

Taking a deep breath, she opened the door, expecting to see Fate in his stoic-warrior pose waiting for her, but the hallway was empty. She'd taken two steps toward the lounge when Bracca's body came flying down the hall. She squeaked and flattened herself against the wall as he landed at her feet with a grunt. The opening to the lounge darkened with bodies and fear whirled through her for a moment before she recognized Fate, Kiel, and Sarreth. She started to relax, but then saw their expressions, and the fear returned, bringing dread along for company.

"What's going on? What happened?" she demanded as Bracca slipped the blindfold off and came quickly to his feet. She tried to put herself between him and the others, but he wouldn't let her, blocking her way with his arm.

"Black Blades. They have attacked the men who were with us. Some are coming this way," he said never taking his eyes off the Silver Blades.

She looked from him to the three warriors ranged in the hall. "How did they find us so quickly?"

"How else," Kiel said. He nodded toward Bracca.

"But he was blindfolded the whole time," Avera insisted, her frantic gaze going to Fate as she clutched Bracca's arm. The way he held his arm in front of her gave the impression he was shielding her from Fate and the others. She had no idea why he would think she needed his protection, or even why he would offer it. He was the one in danger of being killed here, not her. "I thought that's why you covered his eyes, to keep anyone from using him to find us."

"A Bloodsworn does not need a Blade's eyes to know where he is," Bracca said. "A Bloodsworn's sword draws him through the blood-link." Slowly, Bracca's other hand moved to his sword belt and began unfastening the buckle. "One way or another, my link must be broken."

"Agreed," Fate said, holding out his hand.

Bracca shook his head. "The task is mine."

Fate stared a moment before nodding. "Sarreth, Kiel, guard the hallway." The two men muttered, but turned and faced the lounge, planting themselves shoulder to shoulder in the narrow hall.

Her heart pounding, she shook Bracca's arm. "You can't do this." She looked wildly at Fate. "Don't make him do this. You said it would kill him."

"Most likely, but we have no other choice. The Dark Bloodsworn will continue to use Cu-Laurian's link to send Blades after us. I will risk your life no further."

"Damn it, it's my life." She tried to push her way around Bracca but the big warrior's arm curled around her. The look on his face stopped her protest before she could utter the words. His eyes held so much regret she felt her own eyes tear up. Then determination steeled his gaze.

"This must be done. I would have you know one thing, my lady. Though sent to kill you, I would never have taken your life. From the moment I set foot on this world, I felt you here," he touched his chest. "My sword belongs to Camarie, but my life is yours."

"Bracca..." She couldn't get past his name, her throat too clogged with tears. What could she say to a declaration like that anyway? How was it possible that she felt so strongly about this man when they'd just met? She stepped back when he gently pushed her away from him, feeling like she was the one dying inside. She didn't know this man, didn't love him. But his words, coupled with the knowledge he was willing to risk his life to protect her, made her want to fling her arms around him protectively and bare her teeth in defiance at Fate.

Under the Silver Blade's watchful eye, Bracca lifted his sword-belt free and slipped his sword from its scabbard. Avera watched him slide the sword between the door to the ladies room and the metal doorframe. Forcing the door shut, he took the hilt in both hands and shoved it toward the wall.

Avera wondered how much pressure would be required to break a sword. Apparently it was a lot as she watched Bracca strain, arm muscles bunching. He braced his feet and shoved hard. The sword broke with a sudden snap, sending him stumbling into the wall. He fell to the floor with a grunt and didn't rise. She rushed to crouch down beside him. She didn't think he'd hit the wall that hard but his eyelids fluttered, then closed. He groaned, his body going stiff. She looked up at Fate.

"Is this normal?"

"Yes. The link is breaking. He will live or die now according to his life skein." The sound of yelling jerked him around and he jumped to backup Kiel and Sarreth. They didn't have to worry about anyone coming at them from behind since the hall was a dead-end and there were no windows. Nowhere to run.

Avera dismissed the idea as quickly as it came. She couldn't leave Bracca.

The warrior groaned again, a sound of deep pain, and his body began to shake. Sweat beaded his skin and thin trickles of blood started leaking from his nose and ears. He thrashed. She tried to hold him down. Big mistake, she realized, as a powerful arm swung out, knocking her against the wall.

"Stay away from him," Fate shouted.

Shaking the stars from in front of her eyes, Avera decided to follow his order this time. Bracca could probably kill her without even knowing it. She scooted back, watching, biting her bottom lip, as Bracca's body tried to shake itself to pieces. Beyond him, Fate, Kiel, and Sarreth, fought for their lives...and hers.

Avera hated feeling helpless. Not even the gun at the small of her back was of any use. She had no target to aim for.

Suddenly Bracca's body arched stiffly, then fell back to the floor and lay still. She crept closer, and when he didn't move, she reached out a hand, expecting to find no heartbeat at all. But it was there. Very slow, very faint, and seeming to slow further right under her hand. Just like the heart of the man in the hallway back at Barrett's.

Bracca would not last until they reached Fate's Bloodsworn.

"Fate, he's dying! We have to do something!" The Silver Blade barely spared her a grunt as he blocked a sword thrust and delivered one of his own. Blood spurted against the wall and she turned away quickly, covering her mouth. The heart beneath her hand faltered. Tears spilled over onto her cheeks. Tears born of anger as much as sadness and horror. She sniffed, wiping away the moisture. There had to be something she could do. Her father had taught her there were always alternatives. Sometimes the alternatives weren't what one wanted or expected, but often it was better to take what you could and run with it rather than sitting around waiting for something else to come along.

Avera knew of only one alternative to sitting around and watching Bracca die. The man had saved her life. The least she could do was try to save his.

The fighting at the end of the hall was fierce, the clash of swords deafening in the narrow hallway. Bodies had begun to pile up and Avera's eyes locked onto the now dull gray swords of the fallen. One sword had even been kicked somewhat behind where Fate stood. A definite sign, she decided, her resolve locking into place with no further thought.

She had no idea if what she was going to try would work. All she knew was that Bracca needed a Bloodsworn, and he believed she could be one. Staying on her hands and knees, she slid closer to the fighting. The discarded sword lay only a short distance away. She waited, and when Fate lunged forward, stabbing between Kiel's and Sarreth's shoulders, she snatched up the weapon. She didn't look too closely at the sword until she again knelt next to Bracca. Thankfully it was free of blood.

Staring at the weapon, she realized suddenly she had no idea what she needed to do next. Her mind whirled as panic took over. She beat her fist against her thigh as she tried to think. He'd told her this. Bracca had told her how a link between a Bloodsworn and Blade formed back in the warehouse. Something about feeding the sword blood, right? Her clenched hand relaxed as a resigned calm settled over her. Well, she knew of only one way to feed blood to a sword.

She shoved her sleeve up, baring the healing scars on her arm. What was one more? Gritting her teeth, she rested the sharp edge against her arm and drew her hand back quickly. She couldn't suppress a shudder as the cold steel bit into her skin. The sting reminded her of another time and place, one she had no intention of returning to, even in her memory.

She left the blade resting in the wound wondering how she was supposed to make the thing drink her blood. Then she felt a slight, not quite painful, pull from somewhere deep inside her. The wound on her arm began to throb in time to her heartbeat. The sword took on a faint glow, and the pulling inside her grew. She had a moment to wonder if she was doing something incredibly stupid, and then the sword flared, the pain inside blossoming, taking her breath away. She heard Fate's shout behind her and quickly, before he could stop her, she ran the sword across Bracca's bare arm.

Hands snatched her away from the unconscious man's side. She let them take her, but left the sword behind, its edge lodged in the deep cut.

"What have you done?" Fate's voice snarled in her ear.

Kiel slipped past her, reaching for the sword.

"Stop," Sarreth warned, jerking the younger man back. "It is too late. If we try to stop the blood-link now it could kill her."

"I had to, I had to," she chanted, aware her body was shaking and that Fate knelt behind her trying to hold her steady. "W-w-what now?" The pain was gone, but its affects on her remained. She was shaking so hard her teeth chattered. Her insides churned, and her body felt cold while her head felt like it was on fire. Inside, behind her eyes, images flashed. Things she knew she'd never seen or even dreamed of.

A hot, coppery scent rose up around her making her gag. Blood. She smelled blood.

The odor was overwhelming.

The bodies of the men Fate and the others killed were too close.

Avera closed her eyes, swallowed hard, fighting back nausea.

Chapter Twenty-Seven

"Stay conscious," Fate ordered, adding his shake to her body. "You must complete the link."

"Howwww?" Her teeth chattered together, stretching the word into a moan.

Her eyes still closed, she felt him shift her, pick her up. Then she was on the cold bare floor again. Someone started tapping her cheeks with none too gentle slaps.

"Stop it," she said, reaching up weakly to bat the hand away. "I'm not a damn punching bag." She blinked her eyes open. Fate stared down at her, a smile on the stoic Blade's face that was gone so fast she wasn't sure if she'd imagined it or not.

"Listen to me," he said, his hands urgently squeezing her shoulders. "You must take the sword and put it in his hand. We cannot help you with this. We cannot touch the sword or you, once you touch it. Do you understand?"

Avera pushed herself up, bracing her arms against the floor to keep from falling over. She nodded carefully, dizziness making her head spin. "Okay, okay. Sword in his hand. Then what?"

Fate stood and stepped back. "Then put your hand over his. The sword and blood and your Bloodsworn magic will do the rest."

Okay, sword and blood she understood, those being tangible things. But magic? She supposed it was too late to tell him she had none of the imaginary stuff. Instead, she simply nodded again. They would find out soon enough anyway when this blood-link thing didn't work. That didn't keep her from wishing, hoping, it would.

The scent of blood grew stronger. Her stomach rolled and she gagged again. She looked down at herself, but the only blood she saw was on her arm. She wasn't wallowing in the deep red liquid, so why did it smell like she was in it up to her neck? More images flashed through her mind, thankfully distracting her.

"Concentrate," Fate ordered.

Right, concentrate. She had a task to complete. A man to save. She didn't want Bracca to die. It took her a moment to get her brain in the right gear. She had to stare at her hand and consciously think about what she wanted it to do. When she finally gripped the sword hilt, she could feel heat coming through the leather wrapping the hilt. Or at least she thought she could feel heat. She wasn't sure of anything anymore.

The images continued to crowd in, visions of another time and place, a whole other life. Bracca's life, she realized with a start, flashing by like a movie in fast motion, leaving her with only a sense of what he'd done and felt—some good, some bad. Some so dark, the moments filled with such self-loathing and despair, Avera found herself choking back a sob. She squeezed her eyes tightly shut against the pain that pierced her heart.

This had to stop. She didn't know how much more she could stand.

Desperately she fumbled her way down Bracca's arm to his hand, shoving the handle of the sword into lax fingers. She used both hands to close his fingers around the hilt and gasped when a jolt hit her, as if she'd just closed the circuit on an electric current.

Lightning shot behind her closed eyes. She cried out, but in amazement, not pain. The color of the lightning wasn't the brilliant white of a thunderstorm's rage, but the dark orange-gold of a flame's heart. The rich amber veins flashed behind her eyes and into her body, warming her as they repeatedly flashed down her arms to where her hands wrapped tight around Bracca's. One after the other, the jagged forks morphed into amber fire, building into a ball around their joined hands, pouring into the sword, and from there, into the man. Heat bathed the cold, hungry soul that was Bracca Cu-Laurian. She felt the fire fill him, knew the instant his stuttering heart caught and began to beat with a steadily growing rhythm. As the amber fire blazed through them both, Avera felt a sense of well-being fill her, calming her enough that she realized the fire had a taste and smell; sweet, like maple syrup, but with a different odor, one she couldn't place though its familiarity teased her senses.

Then suddenly, like a vacuum sucking air from a room, everything—visions, lightning, fire and all, disappeared in a whoosh, leaving behind a feeling of intense satisfaction.

Gasping, Avera opened her eyes.

"Wow," she whispered, blinking. "Wow."

The fingers beneath her hand moved. Jerking hers away, she looked down. "That was so...amazing," she said, rubbing her palms against her jeans while taking in the sight of the sword lying across Bracca's body. Not gray, not black, not even silver. The new color was a cross between a tiger's gold stripe and dark whiskey. And it wasn't shaped the same either.

Where the other swords were maybe two inches wide at most with close to three feet of straight blade, this one was at least three inches at its widest and a little over two feet long with a graceful curve to the steel. Scrollwork covered the sword from pommel to blade tip. Some of the squiggles looked like writing, runes maybe, though she didn't remember enough of her one ancient languages class from college to read any of it.

She glanced up at Bracca's face and found him staring at her. A wealth of emotions flooded her—elation, awe, gratitude, concern, just the slightest hint of fear. The heady mixture was too much. She tried to bring herself under control, and realized not all the emotions were hers. The relentless waves kept coming, one after the other, barging into her too fast, too strong. She didn't know what to do with so much extra emotion. Her mind cringed, crying for protection.

Suddenly it was there, a mental barrier, a wall, slamming into place, cutting off the flood.

Bracca winced.

Avera sat back on her heels, pushed her hair from her face and regarded the man lying on his back. "That was you, wasn't it? Those feelings were from you."

He nodded once. "Forgive me. I meant no harm. I should have realized you would not know how to control our link."

That was an understatement. She took a deep breath and gave him a shaky smile. "So it worked? Your link with this Camarie guy is broken, and now you're linked somehow to me?"

Bracca sat up slowly, took her hand, and stared intently into her eyes. "I am your Blade, Avera St. John, bound to you by blood and magic from this moment forward. Your life is my life. Your will is my will. The sword in my hand moves at your command until life or link is sundered. Thus do I swear my allegiance to you, my Bloodsworn, in the presence of these witnesses." He kissed her hand.

"Okay," Avera said slowly. "I guess that's a yes to my question. So is there anything I'm supposed to say back to you?"

"Only that you accept me into your service."

She squeezed his hand. "Then I welcome you into my service, Bracca Cu-Laurian." Something occurred to her and she added, "And I make you a promise. You never have to worry about me breaking our link, not for any reason. I'll only do that if you ask me to." She gave him a stern look. "And if you ask, you better have a darn good reason." His answering smile came slowly, as if his lips were out of practice. "So," she said briskly, "we should probably get out of here before more warriors show up. How do you feel?"

He blinked, tilted his head to one side as if taking stock, then answered. "Good." He stood and held out a hand to help her up as well. She moved back, giving him room to lift his new sword for a better look.

"That doesn't even look like a real sword." Kiel's lip curled.

Avera bristled, but Bracca took the scornful comment in stride. She saw his mouth kick up in a one-sided smile. He hefted the sword, twirled it in his hand, threw it up and caught it, finishing with a flourish that left it pointed at the young Silver Blade. "Care to find out for yourself how real it is?"

Avera shook her head. "Not now," she said, and grinned. Fate had said the same thing at the same time. He didn't seem to find it as amusing as she did. She shook her head at the dour man. Then her eyes caught the pile of bodies at the end of the hall, and she sobered quickly.

"Did they kill all the men with us, the pilot, too?"

Fate looked at Sarreth who shrugged. "Most

205

likely. Kiel and I saw the Black Blades kill one man and chase the other two into a building."

"We will have to look for them," Fate and Bracca said together.

If things hadn't been so grim, Avera would definitely have laughed at the looks on both their faces. As it was, she kept her smile hidden and stepped between the two scowling men. She made a shooing motion with her hand toward Fate. "Go, go, let's just go. God, I wish there was another way out of this hallway." She didn't look forward to climbing over the pile of dead bodies. The heavy scent of blood had faded, but she could still smell it.

Before she could take another step strong arms swept her up from behind to cradle her against a broad expanse of chest. The breath rushed out of her in a squeak, and she slid her arms around Bracca's neck in reflex. Embarrassed, she started to tell him to put her down, but the look he gave her made the words catch in her throat. He was looking at her like she was someone special, someone precious. His eyes held a touch of awe, as if he didn't believe she was real, while his arms held her possessively, as if, real or not, he wasn't about to let her go. She had a moment to wonder just what she'd gotten herself into before he turned to the three Silver Blades.

"After you," he told them, motioning with his bare sword.

Chapter Twenty-Eight

How much longer? Devlin asked Karess, glad he didn't have to speak the words aloud. He wasn't sure he'd be able to get them through his clenched teeth.

Another hour.

Devlin swore silently and wiped the sweat from his forehead. Karess and his other Blades stood shoulder to shoulder, like a wall, shielding him as best they could from the increasingly curious gazes of the other Bloodsworn and their Blades. Worry colored Karess' link. *Will you be able to last that long?*

I don't know, I... The Bloodsworn Council Hall receded as the strongest wave of magic yet rushed the barriers in Devlin's mind. Panting, he fought it back into submission, but not before it released something else inside him. Something that locked his muscles and took his breath away. Latent instincts, ones he hadn't even known he possessed, surged to full awareness. His heart stuttered a moment before settling into a wild, pounding rhythm. *Avera!*

Devlin pushed roughly between his men, ignoring their startled outbursts as he headed for the huge chamber doors. His Starmate was in danger, he had to get to her. He barely heard Caveon call to him through the rage roaring in his head like an infuriated beast.

"Tragar, where are you going? Your presence is required. When Camarie arrives you must be here."

Devlin spun, pinning his gaze on the head of the Council. Somehow he found the ability to form words. "Camarie is not coming, Caveon. You know that as well as I. This has all been a trick, a means to keep me away from my Starmate. She is in danger."

"Nonsense." Kapatree's sharp voice filled the chamber. "Come now, Devlin, you cannot expect us to accept such a feeble excuse for your sabotage of this meeting. How can you know if your prophecy bride is in danger or not? She is a world away. Besides, all here know of your hatred toward your uncle. It is more likely that you wish to ensure Camarie has no chance to redeem himself. He is, after all, your father's *elder* brother. If reinstated, he could pose a threat to your status as Illian's ruler."

Sweet power surged, straining the chains of Devlin's control. Magic pricked his skin. He took a step forward. A part of him welcomed the sight of Kapatree taking a hasty step back.

"Avera St. John is no mere prophecy bride. She is my Starmate. We already share an awareness of one another. I can feel the threat to her life. If Camarie is involved, either directly, or indirectly, I claim the right of his life."

Kapatree sputtered. "He is Bloodsworn. You cannot take his life. His Blades—"

"From the rumors I've heard, his Blades will thank me." Devlin swung toward the doors, anxiety pushing at him to hurry.

Before he'd taken three steps, the double doors to the council hall banged open. Not an easy accomplishment considering their massive size and the fact they weighed several tons each. Even with all the magic at his disposal, Devlin could only push them as fast as a man could walk. That they had swung aside as if they weighed nothing was cause enough for the entire council to jump to their feet, magic poised in their hands. The numerous Blades scattered about the hall formed a protective shield in front of their Bloodsworn, swords at the ready. All of which would be as nothing against the child-like woman who strode through the doorway. Pure magic swirled in her wake like churning water behind a fast ship.

"Devlin Kel-Tragar," Luma called out. Her voice matched both her expression and her stride—sharp, angry, and impatient.

While the other men in the room dropped to one knee in deference to Avalyr's Avatar, Devlin didn't think twice about meeting her advance. "My lady," he said, somehow managing to pull himself to a halt and incline his head dutifully when what he wanted was to run past her and through the open doors. Muscles twitching, he forced himself to wait, to hear what she had to say, though something inside him already knew the gist of her message.

Danger stalked his Starmate.

"Your First Blade sent a message requesting your presence on Earth. Something to do with two dead Feyune Blades, and no, before you ask, they are not Sarreth and Kiel. Apparently these two were found sniffing around the place where your Starmate works."

Even though he'd known she was in danger, fury smashed into his chest like a fist, the impact shattering the walls around his bound magic. He grasped the thrashing essence with the last of his control. "Whose Blades?" he growled.

Luma shrugged. "Difficult to prove with both men dead. However, since I'm not allowed to directly interfere in Feyune lives I have a suggestion. Were I you, I would stop playing this wooing game of yours and bring your Starmate to Avalyr before some *other*

Bloodsworn with an agenda of his own gets his hands on her. Again, just a suggestion. Feel free to stay here and wait a few more hours if you like."

She spun around and began walking back to the doors. Between one step and the next she simply disappeared, leaving behind a ripple of magic to haze the air. Devlin was so close on her heels the concentration of Avalyr's magical essence washed over him, filling him with such a strong sense of urgency he could hardly breathe.

He broke into a run as the magic inside him finally spilled out in a rush. He had just enough control to force it into a gate. The huge oval snapped open on the other side of the council room doors. He and his Blades poured through, emerging into the very Gate room of the Enclave itself.

Luma waited, the Outer Gate already open. "Good choice," she said with a grim smile. She reached out toward him and made a grabbing motion with her hand.

Devlin felt the massive power running rampant inside him vanish. The sudden comparative emptiness made him gasp and stumble. Hands grabbed him—Karess and Strum he dimly realized—keeping him on his feet. He shook off their hold, not caring if Luma took offence at his glare or not.

"What have you done," he demanded, though he already knew. She'd just stripped him of nearly every bit of his magic. Even blocked his access to more.

Her ageless face screwed up in a grimace. "The rules covering your visits to Earth are still in place. I haven't had a chance to contact the other Avatars yet to inform them of the extenuating circumstances."

Devlin clenched his fists. "Damn it, Luma, my Starmate is in danger. I need my magic." He couldn't assume Fate and the others were with Avera, protecting her. And he couldn't afford to wait on the mercenaries for transport. He had to reach Avera as soon as possible. He had to protect her himself.

"Stop wasting time," Luma said, her voice exasperated. "I left you enough magic for one gate plus a little left over. When I explain things to the others I'll come to Earth and re-fill you myself."

"And if you arrive too late, what then, Luma? Your actions threaten the very Prophecy you've charged me to see fulfilled."

Sadness touched her eyes before they hardened. "I know, I'm sorry, but it's the best I can do. I can't afford to break any more rules right now. Just go." She waved impatiently toward the open gate.

He cursed, knowing he had no time to argue with her further. Something was happening to Avera. He had to get to her. Now.

Chapter Twenty-Nine

Bracca held the precious woman close as he stepped over the bodies. Her arms tightened around his neck, and she buried her face in his shoulder as the hot smell of blood and visceral fluids rose up around them. He quickened his steps, anxious to get his Bloodsworn clear. *His Bloodsworn.*

Luma's blood and tears, he had a new Bloodsworn!

He still could not quite believe it. Not even with her soft body in his arms and the hard, smooth hilt of her amber sword in his hand. The only thing lacking to make it all real was the touch of her mind through the link, feeding him the sweet flow of magical essence that he craved. She'd snapped their link closed from her side, overwhelmed by the emotions he'd been unable to keep to himself in that first rush of awareness. There was no reason, at this point, for him to try to coax her into re-opening her mind to his or to explain to her what he needed. She may have been able to form a blood-link with him, but she was not Feyune, and knew nothing about Blades and Bloodsworn beyond what she'd learned in the past hour. He would wait until they were back on Avalyr, surrounded by the magic he could not touch. Time enough then for her to learn her Bloodsworn duties.

And if the worst happened, and she was unable

to feed him after all? Well then, he could at least request Solace from the Tragar and die with some dignity. The First Bloodsworn owed him that much for saving his bride's life.

Still, even knowing it was useless, he had to keep his side of the link open. The craving for Avalyr's essence forced him to do that much. And he was craving it, like a starving man just up from a month long illness. He'd been hungry even before the sundering and re-linking. Camarie was stingy when it came to feeding his Blades, keeping them on the edge of hunger before a battle, in some cases the edge of madness. It made them vicious fighters, ready to kill at the slightest provocation. Most Black Blades carried out their orders with a swift, merciless detachment so they could return for their reward—an unstinting flow of essence. The end of a successful assignment was the only time they were given what they needed. And even then, he'd always felt something was missing.

Now he knew what that something was.

He waited until they were outside the building before reluctantly releasing Lady St. John. She might not be feeding him magic right now, but she was his only hope of remaining alive. Her life was his life, and with his former Bloodsworn's Blades and hired mercenaries gating in right and left, he knew she was not safe.

"Wait," she said, before they'd gone a step. "What about the girl behind the counter? Is she...did they kill her?"

Fate An-Derrith shook his head while his eyes scanned the area. "Sarreth sent her out a back way. Come, we must leave here quickly before more of Camarie's Blades gate in." He reached over to take her arm and Bracca's hand shot out, catching his wrist before the Silver Blade could touch her.

Three silver swords were suddenly poised at his

throat. Bracca did not back down. A Blade's foremost duty was to see to the safety of his Bloodsworn, a duty which Bracca Cu-Laurian had never taken more seriously.

"She is my Bloodsworn, the linking witnessed by you all. Until such time as she takes another, I am her First Blade." The pleasure of that simple statement inundated him. He couldn't resist baring his teeth a little as he watched the Tragar's First Blade realize they were now on equal footing. The statement also reminded the Silver Blade that Bracca had certain duties...and privileges.

Fate's sword pulled back slowly. The other two dropped away as well. "Bring her," he snapped before turning toward the flying machine.

Bracca knew better. Avera St. John was not a meek Feyune female who came at a male's bidding. He bowed to her and waved a hand for her to go before him. "My Bloodsworn?"

"I knew you were a wise man, Bracca," she said, her eyes glaring at Fate's back. Bracca fell into step beside her, her praise more precious to him than a thousand rare gems.

****

Avera recognized the man who met them at the open doorway of the helicopter, a pistol in his red-smeared hand, as the one who'd told them about the refueling stop. Dark splotches glistened wetly on his green fatigues.

"Change of plans," he said. His eyes reflected the tension in his voice as his gaze swept the area behind her and the others before settling on Fate. "We're not flying to the Gate."

Kiel stepped forward, and used his sword to point at the man. "You are under contract. You were paid—"

"You'll get your money back if that's what you want, but it'll have to wait." He pointed a thumb inside the helicopter. "My son took a sword to the gut. I'm taking him to the hospital in Redding."

She leaned forward until she could see a young man lying on the floor, eyes closed, his face locked into a grimace of pain. The wide bandage around his middle was mostly red. Her hand flew to her stomach. She hated knives. She couldn't imagine being stabbed with a sword. A sense of urgency gripped her. They needed to get the man to the hospital as quickly as possible.

"What are we waiting for? Let's go." She reached for the side of the door to pull herself up and found her way blocked by Fate's tall body.

"We are not going with them." He looked toward the man with the gun. "I understand your need. You have lost enough men. The Tragar would not wish you to sacrifice your son as well."

The man shrugged. "Not that I care about you or your Tragar at the moment, but I appreciate the sentiment." He turned and yelled into the cockpit. "Billy, why aren't we off the ground yet?"

The engine coughed and sputtered.

Avera moved around so she could look Fate in the eye. "What are you doing? Why can't we go with them? Seems to me a hospital would be a safe place to be for a while. Lots of people, plenty of security. And without Bracca's sword for a homing device, we don't have to worry about more warriors coming after us, right?"

"Camarie will not care how many people we surround ourselves with. He has already shown this by his earlier attacks."

He was right. All told, about a hundred people worked at Barrett's. That hadn't stopped the mini war on the front lawn.

"But he can't find us now. His link with Bracca is broken."

The older mercenary shook his head and raised

his voice over the engine's growing rumble. "If he knows how to use Earth technology, he can find you quick enough if all of us show up at the hospital. You can't hide swords like you can a gun. Hospital security would call the cops before you got through the doors."

He stood and grabbed the edge of the door. "Don't hang around here too long. My cleanup crew will be here soon, but you don't want to take a chance on someone else showing up first. Believe me, it's a lot easier to explain away an army of dead aliens than four live ones." Looking at the four men meaningfully, he slammed the door closed. The rumble built to a whine in a matter of seconds. The machine rose, moving across the field before it had barely gained enough altitude to clear the trees at the far end.

Avera felt a little dizzy as she looked at the four warriors standing around her. Every one of them stared at the departing chopper, a look of disbelief on their faces. One, she imagined, that mirrored her own. The mercenary had used the A-word.

Aliens. i.e. men from another planet.

God, it was so much easier when she believed in the WarCraft-nerd-theory.

After several tries, she finally got her throat cleared of the lump of hysteria trying to choke her. "So. What now?"

"Now we get you back to Avalyr," Fate said. "It is the only way to be sure of your safety."

Avalyr. Of course. See aforementioned planet.

The dizziness got worse. She wasn't so sure about Fate's plan. Leaving Earth had definitely *not* been on her agenda for the day. Then again, neither had all of the other things that had happened to her so far. She glanced up at Bracca and found him watching her expectantly. If Avalyr was his home, he probably wanted to get back to it.

"Okay, how do we get to Avalyr? In case you didn't notice, our ride just flew away, which means, unless you can call your spaceship to us, we're going to have to find another form of transportation."

"Spaceship?" Kiel asked. He sounded like he'd never heard the word before.

"Yeah, you know, a machine like the helicopter only built to fly between worlds." The men looked at each other, brows wrinkled in confusion. They were from another planet and didn't know what a spaceship was? "Okay, if you didn't come by spaceship, just how did you get to Earth?"

"We came by way of an Outer Gate," Kiel said. He hesitated and added, "A path created by magic between one planet and another."

And there was the M-word again. Jeez, she would have to really update her current working vocabulary at this rate.

"All right, so how do we get to this Outer Gate?"

Sarreth and Kiel looked at one another with blank expressions, while Fate said, "We are unfamiliar with the geography of your world. That is why our Bloodsworn hired the mercenaries."

Avera closed her eyes and pinched the bridge of her nose. "Are you telling me you don't know where the Gate is?"

"The Trinity Gate is on the side of a mountain," Fate said.

"Near a large body of water called Trinity Lake," Sarreth added. "I saw the water from the Gate Watcher's roof and asked its name."

She wasn't even going to ask what he'd been doing on the roof. "Okay, I've heard of Trinity Lake. Now all we need is a map and a vehicle. Come with me, guys." Excitement spilled into her veins as she turned and headed back to the airstrip's little office. Was she really going to visit another planet?

Kiel and Sarreth ran ahead of her, swords held

ready, eyes scanning, looking for danger. Bracca marched beside her, Fate a few steps behind. She could feel the edginess of all four men. They had to be worried about more enemies showing up. She was more worried about the police. No matter what the mercenary said, a dozen dead men, alien or otherwise, would be impossible to explain. She broke into a trot as she veered over toward a dusty van parked next to the office. The van's doors were unlocked, but the keys were missing. And hotwiring was not a talent she'd yet to embrace. She checked the visor. No keys dropped out like they did in the movies. Frustrated, she slammed the door and headed for the building full of dead bodies. There would be maps there, and if they were lucky, maybe a set of keys behind the counter.

Fate reached the door first, opened it, and stepped in. He froze in the doorway. Avera found herself suddenly surrounded by large bodies. She couldn't see a thing except broad backs and shoulders. "What? What is it?"

Fate stepped slowly aside and motioned them into the empty room. The bodies left bleeding on the floor from the earlier fight were gone, along with all their physical traces. Swords, blood, everything.

"What's going on?" Goose bumps covered her arms as she looked around. If she hadn't felt before like she was in a Twilight Zone episode, she did now. Dead bodies did not just disappear.

Bracca took a step back toward the door. "Camarie gated them back to Avalyr." His eyes darted around the room and he held his amber sword out in front of him. A wave of possessiveness came out of nowhere and she reached out and took his hand.

"He's not getting you back," she said fiercely. Then, because she knew she was in over her head, she asked, "He can't, can he? Your link with him is really broken, right?"

Sarreth motioned toward the floor in front of the hallway. "Their links were supposedly broken as well as soon as they died. What magic is he using Cu-Laurian? And how many Blades does he have that he would send more than two decca to their deaths?"

"It makes no sense," Kiel said. He walked back and forth across the bare floor in short, angry strides, as if to make sure the bodies were actually gone. "Camarie would not give away this much power."

"Not all of the warriors who have died today were Blades," Bracca said, still looking like a man about to confront his worst nightmare. Avera gripped his hand tighter. She hoped she never had to meet this Camarie. Not if he could fill someone like Bracca, a man she knew from the visions could kill without flinching when he had to, with such dread.

Fate walked up to Bracca, capturing his attention. "Explain."

"Camarie brought only six Black Blades to this world. The others were a contingent of common foot soldiers, mercenaries. Camarie spells their swords black so they appear to be trained Blades."

Fate gave a low growl. "And he spells the men themselves so that when they die, their bodies and weapons return to him. He is covering his tracks. He does not want to leave any evidence behind that our Bloodsworn can present to the Concourse." His gaze jumped to her. "We need to leave here. Now."

She more than agreed. "Okay, okay, keep your tunic on." She went to the snack counter first as there was a display of maps on one corner. She didn't want to let go of Bracca's hand and was glad when he went along with her. She fingered through the maps one-handed until she found one for Trinity County. Trinity Lake wasn't that far away from where they were now as the helicopter flew, but it would take them a couple of hours by car. Assuming she found the keys.

"Keys, keys," she chanted under her breath, going around the counter. She needed both hands to search and reluctantly pulled hers free from Bracca's grip. She pointed a finger at him. "You even feel like someone's tugging on you other than me you better say something." She knew how ridiculous she sounded even before the man's lips twitched. He didn't laugh at her though, but inclined his head. She swung her pointing finger toward the cabinets and drawers running along the back wall "You can start looking there. Pull out any keys you find." She turned to the clutter under the front counter.

"Kiel, Sarreth, search there." Fate pointed to a door on the other side of the room with a little sign reading Employees Only.

Their search resulted in three sets of keys, two of which had a Ford logo imprinted on them—the same make as the van. She jingled them in her hand. "All right, gentlemen, let's see if we have transportation."

Sarreth and Kiel went first, checking outside before allowing her to leave the building. She followed Bracca out and headed for the van, stopping suddenly when he grabbed her arm.

"An-Derrith..." Bracca said softly.

"I see them."

Avera glanced from Bracca to Fate then followed their gazes to the large hangar on the other side of the airstrip. Despite the huge doorway gaping open, the inside reminded her of a shadow-filled cavern. She couldn't see whatever, or whoever, had caused all four of her guardians to become tense statues. She couldn't see, but quickly realized it didn't matter. They were only concerned about one thing.

Her suspicion was confirmed when some of the

shadows separated from the dark interior, emerging into the light.

"Sardis," Bracca hissed. It sounded like a person's name, but she couldn't be sure. It could just as easily been his version of "oh, shit" since the flood of men continued to pour out of the warehouse.

Avera stopped counting at twenty, fear rising into her throat, threatening to choke her. She covered Bracca's hand on her arm. "Let's get to the van."

"No," Fate said, his tone flat and uncompromising. "The time for running is past. We remain here."

"Are you crazy?" She eyed the wave of men. They'd begun crossing the wide pavement separating the hangar from the office building. None of them ran, but then, why should they? She and the others were just standing there, waiting for them. She clutched Fate's arm. "Give me one good reason why we're not already in that van and burning rubber out of here? In case you can't count, we're so outnumbered it's not even funny."

"We will not be outnumbered for long."

She stared at the tall warrior, wondering if the sudden light in his eyes meant he'd gone crazy. Sarreth chuckled deeply, drawing her attention. He threw her a glance over his shoulder, a wicked smile on his face. "Our Bloodsworn comes, my lady."

All of them were crazy, she decided, as the three Silver Blades stepped between her and the approaching warriors.

"Yeah," she muttered, "But is he going to get here in time to make a difference."

Chapter Thirty

As soon as he stepped through the Outer Gate onto Earth, Devlin reached for Fate's mind through their link. A quick response met his quest. Though the distance was too great for them to share mental speech, he still felt his First Blade's acknowledgement of his presence. He closed his eyes and stretched his Bloodsworn senses further, touching Sarreth and then Kiel, before returning to Fate. He sent the image of Avera standing beside Fate, alive, safe, unharmed, and wrapped the image in inquiry. *Are you with Avera? Is she safe?*

Acknowledgement once again, accompanied by a hint of urgency and...exasperation? He didn't have time to wonder at the unusual emotion in his stoic Blade's link.

"Is that all the men you brought?"

His eyes snapped open. The eldest Saunderson stood directly in front of him, sadness and anger simmering in the depths of his aged eyes. He waved toward the five men crowding Devlin's back.

"From what Everett said, that handful there won't be near enough. Damn aliens swarmed over Barrett's like a plague of locusts. Killed three of his men, maybe four. They couldn't find Gerald before your boys came back with your woman. You got an Avatar with you?" He stretched his neck, peering anxiously past Devlin and his men.

"Luma said she would come later. She had to take word to the Concourse."

Saunderson harrumphed. "Don't suppose she let you gate here with a bunch of magic either, did she?"

"No, she did not." He couldn't keep the anger out of his voice.

"A lot of help you're gonna be stuck here with me," Saunderson grumbled. "Everett said they were on their way back, but they had to set down to re-fuel. Be a while before they get here. No telling what they'll run into with some law-breaking magic-user running loose." He rubbed his whiskered jaw, clearly worried.

"I have enough magic to open a gate to my Blades."

The man's eyes lit up. "Then why are you standing around here jabbering? Go. Go!" He waved both hands this time. "I'd come with you if I didn't have to stay here with this darn gate."

Devlin reached for Fate's mind again, using it as an anchor. He called his magic, releasing it slowly and constricting the flow as soon as the shimmering oval appeared large enough for them to squeeze through. He took a step forward, only to have Karess slip ahead of him. His friend's grim laughter filled his mind.

Have mercy, Dev. You know Fate would have my head if I let you go first.

Chapter Thirty-One

Avera pulled the Glock from her waistband. She might be able to take out a couple of the enemy before they turned on their invisible shields. That still left far too many for four warriors and a scared-to-death chemist to face. "We're in so much trouble," she whispered.

Joining their meager line of defense, Bracca glanced at her. "Open our link."

"Our what?"

"Our blood-link. You must open your side of our mental link."

Was he kidding? He wanted her to open herself up to all those overwhelming emotions now? She licked her lips. "I don't think right now is a good time for us to be experimenting, Bracca."

"You must. We will be able to communicate during the battle. I will know where you are, and if you are in danger. Just do it!"

She shook her head. "I don't know how. I don't even know if I can."

Behind them, the door to the office opened. Avera spun, bringing her gun up and flicking off the safety at the same time. Her finger tightened on the trigger at the sight of several warriors crowding through the doorway. She hesitated. Warriors, yes, but maybe they weren't the bad guys. The swords in their hands were silver. Fate's Bloodsworn with reinforcements?

One of the men pushed his way impatiently to the front. Seeing her, he stopped cold, raising a hand to halt the advance of those behind him. Their leader, she thought, wondering if this was the man responsible for dragging her into this mess. She focused on his unsmiling face framed by thick black hair, and found herself suddenly drowning in the most beautiful deep blue eyes she'd ever seen.

Again.

****

Devlin allowed his gaze to sweep over Avera from head to toe before focusing on her weapon.

"Devlin?" she said, her voice tentative. Her hand holding the weapon wavered, confusion overtaking the determination in her eyes.

He sent a wisp of magic out ahead of him, snatching the gun from her grasp and sending it flying over the building.

Her eyes flew wide. "What..."

Two long steps put him close enough to pull her into an embrace he barely kept from becoming violent. "Thank the gods above, you're all right," he whispered into her hair.

They come.

Fate's warning came just as the bellow of battle cries filled the air.

"Damn you Luma," he muttered. He didn't have enough magic left to power another gate. He couldn't just whisk Avera to safety. They would have to fight. He loosened his arms enough to dip his head and capture Avera's lips. He had to kiss her once before he could let her go. The taste of her hit him hard and he forced himself to break the kiss quickly and pass her to Strum. The bewildered look in her eyes was like a punch to his gut. "Go with Strum, he will keep you safe." *She is your sole responsibility, Strum. Take Kiel with you and keep her safe for me.*

He turned away from her—by far the hardest thing he had ever done—and positioned himself in the line between Fate and Karess. His gaze swept the warriors rushing toward them. Seven men against at least three decca. Lousy odds in anyone's book. He caught the flash of gold from the corner of his eye, an oddity in the glinting line of silver. Eight men, he amended, glancing at the man on the other side of Fate. He didn't recognize the man or the sword.

"Whose Blade?"

"Long story," Fate grunted. And then there was no time for words, verbal, or otherwise.

****

"This way, my lady."

Avera let herself be pulled along until the first of the Black Blades reached Bracca and the pitifully small number of men with silver swords. The clash of steel filled the air, jarring her mind back into motion. Her gaze sought and fastened onto the back of the man who looked like Devlin. He fought with a sword, just like the others, but she noticed flickers of light going off around him, like repeating camera flashes. Each time the light flashed, one of the enemy warriors went flying through the air. More always took their place.

She started to struggle. "We can't just leave them, they'll be slaughtered." Somehow she pulled free and ducked under their arms. Dodging the grasp of a hand, she stumbled. Fire burned her right shoulder. She cried out and dropped to a crouch, nausea rolling through her stomach as she looked at the bloody slice on her shoulder. If she hadn't stumbled when she did, the knife sticking out of the wall behind her would be buried in her chest instead.

The burly warrior called Strum snatched her up. "Vet, woman, do you want my Bloodsworn to kill me?" She heard Bracca shout and looked up to see him charging toward her. Three enemy warriors closed in behind him.

"Bracca, behind you! Behind you!" she shouted, twisting in her captor's arms. Bracca seemed not to hear her. Desperate to warn him, she didn't realize she'd shattered the barriers in her mind until his emotions hit her. The overwhelming flood in her head took her breath at the same time she saw Bracca stumble. The warriors were almost on top of him.

Behind you! She screamed the words in her head. Bracca whirled, cutting down two of the men almost at once. As he fought the third, she pressed a hand to her chest, trying to catch her breath. The warrior carrying her ducked around the corner of the building, cutting of her view of the battle.

"Over here, Strum," Kiel called, running to the van. He pulled open the side door and the man carrying her set her inside.

"Keep watch," Strum ordered. "I have to check her wound.

"I'm fine," she snapped, brushing his hands aside. "Go help the others."

"Forgive me, my lady, but I have my orders." He quickly examined her shoulder, and then flashed her a grin. "A shallow cut, thank the gods. Looks like we both may live through this day." He slashed a swath of material from the bottom of his tunic. Folding the cloth into a pad, he placed it to her shoulder. "Hold this tight," he said, placing her hand over the pad and pressing down.

She wanted to ask him what was going on, if the man who'd kissed her really was Devlin Kel, but Kiel cursed.

"We have company."

Strum spun, his grin widening, anticipation gleaming in his eyes as he joined Kiel. Yep, they were all crazy.

Avera scooted away from the door as the battle commenced in front of her. Kiel's flashing sword sliced into a man's belly. Strum brought his sword down in a hard, over-hand chop, taking off his opponent's hand. The man screamed. Blood spurted, some of it splattering into the van.

Been here, done this. Ready to wake up now. Shaking her head at the carnage, Avera scrambled back and climbed into the front seat. She dug in her pocket for the keys. Nothing. They must have fallen out. How much worse could her day get?

The passenger's door jerked open. A scream lodged in her throat as a man tried to stab her with his sword. Something invisible jerked him back and slammed him against the wall of the wooden building several feet away.

Avera didn't wait for the next man to take his place. She shoved open the driver's door, jumped out, and started running.

She rounded the corner of the building, shoes sliding in gravel, and spied a door near the opposite corner. If she could get back inside, maybe she could use the phone to call for help, find another weapon, something. Anything was better than feeling so damn helpless.

She'd almost reached the door when a man holding a black sword ran around the corner right in front of her. Seeing her, he grinned. She tried to stop and spin around, but her feet slid out from under her. She landed hard, the impact knocking the breath out of her. Gravel crunched as the man advanced.

She scrambled back to her feet, fighting for breath, and finally sucked in enough air to scream for help just as another tidal wave of emotions hit her—denial, anguish, shame, regret, white hot rage, black grief. She grabbed her head with both hands, and dropped to her knees. The black sword whistled just over her head, landing with a thunk in the wooden wall. Tears blurred her vision as she crab-walked backward. The man standing over her swore and lifted his sword again. She kicked at his legs, trying to knock him off balance, and heard what sounded like a roar of rage coming from behind her. The ground rippled beneath her. Heat flashed through the air and light burst around her, so bright she rolled and buried her face in the crook of one arm and covered her head with the other.

An earthquake? An explosion? With her luck, probably both.

"Touch her, and you die."

The harsh words brought Avera's head up. A dozen black-sword warriors stood a few feet away, eyes wide, their faces pale as sheets. They stared, not at her, but at the bloody remains littering the ground between her and them. Her stomach heaved when she finally made sense of the chunks of blood-covered flesh, all that remained of the man who'd just been trying to kill her. She started to push herself up, wanting to get away from that awful scene.

"Stay where you are."

The deep velvet voice sent a tingle across her skin, and teased her memory. *Devlin.* She turned to find the man who'd kissed her a few moments ago standing not two feet away. A man who looked like Devlin Kel, but couldn't possibly be the same man.

This man was no sophisticated businessman, but a warrior in every sense of the word. The thick fall of his black hair hanging around his shoulders made him look like the barbarian prince she'd imagined the first time she'd seen Devlin. He stood, feet braced, hands out to his sides, fingers curled slightly as if holding something, though they appeared empty. Then she heard the whispers coming from the group of men.

"*The Tragar.*"

Shock sent her gaze flying back to the strange man who looked enough like Devlin to be his twin. *He* was the Tragar? Fate's Bloodsworn? She realized she'd been envisioning some kindly, older gentleman, maybe dressed in a sparkly blue wizard's robe. But this was no Gandalf or Dumbledore. She shook her head, her eyes narrowing. She didn't care what, or who, he looked like, he was going to pay for screwing with her life. It would take more than a few answers to satisfy her now.

Avera started to get to her feet again. Without warning, a blinding pain stabbed into the side of her head. She sat back down, sucking air through her teeth and squeezing her eyes closed as a wave of dizziness swept over her. Violent nausea seized her stomach. She moaned, rolled to her hands and knees, and retched. She was going to throw up— right in the middle of a sword fight.

Then the sick feeling vanished, disappearing between one heartbeat and the next as if someone flipped a switch. No more dizziness, no more sharp pain stabbing into her skull. She pressed a hand to her temple then checked her palm. No blood.

What is going on? There's no reason...

Her breath caught in her throat. Oh, yes, there was.

Bracca? she thought. Then, *Bracca, answer me!*

As strange as it seemed—because hearing voices in her head should have scared her to death—the silence in her mind terrified her.

Shouts brought her attention back to her own problem. Another group of warriors came running around the building behind the Tragar led by a man with long, golden blond hair, his face Greek-god perfect.

"I swear, Devlin," he said, pitching his voice low

so only those close by could hear. "If you run ahead of us like that again, I'm telling Fate. He'll chain your ass to your desk and we'll all help him, your magic be damned. This could have been a trap. Camarie might have—"

"She almost died, Karess." Devlin's empty hands clenched. Light bled through his fingers, curling around both fists until they looked like miniature suns.

She scooted until her back pressed against the wall. Devlin. The Greek god had called him *Devlin*. She didn't think she'd spoken out loud but his head tilted down and turned slightly in her direction, allowing her to see into his familiar blue eyes. She swallowed hard. He *was* Devlin. There couldn't be another pair of eyes like his in the world.

The glow around his hands faded, but didn't disappear completely. He pointed one nimbus covered finger at the group of enemy warriors. Every man flinched.

"If you wish an honorable death, step forward and my Blades will send you on your way. I know your Bloodsworn, and I doubt Camarie will be as merciful in the face of your failure to kill one defenseless female."

The men looked at one another, whispers passing back and forth between them. One stepped forward. "Camarie is not our Bloodsworn. We are not Blades."

"Your black swords say you are," Karess said, motioning with his own shining weapon.

"Camarie spells them black," Avera said. She knew it was stupid to call attention to herself, but she was tired of being ignored. After all, this fight was about her, right? She should have some say in the matter.

Chapter Thirty-Two

"Avera—"

"No," she said, jerking back when Devlin reached for her. "You don't get to touch me." Her eyes burned, and she blinked rapidly, determined not to let the rage-filled tears spill over. He'd lied to her. Made her think he was some harmless, civilized businessman who knew how to arrange flowers and surprise a woman with dinner. Instead, he'd been playing a game with her, sending her strange, out-of-this-world gifts and letters designed to drive her crazy. He employed sword-wielding barbarians, for Pete's sake. Not to mention he'd somehow just blasted another person into pieces without a weapon in sight.

He couldn't be the same man she'd laughed with last night over pizza. The same man whose kiss had set her on fire, making her want more of him. All of him.

"Avera, how do you know Camarie spells the swords black?"

It took her a moment to answer him. The way he said her name was like a fist squeezing her heart. She had to look away before her brain could get the words formed for her mouth to speak. "I was told by a former Black Blade. Camarie uses regular soldiers like cannon fodder. They're more expendable than his trained warriors. It's my guess he spells the swords black for psychological reasons, and to keep everyone else from knowing how many Blades he really has...or doesn't have."

She gave a careless shrug, determined not to let him see how shaken she was. Eyes that she'd fantasized about for hours stared back at her intently. Despite the lead ball of hurt in her chest, she felt a rush of tingling warmth unfurl low in her stomach. Resentment flared. How could such a pair of lying eyes still have the power to move her, make her feel things she didn't want to feel? Not now, anyway, not while she was trying to make sense of everything. She wrenched her gaze away only to have it land on his lips. Yeah, she'd fantasized about them, too, even tasted them. Did it matter now?

Her tongue flicked out, wetting her lips. She swore she could taste him still. Hot, hungry male passion burning across her taste buds, making her mouth water.

His jaw muscles tightened. When she looked back at his eyes they weren't just intense, they smoldered. She never understood what that phrase meant until now.

"Will you grant us grace?" one of the men asked. "If you take us back through the Gate, we can swear not to return to Camarie."

Hot eyes left hers with clear reluctance, turning cold and as hard as the sapphires they resembled. "No, I will not. You forfeited any right to ask for grace when you attacked my mate and her escort."

"What mate?" she said, infuriated that he would assume she'd just fall in with his stupid plans. She refused to let him bully her into anything, not for all the deep-dish pizza in the world. He had way too much explaining to do. He was also ignoring her again, going on as if she hadn't spoken. Her teeth ground together.

"You still have two choices," Devlin said.

"Surrender your weapons and we will turn you over to the Concourse for judgment. Their punishments are harsh, though usually swift and fair. Or you can still die as the warriors you pretend to be. My Blades will see that you do not suffer."

Karess shrugged. "Well, not too much, anyway."

The men began to mutter. Some stepped away from the others, tossing their swords aside while the rest stood undecided. Their decision became moot as the air above them shimmered. Before any of them could move, the shimmer dropped over them like a net, erasing them like chalk drawings from a board.

Avera looked down at the ground. All the blood and pieces of flesh and bone and other things were gone from there, too.

Karess let out a string of strange words that sounded like curses. "What is going on?"

"I would say the Dark Bloodsworn is cleaning up after himself," Devlin said.

Avera heaved a sigh. "Yeah. He's done that before."

Devlin held out a hand to her. "Come, we must join the rest of my Blades."

She ignored his hand and started walking. She heard him sigh softly as he fell into step beside her. They rounded the corner of the building, and Avera gasped.

Sarreth lay on the ground, eyes closed, his only movement the shallow rise and fall of his chest. Someone had pulled back his leather vest to expose the large, ragged wound on his left side. *Too much blood.* She'd seen too much blood spilled today, a lot of it in defense of her.

She concentrated her gaze on Fate. "What happened to Bracca? Where is he?" His dark eyes held no emotion when he looked up from inspecting the new bandage on his arm. No fatigue, no pain, even though he had to be hurting from his wounds.

Her worry for Bracca grew. Fate pointed with his thumb over his shoulder.

"If his master has not reclaimed him, he is over near the large building. We chased some of Camarie's Blades there before they disappeared."

She let the "his master" remark slide, too worried to call him on it. "Alive?"

"You would know if he were dead," he said.

"How? I don't feel him. He won't answer when I call."

"Is your link with him still in your mind?" Kiel asked.

Everyone stopped what they were doing, disbelieving gazes shooting between her and Kiel. Devlin moved up close behind her, making her more nervous than she already was. She nodded to Kiel, not trusting herself to speak. He gave a humorless laugh. "Then he is still alive, but unconscious. He took a kick to the head right after he saved Fate's life."

"I did not need saving," Fate said, his expression bland.

Avera wanted to throttle them all. "Unconscious? He's unconscious and you just left him?" What if one of the bad guys found him? Worse, what if one of those gates sucked him up, took him back to this Dark Bloodsworn person? She'd been in Bracca's mind, knew that this was the one thing he feared and loathed most.

Panic latched onto her with painful claws, digging deep inside her. She had to find him. A large hand settled around her arm in a grip she couldn't shake. She glared at the hand. She was definitely getting tired of being grabbed.

"Who is this Bracca that you worry so much about him?" Devlin demanded.

She had a hard time thinking of him as Devlin. The persona of the wealthy businessman, the man she'd been attracted to, no longer existed. What was left was a man she didn't know. A man who apparently thought nothing of dragging her into his very dangerous world. A man who, if she didn't know better, she would swear sounded jealous. Since that was impossible, she took exception to both his tone and his hand.

"Bracca is my Blade," she said precisely. "Now let go of me. I have to find him."

"Your *what*?"

"My Blade. Bracca Cu-Laurian is my Blade."

The familiar sound of strange swear words filled the air.

"That is not possible," Devlin said, the blue of his eyes shifting to a darker shade. "Bracca Cu-Laurian cannot be your Blade, Avera. You are not Feyune. And you are female."

Her skin prickled with irritation. "My, but your powers of observation are remarkable today. Want to try telling me something I don't already know?" Her sarcasm earned her a scowl.

"Females cannot be Bloodsworn, and Cu-Laurian has been a Black Blade for many years."

She pointed at herself. "This female can. And Bracca's not a Black Blade anymore, he's my Amber Blade." She recalled something Bracca had said to Fate earlier. "He's my First Blade," she added, feeling a sense of rightness settle over her at the words.

A few of the men chuckled. She glared at them until Devlin's free hand settled around her other arm, turning her to face him. He looked down at her, his expression smoothing into one an adult might have when explaining something to a child. "You know very little about our world as yet, Avera. It is understandable that Cu-Laurian fooled you with his lies. Don't be embarrassed. You will learn quickly enough."

Avera couldn't remember the last time someone had insinuated she was a fool. That he probably already thought her a fool for falling for his "good neighbor" act only made it worse. She would simply have to show him the error of his ways, she decided. Prove to him his definition of "human female" was so far off the mark it wasn't funny.

The first thing she needed to do was get free of him. She brought her hands inside the cage of his arms then twisted her forearms up and over his in a long-practiced motion. The simple move worked, but at a price. She'd forgotten about the cut on her shoulder. She sucked in a surprised breath and slapped a hand to her shoulder at the unexpected pain. Strong arms instantly wrapped around her from behind, pulling her tight against a hard chest.

She froze. All of her muscles locked as the memory of her attack surged up, trying to overwhelm her. Her breath came in gasps. Her vision darkened. She had to get away. She had to try to fight him off. An elbow jab. A kick. A stiff hand to the face. Something. *Anything.*

"Shh, be still, Avera, I am not hurting you. See? You are bleeding. Let me see where you are injured."

Devlin's voice crooning in her ear, tenderness edged with desperation, helped her pull herself together long enough to focus on the touch of his fingers. Not harsh and bruising, but gentle. Nothing but gentle.

Avera drew in a deep breath and sent the painful memories scuttling back to the black pit in her mind where they belonged.

I win this round, you bastard.

She concentrated on the feel of the arms around her. One arm held her arms pinned to her sides while he examined the wound through the rip in her shirt with soft, sure touches. Warm breath bathed the skin of her neck.

She'd wanted to be in Devlin's arms again. But not right now, not like this. The too intimate position played havoc with her current state of mind. She tried wiggling her hips to gain some leverage so she could put some space between them. The opposite occurred when his arm tightened, pulling her even closer. She realized exactly what she'd been wiggling against the moment hot words breathed into her ear.

"Another time, another place, *me`surrasie*, and I would answer your invitation in full measure. For now, trust me when I tell you, you need to be still."

Avera closed her eyes for a second, gulping back a moan while she felt warmth flush her cheeks. How could his words affect her like this? She was still furious with him, yet her stomach had gone all tingly tight with anticipation at his innuendo. "Would you please let me go?" she hissed. "That little scratch is nothing. I've had worse."

The hand examining her wound stilled. "You have been injured worse than this?" His words sounded like they came from between clenched teeth.

Avera swore to herself. She wasn't about to go into her recent life story complete with show and tell. "Yeah. I've been scratched by a cat worse than this, now will you please let me go!" Warmth flared on her shoulder where his hand cupped over her injury. His eyes turned a deep, stormy blue. Deep enough to drown in. She couldn't keep from coming back to that particular metaphor. Clichéd, but oh, so true.

She shuddered. His arms tightened for just an instant, then relaxed slowly. Finally, he released her and took a step back. It was impossible to look away from him.

"It matters little what stories Cu-Laurian has tricked her with, Tragar. If Camarie's Blade is still here, I will make sure he no longer troubles her with his lies."

That caught her attention. She jerked her eyes away and glared at Karess.

He winked at her.

A low, exasperated noise filled her throat. How dare he threaten to kill Bracca and then *wink* at her. "Tell *your* Blades to leave *my* Blade alone," she said, spacing the words out evenly. "Tell them all, but especially this one." She stabbed a finger in Karess' direction.

"Fate?" Devlin called.

"What Lady St. John says is true, my Bloodsworn. Cu-Laurian voluntarily broke his own sword to keep Camarie from locating us. He did not take the sundering well, and I thought him dead. I do not know how, but your lady began the blood-link with him while we were fighting off more of Camarie's warriors. We had no choice but to let her finish the ceremony. I am sorry, my Bloodsworn. I take full responsibility for not keeping Lady St. John safe from such vermin."

"He's not vermin, he's a man. I couldn't just sit there and watch him die. Not after he saved my life."

Chapter Thirty-Three

Stunned into silence, Devlin slowly wrapped his arms protectively around Avera. Bracca Cu-Laurian had saved her life? Why? Cu-Laurian's dark reputation as part of Camarie's Outer Decca painted his heart as black as his sword. Why would he save her?

Perhaps to trick her into linking with him?

A growl built in Devlin's chest at Fate's suggestion. *Show me what happened.*

Fate's memory of the attacks in the warehouse flowed to him through their link. The fight with Kiel. The warrior with the knife in his throat. How Cu-Laurian had later snatched Avera from sure death and dealt it back to her attacker without pause. Had the Black Blade hesitated, even for an instant, she would be dead, lost to him forever.

The woman in his arms took a deep breath. "I need to go find him, Devlin. Please," she said, the words a mere whisper of breath.

Devlin tipped Avera's head up with a finger beneath her chin. Dark, tangled hair, fell back, revealing her heart-shaped face. A face that had haunted his dreams the past several nights. Dirt smudged her golden skin, though it made her no less lovely. He frowned, running his thumb across the red line on one cheek where something had scratched her. Releasing a wisp of magic, he caressed her cheek again. The red vanished, leaving behind smooth skin slightly flushed with warmth.

She made a small noise, a sigh, a gasp, he wasn't sure, and his eyes shifted to hers. Vivid green pools stared back at him, glorious, stubborn, and shadowed with a wealth of worry.

He decided he didn't like that particular shade of worrisome green.

"Karess, take Gideon and Dune and find Cu-Laurian."

White teeth grabbed her bottom lip in consternation. He couldn't keep from tugging the abused lip free with his thumb.

"Bring him to me, unharmed."

She exhaled deeply, her breath bathing his hand in warmth. His body reacted, tightening with anticipation. He controlled the urge to hold her face in his hands and seal his lips over hers as he'd done in her kitchen. Now wasn't the time to press his suit. Later, when he had a chance to explain, to apologize for putting her in such danger, would be time enough for the long, drugging kisses he craved like a Blade craved essence.

A tiny smile flickered across her face, there and gone in an instant. His soul ached at the lingering doubt in her beautiful green eyes. He feared restoring her trust would not be an easy task.

"By your leave, my Bloodsworn, I will go with Karess," Kiel said. "It will save time if I show them where he fell."

Nodding, Devlin waved him on.

"I'm going with them, too." Avera pushed against his arms.

"No." He tightened his hold. Inwardly he grimaced at his behavior. It wasn't like him to dictate to his women. That had been more his father's style. Letting go, however, was out of the question. He'd come too close to losing her far too many times today to let her out of his reach, much less his sight. "For your own safety, you will not leave my side."

Avera glared at him, her eyes bright with green fire, his brief sojourn in her good graces apparently over. "Then come with me," she said, speaking slowly and deliberately, as if stating an obvious solution.

Devlin fought the urge to smile. Such a feisty female, hot-tempered, stubborn, and not afraid to let him know it. Her passionate spirit pleased him, made him hungry to know what she would be like in his bed. "I have better things to do than hunt for a missing Blade you should not have in the first place."

"What things?"

"I must see to Sarreth's wounds."

Immediately her eyes changed color again. Her eyes fascinated him, changing as fast as her mood. They flashed from a bright, stubborn green, back to that softer shade of worry. She looked over to where Sarreth lay.

Devlin already knew the extent of his Fifth Blade's injuries, just as he did the rest of his men. Most bore only minor wounds, and could be dealt with upon their return to Avalyr. Sarreth's injury, however, needed to be healed now, before it siphoned away too much precious blood.

Her worried eyes still on Sarreth, Avera pushed at Devlin's arms again. This time, he let her go, following her as she knelt at Sarreth's side.

"Sarreth?" she said, her voice soft and sweet, fingers gently brushing sweat dampened hair from Sarreth's forehead. Devlin had to lock away a sudden stab of jealousy, shocked at its intensity. That such a simple act could rouse the uncomfortable feeling in him did not bode well for the days to come. While he'd given in to the inevitability of taking Avera to Avalyr against her will, he was still determined to secure her willingness before completing the Starmate-bond. That would take time and patience, and if he felt this way now...

Sarreth's eyes flickered open. "My Bloodsworn."

Devlin held his hand just above the deep gash in Sarreth's chest. "Rest easy, my friend. You will be better shortly."

The large warrior grunted. "It is not as bad as it looks. I can wait until we get back to Avalyr."

"I think not, my Blade."

"Devlin—"

"Peace, Sarreth, this healing will not drain me dry, and we return to Avalyr as soon as it's done."

Avera cleared her throat. "What does that mean, exactly, the not draining you dry part? Is that supposed to be a joke?"

Devlin smiled to reassure her. "No, it isn't a joke. But don't worry, I have more than enough magic to see to Sarreth and still keep you safe. I promise you will not find yourself in danger from Black Blades again today."

"Don't be ridiculous, I'm not worried about me," she said impatiently. "I want to know why Sarreth's worried about you." Green eyes flickered to him, then quickly away.

Could some of that worrisome green really be for him? The possibility was enough to wipe away any lingering jealousy. "I am Bloodsworn, Avera. You will find out soon enough what that means."

"I warn you, I'm not good when it comes to waiting for answers. You already owe me about a hundred. Just tell me what it means now."

"It means that Bloodsworn give of themselves so that others may live. Quiet now, I must concentrate." Closing his eyes, Devlin sank his consciousness into his link with Sarreth. He followed the mental pathway, passing first into the very mind and spirit of his Blade. The cold hunger that characterized a Blade in need of Avalyr's essence rose up, surrounding Devlin with a sharp yearning. The painful feeling never failed to amaze him when he had to enter one of his Blades to heal them. How they could live, much less function with such aching hunger was beyond him.

He set his wonder aside and delved deeper, merging into Sarreth's body, drawn to the damaged area like a plant to sunlight. Quickly he examined the fractured bone, severed veins, and torn tissue to determine the best path for healing. Then he turned his magic loose, letting it flow unstintingly into the wounded area.

Flesh and bone knit, blood cells multiplied. Warmth from the healing flooded Sarreth's body. Dimly, Devlin was aware of Sarreth's deep-throated moan. But it wasn't pain the Blade felt.

The flow of magic into a Blade was better than food to a starving man, or water to one dying of thirst. The taste of Avalyr's essence, freely given—so Karess had told Devlin—was like the pleasurable pain of a man's first orgasm after being hard for a woman for days. The stronger the flow of essence, the deeper the pleasure. The healing itself was accomplished with little time and effort. The drawback came afterward. Instead of the pleasure sating a Blade's body, it had the opposite effect of creating a lust almost violent in its intensity.

Devlin himself had to walk a thin line when deep healing one of his men. He had to keep the link open so the magic could flow freely, but at the same time, he had to fight the backwash of pleasure, the building lust, that overflowed from his Blade. The intense feelings made it hard to concentrate and often left him craving the heat of a woman's body for long hours afterward.

Torturous hours this time, he realized, his Starmate within arm's reach, yet still untouchable.

Sarreth, at least, had other options. Once back at Devlin's palace, he could seek out the comfort of one or more of the shethas, an honored class of women more than willing to ease a Blade's post-healing cravings. The option was open to Devlin as well, but he knew he would not take it. He only wanted one woman now.

Examining the rapidly healing wound, Devlin decided he'd done enough. Slowly, he drew back along the link, leaving the magic he'd released to do its work. He fell heavily into his own body once more. A small hand touched his arm, the light caress sending a mighty jolt of awareness through his entire body. His eyes snapped open, locked immediately on her face.

Luma's bloody hell, how he hungered for her.

He had made a mistake allowing her to remain so close. Just looking into her eyes made him want to pull her across Sarreth's body and up against his own. He wanted to sink his tongue between her lips and plunder the sweetness of her mouth. He wanted more. He wanted everything. Things they did not have time for. Things she was not ready to give him.

"Are you all right?"

With great effort, he brought himself under control. That worried look in her eyes helped. He nodded in answer to her question, which wasn't exactly a lie. Raging desire for her aside, he was fine. A little weak, perhaps, but that was expected when expending a large amount of magic he was unable to immediately replenish. Returning to Avalyr and its Veil of magic would see him completely restored.

Looking as if she didn't quite believe him, Avera turned her attention to his Blade. "Sarreth?" she said, uncertainty in her voice.

It was then Devlin noticed Sarreth's wide eyes fixed on Avera's face. Despite knowing the reason for it, the lust burning hot in Sarreth's gaze raised his hackles. He had to fight back the sudden urge to throttle the injured man.

Then Avera reached to lay a hand on Sarreth's shoulder.

Foolish woman.

"Don't touch him." He grabbed her wrist just as Sarreth's whole body shuddered. Words shot into his mind, tumbling over one another in their haste.

Luma'sbloodyhellgetherawayfromme!

"Get back," Devlin said, standing and drawing her up with him. The words came harsher than he intended, spurred by the panic in Sarreth's link. When confused hurt flashed across her face, Devlin felt as if he'd struck her.

"Avera..." He didn't know what to say to her, how to make her understand he and Sarreth were only trying to protect her. If she *were* Bloodsworn, and he told her about the deep-healing lust, how would she react? Would it give her just one more reason to refuse to have anything to do with him and his world?

As if reading his thoughts her chin popped up and an icy reserve replaced the hurt. "You know, today I've been shot at, chased, knifed, and almost had my head cut off with a sword, but what I'm really getting sick and tired of is being manhandled. Give me my wrist back, and I promise I won't come anywhere near him, or you." She poked him in the chest with her finger.

Having her list all the dangers she'd faced did nothing for his peace of mind, much less his control. If not for that little poke to his chest, a gesture he found ridiculously endearing, the rage and fear her words evoked might have made him do something stupid. Wrapping her in his arms again and not letting her go was the exact opposite of what she asked of him.

Before he could bring himself to release her, however, he used his hold on her wrist to raise her hand to his lips. "I know you've been through a lot, Avera. For that, I beg your forgiveness. I am more sorry than you will ever know that I wasn't here when you needed me."

She blinked, the hard look in her eyes softening a bit. Because of his words, or the feel of his lips against her skin? Both, he hoped.

"Well, you *should* be sorry. If it weren't for you, I wouldn't be in this mess. My life was fairly normal until you moved across the hall. Why don't you take your little war back where you came from and leave me alone?"

He let her pull her wrist free. She rubbed at it, though he knew he hadn't held her tight enough to hurt her. She moved away from him, eyeing him and his men with equal suspicion.

Devlin sighed inwardly. To say his wooing had just suffered a severe blow would be an understatement. If he could get his hands on his uncle right then, he'd cheerfully murder the man.

Grunting came from behind him. He motioned Strum and Thern, telling them through their links to hold Sarreth down. His Fifth Blade was in no condition to be up yet, nor would he be thinking clearly for the next few hours. Or so Devlin thought.

"I didn't mean to... Go after her, Devlin. You can't let her leave. The Black Blades..." Sarreth hissed through clenched teeth, pushing against Strum's restraining hands.

"She isn't leaving, Sarreth, lie still. Your wound needs more time to heal. I swear if you break it open again I'll give you to Bomarr to help catalog the new shipment of books for the Palace Library." The threat was not an idle one. Sarreth had little patience with forced inactivity. To further make his point, Devlin used a fraction of his dwindling magic, enough to blanket the agitated Blade until he calmed down.

Pain mixed with the lust in Sarreth's eyes, making a despairing brew. He stopped struggling. "Forgive me."

Devlin shook his head. "I am to blame, Sarreth, not you. I will explain everything to her later."

Avera's sudden gasp made Devlin wonder if later was going to be soon enough. Then he felt concern cut sharply through several links and spun around, looking for his mate. She stood a few feet away, one hand pressed to her temple in obvious distress. Her green eyes met his, dark with pain and fear. She gasped again. Then she threw her head back and screamed.

Devlin's blood ran cold, his breath freezing in his lungs. He dove for Avera as her knees buckled, catching her and pulling her into his arms.

"What's wrong?" Fate demanded. "Is Camarie attacking her with magic?"

"Not Camarie," Devlin said sharply, aware that Fate and the others moved to form a protective circle with him, Avera, and Sarreth in the middle. They held themselves and their swords ready, eyes searching for an enemy. But there was no one for them to fight this time. He'd seen this type of attack before, though never against a woman, and never with such intensity.

"Avera!' he called. "Avera, you must close your link with your Blade." She didn't answer, too caught up in the violent assault on her mind to heed him. Slender hands latched onto his shirt, balling into terrified fists. The fear in her eyes was unbearable as she gasped, seemingly unable to catch a full breath. He laid a hand against her face, trying to get her to hear him. "Avera!'

Her eyes rolled back, their lids fluttering. Her body went stiff.

Blind panic wrapped itself around his heart. This should not be happening. Women were not Bloodsworn. It was impossible for them to survive such things as a Blade's pain. Every instinct screamed at him that the overwhelming suffering of a mind starved for the touch of magic would be too much for the gentle mind of the female he held. How could she survive such agony?

He shook her again. "Avera, listen to me. Hear me," he begged. "You have to close your link with Cu-Laurian now." Her only reply was a keening moan that cut straight to Devlin's heart. Desperate, he sent a call to Karess and the others looking for Cu-Laurian.

Did you find him? Is Cu-Laurian awake?

Karess answered quickly. *We found him. He is only now beginning to come around. Kiel has his sword, if you can call it that, and it is not black.*

Wake him! Do whatever it takes! Give him back his sword!

Dev—

His link to Avera is wide open, Karess. She feels everything he does. She can't close the link from her side. Wake him now. Make him close their link!

Violent swearing was followed by silence. Several long seconds passed before Avera's body slumped boneless in his arms. Her head lolled and her eyes remained closed.

Cupping a hand around her throat, he checked her pulse. Its rapid beat thundered under his fingers for several more seconds before beginning to ease into a more normal rhythm. Only then did he allow himself a sigh of relief, though it would be a while before his own heart stopped pounding. He gathered his unconscious Starmate close to his chest, one hand brushing back her tangled hair, stroking tenderly over her cheek. So beautiful, so precious. He had yet to know her a full week, and already she'd wrapped herself around his heart.

He traced the arch of an eyebrow with the tip of his finger. The joy of being able to touch her went a long way toward easing the fear that had held him in a tight grip from the moment Luma had entered the Bloodsworn Hall. He'd almost been too late. Another minute and he would have found her with a black sword buried in her breast. The image had him shuddering in denial. He hadn't been too late. She was alive.

Unmindful of the men around him, Devlin pulled her even closer, burying his face in the curve of her neck. Her pulse throbbed reassuringly beneath his lips. The steady beat calmed the frantic pace of his own heart until their pulses were beating almost as one. He breathed in deep, drawing her scent into himself. Such a brave soul, his Starmate. She had faced death numerous times that day already. Attacked, chased, and attacked again. Gods, he wanted her safe.

Kiel arrived first, jogging around the corner ahead of the others. As soon as he saw Devlin holding Avera, he stumbled to a halt, dismay twisting his features.

"Unconscious only," Devlin said.

Kiel's shoulders sagged and he turned away as Gideon and Dune arrived with a groggy Bracca Cu-Laurian, Karess a step behind them. Blood leaked from the split skin on the side of Cu-Laurian's head. When he noticed the unconscious woman in Devlin's arms, he stiffened. The change came over him swiftly, from half-dazed man to a very aware, very dangerous Blade. The sword in his hand twitched.

"What happened to her?"

"You happened." Devlin could barely control his anger. This man was responsible for Avera's current state. "She could not close the link on her side and felt everything when you started regaining consciousness." To his credit, Cu-Laurian paled visibly, though the show of remorse did nothing to lessen Devlin's resentment or cool his temper.

"I did not know."

"Do you think that excuses what you've done? You should not even be linked to her at all! How dare you put her at such risk?"

"She is Bloodsworn—"

"Yes, and you have been a Blade long enough to know what that means. She felt it all, Cu-Laurian. Your head wound, your hunger, everything. Right down to your reaction to Kiel holding your sword."

A harsh bark of laughter had him glancing over to where Kiel leaned against the nearby building. Contempt twisted the features of his young face. "And to think we worried about you and your dark reputation. You fought for her, but did nothing to protect her from yourself. You are not much of a Blade after all, are you, Cu-Laurian?"

"Watch your tongue, *malimes*. I do not have the time or patience to school you."

"School me? And what do you think to teach me? How to come within a breath of killing my own Bloodsworn?" The venomous taunt surprised Devlin. Kiel was not the type to tease someone's temper with a list of their faults. The deliberate insult somehow cooled some of his own temper.

"Enough," he ordered sharply. He was suddenly tired of their bickering. Tired of waiting, tired of being on a thrice-damned magic-less planet. He needed the feel of Avalyr's magic around him. His injured Blades needed to feed on its essence. More importantly, he needed to get Avera home, where she belonged. Where she would be safe.

Where the hell are you, Luma?

He hadn't expected the answering ripple of

feminine laughter in his mind.

Closer than you think, my First Sworn.

Magic surged into him, filling him close enough to full the difference didn't matter. He took a deep breath, settling the essence into place with a sense of relief.

You took your time, he snarled.

No answer this time. Had he really expected her to stick around for him to scold?

"We return to Avalyr, now," he said, anxious to leave before Camarie could send in more mercenaries. He pinned Cu-Laurian with a threatening look. "You may come with us since you appear to have maneuvered your way into becoming my Starmate's Blade. But I warn you, one sign of treachery, and I will sunder your link myself."

Cu-Laurian lifted his amber colored sword in a slow salute. The weapon was unlike any Devlin had ever seen. Broad and curved, with runes etched into the strange colored steel. Grace, strength, and mystery, coupled with a heart of fire. A weapon very much a reflection of the woman he held so close to him.

"This is her sword, I am her Blade," Cu-Laurian said. "There can be no betrayal between us."

Kiel snorted a mocking laugh. "You betrayed Camarie quick enough when you saw a chance at something better." He pushed away from the building he leaned against and sauntered over to stand face to face with Cu-Laurian. "Who is to say you won't do so again? Perhaps you'll find some way to sunder your link with her so you can try to become a Silver Blade. Is that Camarie's plan? Did he send you to sneak your way into our ranks so you can murder our Bloodsworn?"

Devlin tensed. It was as if Kiel begged for Cu-Laurian's attack. Animosity simmered in the air, not just from him but the rest of Devlin's men as well.

As much as he might welcome such a solution to the problem of Avera's Bloodsworn status, he was not the ruler of a realm for the sake of his lineage alone. A wise leader tried not to make decisions based on his emotions. Cu-Laurian had caused Avera immeasurable pain, but he had also saved her life. Devlin owed him.

Stay your swords, my Blades. This man does not die by our hands today. He inserted the order more forcefully into Kiel's link since the young warrior seemed more eager than the others.

Cu-Laurian, however, merely shook his head at Kiel's insult. "I was wrong about you, boy. It isn't your anger that is going to get you killed, it's your lack of control over your mouth."

Karess' laugh drowned out Kiel's snarl. He was suddenly at Kiel's side, clapping a staying hand on his shoulder. "He's only known you a few short hours, Kiel, and already he has discovered your weakness." Devlin saw Karess squeeze the young warrior's shoulder once before he moved to stand next to Cu-Laurian. He flung an arm across Cu-Laurian's shoulders like a long, lost brother. "Come, Amber Blade, you and I will walk together through the Gates, and you can tell me how Kiel gave himself away so quickly."

Cu-Laurian snorted. "You mean walk with you so you can keep me under the threat of your sword, don't you?"

Karess nodded once, his grin unrepentant. "That too."

Chapter Thirty-Four

Devlin paced the hallway outside Avera's room, cursing *time*, that most hated of dictators, with every step. More than anything, he wanted to be at her side when she regained consciousness. But informing the Concourse of Camarie's crimes, making sure they used their considerable resources to pursue him for his misuse of magic on Earth, came first. The dark Bloodsworn had made a grave error this time. He could not possibly come through this without facing sanctions by the Concourse. They might be content to let him run amuck on his home planet, but causing havoc on a protected world was something else entirely. Even if they didn't catch him, Camarie would at least have his hands full hiding from the Avatars. Maybe they would keep him busy long enough for Devlin to seduce Avera to his bed and seal the mate-bond without further interference.

He stopped and listened at the door again, recognizing his mother's voice mixed with that of the palace healers. The worried tones sent his hand to the doorknob. Perhaps he should have taken Avera to the healers at the Bloodsworn Hall. They, at least, knew how to deal with the special psyche of a Bloodsworn. He hoped she would not need their expertise. He didn't want to expose her to the intricacies and intrigues of the Council. Not yet. He needed more time with her alone. Time. Everything came right back to the measuring dictator.

The knob beneath his hand turned. He stepped back quickly as the door opened.

"Devlin."

His mother had a frown of worry on her face. Not a usual expression for her. Devlin felt his pulse quicken. "What is it, Mother? What's wrong?"

She stepped into the hall, closing the door softly. "You said she was attacked by Camarie's Blades. When?"

"Today, when Fate and the others went to pick her up. They were attacked several times. Why do you ask?"

"You know of no other attacks?"

Other attacks? He shook his head. What other attacks could she mean? "I don't understand, what are you asking? If something is wrong just tell me instead of speaking in riddles."

Lady Patria drew herself up, her chin tilting until she looked at him more directly. "I think you should see for yourself." She put a hand on the door knob and paused. "Before you go in, make sure those links of yours are all closed. I do not need a herd of men stampeding through my halls just because you are upset by what you see."

Devlin's hands clenched, already not liking what he was seeing and hearing. One thing he could say about his mother, she was not one to exaggerate. This had to be bad.

He did as she asked, but not before sending word to his Inner Decca. Fate and Karess had already queried him, feeling his rising anxiety. He would get back to them when he found out for himself what the problem was. In the meantime, they were to make sure none of the others entered the Lady's wing. The last thing he needed was to give his mother more ammunition against his

Blades.

A large bed draped in white silk dominated the room. Maids hovered around the bed along with the two palace healers. Seeing him enter, the maids scattered. The two healers, both women, moved only as far as the foot of the bed.

Avera St. John lay still, her black hair making a dark, curling halo round her head against the white pillow. The light golden skin of her face looked paler than Devlin remembered. In fact, she looked so fragile lying there, he could hardly believe it was the same woman who'd faced him down, threatened Karess, and had the courage to blood-link with a former Black Blade. He addressed the healers without looking at them, unable to take his eyes off the woman in the bed. His mate, so still, so pale. He reached out a hand and fingered one dark curl.

"Tell me what is wrong with her."

"Except for a few scrapes and bruises, and the one wound on her shoulder that we have healed, we can find nothing wrong with her," one of the healers said in a quiet voice.

The other added in words clearly reproachful, "There is no wound to her head as we were told, my lord Tragar."

"I never said she had a head wound, only that she felt the pain of one."

"My lord, I'm afraid we do not understand."

He'd wanted to wait before declaring her status. Many, he felt, would not understand. Hell, he didn't understand. "She is Bloodsworn."

Several gasps filled the room, his mother's the loudest. "Devlin, why would you say such a thing? She is your prophecy bride. How can she possibly be Bloodsworn? Surely you are mistaken."

"Trust me, I am not one to mistake such things. She is Bloodsworn by the proof of her one Blade, the linking ceremony witnessed by three of my own."

Her astonishment mirrored that of the two healers.

"But, my lord, she is female..." the elder healer began.

"What Blade?" his mother asked at the same time.

He ignored his mother's question. "A *human* female, as my mother pointed out. Apparently the weaver of Avalyr's future thought it time for some changes and decided to throw all the threads in at once."

Lady Patria clasped his arm, fingers digging into his muscles. Her distress was such that he did not stop her. "I say this is a mistake. The Oracle did not translate the prophecy correctly, or perhaps we misunderstood. There must be two women not one, a Starmate and a Bloodsworn. We can contact the Oracle, ask—"

He shook his head. Prying her hand free, he kissed her still smooth skin. "I have felt the connection between us already, mother. There is only one woman, both Starmate and Bloodsworn, and she lies here. Believe me, if I could, I would deny it myself. Do you think having a mate who is blood-linked to another man is something I would choose?" Devlin felt himself beginning to slip deeper into anger with each word. He'd had all his choices taken away. Some he thought he could live with, but this? This one, he wasn't sure about.

He took a deep breath, pushing back the anger into something more manageable. There were aspects of his coming marriage to this woman he would have to work through, but now was not the time or place. He turned back to the healers.

"Why has she not awakened? Did the link with her Blade damage her?" If it had, he would have the excuse he needed to sunder Cu-Laurian's link. He could do it while she was still unconscious, minimizing her pain and bypassing any protest she might make.

A tempting prospect either way.

"No, my lord, your lady seems to be fine."

"Can you wake her?"

The two looked at one another before the eldest of them answered. "We think it would be best to let her rest until she wakes on her own."

Devlin frowned. He looked at his mother who still appeared to be having trouble believing her daughter-in-law-to-be was a Bloodsworn. "Why, then, did you call me in here, giving me the impression that something is wrong with her?"

"Because something *is* wrong." Clearly agitated, she stepped around him and twitched back the sheet, exposing Avera to the waist. The maids had stripped his mate of her clothes and dressed her in a sleeveless gown of more white silk edged in lace. The way it molded to her body, outlining her generous breasts, was enough to stop the breath in his throat. It wasn't the alluring gown, however, that had Devlin's jaw clenching and his hands curling into fists. It was her bare arms.

So many scars.

Power bled into his eyes as he studied the pink lines and puckers of raised skin. Defensive wounds, experience told him. She fought off someone attacking her with a knife. Fought them off, and lived.

He picked up one limp hand and touched her arm lightly, tracing every scar. A deep gash here and here, a stab wound there. More slices crisscrossing near her elbow. He laid that arm down and picked up the other one, tracing those scars as well, memorizing each one. It didn't help that the wounds had neatly mended and looked to be weeks, if not months, old. Someone had attacked her, and he, by Luma, was going to find out who and why.

Chapter Thirty-Five

Avera crawled up out of dark unconsciousness one slow step at a time. Faint sounds impinged on her awareness, unidentified, un-regarded. The softness of the bed registered first, along with the cool caress of fine sheets. For the moment, it didn't matter where she was. Just the absence of pain pounding her skull to bits was enough. The relief was euphoric.

As much as she hated to move, however, her memory wouldn't let her just lie there. Things had happened to her. Strange, unexplainable, heart-pounding things. And she didn't think the ride was over yet.

She knew, for instance, without opening her eyes and with absolute certainty, she was not in her own bed, safe in her own apartment. For starters, the sheets were too soft and the mattress too comfortable. And the smells were all wrong. Instead of the frankincense and myrrh candles she kept by her bed, she could smell fresh linen, flowers, beeswax, and the lingering odor of burning wood.

In spite of all this, she still might have been able to push the strangeness aside and sink back into sleep if not for the nagging sense that something was missing. She tried to figure out what it was, but every time she got close, the vague whatever-it-was slipped away.

No, not what, who. The missing something was a *someone.*

More than one someone?

It was then she realized she'd been hearing voices and started paying attention to the sounds around her. When she did, she immediately decided to keep her eyes closed.

Two female voices talked in low, hushed tones, the kind used in sick rooms and hospitals.

"She looks strange, does she not?"

"Aye, her skin is so golden."

"Is it natural do you think? I mean, I have heard that females from other worlds often have strange things done to their bodies."

Females from other worlds?

Avera would have groaned aloud if the whispered conversation hadn't caught her interest. Apparently she wasn't out of the Twilight Zone yet.

The voices dropped to conspiratorial level.

"What things?"

"They have skin and flesh removed from some places and added to others."

"How perfectly awful," the second voice said, though the tone implied, "tell me more."

"Yes. And they change the color of their hair, sometimes the shape of their faces." The voice dropped so low Avera had to strain to hear the next words. "I have heard some even change their sex."

Silence stretched for several heartbeats. Avera couldn't believe it when she felt fingers tug on the sheet covering her.

She snapped her eyes open and fastened a hand around the wrist of a wide-eyed young girl who looked barely old enough to be a teenager. The shrill squeal of her companion filled the room, as the other girl bolted for the door. The one whose wrist she held never made a sound. By the look of her she was frozen in fear. Her bottom lip trembled and lovely hazel eyes filled with tears.

"Gwenell!"

The girl shuddered and squeezed her eyes shut at the sharp call coming from outside the door. Tears spilled down her cheeks.

Inwardly, Avera sighed, wondering why she suddenly felt like protecting the little brat. She and her shrill-voiced accomplice should be spanked for sneaking into someone's bedroom just to peek under their sheets.

But not by her. She couldn't find it in her to be angry. She still felt too tired and wrung out from the events of her no-good-very-bad-day to worry about a bit of girlish curiosity.

"Hush," she whispered.

The girl's eyes flew open, wide, blue, and vaguely familiar. Avera tugged on her wrist. "Sit down, wipe your face."

The girl dropped to the bed like an obedient puppy. How refreshing. Avera moved her hand from the teenager's wrist and threaded their fingers together.

It was all they had time for as a woman entered the room.

Swept in, would be a better description.

Avera recalled an old movie she'd once seen about the life of Elizabeth the First of England. This woman could have played the part and still had enough regal demeanor left over to pull off Catherine the Great.

The stately woman came to an abrupt halt at the edge of the bed, frowning in clear disapproval at the young girl sitting so quietly.

"You were told not to disturb Lady St. John, Gwenell. Explain yourself."

"She isn't disturbing me, she's keeping me company."

The woman's disbelieving gaze flew to Avera. "Is

she indeed? Then why, I wonder, did her companion flee this room just now, screaming fit to wake the dead."

"A mouse."

Regal brows rose. "A mouse?"

Avera chanced a quick look at the girl. Her bowed head hid the small smile tugging at her lips. Good, smiles were much better than tears.

"Yes, you know, little brown thing with twitchy whiskers and a long tail? Ran right over her shoe. You might want to think about calling an exterminator. Where there's one, there are usually others, so they say."

"Do they indeed?"

Translation: "I don't believe a single word."

Avera kept her eyes widely innocent, holding the woman's stern gaze the whole time, daring her to call her bluff. The small hand she held squeezed, and Avera squeezed back reassuringly.

The woman broke their staring contest first, making Avera feel like that wasn't something she often did, and came around the bed to place a hand on the girl's shoulder. The gesture was surprisingly tender.

"Gwenell, I believe you should let Lady St. John rest. Why don't you go find Tarazia and see if you can sooth her fear of mice?"

"Yes, mother." Gwenell gave Avera's hand another grateful squeeze. She rose, smiling shyly. "I can come back tomorrow if you like, Lady St. John. I mean, if you get bored and would like some more company..." She trailed off, aware of her mother's frown.

"That would be nice, Gwenell, thank you."

"Just send one of the maids to fetch me." She made her escape then, the door closing softly behind her.

The woman turned back to Avera. "A mouse?"

"That's my story."

Uncomfortable with someone towering over her, she struggled to sit up. Surprisingly, the woman snagged pillows and stuffed them behind her for her to lean against. Once settled, Avera looked around, frowning at the wealth of white silk. Bed hangings, bed clothes, her slinky gown.

"Do you know where my clothes are?"

The woman turned to a side table where a sweat-beaded pitcher and empty glass sat on a silver tray. "I had them burned. Would you like some water?"

"Burned? You had my clothes burned?" She couldn't believe what she was hearing.

"Yes, of course. They were no more than rags. Dirty, torn, and badly stained. Totally inappropriate for someone of your station."

Inappropriate? She could not believe the woman's nerve. The glass of water in her hand, however, looked too tempting to be ignored for the sake of outrage. Avera took it. "So because my clothes didn't meet with your approval, that gave you the right to burn them?" She started drinking thirstily, holding the woman's gaze over the rim of the glass. She was fairly proud of the reasonable tone she'd used.

"I am Lady Patria Kel-Tragar, mother to Devlin Tragar, current ruler of Illian. Until he takes you to his bed, I am the highest ranking woman in this Realm. That gives me the right to do quite a few things."

She choked on the last swallow of water. Coughing, she surrendered the glass to Lady Patria's hand. When she could breathe again, she pinned the woman with as stern a look as she could manage considering she was propped up in a bed that resembled a marshmallow. "Excuse me? What makes you so sure I'll be going anywhere with your son, least of all his bed?"

"You are the foretold bride of the Seventh Prophecy. You have no choice any more than he does. The only question is when, though there is very little choice there either. The solstice is but a few months away. The Prophecy must be fulfilled by then."

She shifted against the pillows, suddenly very uncomfortable. It was clear Lady Patria believed every word she said. "What do you mean, I have very little choice? I assure you, no one is going to force me to do anything I don't want to."

"Did you not read the Prophecies Devlin sent you?"

Avera nodded. "I read them. That doesn't mean I believe them."

"Your belief in them is not required. Only your compliance."

"And what if I choose not to 'comply' as you so eloquently put it? They're your prophecies, after all, not mine."

Lady Patria's face grew even more stern. "As I said, you have no choice. No one has a choice if called on to fulfill one of Avalyr's Prophecies. The very future of Avalyr depends on those words. No one, Feyune or human, will be allowed to circumvent them. The Seventh Prophecy states that you, Avera St. John, will be wed to my son on our summer solstice. Thus it is written. Thus it will be. Even if I have to see to it personally."

Outrage shot through Avera. Now that was taking things too far. No one had ordered her around for years, not since she was a teenager. And as for ordering her to someone's bed?

Ha! She'd like to see them try.

She threw the covers back and her legs over the side of the bed so fast it startled the woman into taking a few steps back. Good. The Tragar's mother had better be afraid of her. Unfortunately, she couldn't just jump right up to follow through with her attempt at cowing the woman. The room was spinning too much, and she had to wait for a wave of dizziness to pass. When she did stand up, it was slowly. She tried to make it look like she was moving slow to control her anger instead of to keep from falling on her face.

"You have no idea who you're dealing with. I do not take orders from you or your son, or anyone else on this planet."

She sat back down abruptly as the realization hit her. Dear Lord, she hadn't even thought about that. Was it possible? Was she really on another planet? "I'm not on Earth anymore, am I?" What had happened while she was unconscious? Where had that high-handed Bloodsworn of Fate's taken her? More important, now that her mind was working she realized who it was she was missing. Where was Bracca?

Ignoring Lady Patria's smug look along with whatever answer she was making, Avera searched for the Link with her Blade, afraid it wouldn't be there. Afraid he'd died while she was unconscious. But she found the link with little problem, still wide open on her end. She sent a tentative thought down its bright length in search of Bracca, amazed at how easy it was for her to do something that, up until a few hours ago, she didn't even know existed.

Bracca?

She waited, holding her breath.

Here.

His one word answer came in a brief spurt, as if he'd opened his side of the link only wide enough and long enough to slip the word through. Even so, she could have wept at the exhaustion and pain surrounding that single word.

You don't sound so good, big guy. What

happened? Where are you?

"Are you listening to me? You have gone pale. Perhaps you should lie down again."

Avera blinked and focused on Lady Patria's face. She had no idea what the bossy woman had been saying and at this point couldn't care less. "No, I'm not listening to you right now, and no, I don't want to lie down again. I want my clothes, any clothes."

"It is already night. If you are hungry, I will have something brought to you. There is no need—"

"Thanks, but it's not food I'm after. I need to find my friend."

Bracca, where are you? Answer me.

"If you are referring to your Blade—" She curled her lip, making the word sound like something foul. "He is in the Blade's Wing where he belongs."

Bracca didn't answer. His silence caused her worry to spike. She crossed the room to a cabinet that looked like an old fashioned armoire. Several dresses hung inside, but no jeans or pants. Fine, she could do dresses. Anything was better than running around in only the silk nightgown. It was a beautiful thing and felt positively sinful, but wasn't something she wanted to parade around in public. Particularly since it had no sleeves. Neither Gwenell nor Lady Patria had commented on her scars but that didn't mean no one else would.

She grabbed the first long-sleeved dress she came to, a dark green with the heavy look of velvet though it felt light as a feather. Turning around, she found Lady Patria staring at her in disapproval.

"I'd like some privacy, if you don't mind." Avera knew she was being rude, but couldn't help it. The woman positively grated on her nerves. And that was before she'd practically threatened to tie Avera to her son's bed.

"Where do you think you are going?"

Avera huffed. "To find my friend. Something's

wrong with him, and I intend to find out what."
Looking around, she spied a privacy screen in one
corner.

"Don't be a fool. I am sure he is being taken care
of."

The words lit a fuse inside her. She stopped
short of the screen and turned around slowly. The
shocks of the day, coming one on top of the other,
had taken a toll on her usual patience. She felt ready
to explode. She walked back, green dress clutched in
her hands, to face Lady Patria. Elizabeth the First
or Catherine the Great, it didn't matter, neither one
had a thing on Avera the Fed-Up-To-Here.

"That's twice I've been called a fool today. Once
by your son, and now you. I don't like it. In fact, I
haven't liked much of anything that's happened to
me today. Don't stand there and tell me Bracca is
okay because I can feel that he's not. Now I
appreciate the use of the room, the gown, heck, even
the glass of water, but let's get one thing straight. I
don't owe you anything, and whether or not I end up
in your son's bed is between me and him. Personally,
I don't see it happening. He's a lying, high-handed
son-of-a-bitch in more ways than one."

Lady Patria jerked her head back as if slapped.
"How dare you!"

Avera shoved her twist of conscience aside. She
didn't normally insult people to their faces, but she
wasn't feeling very normal at the moment. "Now if
you'll please excuse me, I've got better things to do
than stand around arguing with you." She marched
across the room, white silk fluttering around her
ankles, to the privacy screen.

By the time she'd won the fight with the dress'
fastenings and emerged from her miniscule changing
area, Devlin's mother was gone. Avera heaved a sigh
of relief. Sparring with the prim and proper Lady
Patria was almost as bad as dealing with stuffy

Taylor Morrison. Almost.

She searched the bottom of the armoire and came up with a pair of gold strap sandals that fit pretty well. She didn't bother with trying to find a brush for her hair, settling for twisting a few stray locks behind her ears on the way to the door. Getting all the tangles out would take time, and time wasn't something she had a lot of.

Chapter Thirty-Six

Avera stepped into the hall and closed her eyes. Bracca was out here, somewhere. Now all she had to do was locate him. She touched their mental link, the desire to find him utmost in her mind. Slowly, like a compass needle, she turned until she felt the pull the strongest. Her eyes snapped open. He was somewhere in this direction. Somehow she could even tell he was trying to shield her, to keep her from knowing how much pain he was in.

I'm coming, my friend, hang on.

She had to double back twice trying to find her way out of the wing she was in. Wherever she was, the place was huge. She finally asked a maid for directions. The young girl took pity on her, leading her in person to a pair of very sturdy looking doors at the end of a hallway. The maid knocked softly and a moment later both doors swung open, pulled by a pair of footmen who bowed as Avera marched out.

The two footmen closed the doors behind her and snapped back to attention, apparently waiting for someone else to enter or leave just so they would have something to do. Avera shook her head thinking it had to be one of the most boring jobs she could imagine.

Then she saw the Blades.

She would have known they were warriors immediately, even without the swords strapped to their sides. She'd seen enough barbarians today. She didn't recognize these two, however.

Each man occupied a small alcove just a few feet from the door, standing with legs braced, arms crossed over their chests. Still as statues they were, eyes staring straight ahead. Neither one gave any sign they were aware of her.

She thought about asking them the way to the Blade's wing, but dismissed the idea. Her link with Bracca was already stronger. Using it as a guide, she should be able to find him on her own. She turned and started down the hallway, and then stopped as she heard the two Blades fall into step just behind her. Not surprisingly, they stopped too. She took two steps. Her new shadows each took one. She sighed and turned around expecting to find a pair of stoic warriors. Their grins took her by surprise.

Hands on her hips, she regarded the pair. "Gentlemen, is there something I can do for you?"

"I am Paxx, my lady, and this is Mallion. If it pleases you, simply continue your walk." His head inclined toward her, long, light brown hair sliding over his shoulders. A pair of braids at each temple framed a narrow face. He looked about as old as Kiel. Mallion looked older, her age maybe, with blond hair, clear blue eyes, and a nose that looked like it had been broken a time or two.

She calculated the possibilities for why they were there. "Am I to assume you two have been appointed my keepers?"

Both of them managed to look offended. Mallion said, "Nay, Lady St. John, not your keepers. Our Bloodsworn merely wanted to make sure you had an escort if you felt the need to leave the Lady's wing."

Yeah, right, an escort. More likely he just wanted to make sure she didn't try to run out on him, though where he thought she could run on a planet that wasn't her own, she didn't know.

Assuming she really was on another planet. Her belief hadn't quite extended that far yet.

"Uh-huh. Okay, escorts, how about escorting me to the Blade's Wing?"

They both looked at her in surprise and then Paxx's eyes lit up with understanding. "Ah, you wish to find out about the Black Blade."

"Amber. Blade." She spaced the words deliberately. "In case you didn't get the memo, he's not a Black Blade anymore."

Mallion's face darkened in disapproval. "A change of sword color does not wipe away the wrongs he did as a Black Blade. He is still the same man. His heart is just as black—"

"Don't tell me what his heart is like," she said, feeling outrage on Bracca's behalf. "I've touched his mind. I know the disgust he feels for the man he was forced to serve, the things he was made to do. How many Bloodsworns have you served?"

"I have always been the Tragar's."

"Right, and how many times has he asked you to do something you didn't think was right? Never? My, how fortunate you are. But what would you do if he did, I wonder?"

Mallion's lips curled. "I would break my own sword before sullying my honor."

Avera nodded her head. "Good answer. Very nice and noble. But what if the lives of your family were at stake? Would you still resist?" She nodded again when the blue eyes flickered. "Yeah, that changes things a little, doesn't it? You misbehave and someone you care about dies. Or, if you're lucky, the only one he'll punish is you. He could lock you up somewhere to keep you from killing yourself and just not feed you. Let you go mad, slowly, painfully." From what she'd learned by sharing Bracca's thoughts, that was one of Camarie's favorite punishments. The man was a sadist. He kept his

271

Blades half starved most of the time. She moved closer to the warrior, her anger making her reckless. "Think about how hungry you were before you linked with your Bloodsworn. Now think about being that hungry all day, every day. You want to judge Bracca Cu-Laurian, you better walk a bit in his shoes. Until then, keep your mouth shut about him around me. I'm the kind of person who protects the people I care about. You don't want to mess with my friend."

She turned her back on the two Silver Blades and stalked away, not caring if they followed or not. She'd find Bracca on her own.

They followed her, of course. They even tried to stop her outside of the Blade's wing, but she wasn't in the mood to listen. And thankfully, they weren't prepared to use force. Shoving the doors open, Avera strode inside. The room was large, with a high, vaulted ceiling. Rows of tall windows marched along two walls. About a dozen men, lounging in wide chairs or sitting at tables spaced around the room, shot to their feet as soon as they saw her. Avera ignored them, her sense of Bracca leading her to a door in the far wall.

"My lady, stop, you cannot go in there."

"Our Bloodsworn is going to kill us all."

The last was muttered, she thought, by Paxx, but she ignored it along with Mallion's order. The pull to Bracca was so strong she was almost running. She snatched open the door. The room beyond wasn't as wide as the first one, but it was long, with a double row of beds bordering a wide center aisle. A barracks; she'd seen enough of them to know. This one was occupied at the moment by another dozen or so men. She jerked to a halt as soon as she saw them. Not out of fear, but embarrassment. At least half of the warriors were extremely, and she had to admit, gloriously, naked. Hard, muscled bodies sat, stood, or moved between the rows of beds with complete unconcern. Then they noticed her. One after another, the warriors froze in place and just stared at her. The effect was almost comical, rippling around the room as if a curtain was being drawn back to reveal her. She felt every speculative gaze.

One of the men moved toward her, then another. She soon found herself surrounded, her personal space invaded. She felt like a pigeon in a room full of hungry cats. Very large, very naked, cats.

"Is she a new shetha?"

"She has to be, not even the maids come in here unless they know we're out."

"She's bold, even for a shetha."

"I don't care. Someone stab me and call our Bloodsworn. Better yet, forget about a deep-healing. I don't think this one will mind." The speaker reached out toward her hair. Avera tensed. Fighting them off was not going to be easy.

"Our Bloodsworn will do more than stab you if you touch her, Tor. She belongs to him."

"Vet!" The hand jerked back, its owner back-peddling several paces with a look of horror on his face. Her personal space magically increased by a factor of four as the rest of the warriors went with him. Every face showed some level of horror, though curiosity and speculation appeared in equal measure. Some even blushed in embarrassment. Clothing and other concealing wraps appeared with frightening speed.

Avera felt her own mix of emotions, resentment topping the list. "For your information, I do not *belong* to anyone, least of all Devlin Tragar."

"You are his Starmate. You belong to him."

Paxx's simple statement made her grind her teeth. "I am not some kind of souvenir he decided to bring home. I am a free woman. No one owns me."

After sweeping her eyes around the group of

men she marched down the aisle between the beds. The smooth, light colored wall at the far end was broken up by several dark wooden doors. She headed unerringly for the one on the far right. Bracca was there, her new senses told her, behind that door. Waiting for her.

A door which was securely locked.

She glared at her two escorts. "Open it!"

Mallion crossed his arms stubbornly. "Not without the Tragar's orders."

Her simmering anger began to boil. So this Tragar—she still had trouble calling him Devlin—had ordered Bracca locked up like some kind of criminal, had he?

"And just where is the Tragar?"

"Not here," Paxx offered helpfully.

Avera clinched her teeth. "When do you expect him back?"

A dismissive shrug from Mallion. "When he decides to return."

Stifling the urge to scream, Avera turned back to the door and pounded on it with her fist. Bracca still hadn't responded to her calls through their link and her worry was starting to lean toward panic. "Bracca? Bracca, can you hear me? Are you all right? Bracca!" There was no answering rumble, at least none she could hear though the door. She slapped the solid wood with the flat of her palm fighting back tears of frustration. He was hurting. Even with his side of the link closed she was close enough she could feel the dull edge of his pain. If only she could get to him. If only she had the darn key. Her hand dropped down to grip the metal handle as she stood there, not knowing what to do next. The handle moved.

She held her breath and applied a little more pressure. The latch continued to move until she heard a soft, unexpected, click. Her breath rushed out as she pushed the door open, slipped through, and shoved it closed again before anyone could stop her. Someone called her name from the other side, and the handle jiggled beneath her hand. She braced herself against the door, holding the latch as tight as she could. "Go away," she ordered, wishing she had the key this time so she could lock the stupid door. She couldn't help Bracca if those warriors just dragged her out again.

A sharp tingle, like a small electric shock, ran through her hand. She jerked back in surprise just as several sharp oaths sounded from the other side of the door. Stepping back, she crouched, waiting for the door to swing open. If she fought them, would they decide it best to go away and leave her alone? She didn't think they'd want to use force on her, not with their belief that she belonged to their boss. They wouldn't want to damage her. A point in her favor, however small. There were numerous ways to subdue a person without hurting them.

Remarkably, the door stayed closed. The rumble of angry male voices grew fainter. Maybe they had decided to wait for their precious Tragar to get back to deal with her. That was fine with her.

She turned around, looking for Bracca, and found him quickly. He lay on his back on a comfortable looking bed. A small white bandage covered his temple, bright against the large, angry looking bruise spread across the side of his face. His eyes were closed and lines of pain wrinkled his brow. He looked very ill.

Avera rushed to his side. She touched his hand, his face. He was cold, his body shaking with small shivers. "Bracca?" She used both voice and mind to reach out to him.

It was a moment before his eyelids fluttered open. "My lady..."

Her chest tightened in alarm. "Bracca, what's

wrong? Is it your wound? Why didn't the Tragar heal you?"

"The Tragar...cannot help me. Only you..."

"Me?" She shook her head, alarm spreading through her. "I don't know the first thing about healing like he did."

"You are...my Bloodsworn. Only you can heal me...feed me Avalyr's essence..."

She felt movement in the link, felt it open just the tiniest bit from his side, just a slit.

Voracious hunger hit her like a sledge hammer, taking her breath and making her rock back physically. She fell to the floor. Her hands went first to her stomach, then to her head as she tried to sort out what she was feeling. Hunger, yes, but not a hunger for food. Bracca's mind was starving for the magical essence all Feyune needed to survive. An essence he could no longer touch without the aid of a Bloodsworn.

And she was his Bloodsworn.

Suddenly, a vast pressure pushed against her mind, seeking entrance. She realized she'd been aware of the building pressure for some time, just too preoccupied with finding Bracca to pay it any attention. Now, it demanded more than just her attention. It demanded to be let in.

Terrified, She threw up every kind of barrier she could imagine. Walls, towers, anything to keep whatever it was out.

Bracca's body jerked and he groaned.

Tears in her eyes, she got up from the floor and sat beside him on the bed. The lines of pain etched deeper into his face. She took his hand. When she spoke, her voice shook.

"I'm sorry, I'm so sorry," she whispered. "I know I'm not doing this right. Please, you have to tell me what to do." He didn't answer.

Without giving herself time to think about what

she was doing, she closed her eyes and opened her door to their link. Pushing her way through the punishing hunger, she imagined her mind reaching for his, reaching back along that strange, mental pathway. Scrabbling, fumbling, feeling completely inept, she kept trying to reach him. She couldn't let him die. He'd saved her life. She'd touched his mind. She may have only met him a few hours ago, but she felt closer to Bracca Cu-Laurian right now than anyone else she knew.

Another shudder passed through his body.

Avera pulled back, afraid she was hurting him instead of helping. Safe once more behind her closed mental door, she tried to gather her self-control. Tears coursed down her cheeks. It wasn't like her to go all to pieces when faced with a problem. She was a scientist, used to planning and executing each logical step needed to take her to a successful conclusion.

But there was nothing logical about watching Bracca suffer. He was dying, second by second, and she had to figure out what to do, fast.

"Bracca!" She called his name, and shook him. She had to get him to wake up, tell her what to do. Why had no one woken her sooner? Where was that high-handed jerk, Devlin Tragar? This was all his fault. If he was here, he could at least tell her what she needed to do.

Her Blade's eyes opened slowly. "Do not fear for me, Avera St. John."

She felt relief, followed by a surge of anger. "Don't you dare start telling me goodbye, Bracca Cu-Laurian." He smiled slightly at her order. "Come on," she urged, aware her voice sounded wheedling and not caring one bit. "We can do this. Just give me a little hint, okay? I'm smart, I can figure out the rest. Just get me started."

His eyes drifted closed. "I have been a Blade for

many years. There were times, only a few, when I was able to sense the raw magic of Avalyr through my link. It is like a vast ocean. Warm. Soothing. Wild. Raging. All of these things. It must be ecstasy itself to be able to touch it."

"But how? How do I touch it? How do I get it to you?"

"Open your mind. Let the essence know you. You are Bloodsworn. The magic and our blood-link will do the rest."

She felt the first stirrings of hope. Bracca's words were so close to Fate's when she was blood-linking to Bracca that it couldn't be coincidence.

Instinct, not science.

Magic wasn't something to be studied under a microscope or captured in a test tube. It was elemental. It filled empty places just like water and air did, flowing where it was needed. All she had to do was let down the barriers and open the link. Hopefully, the magic would do the rest.

Closing her eyes, She gripped Bracca's hand tightly, turning him into her anchor. Something told her this was going to be a wild ride, and she'd never been a fan of roller-coasters. Taking a deep breath, she pictured the barriers in her mind and, one after another, took them down.

Like the ocean of Bracca's description, the pressure rushed in like a turbulent wave against an empty beach. Caught in the deluge of raw power, all Avera could do was gasp and shake. She'd never felt anything like it before. Totally terrifying and exquisitely rapturous all at once. The power filled her completely. And as it filled her, it shifted, changing from something elemental into something almost...alive.

Avera shuddered when the pressure equalized between herself and Avalyr's magic, and the power stopped flowing into her. It didn't stop swirling in her head, though. She realized quickly she had a fight on her hands.

Eyes squeezed tight, she clutched her head trying to make sense of what she felt. This magic, this...thing inside her mind didn't want to cooperate. Not at first. She had to really concentrate hard to get it to do what she wanted, which, at the moment, meant getting it to settle down so she could think. It took several precious minutes. Finally, she was able to corral the essence of Avalyr's magic into one corner of her mind. A corner where she knew she would always feel it, waiting, ready to answer her needs.

She needed it now for her Blade.

"Open our link, Bracca," she urged, tears in her voice. To be able to do this for him touched her as nothing else ever had. It was like donating blood, no, like donating your heart.

She felt the link on his side open, felt it fall away as if he had no more strength to hold it closed. No more strength for anything.

Ignoring the gnawing hunger battering at her, she called the essence forth and sent it in a slow, steady stream through the link. She knew the instant it touched him. His body stiffened, arched, then sank back onto the bed with a long sigh. There was a pull along the link which she automatically answered, increasing the flow of essence from a meandering stream to a rushing river.

With a sigh of her own, Avera watched the lines of pain ease on Bracca's face. His skin warmed noticeably beneath her hand.

Instinct, she decided, was a wonderful thing. Not as good as science, but damn close.

****

Bracca drank in the essence like the starving man he was. He tried not to pull it from his Bloodsworn too quickly, fighting down the urge to

279

swallow the delicious stream in huge gulps. This woman was not Camarie who often cut his Blades off before they'd had their fill. Avera St. John was the exact opposite. If anything, he would have to be careful she did not tire herself trying to care for him.

Already he knew her well enough to know she would want to heal him next. A dangerous undertaking in more ways than one. He didn't think she was aware of what a deep healing could do to both of them.

Usually he had no trouble handling his own post-healing desires, but with her here, in the same room, feeling what he was feeling, the situation could become...complicated.

Bracca quickly shifted his mind away from that train of thought. Already, the glorious essence flowing into him had his body reacting, growing hard, hot, and needy.

Chapter Thirty-Seven

The glow from the Inner Gate illuminated the practice courtyard as Devlin and his men returned to the palace. He dismissed the gate with a sharp gesture, plunging the courtyard into darkness. A perfect match to his current mood. Thanks to Camarie's retrieval magic, Devlin had had no evidence, not a single drop of blood, to present to the Concourse. The wounds his men had suffered did not matter. The Avatars assured him they had found no evidence of tampering with Earth's Outer Gates. Therefore, the warriors who had attacked Avera had to have originated on Earth. Since Avera was now safely on Avalyr, further conflict was impossible. Case closed.

Even Cu-Laurian's presence was of no help now that his sword was not black as sin.

Thinking of the Amber Blade brought Avera to the forefront of his mind. Anxious to see her, he headed for the Lady's Wing. He sent his mind ahead to find out if Mallion and Paxx knew whether or not she had awakened. He frowned when he sensed them in the Blade's quarters instead of outside the Lady's Wing. They knew better than to desert their post. The only reason they would have left would be if Avera had. Instead of wasting time querying them, he set off at a run toward the Blade's wing. Curses broke out from the Blades who'd accompanied him to the Enclave, Fate, Karess, Strum, Sarreth, and Kiel. Drawing their swords, they sprinted after him.

A knot of men stood at the far end of the Blade barracks, right in front of the room he had locked Cu-Laurian in. There were those of his Blades who'd had friends killed by Black Blades in the past. Devlin thought it entirely possible someone might consider taking their revenge out on Cu-Laurian worth the risk of reprisal. He had done what he could to keep that from happening, but apparently it had not been enough. Conflicting impressions from his Blades tumbled into his mind, making it difficult to discern exactly what had happened. His main concern at the moment, was finding out where Avera was and how she fared. He'd worry about her Blade later.

"Mallion, where is Lady St. John?"

The blond man he'd set as one of Avera's guards broke away from the others. "Your mate insisted on coming here to check on her precious Black Blade." There was such a wealth of contempt in his voice that Devlin's fist shot out in reflex, catching the man on the jaw and sending him to the floor.

Devlin stood over him, shaking in shock as much as anger. He had never struck out like that at anyone before. He'd always made it a point not too. The fact he'd done so now disturbed him greatly, though he knew he would do so again under the same circumstances. No man would be allowed to insult Avera without consequences.

"You will use respect when you speak of her." His eyes roamed over the other men, some shifting nervously. "She is Bloodsworn. Believe it, accept it, and show her the deference her station is due. And if you still find it too difficult for you, consider that as her mate, I will take it as a personal offense if you slight her in any manner. That includes attacking her Blade without provocation. Have I made myself clear?"

They all looked at him, some in shock, and nodded. "Good," Devlin said. He offered a hand to Mallion to help him off the floor. To Devlin's inner relief, the man took it. He checked his link with his Twelfth Blade as well as several of the others. He'd worked too hard to instill trust in his men to let one un-controlled moment wipe it all away. He was a bit surprised to find only respect and admiration in their minds.

There is nothing wrong with a Bloodsworn showing his teeth now and again, even to his Blades.

Devlin glanced at Fate. Other than Karess, he had been with Devlin the longest, knew him best. There was not much the man missed, even when their link wasn't fully open.

A woman's low cry coming from Cu-Laurian's room drove every sane thought out of Devlin's mind and had his blood suddenly boiling. The cry started out sounding distressed but ended in a low, seductive moan.

A path to Cu-Laurian's door quickly opened. "We cannot touch the door, Tragar," one of the warriors said. "It is protected by magic."

The information wasn't necessary. Devlin could sense the magic swirling over the heavy wood. The essence was clearly of Avalyran origin but at the same time it felt strange, different from any he'd felt before, and surprisingly strong. But not as strong as his.

He slammed his hands against the thick door, sending out a flash flood of his own magic. The door popped off its hinges and disintegrated into a shower of splinters. Physical touch hadn't been necessary any more than the complete destruction of the door, but just watching the splinters rain down in a cloud of wood dust made him feel better. He stepped into the room, looking for another target. Cu-Laurian would regret touching his woman.

The scene inside the room was not quite what he had expected. True, Avera was there, but she was on one side of the room while Cu-Laurian crouched in a far corner. The warrior appeared whole, the badly bruised wound to his temple healed, yet his pale skin was flushed, eyes half lidded, breath coming in heavy pants. A Blade fully engulfed in the throes of deep-healing lust. Only the fact Avera was on the other side of the room, her back to a wall, fingers curled into the stone like claw anchors, made it possible for Devlin to stop the call of magic he'd already begun that would have killed the Blade in a heartbeat.

Avera made a soft noise, as if gasping for breath.

"Get her out! Get her out, now!" Cu-Laurian's voice commanded harshly.

Devlin ignored the tone, too concerned by Avera's distress to care. He moved quickly, putting himself between her and Cu-Laurian. When he was close enough to touch her, her body arched toward him, the movement making her breasts strain against the dark green velvet of her dress. Her eyes were filled with desire and lust, and not a little fear.

"Help me," she moaned, the words coming out in a throaty purr. She shuddered, and then gasped, "I don't know what's happening to me."

Devlin's entire being responded to her plea. He was not entirely over healing his own men yet and the unconscious seduction of her voice had him hard in an instant. He had to fight down the urge to crush her to him right there. He could easily give her what she needed while taking what he suddenly craved. She wouldn't deny him. But she would probably hate him later, almost as much as he would hate himself. And there was still the matter of her Blade. Devlin imagined he could feel the man's hot breath on his neck from across the room.

"Shhh, it's all right," he soothed, pushing her dark hair back from her face. "What you feel is normal."

Though she didn't speak, her head rocked back and forth in denial.

"Yes, it is, trust me. When a Bloodsworn deep heals a Blade, the Blade's body reacts to the use of magic. It stimulates him, and his arousal flows back along the link to his Bloodsworn. You are feeling Cu-Laurian's natural reaction to the deep healing."

She leaned a little as if trying to see around him to her Blade. Devlin urged her face back to him. "No, don't look at him. He is having enough trouble dealing with this as it is. He doesn't need you here. He doesn't want you here. Come with me," he coaxed, his hands brushing her shoulders and skimming down her arms. He noticed her flinch as his hands brushed over her scars. Perhaps it gave her something else to think about, because the lock on her body loosened and she took a step away from the wall.

Devlin had a moment to be thankful for that small step of trust before he couldn't think of anything else but the soft body pressed so hotly against his. She moved, moaning and rubbing against him helplessly like a small kitten. With a groan, he closed his arms around her, dragging her closer. She felt so good, so right, her body fitting to his perfectly. A low growl came from the corner behind him.

"Devlin, you need to take her from here. Cu-Laurian's control won't last much longer."

Devlin couldn't concentrate on Karess' words. He was swamped by feelings he hadn't expected to feel so soon. He wanted to explore them, just as he wanted to explore the luscious body in his arms. A hand on his shoulder had him snarling at its owner.

For the first time ever, he saw Karess flinch

away from him. "Listen to me," his friend said. "You have to go, Dev. Call a gate. Take your lady somewhere private."

Somewhere private. Yes, that would be best. He needed to take Avera somewhere private so he could help her deal with what she was feeling. He had to help her understand. He just had to help her, period.

He opened a gate with a scattered thought and, sweeping the trembling woman up in his arms, carried her through the shimmering circle.

Chapter Thirty-Eight

Avera moaned. The brush of her clothes, the very touch of air against her sensitized skin threatened to drown her in a flood of sensual emotions. Something else brushed against her, enveloped her for a brief second, as if she passed through a sheet of warm water. Her body writhed at the intensely erotic sensation. Strong arms tightened around her. Devlin's arms.

Part of her said she shouldn't want to be there, cradled so close to his body she could hear his heart pounding. But for the life of her she couldn't find it in herself to object to his possessive hold. The best she could do was clamp down on the sudden desire to snuggle into his embrace. She felt so out of control it frightened her.

The warm smell of growing things assailed her nose. Slowly, Devlin let her feet fall, holding her tight against him as she slid down his body. It was torture. It was heaven. She didn't want the ride to stop. When it did, feet touching the ground, she heard herself whimper. A small, sane corner of her mind cringed at the needy sound.

"Luma's hell, woman, how you tempt me."

His voice sounded strange to her. Hoarse, as if he struggled just to speak. Lips brushed her hair, her temple and traveled down her neck. She shivered in response and pressed closer to him, tilting her head so he could reach her neck easier. Her hips pushed against his in invitation.

This was crazy, a part of her shouted. She wasn't like this. She wasn't a prude, but she'd never been this bold before, this brazen. How could she be like this with a man she didn't even know, one who had lied to her? Part of her knew she would hate herself later. The rest of her didn't care. She was no more able to prevent her hips from rubbing against the bulge at his crotch than she was able to stop breathing. She was simply too needy, too caught up in the moment to worry about modesty and restraint.

Rough hands roamed over her back and moved down, cupping her bottom and pulling her even tighter against that enticing hardness. A shot of fire pierced her belly and moved down between her legs. Damn, it felt good.

She wound her arms around his neck and fisted a hand in his thick hair. Roughly she pulled his head to the side so she could nibble the skin of his neck before moving up to lick and suckle the lobe of his ear. He groaned and she felt his body jerk. She added a scrape of teeth. He tasted so good. She'd known he was going to taste good.

Avera moaned and hooked a leg around his thigh. It had been a very long time since she had let herself get close enough to someone to indulge in a good old-fashioned petting session. The thought amused her for some reason, and she chuckled low in her throat. Devlin's body shivered beneath her hands and lips, giving her a feeling of power over this strong, virile man. Perhaps being his wife would not be such a bad thing. Perhaps she could even learn to like him, high-handedness and all. Perhaps—

"Avera, we cannot do this."

His rasping words were like a bucket of cold

water. She froze and pulled back enough so she could look at him. His eyes weren't saying the same thing as his lips.

"You don't want to stop."

His arms tightened. "No, I do not. But unless you tell me you are willing to accept me as your mate, stop we must."

"Maybe I am." Maybe, right now, she didn't care about worlds, or prophecies, or anything else.

His hands came up to cup her face. His eyes, so much like orbs of dark blue fire she imagined she could feel heat coming from them, searched her face. Whatever he saw had him shaking his head slowly, disappointment replacing some of the fire. "Avera, the bonding of Starmates is begun by the act of intercourse. I would like nothing better than to take you, now, right here in my garden, but I will not. Not unless you can convince me it is you who want this and not Cu-Laurian's lust driving you to it."

Even in her aroused state, Avera knew that wasn't likely to happen. Yes, she wanted him, but no, she couldn't say it wasn't the lust talking. At this point, her body didn't care.

But he did.

His hesitation allowed her to pull herself together. She even had enough sanity left to appreciate the sacrifice he made by not simply taking what she offered. That didn't keep part of her from weeping with frustration as she reached up and carefully pulled his hands away from her face. His arms dropped to his sides the moment she released him. When he didn't move, she forced herself to step back. Once, twice. His expression never changed. He still wanted her.

She turned away to keep from flinging herself back into his arms. "Stop it. How can you look at me like that and just stand there?" She wasn't that strong. She wanted him so bad, it hurt, and she had no way to deflect the pain, no shields to hide behind. She crossed her arms over her aching breasts, partly to try to relieve some of the pain and partly to hide the trembling of her arms. For the first time that day she really did feel like a fool.

****

It took all of Devlin's willpower not to pull Avera St. John right back into his arms. Luma's blood and tears, but he wanted her. He didn't care that she was from another world, didn't even care that she was Bloodsworn. Didn't care if, by bonding with her, he was doing exactly as his mother wanted, exactly as the damned prophecy demanded. The only thing stopping him from taking her was the fact that if, no, when, she came to him, he wanted it to be with her eyes wide open, not clouded with another man's lust.

But he couldn't leave her like this either. Aching. Wanting. Holding herself so tightly it was painful just to look at her. He knew what it was to want that badly.

He approached her slowly, a careful stalking motion. When she would have turned to face him, he moved fast, wrapping his arms around her and pulling her back to his chest. It was safer this way, he told himself, though his mate may not have thought so. If possible, her body stiffened even more. She became as still as a statue in his arms. Not a statue of cold stone, but of heat. Even through the cloth of her dress, her skin burned like fire beneath his hands.

Devlin closed his eyes, praying for strength. Ignoring the call of her body was going to be next to impossible. Already he felt an edge to the lust still lingering in him from his own deep-healing sessions with Sarreth and Fate. His First Blade had suffered two broken ribs in his last fight and hid the knowledge until they returned to Avalyr. The stubborn fool.

The statue in his arms moved.

"Relax," he murmured against her hair. "There are other ways I can help you. I will not leave you to suffer this alone. The lust from a deep-healing can last for hours if you do not find release somehow."

A pause, and then she spoke, her voice husky with need. "Let me go. I don't need your pity. I can handle this fine on my own."

Devlin bit back a laugh. Pity was the last thing he was feeling. Couldn't she tell that? His body wasn't exactly being subtle in making its wishes known. But this wasn't about him. It was about the remarkable young woman in his arms who continued to astound him with her strength and courage. She'd faced numerous challenges today. Faced them, and conquered every one with nothing more than her quick mind and strong will. He was determined she not face this last trial alone.

"Peace, Avera. Forgive me. I mean no offense." He kept his words soft, coaxing. "Are our worlds so different? Can one not offer help to a friend in need on your world without being motivated by pity?"

"We're...we're not friends."

Her words cut through him like knives. "Perhaps not, but I would like to believe we have the beginnings of a friendship. I know this day has been difficult for you, and I apologize once again. I planned to come to you this morning to tell you everything. To ask you to come back to Avalyr with me."

Her body relaxed just a fraction. An encouraging sign.

"Why didn't you?"

"Camarie, the man who sent his Blades after you, fooled the Bloodsworn Council into thinking he was ready to give himself up. But only to me. I didn't want to go when they called me. If I'd ignored them, none of this would have happened." No Bloodsworn status, no Black Blade linked to his mate. Gods, his uncle owed him.

"You sent Fate and the others?" Her body softened a bit more.

"Yes." He whispered the word warmly against her hair. "Sarreth and Kiel were already there, in the rooms across from yours."

Her breathing hitched. "You left them to spy on me?"

"To watch over you, to keep you safe. As a magic user, my time on your world was limited. I couldn't be with you as much as I wanted. I needed to know you were safe. Sarreth and Kiel volunteered to stay to ease my mind."

"Fate?"

"I sent him this morning. Camarie's demand that I attend his meeting with the Council made me suspicious. Not enough to call his bluff, but enough that I sent Fate ahead to make sure you were safe. He sent word back to Avalyr about strange Blades found around the place where you work. He knew the message would take some time to reach me and went after you himself." Another reason Fate An-Derrith was Devlin's First Blade. If he had stayed at the Gate Watcher's house and waited for Devlin, Avera would be dead.

"I'm sorry," he said again, the thought of losing her making his voice crack. "I'm sorry you had to run, that you were scared. I'm sorry you were hurt." He pressed a kiss to the spot on her shoulder where the shallow knife wound was not even a fading scar, completely erased by healing magic.

She shivered at his touch and let her head fall back against his chest. "You came," she said softly. "That's what matters."

He had yet to move his hands, waiting for her acquiescence. When he felt her arms loosen from their tight grip around herself, he loosened his slightly as well, setting her hands free. Small, smooth palms slid like silk along his skin, making the hairs on his arms stand in their wake. Slim, feminine fingers settled over his broad hands. She squeezed, and he knew she was his.

Her hands stayed on top of his as he slowly brought one hand up to curl possessively over her breast. Her breathing picked up as he strummed the taut nipple trapped behind smooth velvet with his thumb. Their other joined hands moved low, where he cupped her through her gown. She moaned and leaned into his touch.

Devlin swallowed, fighting back the damn lust that threatened his control. She was so receptive, so responsive to his touch. He couldn't help but wonder how she would be with her own lust riding her instead of her Blade's. The mere thought of her responding to him like this of her own accord caused him to swell in a rush bordering on pain. It also brought something else to mind.

He leaned over her, his lips finding the corner of hers. He murmured against them. "Tell me your link with your Blade is closed." He needed to know it was. He didn't want to share this part of her with anyone.

"Yes," she whispered, her breath hot against his lips. "We closed both sides as soon as he was healed. It didn't help. I'm still burning up."

"I can help you. Let me help you, Avera." He settled his lips over hers, swallowing her whispered assent. His tongue slid across her lips, pushing inside easily, delving, seeking, mating with her own. For a while they simply fed off each other in long, panting kisses while Devlin's hands worked their own magic on her needy body.

They kissed until she writhed in his arms, her fingers digging into his thighs, kneading, stroking.

"More." She breathed the word into his mouth.

Holding tight to his fraying control, Devlin backed up with her until he was half leaning, half sitting against one of the boulders surrounding the pond, her lying atop him. Hooking his ankles around hers, he slowly spread both their legs. He held her there, unable to move, while he gathered her skirt, handful by slow handful, and pulled it up until it bunched at her waist.

She was wide open for him, bare, the cool night air of his garden bathing her heated flesh. He pressed his hand to her wet core. Both of them shivered at the touch. Her hips moved, pressed first against his hand and then back against him, rubbing at the hard length of his manhood pressed against her bottom.

His own lust lashed at him.

The thought that he would be lucky if this didn't kill him skittered through his mind and was gone, chased away by the touch of her tongue sliding in a long lick up his neck. Closing his eyes, he cupped her face, held her in place while he indulged his hunger and ate at her sweet mouth. When he would have pulled back, he found his own head held captive by a small hand buried deep in his hair. Devlin surrendered, not really wanting to escape anyway.

But if he didn't bring her to a peak soon, cool some of the lust raging through her, all thoughts of honorable intentions were likely to be forgotten.

He pressed a long finger between her slick folds, pushing deep into her body while his thumb circled the tight bud of her sex. She moaned, a needy sound he answered by adding a second finger. Her legs stiffened, hips pressing forward helplessly. He took her mouth again and again, his tongue settling into the same mating rhythm as his fingers as he brought her higher and higher, circling the pinnacle. Finally, her body arched. She threw her head back against his shoulder and cried out. He could feel the pleasure ripple through her body, her inner muscles clutching around his fingers in satisfyingly tight contractions.

Merciful Luma!

There was no help for it. Her release pulled at him, and he was too close to the edge himself to resist. Devlin held her tightly against him, his hips thrusting blindly against her firm backside once, twice, and then his own climax roared through him.

Chapter Thirty-Nine

It was a long moment before he could move enough to release her ankles and twitch the skirt of her gown back over her bare legs. She brought her legs together and rolled off him, but didn't try to get up right away. He took that as a good sign.

For a while he was content just to hold her. The sound of lapping water, chirping insects, and wind rustling the leaves grew more pronounced as their breathing slowed. He moved first, nuzzling his lips against her hair.

"Better?"

She stirred in his arms. "Yes." Her voice still sounded breathless. Devlin thought he heard embarrassment there as well. Not surprising. She didn't strike him as someone used to losing control. Neither was he, for that matter.

Still, all things considered, it was the best he'd felt in a very long time.

Avera finally moved, making it plain she was ready to get up. He helped her stand. She stepped away at once, head bent, hair hiding her face as her arms crossed over her breasts again. Her embarrassment was almost palpable now. She looked so distressed, so vulnerable, Devlin felt a fierce need to take her back in his arms and comfort her.

As if sensing his desire, she glanced at him

before moving further away. Her eyes were wary, but he could still see the lust lingering in their green depths. He knew from his own experiences one climax would never be enough to cool it all. At least now, though, it wasn't riding her so hard.

Devlin hid a grimace. His own release as evidenced by the dampness of his pants had gone far to cooling the remnants of his remaining lust. So much for his self control. This woman's very presence easily shred it to tatters. He hadn't come like a rank juvenile since...well, since he'd been a rank juvenile. If Karess or the others found out about it, they would never let him live it down.

He spared a bit of magic to clean himself and dry his pants. She had to know he'd found his own release, but Devlin wasn't of a mind to parade it in front of her. Already there was a distance growing between them he didn't like.

"I should..." She cleared her throat and started again. "I should go back to my room, I suppose." Her voice sounded small and lost. It tore his heart, and made him a little angry, too, to see her this way, her shoulders bent as if she were ashamed of what they had just shared. She had nothing to be ashamed of!

He cursed himself, unable to think of any simple words to mitigate what she was feeling. For her to understand she would have to first understand fully what it meant to be Bloodsworn, something which would only come with time. All he could offer her now was privacy. "I can open a gate for you, if you like," he offered.

"A gate?"

"The magic version of a short-cut."

His explanation earned him a raised brow and a curious smile. "All right."

Pleased, he took a step toward her, only to have her step back hastily. Devlin frowned. Why would she fear him now? He had been nothing but gentle with her. It was not as if he had attacked her, forced himself on her. Luma's hell, he'd come close to castrating himself just to protect her honor.

"There is no reason for you to fear me."

She gave a small snort, looking at him with the same fire he'd seen in her eyes back in the woods on Earth. "Don't flatter yourself, Tragar—"

"Devlin. My first name is Devlin, remember? After everything we've shared, you can at least call me by my first name, I think." He took a chance reminding her, but he couldn't stop himself. He didn't like seeing that distant look in her eyes, like she was looking at a stranger. He wasn't a stranger, damn it, he was her mate. A fact he was coming to accept more and more.

Her chin came up a fraction. "Devlin, then. And I'm not afraid of you. If you must know, I'm afraid of myself. I'm...I'm not myself right now." Moonlight caught the flush staining her cheeks. "I don't make a habit of having sex with a complete stranger."

"I am pleased to hear that, Avera, but you must know you and I are far from being strangers." Determined to hear her admit it, he took another step toward her. She retreated.

"Well, you may not think we're strangers, but I do. We only met a few days ago, and what just happened aside, I don't know you." She gave a shaky laugh, running her hand through her dark curls. "I *so* don't know you. I know Bracca better than I know you. At least I've been inside his head."

Jealousy cut through Devlin, his whole body filling with tension. He rolled his head on his neck to get rid of it, tight muscles stretching, vertebrae popping.

"It would be best if you did not mention Cu-Laurian too freely around me. Knowing he has been in *your* head, that he could be there now, is not something I take lightly."

Avera's arms unwound, hands going to her hips. At least their argument was having one positive affect. She seemed to be forgetting all about lust and need, so why wasn't he happier with that?

"Don't start," she told him. "Just don't start with me about Bracca. You're the one who locked him up in that room knowing he was dying. You didn't even try to heal him, did you?"

"Is that what Cu-Laurian told you?"

"Well, no, actually, he told me only I could heal him because of our link. But there had to be something you could have done. What if I hadn't woken up in time? What if I hadn't tried to find him? He could have died."

"I had my healers dress his wound. There was nothing else we could do for him. If you were still sleeping in the morning, I would have tried to wake you then."

"Didn't you hear me, I said he was dying. He wouldn't have lasted till morning."

Devlin gave her a less than patient look. "Your pardon, my lady, but I was under the impression you knew nothing of Blades and Bloodsworn except for the mention of them in the Prophecies I sent you, and what you might have learned from Fate and the others today. I was not aware you were an expert."

"Believe me, I know a dying man when I see one."

"Yes, but can you judge how long it will take that man to die? Cu-Laurian could have lasted several days. True, they would not have been pleasant days, but he was in no danger of losing his life if you had slept through till morning."

"I can't believe how arrogant you are. How dare you presume to play with another man's life, much less my own."

"I cannot see where I have played with your life, Avera."

"No? How about the fact you've dragged me back to your home against my will like some flippin' caveman."

"I did not bring you here against your will."

"Hello? That's because I was unconscious. You didn't bother to find out if I wanted to go with you or not. Don't stand there and tell me I had a choice. I can't see that First Blade of yours going back to you empty handed if I'd told him no and sent him and his buddies packing. He'd have hauled me to you in chains if need be, wouldn't he?"

Devlin couldn't keep his lips from twitching. He'd seen through Fate's, Sarreth's, and Kiel's memories how confused his Blades had been by Avera's strong will and outspokenness; traits Devlin didn't mind at all. Seeing her like this—skin flushed and eyes bright with outrage—was far better than seeing her racked with guilt and pain. "I am sure he would be a bit more diplomatic than resorting to chains, but yes, he would not have returned to me without you."

"See, see there! High-handed. That's just what I told your mother." She started pacing, the hem of her gown swishing angrily around her ankles. "I so don't need this. You need to take me back home, right now."

He stiffened, no longer amused. "Impossible."

"Don't tell me it's impossible," she snapped. "You brought me here, you can bloody well take me back."

Not used to anyone defying him, much less giving him orders, Devlin's first reaction was the desire to grab her and shake her into submission. That, or kiss her until she was senseless, until she clung to him willingly as she'd done a few moments ago. He did neither. As difficult as the day had been for him, he couldn't begin to imagine how bad it had been for her. Attacked, her life threatened numerous times, not to mention having to accept the impossible as reality. She had every right to be upset. But that still didn't mean he was going to let her go.

"Avera, you have to be reasonable. What part of today's fiasco with Camarie's Black Blades did you not understand? He is trying to kill you."

She stopped pacing and turned to him. Lifting first one arm, then the other, she jerked the velvet of her sleeves up to her elbows, exposing her scars. "In case you hadn't noticed, I don't kill easily."

Devlin felt his anger stir to life at the sight of her slashed arms. He reached for her. "Tell me how you came by these. Tell me who is responsible." A quick trip back to Earth would see the bastard dead.

She made a sharp twisting motion, dodging his grasp and tugging down her sleeves, her expression suddenly wary.

"Tell me," he insisted.

"No."

Luma's hell, the woman was stubborn.

"I didn't show my scars to you to talk about them. I showed them to let you know I'm not afraid to fight my own battles. I want to leave. Now. I demand you take me back to Earth right this minute."

Devlin crossed his arms, partly to keep from reaching for her again and partly in anger at himself. This was just the situation he'd wanted to avoid. Lucky for him he didn't have to think twice about how to deal with it. Her Bloodsworn status provided him the perfect answer. "Assuming, for a moment, I were to grant such an unwise request, would you be leaving your Blade here to die or would you rather take him with you to watch him die on Earth?"

"What?"

"Cu-Laurian is Feyune, Avera. We require the magical essence of our planet to survive. He is also a

Blade, meaning he can only touch the magic with the help of a Bloodsworn, and you, as unbelievable as it seems, are his Bloodsworn. If you return to Earth without him, I will have no choice but to show him the mercy of Solace, the ritual death." Not completely true, since his honor would demand he at least attempt to link with the man in return for Cu-Laurian saving her life. However, nothing was certain, especially when it came to blood-links. "On the other hand," he continued in a merciless tone, "if you take him with you, he will survive for a time, but once the magic you had stored up is gone, he will die a slow, agonizing death. As your Blade, his life is in your hands."

Chapter Forty

Avera swallowed hard. She couldn't go back home. Not ever. She hadn't possessed that pertinent piece of data when she'd chosen to help Bracca. The whole Bloodsworn thing hadn't seemed real at the time. It had all been part of a fairy tale someone had made up. Having magic flood her mind and turning around and feeding it to Bracca still hadn't hammered home all the responsibility involved. It took Devlin to point it out to her.

Committing to being Bracca's Bloodsworn really meant she'd sealed her fate to his. Was that something she could accept?

Several scenes flashed through her mind in quick succession. A man holding a black sword over her head while gagging around a knife in his throat. Another man sprawled on the warehouse floor, his neck broken. Bracca running toward her, fighting to reach her, her mind flooded by his desperate need to keep her safe.

On his knees in front of her, swearing his loyalty.

She wasn't the kind of person who could turn her back on something like that. It wasn't his fault her impulsive nature landed her in a situation so hard to accept. She couldn't even blame Devlin. The choice of trying to keep Bracca alive had been all hers.

Avera heaved a deep sigh. "I guess I don't really have a choice, do I?"

She was looking right at Devlin, so she saw his shoulders relax, ever so slightly. "No," he said. The accompanying smile looked forced. "I am afraid neither of us do."

That was strange. She'd figured he would pounce on her admission with relish. Maybe he and his mother weren't so much alike after all. Maybe he didn't like this whole prophecy thing ordering their lives around any more than she did.

A disturbing thought occurred to her.

What if Devlin had made plans to marry someone else, someone he loved, but was forced to give up because a crazy Oracle told him to marry her instead? She didn't even want to think about that possibility. Being forced into a relationship was bad enough without it being doomed to failure right from the start. This whole situation was getting way too complicated.

A finger touched her cheek with a gentleness that surprised her. "There is no need to look so defeated. I promise you your life here on Avalyr will not be such a heavy burden. Our worlds may be very different in some ways, but in others, we are much the same. We live, we work, we play, we lo..."

"Do you have horses?" A silly question, all things considered. She couldn't begin to understand why she'd blurted the question out except she loved to ride and never had the opportunity to do it as often as she wanted. If she had to give up her life back on Earth there had to be a few things here she could look forward to as compensation.

"Yes, of course. Horses are our main method of transportation." He must have seen her eyes light up because he smiled. "Ah, so you like horses, do you? Can you ride?"

"I've been riding since I was ten. Not often now,

304

of course, but I try to get out to the stables every couple of months or so."

"You had a mount of your own?"

She shook her head. She had no place to keep a horse much less the extra funds to take care of one. "No, the stables I went to had horses for rent. Flash your plastic, sign a waver, and the horse was yours for however long you could stay in the saddle. I did have a favorite though, a frisky buckskin mare. She and I used to love to run..." Avera trailed off. There were a lot of things she was going to miss.

"I have many horses, my lady, one or two of which might serve as a suitable mount in place of your mare. I will speak to the stable master and have him bring them in from the pasture."

Avera felt a brief surge of anticipation followed by a wave of guilty homesickness. One or two horses really weren't going to make up for leaving everything else on Earth behind.

Devlin reached out and tipped her head up with a finger. "There are other benefits to living here that you might not have considered."

"Like what?"

He quirked a smile at her laced with mischief. "Well, since you are Bloodsworn, you will be able to do more with Avalyr's magic than simply providing it to your Blade. It will take time for you to learn to control it, bend it to your will, but once you do..." He waved a hand in a casual gesture.

Tingles ran over her body, and she looked down, gasping in shock. Her green dress was gone. In its place were the same black jeans and knit blouse she had put on that morning. At least they looked the same. Hardly daring to breathe, she ran her hands up her thighs, across her stomach, down her arms. Soft, worn denim and stretch cotton.

Assuming the clothes were real, and she wasn't dreaming or hallucinating, the hypothetical possibilities were immediately apparent. No more shopping, no more fumbling with buttons and zippers when she was running late, not to mention, no more laundry. She really hated doing laundry.

She looked up at him, cocking her head and asking to make sure she hadn't made the wrong assumption. "Are you saying I can wish up my own clothes?"

"Eventually, yes. As I said, you will have to first learn how to harness the magic you have access to."

"Really?" she said, her mind already cataloging the possibilities. "So, once I learn to rein in this magic, can I do other things with it?" She couldn't keep the growing excitement out of her voice.

He must have heard it, or seen it on her face, because he chuckled at her. "A myriad of things, too many to name."

"How? Can you teach me? Will you?" Could she really learn how to wield magic?

His hand reached out and tucked some of her hair behind her ear. "Of course. As your mate, it will be my pleasure to teach you to use your magic, among other things." His voice lowered to a seductive drawl that crawled lazily across her skin.

Avera wet her lips as she stared into his eyes, trying not to think about what kind of other things he might be referring to. She was already having enough trouble with the things his light touch around her ear was doing to the rest of her body. There was no doubt she was attracted to him. Had been since the moment she'd looked into his deep blue eyes outside her apartment. But they were still strangers. She had no business just falling into bed with him, especially when doing so might be the same thing as accepting a marriage proposal. Or was it the same as the wedding itself? She didn't know. There were just too many things she didn't know. How was she supposed to make any kind of life altering decision with so many unknowns.

She needed data. And she needed time to collect that data.

Avera cleared her throat. "Maybe...maybe we could step back a bit, take things a little slower. I really think it would be a good idea to get to know each other better, don't you?"

She tried to sound like a rational, reasonable adult discussing some mundane subject. It wasn't easy. She had a feeling she'd left the rational and reasonable side of herself cringing in one of Barrett's hallways. Everywhere she'd turned since then, there'd been nothing but complete irrationality.

Her attraction to Devlin, for instance.

He'd lied to her, spied on her, played her for a fool. He'd even kidnapped her from her world. Yet, here she was, wishing he'd take her in his arms again. And she was honest enough to admit it wasn't just because of the lust playing havoc with her senses. How could she still want him so much?

Too close, he was standing too close, that was the problem. Every time she took a breath she inhaled his scent, something masculine and spicy. Exciting. It was starting to drive her a little crazy. She wished he would either step away or step closer, because she didn't seem to be able to move at all. He smiled at her, making her heart pound faster.

"If that is your wish. Perhaps it would be best if we began anew in the morning. It has been a difficult day for us both." He held out a hand to her. "Would you like to return to your room now?"

She looked at his hand, but didn't take it. She didn't dare. He had to know what he was doing to her already. It had to be plain in her eyes. But if she touched him, he would definitely feel her trembling. She couldn't give him that. "Yes, I think it would be a good idea if I went back to my room. Alone," she added hurriedly.

With a knowing look, he let his hand fall, and dipped his head in understanding. "Very well." He made a gesture with his hand. A few steps away a shimmering oval appeared. Avera took a cautious step back.

"What's that?"

"The gateway I promised you. It's how I brought you here to my garden from Cu-Laurian's room."

She felt amazement widen her eyes. This was his magic short-cut? "What is it? A mini worm hole or something?"

"Or something. I picture where I want to go, release the magic—"

"—and it does the rest." She finished the sentence for him, shaking her head. People who lived and worked with magic took so much for granted. They didn't seem to even want to look into the mechanics of how something worked. She, on the other hand, wasn't comfortable with trusting her mortal body to some sci-fi form of transportation. Even if she had already been through it once.

Lured by the prospect of the unknown, Avera walked up to the gate to inspect it. The shimmering edge held power, that much she could feel without even touching it. Something close enough to electricity that it made the hairs on her arms stand on end.

The softly glowing edge framed part of a dimly lit room. She could see the bed she'd left earlier, a cloud of white silk surrounded by dusky shadows. Curious, she circled the gate. No glow came from the back side. In fact, the only way she could tell the gate was there at all was a haziness hanging in the air like a thin veil through which she could see Devlin watching her patiently. Walking completely around it, she asked him, "So what happens if someone steps through it from the back?"

He shrugged one shoulder. "Gates are one sided.

At worst, the person would disrupt the magic field holding the gate open, and it would collapse. If the Bloodsworn who opened the gate was strong enough, there would be no disruption at all."

Still examining the gate she asked, "And only Bloodsworn can open gates?"

"Yes, only we have the ability to tap into Avalyr's veil of magic to that extent and harness it for our own use. It is a benefit, you might say, for our willingness to provide for those who cannot touch the magic themselves."

"Men like Bracca and Fate."

Devlin nodded. "Men who fall prey to the illness that strips them of a Feyune's natural ability to mentally touch the veil. Without our intervention, they would soon die."

"Do they ever recover? I mean, you called it an illness. Does anyone ever get better so they don't need the link anymore?"

He walked up to her, close enough to touch, but he only looked at her intently. "No, Avera, Blades never recover. Linking to a man with the blade-illness becomes a life-long responsibility."

Avera frowned. Life-long? Bracca would need her as long as he lived? She thought about that for a long moment. If she looked at it from a different perspective it wasn't really so bad, she decided. She and her father were committed to one another, or had been, until he disappeared. It would have been the same thing, a life-long commitment of looking out for one another.

Okay, she could deal with that. But what if she died before Bracca did?

"What...what happens when a Bloodsworn dies? What happens to their Blades?" He didn't answer right away, and for a moment she thought he wasn't going to. Was the answer that bad?

"An older Bloodsworn, one who is close to death,

can bequeath his links to another, though it is rare for all of the Blades to transfer successfully. Some are simply tied too closely to their Bloodsworn to survive the sundering of their link." He paused and his face tightened as if recalling something painful. He shook his head slightly and continued. "If a Bloodsworn dies quickly, unexpectedly, those Blades who have such close ties to him die immediately. The rest merely go unconscious or are not affected at all. At least, not at first. But they, too, will die, unless they find another Bloodsworn who will accept them in a blood-link. A task harder than one might think."

"A question of past loyalties." When he looked surprised at her understanding, she said, "My father was in the Marines for almost twenty years. The Marine Corps is a branch of our military," she explained. "He was a Colonel for fifteen of those years, specializing in troubleshooting. If some base started showing a breakdown in command, decrease in efficiency, you name it, he was sent in to fix things. That meant we moved around a lot, and he had to step on a lot of toes. It was never easy. Most of the other officers resented him, even if he was there to bail them out. And as for the regular jarheads...warriors you'd call them," she shrugged. "They obeyed his orders because of his rank, but he was never in one place long enough to build any kind of trust with them." She reached up, and hesitantly touched the edge of the gate. When its power didn't bite, she ran her hand through the shimmer. The magic made her fingers tingle.

"I think that's one of the reasons we were so close. I was the only constant in his life, the only person who trusted him completely."

"Trust is a precious commodity," Devlin said. "One purchased with loyalty and faithfulness.

She nodded and sighed. "Semper Fidelis." When he raised a brow, she translated for him. "Semper

Fidelis means 'Always Faithful'. It was our family motto, even if it did belong to the Marines first. Dad and I depended on one another." And then he'd disappeared.

Grief welled up quickly, as it always did when she let her guard down. Blinking back tears, she wished with all her heart that just once, she could think about her dad, remember the good times, without feeling the pain of his loss. She'd been waiting over a year for it to get better, but the pain was still just as sharp and fresh in her heart as the day the military had declared him dead. She was so deep in the memory she started when Devlin reached out and took her hand, holding it gently in his. Surprised, she looked at him, and all thoughts of her father fled.

Chapter Forty-One

The faint glow from the gate cast highlights across Devlin Tragar's handsome face and flickered in his eyes. The mix of light and shadows made him look even more hauntingly mysterious. She liked mysterious. He opened his mouth slightly, his tongue flicking out to moisten his lips. Avera got the feeling he did it deliberately, just to distract her, and she was grateful. She really didn't feel like indulging in a bout of tears.

Watching him, she suddenly found it impossible to think about anything else but the memory of his kisses and the touch of his hands. Slowly he lifted her hand to his mouth where the brush of his lips sent tingles running up her arm. The tingles had nothing to do with magic this time and everything to do with desire. Sweet Lord, but the man was pure seduction. The last of her sadness vanished.

"I have spent many years trying to earn and be worthy of the trust of my people and my Blades," he murmured. "Good practice, I would think, for the daunting task I now face."

"And what task is that," Avera whispered, watching him rub the pad of her finger against the edge of his teeth.

"Earning back your trust."

He looked at her through his dark lashes, and Avera's breath caught in her throat. She'd swear trust was the last thing on his mind. It was certainly the last thing she was thinking of, though her common sense said it should have been the first. Trying to gather her thoughts, she tugged her hand free. He took several steps back and then bowed, never taking his eyes off her.

"I bid you good night and pleasant dreams, my lady."

He was dismissing her, and she didn't know whether to be relieved or offended. Goodness knows it wouldn't take much convincing for her to be back in his arms. If only she could be sure of what she felt, what *he* felt, like she was with Bracca.

Thinking of Bracca reminded her of what she'd experienced while healing him. Some wild ride. The echo of his pleasure as the magic filled him had been bearable, even nice. The raging lust, as that same magic drove deep into his body, repairing cells, generating tissue...? Not even close to nice. She still felt it running through her veins despite the exquisite orgasm Devlin had given her. If that heavy dose of desire still rode her, what about Bracca?

She hesitated at the edge of the shimmering oval. Her mind shied away from opening their link to ask him if he was all right. Asking Devlin about him was probably looking for trouble, but she had to know. "Um, what about Bracca? Is he... I mean, will someone..." Well, this was more embarrassing than she thought it would be. "Is he going to be all right?" she finally blurted.

Devlin's eyes tightened, flickered for an instant. "Cu-Laurian is fine. One of the shetha is with him."

Shetha. His men had wondered if she was a new shetha. She thought she understood the word now, but asked, just to be sure. She'd been in enough foreign cultures to know not to assume. "And a shetha is?"

"A woman of great heart and compassion.

313

Shethas take it upon themselves to see to the needs of Blades and Bloodsworn after a deep healing. Their caste is honored, holding the same status as our healers."

An honored caste. She was glad she'd asked. But, Blades *and* Bloodsworn? Did that mean Devlin had...

Of course he had. He's a man. He's single. And chances are good he's had to deep-heal an injured Blade more than a time or two. She recognized the sharp edge of jealousy cutting through her and decided right then she didn't want to meet any of the shethas living at the palace. She wouldn't be able to keep from wondering which ones had shared Devlin's bed.

"I see," she said, quickly tamping down the jealousy before it showed. Definitely time to call it a night, she decided. She ran her hand slowly down her newly conjured blouse and jeans, smiling when she saw how his eyes followed the movement. "Thank you for the clothes, by the way. I would have missed my jeans. Good night." Without waiting for a reply, she turned and stepped through the gate.

The cloud-like bed, seemingly far too big and austere in all its whiteness before, now beckoned to her tired body. She made sure Devlin's gate was gone before she removed her clothes and slipped between the sheets sans the nightgown she'd had on earlier.

Not the smartest thing she'd done that day, she realized, as the feel of those cool, soft sheets on her bare skin sent a shaft of fresh need scampering through her belly. With a groan, Avera flopped back on the pillow. The top sheet settled down, caressing her breasts and stomach and pooling between her thighs. "Damn," she whispered into the darkness. It was going to be a long, uncomfortable night. A perfect match for the rest of her day.

Then her lips curled into a resigned smile. Yeah, her day had been a bitch, but, despite everything, she couldn't find it in herself to wish it all had never happened. Not only did she have a whole new world to explore, but it was a world of magic.

She caught herself wincing at the M-word and chuckled. Her poor scientific mind still hadn't quite come to grips with her new reality. Magic was real, and she'd just been promised she'd be able to experiment with it. How cool was that?

And the rest of it? Her connection to Bracca Cu-Laurian, her attraction to Devlin Tragar?

Avera sighed deeply. To say she was confused as hell would be an understatement.

She already knew she'd do just about anything for Bracca. The images of his life that had flashed through her mind when their blood-link popped into place sealed the deal as far as she was concerned. The man's gentle soul had been so badly abused by that damned black Bloodsworn of his, it made her spitting mad just to think about it. How they were going to cope being tied mind-to-mind was the real question.

And Devlin? She simply didn't know what she was going to do about him. The man made her absolutely crazy. All he had to do was touch her and all her common sense flew out the door.

That didn't mean she was ready to forgive him for deceiving her. Getting over that was going to take time.

Then she thought about the man he'd killed to protect her. The gentle touch he'd used when examining her wound. His delight when he'd discovered how good pizza tasted. Her delight when she'd finally gotten a taste of him. His lips, his mouth, the skin on his neck where she'd licked him.

How good his hands felt on her body.

Avera groaned again and rolled to her side.

Okay, so maybe forgiving him wasn't going to take as long as she thought.

****

Devlin allowed the gate to Avera's room to close, blocking out the sight of her moving toward her bed. A bed he very much wanted to join her in despite the anger simmering in his veins. He closed his eyes, fists tight at his sides, and let the image of her backside swaying back and forth in those tight jeans of hers replace the jealous anger he'd felt at the mention of her Blade. Having a mate who was also a Bloodsworn was not going to be a pleasant experience. He just hoped he would be able to find a way to deal with the situation before he made it worse by killing the Amber Blade.

He took a deep breath to calm himself. The hint of sexual encounter mixed with the scents of exotic blooms and rich earth flooded his senses.

Their scents, his and hers, mingled together.

A rueful smile tugged at his lips as his body responded forcefully, reminding him he was far from satisfied in more ways than one.

He had to console himself with the fact that at least he'd attained the first of his goals. Avera St. John was on his world. More, she had agreed to stay. Maybe not for the reasons he wanted, but at least she was here, and so far didn't seem to hate him completely for turning her life upside-down. All he had to do now was convince her to take the next step in tying her life to his. He had to make her realize that she wasn't just a name to him, a way to fulfill a prophecy even if prophetic words were what brought them together. Avera St. John was more to him than a means to an end, much more. All he had to do was to convince her that he saw her as a person, someone with feelings. A woman with desires, hopes, dreams, and memories. A woman he cared for.

Suddenly, an idea came to mind and Devlin

smiled. Perhaps there was a way for him to do the impossible after all. A way to show her the value he put on her presence in his life. Would he have time to complete his task, was the question.

A quick flick of his hand opened another gate as he sent word to his Inner Decca to meet him in the practice courtyard. He had to at least make the attempt. Hopefully Luma would still be at the Enclave or at least within easy reach. Her assistance was vital if he was to complete his mission before dawn. Oh, he would still do as he planned regardless, but later would lessen the impact. He had to have things in place when Avera woke up.

Chapter Forty-Two

Birdsong woke Avera from her night of torture. She was more than grateful. It had taken a long time for her to fall sleep, and when she'd finally succumbed, dreams had made for a long, restless night.

Hot dreams. Erotic dreams. Dreams filled with whispered words, gentle touches, and far too many groans of pleasure. Dreams filled with only one man's hard body and haunting face. Dreams so sensual, she expected to wake and find that man in her bed.

Devlin Tragar.

Avera shifted and rolled over, biting back a moan. The bird song got louder. She opened her eyes, blinking at the sunshine flooding the room.

At first she thought the red bird sitting on the edge of the stone balcony she could see through a pair of open doors was a cardinal. After a minute of staring at it, she realized she was wrong. Though the same vibrant red as a male cardinal, this bird didn't have the little flipped crest. Nor did it chirp the one-note song she was familiar with. This bird trilled. Its song flowed into the room, a light and airy accompaniment to the breeze fluttering the gauzy white curtains lining the doors.

Avera smiled, letting herself enjoy the serenade. All too soon she'd have to get up and face reality in all its insanity. If anyone deserved another few minutes snuggled deep in warm covers, it was her.

Another sound erupted, a sharp, repetitive note that cut through the bird's song, sending it winging away in fright. Avera gasped at the familiar sound and rolled away from the window in search of the noise-maker. Her hand automatically reached out, smacking down on the alarm clock on the bedside table. She glared at the red numbers. "Stupid alarm clock," she muttered.

Then she froze.

For a full minute she stared at the obviously glowing display trying to reconcile it with the fact that the bare prongs of the clock's power cord lay on the table next to it. Her clock didn't have a battery backup so where was it getting the power to run? For that matter, what was it doing here?

One by one, she noticed the other items on the small table. Things that were supposed to be a world away.

A pen and pad of sticky notes—she always kept them by her bed to scribble things down in the middle of the night. The blue and green night-light thingy her secret admirer—or rather Devlin—had given her. The first flower he'd sent her—still as perfect as the day Steven had handed it to her. Hadn't she taken that to her office?

What really made her hand start to shake was the simple double frame holding two 3 x 5 photos.

Avera reached for the pictures of her parents, half expecting them to disappear. Tears welled up as her fingers closed on the plastic frame. With a quiet sob, she closed her eyes and hugged the pictures to her chest. Not until then did she realize how devastated she would have been without the photographs.

She'd told Devlin last night she understood she couldn't go back home. Part of her knew she would be leaving everything and everyone behind. Her friends, work, everything she owned. No biggie, she'd thought. Moving around so much in her youth taught her not to hold on too tightly to people or things. She wasn't a very material person and kept her friendships casual.

Still, some things were irreplaceable. She could admit now that having to leave *everything* behind, these pictures for instance, would have been a serious barrier to adjusting to her new life. It would be like someone losing their home to a fire, the mementoes of a lifetime reduced to smoke and ashes. Memories were harder to hold onto without some kind of tangible evidence. And memories were all she had left of her parents.

Devlin Tragar had given her back something precious. She didn't even question how she knew he was the one responsible. Who else could it have been? Fate?

Avera laughed.

Wiping away tears, she sat up and looked around. A gasp flew out of her as her hand came up to cover her mouth. Unbelievable!

The large bedroom had changed quite a bit since she'd drifted off to sleep last night, starting with the table and two chairs sitting at the foot of the bed. She easily recognized the little bistro set she'd bought for her kitchen a month ago. Her microwave, toaster and electric can opener crowded together on the table, the cords of all three appliances wound up and neatly tied with pieces of leather string.

Other, equally familiar pieces of furniture were scattered about the room interspersed with several unfamiliar chests, some stacked two high. Avera spotted her comfy old recliner and leather loveseat over near the bedroom's fireplace, along with the floor lamp and both end tables from her living room. The mattress and box spring of her bed leaned against a wall. The rest of that wall was taken up by, not one beautiful armoire, but two, both flanking her generic-looking little dresser. One of armoires had to contain the dresses she'd riffled through last night. The other?

Curiosity drew her from the bed. Her heart pounding, Avera tugged the sheet off and wrapped it around her. Still clutching the picture frames, she wound her way carefully through the clutter, trailing a finger over several items. They all felt very real, so maybe she wasn't dreaming.

Reaching the armoire, she opened both doors. Fresh tears filled her eyes as she saw clothes, *her clothes,* hanging on satin-padded hangers. Jeans, pants, skirts, blouses, even her old bathrobe, hung precisely and carefully. Her meager collection of shoes stood in a neat row along the bottom.

Blinking her eyes to clear them, Avera turned to one of the chests and heaved it open. A watery giggle bubbled up as she ran a finger along the spines of well-loved and often read books. English, chemistry. The History of Guns. Even an odd romance or two.

A smaller chest held the few knick-knacks she owned, each carefully wrapped in a piece of butter-soft leather. Dishes filled a third chest. Glasses. Silverware. Towels. Sheets. She found them all, everything she owned. The only things not packed in a chest was the food from the refrigerator and the stuff in the dresser—her underwear, along with the more mundane items such as socks and nightgowns.

Avera sniffed and felt her cheeks heat as she ran a hand over the dresser's old veneer. Devlin had thought of everything. Even her need for privacy.

"Avera?"

His voice didn't startle her, not really. It was as if she'd felt him there all along, watching her.

"You did this for me," she said without turning.

"It was the least I could do, considering the

compromises you have made. I would do more. My desire is to make this change as painless as possible for you. Just tell me what to do, my lady. Command me, and I will see it done."

Avera had no choice but to believe him. There was no doubting the conviction in his voice, the pure determination. He really would do anything she asked. She turned slowly. Devlin stood in the open doorway to the balcony, watching her with those blue eyes of his. Her heartbeat quickened. He was even more handsome than she remembered. Hotter than her dreams.

"This is more than I expected." More than she would have asked assuming she thought to ask in the first place. She tightened her hold on the sheet as he moved into the room, grateful she hadn't just popped up and ran around naked. What was he even doing here?

Acutely conscious of her lack of proper clothes, she said, "Um, don't think I'm not grateful for all this, but mind if I ask what you're doing in my room? I'm not dressed for company."

His lips curved into a wry smile as he stopped and patted the lid of a chest. "Delivering the last of your possessions. I intended to be gone before you woke up, but the harper sang you awake before I could leave."

"The harper?"

His head nodded toward the balcony.

"Oh," she said, realizing he was referring to the red bird. The name fit.

He took a few more steps, moving closer. "I'll leave now," he said. "I'm sure you will want to look through everything to make sure it is all here." He looked apologetic. "I tried to be thorough, but please tell me immediately if something is missing."

She looked around at the jumble of stacked chests and furniture and laughed. "I don't see how you could have possibly missed anything. In fact, I think I see an item or two that should probably have stayed in the apartment." She nodded to a corner where several long, fat rolls looking suspiciously like carpet, leaned against one another.

She saw him glance at the corner before shrugging easily. "I had no way of knowing what had value to you and what did not, so I'm afraid I may have erred on the side of excess. Whatever you do not wish to keep can easily be returned."

The man had pulled up carpet to try and make her happy. Un-freakin' believable. Staring into his blue gaze, she finally noticed the dark smudges under his eyes. He looked tired, she decided, then mentally slammed her palm against her forehead. Of course he was tired. He'd stayed up all night packing and shifting several rooms of things from one world to another just to make her feel better when she woke up. What kind of man did that?

One who cared, was her answer.

She took a step toward him without thinking. The sheet immediately tangled around her feet. She stumbled.

"Careful." His hands closed on her shoulders to steady her. He didn't let her go right away, and Avera felt the heat of his palms through the thin sheet.

"Thank you," she said softly, her eyes staring into his letting him know the words were for more than his steadying hands.

"You are very welcome," he murmured.

She felt his fingers flex, like he was going to pull her closer and, oh, how she wanted to be closer. Heat flared low in her belly. Not the fiery lust she'd felt last night, a lust that held her at its mercy. No, what she felt now made that uncontrollable lust feel like an echo. This was completely different.

Different, yet still familiar. This searing burn of

desire she'd felt before, in her kitchen, in Claudia's kitchen, in the long, dream-filled nights in her bedroom. Oh, yes, she knew this feeling, welcomed it with a surge of relief, in fact. Not everything had changed with her change of worldly residence. She still wanted Devlin Tragar. And unlike last night, this time she was sure the want was all hers.

Some of what she was feeling must have shown in her eyes, because she heard his breath catch. His own eyes darkened to a stormy blue in the matter of a few heartbeats. He suddenly looked like a man who was finding it difficult to breathe. Like a man who wanted nothing more than to crush her body to his and lick her from head to toe.

The mental image made the desire inside Avera flare white-hot. Disappointment dampened the heat like a splash of cold water in the next instant when, instead of pulling her closer, Devlin snatched his hands away from her. His eyes jerked down and away from her face, too, and he cleared his throat. "I should—" He broke off, his expression becoming a fierce mask.

He should put his hands back where they were, is what he should do, but instead of telling him that, she asked, "What is it?" reaching out automatically.

His larger hand closed gently but firmly around her smaller one. The touch of his other hand on her bare forearm made her realize she was showing him a part of herself she would just as soon no one saw. Her scars were personal. A private reminder of the pain and fear she'd suffered. An ugly reminder of a very costly mistake. She tried to pull away, but he wouldn't let her.

Then he did the strangest thing. Something she'd never imagined anyone would ever do in a million years. One after the other, Devlin treated each scar to a gentle brush of his lips. With each touch Avera felt something else, something besides the softness of his lips or the warmth of his breath. She felt something...magical.

"What are you doing?" she asked breathlessly. His answer came between kisses.

"I cannot wipe the scars out completely. No one can. They are a part of who you are now. A sign of your strength. Still, they need not be painful, or so evident."

"They...don't hurt. Not anymore."

"Don't they?" He finished with her left arm and, tucking it inside the sheet, motioned for her right one. She drew her arm out, half dazed, part of her amazed she obeyed him so easily. Was he using more magic on her? Controlling her? She didn't think so. Her willingness came from another source. She was completely mesmerized by the look in his eyes. Devlin wasn't repulsed by her scars.

He didn't pity her, he respected her. He accepted her, scars and all.

More kisses, more whispers of magic. Avera could see the scars getting fainter right before her eyes. Puckered pink lines faded into smooth, thin white ones.

When he was done, Devlin started to release her, his fingers leaving her with clear reluctance. Avera snatched his hand in a tight grip. How did she tell him? How did she tell this man that what he'd just done—seeing her scars as something other than ugly reminders—meant more to her than anything, even the pictures and other material memories he'd so thoughtfully retrieved for her? Knowing he saw her as a strong person and not someone to be pitied was a gift beyond measure. She'd face all the craziness of the previous day again, go through it all again, because she suddenly realized having Devlin in her life meant more to her than she could ever have imagined. How could she admit that to him when she'd barely admitted it to herself?

Things were still happening too fast. Her brain was having enough trouble adjusting to the rapid changes. Her heart didn't have a prayer of keeping up.

She locked her gaze on his lips. He wasn't getting away without giving her a proper kiss, she decided. She wanted to feel the magic of those lips against hers.

She tilted her head up and leaned closer. It only took him a second to understand what she was asking for, less to give her what she wanted.

Avera felt a jolt go through her as soon as their lips met. Magic or desire, she wasn't sure which and didn't care. She felt another powerful jolt when his tongue slid urgently against her closed lips. She sent her tongue out in answer, joining his in a dance full of tasting licks and sensual caresses.

Ah, yes, taste.

Devlin Tragar tasted so good, so sinfully male. So damn right. Avera couldn't hold back a moan of pleasure.

"Lady Avera, are you awake?"

Immediately Devlin broke the kiss. Avera tried to get her racing heart under control as he held her close, their panting breaths mingling. "What is she doing here?" he finally managed in a low voice.

"You know who it is?"

"My sister, Gwenell. I was not aware she even knew of your arrival yet. Do you know why she's here? So early?"

Right, Gwenell, his sister. "Um, she and I met briefly last night. I saved her from a tongue lashing from your mother, I think."

Devlin pulled back, clearly surprised, and smiled widely. "Did you, now? I would have liked to have seen that."

Another knock, more insistent this time.

"I guess I better see what she wants."

Devlin stopped her, his expression shifting to one of mock solemnity. "If you rescued her from our mother you realize you are now stuck with her. She'll probably want to have breakfast with you and show you around the palace. Prepare to be dragged from the east tower, to the ballroom, to the—" He stopped speaking, a speculative look coming into his eyes. He flicked out a hand, commanding a gate to appear in an open space by the balcony doors. "Come with me."

Was he serious? "Come where? Devlin, I can't just leave, she's your sister—"

"Yes, and if I leave you to her now I will be lucky to get you alone to myself for even an hour today. I will make it up to her later, I promise. I'll even give up breakfast with you tomorrow. But you must come with me now. There is something I wish to show you."

Chapter Forty-Three

Devlin tugged on Avera's arm, urging her toward the gate. He should have known gaining her cooperation would not be so easy. She set her feet, her soft laugh causing his insides to clench. Leaving her room with the rumpled bed so nearby was becoming imperative. He still wasn't sure she understood the full implications of what intimacy between them would mean. Perhaps he was being selfish, certainly reckless, considering the importance of the Prophecy, but he wanted her choice to be based on something other than prophetic words or spur-of-the-moment passion. He wanted forever with her, and wanted her to choose forever with him. He wanted her love.

"You are crazy. I'm not sneaking out with you. I can't go anywhere at the moment anyway. In case you haven't noticed, I'm not exactly dressed."

Oh, he'd noticed. He'd seen her bare back as she'd tugged the sheet from the bed and wrapped it around her. He'd noticed every bare inch. She was right, though, she needed proper clothes. Too bad they didn't have time for her to change.

Grinning, he sent out a swift wave of magic, enjoying her gasp as the essence hit her skin. The white sheet became clothes similar to those he'd conjured for her last night, except this shirt was a soft silk in a shade of green to match her eyes. The pants were the same dark material as her jeans, cut snug enough to hug her legs and bottom. There was something to be said for the clothing styles of Earth, he decided.

"You were saying?"

Without a word she raised her brows and pointed down. Devlin's grin widened and a chuckle spilled forth when he saw her bare toes wiggling in the thick pile of the rug. Another wave of magic and her feet became encased in a pair of soft leather boots.

She made a show of examining them. "Much better," she said, "though a little contrast stitching would have been nice."

More voices sounded outside the door, one of which he recognized as his mother's. He moved fast, scooping Avera into his arms. She gave a small yelp of surprise that he quickly silenced by the simple method of pressing his lips to hers. Still kissing her, he carried her through the gate, not sure if it was the brush of gate magic or the feel of her lips under his making him shiver. Habit alone had him closing the gate behind them. He was enjoying himself too much to bother with coherent thought. Then she uttered a soft moan, one he felt with every fiber of his being. Her lips parted in invitation.

Dangerous, so very dangerous. Devlin had to force himself to end the kiss right then. Taking advantage of an opportunity might win the battle but strategy was what won wars.

He pulled back, aware he could feel the pounding of her heart against his chest. Staring into her green eyes dark with passion, he was hard pressed to remember what part of his strategy included gating them to the stable instead of his rooms. He tightened his arms, pulling her even closer. Her breasts rose as she drew in a deep breath.

With his lips inches from hers, he felt her body go still. She sniffed. Leaning back, she took a deeper breath and looked around. Tamping down his frustration, he watched her eyes widen, their dark color lightening to an excited peridot green. A keen sense of satisfaction shot through him. Bringing her here had been a sound bit of strategy after all.

She wiggled in his arms until he had no choice but to set her on her feet. "You snatched me from my room to show me your stable?" He could tell she was trying to sound scolding, but her excited expression as she looked from one row of stalls to another had him holding back a pleased chuckle.

"Not just the stable." He took her hand, leading her down a wide aisle lined with stalls of various sizes. She followed willingly at first but he could feel her hesitation grow with each occupied stall they passed. He hid his grin. He'd never seen a female so enamored with horses.

"Here," he said, stopping in the middle of the aisle and gesturing to a stall on either side. A gray horse stood in one, and a larger, almost all black horse in the other.

"Here what?" she asked, her head whipping back and forth between the two.

"These are the horses I mentioned earlier, the ones I promised you. I had them brought in last night."

Her eyes lit up, but she shook her head. "You didn't have to do that. I'm really not that picky. Any one of those we passed would have been fine."

Slowly, he stalked back to her side. "Ah, but none of those are for you. These two are. You will need them if you wish to travel any distance on my world. At least you will until you learn to call gates."

He waited, sure she would be pleased with his gift. Instead of looking pleased, however, the excitement in her eyes dimmed. She nodded gravely.

"You're right, thank you for the loan. It's not like there's a gas station on every corner where I could fill up my Rav4. Besides, when in Rome and all that... I should probably try to blend in as much as possible."

"You misunderstand, Avera. I am not loaning you the horses, I'm giving them to you. They are a gift."

Her mouth dropped open. "You're giving me two horses?" Her eyes grew bright with tears and she threw herself into his arms. "Oh, Devlin!"

****

Avera paused in brushing the mare's smooth gray coat and shook her head sadly.

"You're a shallow creature, Avera St. John. Seduced by a pair of horses. Pitiful, just pitiful. One day that impulsiveness of yours is going to land you in big trouble." Like it hadn't already?

She kept her muttering very low, so the man brushing the gelding tethered on the other side of the mare couldn't hear her. He'd been so pleased with her acceptance of his gift. The smile on his face had almost melted her on the spot. She couldn't have changed her mind even if she'd wanted to.

The mare turned her head and nudged Avera's shoulder impatiently. Avera laughed. "All right, all right, I'm brushing. Something tells me you're going to be a spoiled diva. Next you'll be asking for a bowl of sugar cubes for your stall."

"She prefers apples."

She turned to find a man wearing a blacksmith's apron standing nearby. He was tall, easily over six feet, lean but with bulky muscles in his arms and a thickness to his chest that made her think he could take Sarreth in a wrestling match. His hair was a mixture of browns and grays, cropped close to his head. She didn't make the mistake of assuming the gray meant he was old. He could have been

331

anywhere from thirty to sixty.

"Heleron," Devlin said in greeting.

"My lord Tragar." The man tipped his head respectfully. He could do little else with the large, heavy-looking roll of leather balanced on one shoulder. His other hand held a knife, long and wide, with a single edge and a wrapped handle. A plain, utilitarian tool rather than something meant for combat.

Devlin came around the gelding and motioned for Avera to join him. Curious, she ducked under the mare's neck.

"Avera, this is Heleron, the master of my stables. Heleron, Lady Avera St. John."

Somehow the tall man managed to add a slight bow to the tip of his head. A pleased smile warmed his face. "My lady. A pleasure to have you in *my* stables." He winked at her, ignored Devlin's indignant huff and asked, "Are the horses to your liking?"

"Yes, thank you. They are both beautiful."

"Good. The gelding is patient and steady and has more sense than he looks. He'll not balk at crowds or jumps." He turned to Devlin. "I'm still not sure about your choice of the mare."

"Why, is something wrong with her?" Avera asked, glancing at the pretty filly. She hoped not. She felt like she'd already made a connection with the gray horse and couldn't wait to ride her.

"Nothing is wrong with the mare," Devlin assured her. "Heleron is simply concerned she might be too spirited for you."

"You will need to be on your guard with that little female, my lady," Heleron insisted. "She'll not be a placid ride. She enjoys running far too much and is still young enough to think she should have her way."

Avera laughed. "Don't they all? She sounds

wonderful, really. As I enjoy running, too, I think she and I will get along fine."

Heleron didn't look convinced. Devlin slapped the man on the shoulder and said, "Stop worrying, old friend. I will be with her at all times. I'll not let her or the mare come to harm."

That pronouncement seemed to be what Heleron wanted to hear. The worry on his face cleared and he nodded. "I'll send the boys with the saddles. Will your Blades be joining you?"

"A few. I'll call them shortly. Come, before you leave, take a look at the gelding's rear hoof. I know you would have checked him the moment he was brought in, but the shoe appears loose. He's favoring that foot."

The stable master snorted and winked again at Avera. "Horses are an unpredictable lot are they not, my lady. With them, anything is possible." He crossed the aisle to a bench and shrugged the roll of leather off his shoulder. The knife joined an assortment of grooming tools lined up on one end.

"Yes, I see," he said, after examining the horse's left rear hoof. "He must have kicked the stall some time this morning. Not only is the shoe loose, but there is a crack in his hoof."

"Is it deep," Avera asked, peering worriedly over his shoulder. This was her horse now, after all.

"We shall see." He pulled a small hammer from an apron pocket and began removing the shoe. "Would you mind handing me the file and clippers from the bench, my lady? I'd ask the Tragar, but I'd rather he stay at the gelding's head. He has a way with animals and as steady as this one is for riding he's never been comfortable with the shoeing."

She smiled at Devlin, who stood with one hand on the black's halter while stroking the animal's thick neck with the other. The smile he gave her in return sent a rush fluttering through her stomach.

Really, the man was just too damn handsome. "Of course not," she said, dropping her eyes quickly.

She picked up the file and reached for the clippers. A deafening neigh rang out from behind her. She spun around, her hand sweeping several items off the bench, to find a chaotic scene.

The black gelding was trying to rear. He jerked back against the lead rope, ears laid back, a ring of white around his large, dark eyes. Almost directly under him, Heleron rolled on the ground, dodging the gelding's stomping hooves. Devlin still held firmly to the horse's halter. She watched wide-eyed as he slowly, inexorably, pulled the large head down. Avera's heart jumped into her throat as the powerful animal suddenly surged forward, pinning Devlin to the wall.

"Devlin!" She started forward, unsure of what she could do, but unable to stay still.

"Stay back," he ordered.

Avera hesitated. He didn't sound like someone who'd just been rammed by a half-ton of horse flesh. In fact, he didn't even sound out of breath. She tried to see him better, to see if he was hurt, but the air around him and the horse was blurry. She squeezed her eyes shut and rubbed them. Now was not the time for blurry vision.

"Avera, look out!"

Her eyes popped open to find hind-quarters whipping in her direction. The gelding's head was down. Too far down. She could see the kick coming. Raising her arm up to protect her face, Avera threw herself back. She didn't fall far. A brief whoosh of air and her back suddenly hit a wall. The blow wasn't hard, but hitting anything other than the floor was disconcerting. The wall should have been several feet behind her. Surprised, she lowered her arm to find she wasn't imagining things. She was several *yards* away from where she'd just been standing.

Two stalls away to be more precise.

Shouts, the sound of running feet, the gelding and mare neighing together, other horses echoing their distress. The cacophony of sound cut through her shock. Stable hands converged. Avera took a few steps, intending to help, and stopped when she realized her vision was still hazy. She blinked hard, trying to clear her sight, but the haze remained. She couldn't understand what was wrong. No pain in her head, no dizziness. What was causing the problem with her eyes?

It wasn't until she glanced down and saw her body clearly that she realized her eyesight was fine. It was the air surrounding her that was the problem. She put out a hand and felt resistance, like trying to push her way into thick clay. She tried walking through, but every time she took a step the haze moved with her, keeping her in its center. A prickle of unease ran across her scalp and down her neck. Was this some kind of magical attack?

She turned to call for Devlin and found him already walking toward her. Behind him, two men soothed the gray mare. Heleron held the gelding's halter and was speaking in the horse's ear. Except for a fresh sheen of sweat on his dark coat, the animal appeared calm.

Her barbarian prince, however, was another matter. Brows lowered over slightly glowing eyes, shoulders tight, fists clenched, he looked ready to explode. Avera's heart rate spiked, and she pushed against her prison with both hands. How was he going to get her out? Could he?

Devlin's stiff strides ate up the distance between them in long gulps. The haze around her vanished as he reached her, and she stumbled forward into his arms. Clenched fists opened and closed again on her shoulders. Before she could get out a word of thanks to him for freeing her, she was being shaken. Not enough to rattle her teeth, but enough to shock her into momentarily forgetting about the haze thing.

She couldn't believe he was actually shaking her like an angry parent would a disobedient child.

"You will never do that again." His words came out through clenched teeth.

Shock gave way to anger. "Do what?" She wind-milled her arms, breaking his hold on her shoulders, and took a step back. "Try to help you calm a scared horse? Or maybe you're referring to when I wanted to see if you'd been smashed flat against a wall? Pardon me for caring."

"Neither," he snapped, looking as if he'd like to shake her again. "That is not what I mean, and you well know it. Using your magic without training is dangerous. You could have injured yourself."

Confusion made her blink. "Using...what? What are you talking about? What magic?" He thought she'd used magic? When? How?

Devlin stared at her a long moment, his glowing gaze searching her face. Avera wished he'd just spit out the answers to her questions. She hated being in the dark about things, especially things that concerned her. "Ah," he finally said. He took a deep breath. She watched, fascinated, as his eyes lost that freaky glow, returning to their normal shade of blue. He looked worlds calmer. Maybe even a little chagrined.

"My apologies, Avera. When you dodged the black's kick you used magic to send yourself flying back too fast and hard for my liking. That's why I placed the shield around you. I see now your reaction was purely instinctual. He reached for her hand. "When you—" He broke off, frowning down at their joined hands.

Avera didn't notice at first. She was too busy trying to assimilate what he said.

Devlin thought she'd used magic to move herself

a dozen yards in the blink of an eye. Devlin had been the one responsible for the hazy barrier around her. He'd been trying to protect her from herself. Had she really used magic? She hadn't felt a thing in that place in her mind where the magic waited. Not a twitch. Nor could she recall thinking about tapping into that reservoir at any time.

The possibility she could use magic without consciously thinking about it was a bit scary. What if she did something dangerous? Could she hurt someone without meaning to?

"Vet!" Devlin muttered, "I thought I placed a shield around you in time. Are you injured anywhere else?"

The touch of his fingers moving lightly over her body snapped her back to attention. "What do you think you're doing?"

"Trying to see if you injured yourself anywhere other than your hand." He shook his head, and she realized the fierce frown on his face was for himself, not her, when he said, "I need to do a better job of protecting you in the future. I *will* do a better job."

She glanced down at her injured hand held in his tight, but gentle grasp. The thin line of fresh blood didn't look worth frowning over. She shrugged. "This is nothing. I've been—"

"Scratched worse by a cat, yes, I know." His lips tilted up in a warm smile that didn't quite erase the somber look in his eyes. He was serious about protecting her, she realized. Even from something as simple as a scratch. Part of her melted inside when he raised her hand to his lips, and kissed the back of her fingers.

"Do not worry, Avera. Shallow scratches such as this are easily healed." He cupped his hand over hers.

"My lord!" Heleron called, his voice shaking and urgent.

She and Devlin both turned to find the stable master pointing to the bench. "The leather cutting knife, my lord!"

Avera felt the bottom drop out of her stomach as soon as she saw the knife lying on the ground, glowing softly like some macabre nightlight. She'd seen something like that before. Her gaze shot to her injured hand. She must have cut herself on the knife when she knocked it off the bench. She'd inadvertently fed the knife her blood.

"Does that mean what I think it means?"

She asked the question at the same time that Devlin began muttering a string of words she didn't understand. Of course, she'd grown up around military men and didn't have to understand to know cussing when she heard it.

"Yes," he growled. "When you cut your hand the combination of steel and blood and your Bloodsworn magic automatically began a link."

"A link with who?" She looked around. Only Heleron and two of the stable hands were nearby and none of them looked like Bracca had. But then, Bracca had been dying. She had no idea what a man freshly stricken with the blade-illness looked like, what kind of symptoms he manifested. Just how did they go about finding someone who couldn't touch magic with their mind, she wondered?

Before she could ask, Devlin bent and pulled a dagger from his boot. Avera gasped as he slashed the edge of the blade across his forearm. It wasn't a shallow cut.

Blood welled up thick and fast, running down his arm.

She grabbed his wrist. "What are you doing?"

"My Bloodsworn magic is strong. It should be able to over-ride yours." He reached out, his fingers caressing her face. His dark blue eyes bore into hers. "I will link to this man, not you. I'll not have you risking your mind, Avera."

A chill swept through her at his words.

Risking her mind? No one had ever said anything about a risk to her mind.

The glow of the knife on the ground flared brighter.

She felt a strange sensation pulse through her body and settle in her chest. She wasn't sure that it wasn't fear.

Devlin swore again, drawing her attention. He was staring at his own dagger. The weapon wasn't glowing in the slightest.

"It's not working, is it?"

"No, it is not."

She thought she saw tiny sparks dancing across his skin as he wiped the dagger clean on his pants and shoved it back into his boot. He accepted a strip of cloth from Heleron and wrapped it around his arm. Then he gripped her hand. "Quickly, we haven't much time."

"Time for what? Devlin, would you please stop being so cryptic." She let him pull her to the bench until the knife was at her feet.

"Pick up the knife, Avera."

She sighed in exasperation and started to reach for the knife with her bloody hand, only to have him grab her wrist.

"No! Not with that hand. No more blood. It will only incite your magic, make it stronger. All we want to do is locate the sick man. Once I gate him away, your magic should calm down."

"Gate him where? Devlin, I don't understand. I thought the glowing knife meant I had to link with someone to keep them from dying. How can I do that if you take him away?"

"I will take him to the Bloodsworn Hall. The Bloodsworn High Council will try linking with him."

She frowned, feeling her anger begin to stir.

He'd said forming a link was a risk to her mind. What about the risk to his mind, to the other Bloodsworn? Why should their risk be any less than hers? "And if they can't?"

"There are many other Bloodsworn. Avera—"

"No."

"Avera, listen to me."

"No, you listen. I understand what you're trying to do. You're trying to protect me, I get that. But, Devlin, don't you see, you can't protect me from this. There has to be a reason why I'm Bloodsworn. I have to believe that. If not, then why am I here?"

He moved fast, his hands closing around her upper arms and jerking her forward before she'd even blinked. Light flickered in his blue irises like lightning inside the clouds of a storm.

"You are here because you are mine," he said emphatically.

"Only because one of your prophecies said so," she said quietly. "Why would it do that, send you to a woman from another world, if there wasn't a darn good reason?"

"We are Starmates."

She laid a hand against his tight jaw. "And if not for your mystical Oracle, you'd never have known I existed. Tell me, Devlin, have any prior prophecies ever granted someone a reward without first demanding a price?"

The lines of his frown deepened, the jaw under her hand flexing as teeth ground together. Taking his silence as a no, she continued.

"I thought I stumbled onto this Bloodsworn thing by accident, trying to repay a man for saving my life. But what if it wasn't an accident? What if it was meant to be? There has to be a reason why I'm able to tap into another world's magic."

She stared into his eyes, willing him to understand. "Devlin, my life has been turned upside-down. My plans, my goals, everything I've worked for is gone. I don't have a career anymore. I don't have a purpose anymore, and I need a purpose. I need to do this."

Chapter Forty-Four

Her barbarian prince looked far from convinced. Avera almost expected Devlin to wrap her up and whisk her away through one of his magic shortcuts. She prayed he wouldn't. She wasn't the type who took well to being caged, not even by someone who was trying to protect her. Her father had always given her room to make her own choices. And her own mistakes.

Hopefully, she wasn't making one of those mistakes, now.

The fierce tightness in Devlin's faced eased by degrees. The storm in his eyes slowly calmed. He rested his forehead against hers, his expression settling into one of cautious resignation.

"Heleron," Devlin called.

"Yes, my lord?"

"Are any of your workers ill?"

"No, my lord Tragar. I have no one..."

The stable master stopped speaking. His face paled and his eyes widened. He looked frightened.

"Heleron?"

Avera saw the stable master swallow twice before finally spitting words out. He sounded like he was choking.

"My son... My son, Tyr. He has been abed these past four days." He staggered forward, moving like his legs were numb. His words came faster, tumbling out one after the other. "He is often sick, my lord, as you well know. We thought this illness just like all the others. And he is not yet fifteen summers, not yet a man. Can it really be him?"

Devlin laid a calming hand on the man's shoulder. "We shall see, my friend. Avera, would you pick up the knife, please."

She held up both hands. "Does it matter?"

He gave her a smile that looked so sad she wished he hadn't smiled at all. "No, not anymore."

She looked at the knife for a moment. Did she really want to do this?

Did she really have a choice?

She bent and scooped the knife up quickly. The blood on her palm made her hand stick to the wrapped handle. She grimaced.

Then she felt that strange sensation in her chest again. Not fear after all, she decided. The feeling grew tighter, as if a hand buried in her chest had just closed into a fist.

The fist tugged.

Avera cocked her head and thought about what she was feeling. Something was definitely pulling at her.

She pointed the knife down the aisle. "That way, I think."

She felt the heat of Devlin's body before his hand touched her shoulder. "Are you sure?"

She took a step back. The fist tugged again, pulling her forward. At the same time she felt a tingling, like brief fingers of lightning, shoot up her arm. Neither sensation was painful, nor were they so strong she couldn't ignore them if she wanted to.

"Yeah, I'm sure." She started forward. Devlin stayed by her side and Heleron at her back. She could almost feel the stable master's anxiety growing.

The tugging fist led her out of the stables, down

a short path to another building. The stable master's home, she guessed, since Heleron hurried ahead and opened the door for them. They passed through a cozy room, the details of which were lost on Avera. Her concentration was solely on the growing awareness inside her. They were close. She saw Heleron hesitate outside a closed door. Avera didn't realize she was shaking until Devlin put an arm around her. When they entered the small room, a woman seated beside a narrow bed looked up.

"Heleron?"

Then she saw Avera and Devlin. She stood quickly. "My lord Tragar. You honor our home."

"Malia, it is good to see you." Devlin took her hand, surprising Avera when he leaned down and kissed the woman's cheek.

A small part of her heard him explain that Malia was Heleron's wife. Then he introduced Avera to the woman. Avera tried to make the correct responses, but her main attention was too caught up by the slight form lying beneath the covers of the bed.

This was the blade-sick *man*? Child was more like it. Heleron had said his son wasn't fifteen yet. That had still left Avera picturing a gangly teenager. But this frail child looked no more than eleven, twelve tops. She must have made a mistake. There had to be someone else. She took a step back, shaking her head.

"Avera?"

"This can't be right. I'm sorry, Devlin, I must be doing something wrong. He's only a child."

"Peace, Avera. You have done nothing wrong. I like this situation no more than you, but it appears Tyr is indeed the one. Even I can sense him now."

"Sense what? Heleron, what is going on?" Avera heard the wariness in Malia's voice. She wished she could reassure the woman.

Then Malia noticed the glowing knife Avera had tried to hide behind her back. The woman gasped. Her wide-eyed gaze shot from the knife, to her son, then locked onto her husband with a desperate intensity.

Instead of the denial and fear Avera expected, hope filled the woman's voice. "Heleron, do you realize what this means? If Tyr is blade-sick, he can be made well. Our son can live." She turned to Avera, reaching out to take her hand. "I have already heard the news that you are Bloodsworn. I did not believe it. But, my lady, if the stories are true, I beg you to save my son. None of the healers can find the cause of Tyr's recurring illness. But if he is your Blade you'll have a deeper connection to him. Please, I beg you, make him your Blade. Heal him."

The last words came out a fervent plea, one Avera couldn't ignore even if she'd wanted to. She nodded, squeezing the woman's hand. "I'm new at this, but I promise I'll do what I can."

Heleron drew his wife aside, and Avera took her place beside the bed. She sat in the chair and searched the child's pale face, brushing back damp hair. He looked so small, so innocent.

"He opened his eyes a few moments ago," Malia told them. "He acted as if he wanted to get up, but he is too weak." Her voice caught on a sob.

"He must have sensed the beginning of the link," Devlin said. He drew one of Tyr's thin arms out from under the covers. "Do you remember what to do?"

Avera nodded. It wasn't something she was likely to forget.

"Do it quickly." He brushed the back of his fingers down her cheek. "You know I would do this for you if I could."

"I know." She leaned into his caress for a moment, then straightened. Devlin moved behind her, squeezing her shoulders once before stepping back. She started to ask him to keep his hands there, then remembered Fate's words. No one was supposed to touch her. She had to do this on her own.

Taking a deep breath, she placed the knife against the boy's skin and drew the blade back in a quick motion. The razor sharp edge bit easily, almost hungrily.

Immediately, her senses were inundated. A rushing sound filled her ears. She felt power zoom through her, heating her body. Amber lightning flashed behind her eyes. And cinnamon. She would swear she smelled cinnamon. So heavy it burned her nose. So strong, she could taste the sharp spice biting her tongue. Half-blind, she shoved the handle of the knife into the boy's slack fingers, closing hers around his.

The visions started, racing through her mind in quick succession, blotting everything else out but that sharp cinnamon odor. The carefree life of a child interspersed with periods of darkness, the pain of an illness no one could fix. A keen sense of frustration dominated. The boy hated his life. He wanted to be big and strong, like his father, not tied to a bed several times a year. The sense of frustration increased as the boy's brief life flashed by. Avera felt a slight shock when she realized Tyr was several months past his fourteenth birthday. The constant illnesses had stunted his growth, weakened his body, until he was unable to run and play much less lift even the smallest saddle, the lightest sack of feed. He had a child's impatience with such limitations. He wanted so much to be well.

Very soon, much sooner than she remembered with Bracca, the visions began to fade. Her senses slowly returned. She could feel the small hand beneath hers, hear her own rapid breathing. The scent of cinnamon lingered. It was all she could smell as her consciousness fell deeper into the growing connection. She could feel Tyr, now, knew he could feel her. Bracing herself, she opened their link wide and sent the essence to him in an unstinting flow.

What would the flow of magic do to the boy?

Bracca had responded on a primal level. She'd felt the echo of his pleasure even before she'd deep healed him. She wasn't sure if she was prepared to deal with a horny teenager.

She waited, but all she felt coming from Tyr was a deep sense of well-being coupled with a longing so sharp it brought tears to her eyes. He wanted to be well more than anything else in the world.

Avera wanted that for him, too. She wasn't even aware of what she was doing until it was already begun. Until it was too late to stop it. She had no choice but to trust in the magic at that point. Manipulating someone on a cellular level was dangerously beyond her knowledge. That didn't seem to matter to the magic eagerly swirling up, flowing out of her and into the boy. Again the words, "Think about what you want, and the magic does the rest," flashed through her mind.

Damn if she wasn't beginning to like this whole magic business.

A few moments later, she felt herself rising, becoming more aware of her surroundings. Tyr's sense of well being followed her. She could actually feel him getting stronger. The overpowering scent of cinnamon started to fade. By the time she heard Devlin's voice calling her, the spicy aroma was no more than a lingering memory.

Avera opened her eyes, blinked, and found herself staring into a pair of wide blue eyes. Tyr's weren't the same intense blue as Devlin's but they were beautiful nonetheless. The excitement in them was mixed with a worshipful awe that made her slightly uncomfortable.

"You are my Bloodsworn?" The hesitant question, asked in Tyr's little boy voice, tore at her heart. Their link was wide open, he could feel her, and still he doubted. He'd given up hoping a long time ago.

She couldn't speak for a moment so she answered him in her mind. *Yes, I am.*

If possible, his eyes widened further. She saw him swallow hard. *Thank you, my lady, my...B-Bloodsworn.*

Then Malia was there, unable to stay away from her son any longer. Avera let the weeping mother push her way between them. She felt tears prick her eyes. Devlin's arms closed around her.

She heard him speaking to Heleron, the two men discussing Tyr's new status, the possibility of training. Much would depend on how well the magic had done its work, and how his small body responded to the flow of essence. He had a long way to go to be a fighting Blade, if ever.

The murmur of two conversations filled the room, but Avera was only partly listening to either of them. She was too busy going over what had just happened, especially the part about the cinnamon smell.

When she'd linked with Bracca, the only thing she'd smelled out of the ordinary was blood. At the time, she'd thought it due to the dead bodies piling up nearby. Thinking back, however, she couldn't remember smelling it much after the ceremony was over. Not until Bracca had carried her over the bodies themselves.

She shuddered at the memory.

Blood and cinnamon, what a strange combination. They had to mean something, she was sure of it.

Devlin's arms tightened around her. "Are you

well?"

She tilted her head back so she could smile at him. "Yes, I'm fine. Just a little tired." She wanted to ask him about the odors, but decided to wait until they were alone.

A stab of anxiety coming from Tyr had her turning to reassure him. Her gaze was immediately caught by the amber knife he cradled close to his body.

No longer plain, the long, gracefully curved knife covered in scrollwork looked out of place against the bed clothes.

Too dangerous, part of her said. Sharp objects and children didn't belong together. Who would have thought she had a maternal side?

Perfect, said another part of her—the Bloodsworn part, of course. The long knife was the perfect length for her new, young Blade.

Tyr wiggled and pushed himself up. His mother clucked and murmured encouragement, stuffing pillows at his back for him to lean against. The woman's joy was palpable. Though far from being fully recovered, they could all see Tyr was already stronger.

Avera went to him and laid a hand over the one clutching the knife.

"Don't worry, I'm fine. You're going to be fine, too. We'll be able to check on each other through our mind link, even when I'm not here. I have another Blade, his name is Bracca. He'll want to come see you."

"I have a blade-brother? Will he train me?"

She hesitated.

"There will be no training for a while yet, Tyr," Devlin said. "You will need to regain your strength."

If she hadn't been able to tell from their link that he was feeling a little giddy, Tyr's wide, boyish grin would have been a dead giveaway. "I know, but

I already feel stronger. It feels...strange, but good."
He ran his fingers along the flat of his new knife.
"For the first time in my life, I feel really, and truly
good."

Chapter Forty-Five

Once outside Heleron's home, Devlin pulled Avera close, loving the way she fit against him as they walked back toward the stable.

"I am proud of you," he said.

She looked up at him, both brows raised in question.

"You handled your first linking well. Better than most new Bloodsworn I have known."

"Don't you mean second?"

"No. Your linking with Cu-Laurian was more in the way of an accident. You were not aware of what you were doing. Yes I understand you were trying to save him," he said quickly, seeing her disagreement. "But you had no way of knowing the commitment involved. With Tyr, you knew the consequences of your actions and accepted them." Or most of the consequences, he corrected himself.

As if she heard his thoughts, she said, "I don't think I know quite everything. What did you mean earlier about me risking my mind?"

He stopped and drew the tips of his fingers across her forehead, smoothing out her slight frown, then let his hand drift down the side of her face to her neck. Her pulse beat beneath his palm, a rapid pace belied by the calm in her green eyes. How he loved just touching her, feeling her respond to him.

"The risk?" she reminded him.

She was right, she needed to know everything. Not that he had any hope she would walk away from the next blade-sick man she came across. He was coming to understand his Starmate had a sense of honor to rival his own. "There is a danger posed by Avalyr's magic, one not well known. It stems from the capricious nature of the powerful essence. Predicting its effect on individual minds is difficult. Some people chosen as Bloodsworn have proven incapable of controlling the magic. It eventually drives them mad."

Her pulse skipped a beat before settling down once more. "Is that why you don't like the idea of me being Bloodsworn?"

"One of the reasons, yes," he said, striving for truth. "I know you have a strong will, but watching you battle alone for a person's sanity is difficult for me." He balked at telling her jealousy was the other reason. That the damaging emotion ate him alive every time he thought about the intimate connection between her and her Blades. Her hand came up to stroke his jaw, soothing, the simple gesture a balm to his soul.

"Thank you for understanding that I had to do this. Like I said before, I need a purpose, and I think I must be Bloodsworn for a reason."

He sighed and leaned into her touch. "I do not understand, but I am trying."

The stone wall of the stable splintered a foot from Avera's head. Devlin grabbed her shoulders, pulling her into the shelter of his body as a crack of thunder rumbled in the distance. Her hands fisted in his shirt and she crouched, pulling him down with her.

"I thought you didn't have guns here," she gasped.

"We don't." Devlin didn't stop to wonder how a weapon from Earth could possibly be on Avalyr. He reached for his magic, snapping a shield around them an instant after something slammed into his back, shoving him forward. He grunted, reaching out a hand to brace against the side of the stable to keep from crushing Avera. Pain stabbed into his mind, threatening his concentration. He ripped open the links to every Blade stationed at the palace.

Ambush! The upper stable! Now!

"You're bleeding!"

He felt Avera's fingers probe the warm stickiness of blood running down his back, soaking his shirt. More pain blossomed as she found the well-spring of blood and pressed her palm against the wound. The shield around them flickered. He gritted his teeth and tucked her closer, knowing he needed to get her inside the stable before the pain became too much.

Two more peals of false thunder echoed as he forced himself up. The impacts against the barrier shielding them were easier to ignore than the pain streaking down his back at every step. His vision blurred. Half a dozen steps from the corner of the stable, his knees buckled. The impact jarred his injury sending a storm of fresh pain bursting through his body, shattering his concentration.

The barrier around them winked out.

****

Avera's already pounding heart jumped when the air around her and Devlin went from hazy to clear. No more invisible shield. Another bullet could tear into them at any second, but that wasn't what had her worried. Devlin was bleeding. Bad. She pushed up and twisted, trying to peer over his shoulder at his back.

"No. Stay down." His fingers dug into her hair, pulling none too gently until she relented and let him tug her until they were nose to nose. Pain had leached the color from his eyes until they were a pale blue. "Call your Blade," he ordered between clenched teeth. "He will protect—" His head jerked and twisted as another bullet plowed into the wall next to them. Stone splinters peppered the side of her face like bird shot. She ignored the stings, catching Devlin as he fell, his body limp, his eyes closed. The sound of the shot echoed like a death knell across the secluded meadow.

"Devlin!" She screamed, wrapping her arms around him as they both collapsed to the ground. She had to fight back panic when blood began pouring from his scalp, covering the side of his face. "No, no. You can't die. Not now." Not after he'd made a place for himself in her heart. Losing someone else she loved would kill her.

A sharp sensation filled her mind, as if someone jerked on a fishing line, the hook buried deep inside her brain. Bracca!

She fumbled to open the link, despaired for a moment, then simply blew the barrier away with an imagined mortar round.

My lady! Relief flooded the link, then concern. *The Silver Blades say their Bloodsworn called them, but they can no longer reach him.*

Devlin's been shot. He's unconscious. A sniper has us pinned down outside the stable. Hurry, Bracca.

Across the wide yard, the door to the stable master's home open. Heleron stopped in the doorway, and stared up at the cloudless sky with a puzzled frown.

"Heleron!" Avera shouted. He looked around quickly, searching for her. She held up a blood-stained hand for him to stop and cringed when a shot slammed into the wall just above her head. More splinters showered down. She moved, covering Devlin's body as best she could as the shot's echo rumbled over the meadow. The rolling sound seemed to go on for a long time.

"What magic is this, my lady?" Heleron called. He took a step away from the cover of his house, and she held up her hand again, lower this time.

"No, stay where you are. If you come out here, you might get shot."

"Shot?"

"Attacked from a distance. The shooter might aim at you if you try to help us."

His face twisted in indecision. "The Tragar is injured. I can see the blood from here. What can I do?"

Good question. "Stay there. Help is coming." She went back to pressing her hand against the wound in Devlin's back, telling herself it was the injury she needed to worry about, not the head wound. Everyone knew head wounds bled like crazy. This was nothing. Just a scratch. A graze. Devlin would wake up and be fine. As long as he didn't get shot again, he'd be fine.

She glanced up at the holes bored into the stable wall. Those bullets had been meant for her, she was certain. A gun from her world instead of magic? It couldn't be coincidence. Camarie was still trying to kill her. Devlin had known and protected her just like he said he would by shielding her with his own body.

Anger began pushing aside her panic. Here she was, just beginning to find a place for herself on a new planet, and someone was trying to take it all away. She eyed the three holes, looking longest at the one closest to her, then let her gaze roam over the paddocks and small buildings off in the distance. Geometry wasn't her field of expertise, but anyone who'd shot a gun as often as she had could estimate trajectories.

She called to Heleron. "That cluster of buildings on the slope, what are they?"

"Homes for the stable hands."

"The shots came from up there, I think. We need to—"

The sound of pounding feet drew her gaze to a separate path leading to the stable. Men appeared over the rise, running hard. Karess, Fate, Kiel, Sarreth, others she didn't recognize. A veritable army. Bracca ran in front, stride for stride with Karess and Fate.

She started to yell at them to take cover, but realized by their expressions it wouldn't do any good. Instead, she kissed Devlin's forehead and whispered, "Help is coming, Devlin, just hang on. Please, please, hang on."

Chapter Forty-Six

The assassin was dead. Apparently killed when the rifle he was using exploded in his face. There weren't even enough of his features left to identify him.

Avera handed the bit of twisted metal with the manufacturer's name on it back to Karess without looking at him. He and Fate stood with her in a corner of Devlin's large bedroom. She'd been half listening to Karess' whispered report when the mention of the ruined weapon caught her attention. Curious, she'd asked to see the pieces, wondering what firearm would have malfunctioned so badly.

"We got lucky. This particular weapon is usually very reliable. It shouldn't have gone to pieces like that," she said, not taking her eyes off Devlin. He lay on his side on a huge bed, so still, so quiet, nothing but the regular rise and fall of his chest telling her he still lived. A woman dressed in a flowing blue robe leaned over him.

"The Essence of Avalyr has its own way of dealing with things not of this world," Fate said.

The tall warrior's actions had demonstrated why he was Devlin's First Blade, taking charge at the stable as soon as he arrived. Two men had quickly field dressed Devlin's wounds while half the warriors left to search the cottages for the assassin. The other half stayed behind, acting as a living shield until she

357

and Devlin were safely back at the palace. Two women attired in light gray robes had appeared almost immediately. Healers, she was told. A half hour later, another healer, the woman dressed in blue, entered Devlin's room. The first two women backed away with a bow of respect.

Avera didn't think anything else could have distracted her, but Fate's words about "things not of this world" struck a nerve. These two men were Devlin's Blades, his comrades in arms. Perhaps even his best friends. If she wanted to be part of Devlin's world—something she vowed she wanted more than life—then she needed to know where she stood with his warriors. "Is that a warning?"

Fate's dark eyes seemed to glitter. "In part."

"Fate—" Karess began, his brows drawing together in a quick frown.

Fate held up a hand. "I simply state a fact. Lady St. John should know these things since she has chosen to remain on Avalyr and accept our Bloodsworn as her Starmate."

Surprise rippled through her. "What makes you think that's what I've decided?"

He nodded toward the bed. "The Tragar shielded you with his body, yet when we arrived, you were shielding him with yours."

Karess' gray eyes widened slightly, a slow grin replacing his frown. "So she was."

Avera squirmed under their combined gazes. "Of course I tried to shield Devlin. I would have done the same for a lot of people." But she wouldn't have felt the same frantic urgency, the fear bordering on terror that she had at the thought of him dying.

The two men said nothing, just continued to stare at her with silent approval. She flushed and turned her own gaze back to the bed and to the man she now realized she was willing to die for. "How much longer?"

"A deep healing takes time," Fate said.

"Sarreth's didn't," she pointed out, lowering her voice to a whisper. She didn't want to disturb the woman healing Devlin, but talking helped keep her anxiety at a manageable level. Maybe Fate could tell she was close to losing it, because the normally taciturn man started talking, his deep voice low and soothing.

"The connection between Bloodsworn and Blade is deeper than that formed between healer and patient. I understand the manipulation of the essence of magic is difficult under the best of circumstances. Working a deep healing on Bloodsworn, especially one as powerful as the Tragar, can be done only by the strongest healers. Even those healers must train for years before they are accepted into the service of the Bloodsworn. Latessa has been senior healer for only a few years, but she is very skilled."

As if hearing her name, Latessa straightened. She turned to the table next to the bed, placed something in a small bowl, then washed and dried her hands. Wetting a clean cloth with fresh water, she applied it to Devlin's back. Avera took a step, barely stopping herself from rushing to the bed. The woman looked up at her, her expression tired, but serene. She smiled.

"You are the First Bloodsworn's Starmate."

Not a question, but Avera nodded. The healer held out a hand.

"Come. He will want to see you when he wakes."

Avera practically ran to the bed. Latessa gently rolled Devlin to his back and motioned Avera to sit next to him.

"Is he all right?" She hesitated before laying a hand on his bare chest. The strong, steady beat of his heart did more to reassure her than the healer's words.

"The worst of his injuries are healed. I left magic working inside to complete the process and remove any scarring. He will be sore, tired from the loss of blood, but nothing rest and a good meal cannot remedy."

Avera smoothed back the black strands of hair from the side of his head where the bullet had blazed its trail. His skin felt warm, smooth except for the prickle of new hair already growing along the narrow path. She shook her head, amazed, and turned to the woman responsible for such a miracle. "What you have done is incredible. I can't thank you enough."

Latessa bowed slightly. "It is my pleasure to serve, Lady Bloodsworn."

Devlin's heartbeat faltered, his breathing stopped.

Terrified something was wrong, Avera spun back around and found herself suddenly caught by a pair of strong arms, tucked against a hard body, and rolled across the bed. Devlin lay atop her, muscles rigid, his breath coming in fast, ragged pants.

"It's all right, we're safe," she told him, trying to wiggle her arms free so she could hold him. His eyes flickered, and she knew he was getting updates from Fate and the others. Slowly, the tension seeped from his knotted muscles. He shifted his body slightly, removing most of his weight from her, but not all.

His gaze focused on her face. "You have my thanks, Latessa," he said without looking away from Avera's eyes.

"You are most welcome, First Bloodsworn."

Avera couldn't take her gaze from his anymore than he could from hers. She heard the rustle of cloth, footsteps, then the click of the door opening and closing. They were alone.

His hand cupped her cheek where the palace healers had removed the scratches from the stone splinters. "You are well? You weren't…struck?"

She shook her head. "No, you…" The tears she'd been holding back filled her eyes. Angry tears, she told herself. "You shielded me. You shouldn't have done that." She touched his scalp again and let her hand drift over his shoulder to his back. "You could have been killed. You almost were. If Fate and the others hadn't come when they did… If Latessa had been a little later…"

His mouth covered hers, lips moving with a desperate urgency that took her breath away. She kissed him back, just as hard, with just as much desperation. Her hands clutched frantically at the hard muscles of his back. She couldn't get close enough, wanting him inside her. Nothing was more important to her than this man. Not her home, not her career, not even her world.

And she'd almost lost him.

She broke their kiss and started pressing her lips everywhere she could reach, ignoring the tears running down her cheeks.

****

Devlin held Avera as she cried, murmuring words to her in ancient Feyune while trying to bring his racing heart under control. Luma's blood and tears, he'd almost lost her again. Not to magic, not to a sword, but to a damn weapon that should not even be on his world. The memory of her terror-filled eyes just before the darkness claimed him would haunt him for years to come.

He welcomed her kisses, her hot tears wet against his skin, her nails digging into his back. One of her legs wrapped over his thigh, locking them together. Her hips rocked up into his. "I want you," she whispered through her tears.

Instant need slammed into Devlin, heating his blood and hardening his body in a painful rush. He shuddered, feeling her call to him, mate to mate.

He smoothed back her hair, tried to get her to look at him. "Avera, *me`surrasie*, do you recall what I told you in my garden last night?" His words came out ragged, his breathing too out of control for anything else. He wanted her, too. Desperately. But not just her body. He wanted her understanding, her complete acceptance. He wanted her love.

"We are Starmates, Avera. If we consummate our bond, there is no going back, no separation. If anything were to happen to your Blades, I would still not let you go. You have to be certain."

She stared into his eyes. The heat of her gaze almost took his control. "I don't know what a Starmate is, but I know what I'm agreeing to, Devlin. This isn't lust talking." Her cheeks flushed. "Well, it is, but it's *my* lust. And *my* heart. I *love* you Devlin Kel-Tragar."

Joy infused Devlin like a wave of brilliant magic. She loved him. He tightened his hold and took her mouth in a kiss he intended to be gentle. But gentle wasn't what his lovely prophecy bride wanted. She let him know by the tangle of her tongue with his, the moans in the back of her throat, the insistent shifting of her hips against him.

Still kissing her, he worked the fastening of her jeans open and slid a hand inside. One finger slipped into damp curls and damper flesh. Relief shuddered through his body She was more than ready for him. Only one last thing remained.

"Our vows," he growled.

"Vows? Now?" she gasped, pushing into his touch. Her hands trailed down his back, nails clawing him lightly, impatiently, making his muscles clench. "Devlin, you can't seriously expect me to recite vows when I can barely remember my own name."

He closed a hand over her right breast and gently squeezed. "There is nothing to recite, beloved.

The words come from your heart."

"All right," she agreed breathlessly. One of her hands covered his over her breast, pushing his grip tighter, the other tugged at the waistband of his pants. "Anything, just get these off."

Devlin held his breath and sent out a whisper of magic, banishing his clothing and hers. They both gasped as their heated flesh touched. Her hips jerked once, and the head of his erection slid to the edge of her wet entrance. Her groan matched his at the sweetness of the pleasure.

Hanging on to his control by the tips of his fingers, Devlin took her face in his hands. "Look at me," he demanded. He wanted to touch her, taste her, spend hours just getting to know every inch of her body. But such a slow perusal would have to come later. Now that Avera had accepted him, the bond demanded completion. The magic between Starmates pulled at them, relentless for fulfillment. When their gazes locked, he began to push inside her. He couldn't go as slow as he wanted and watched her eyes to make sure he didn't hurt her. Leaning close, he whispered the words of his heart against her skin.

"I accept thee, Avera St. John, as mate of my heart, light of my soul, and star of my night. I pledge to thee my love, my honor, and my protection, in this life and forever more. As long as the magic of time flows, I am yours."

Tears sparkled in her eyes when he was seated fully inside her. "Are you all right? Am I hurting you?"

Her lips trembled into a smile. She shook her head. "No, you're not hurting me," she whispered. "I..." Her eyelids fluttered down, and he felt her muscles clench around him. His whole body jerked in response. "I'm fine," she gasped. "I just... I need more. I need you to move."

Devlin shuddered. "Then say the words of your heart, *me`surrasie* , and give yourself to me."

The magic gathered around them, tingling along his skin. Avera's breath caught, and he knew she felt it too. He pulled back slowly until he was almost free of her hot sheath and made himself pause.

"Now?" she gasped, arching to keep him inside her.

He almost choked on the strained chuckle low in his throat. "Yes, now would be good." Now would be very good. His first thrust had been a giving of himself. This time, he would claim her for his own. As she spoke, he slid forward in one long, slow slide of ecstasy.

"I take thee, Devlin Tragar, as my husband, as my..."

He pulled back and thrust again.

"Sweet Lord, yes, as my mate, and m-my beloved. Ah, Devlin, that feels so good!"

Too good. He couldn't keep the slow pace up any longer. Whatever control he'd ever had was gone, swept away by Avera's words of acceptance, and by the fierce hunger rising up, threatening to devour them both. He kept thrusting, hips pumping in time to a rapidly escalating beat, spurred on by the swirling magic now visible around them.

Avera wrapped her legs around him, her hips rising eagerly to meet his every move. When her hands closed around his face, he stared into her vivid green eyes glowing with her Bloodsworn power as she gasped out the final words of her heart.

"I promise to love, honor, and cherish you forever, Devlin Tragar. As God is my witness, I am yours."

Devlin immediately sealed his mouth over hers, feeling their souls touch. He wanted to get closer, wanted to be joined with her like this forever. She made a small noise, almost a growl, and her whole body tightened. A possessive fire flared deep inside him, knowing he would be the one to send her over the edge into ultimate pleasure. Slipping a hand beneath her hips, he tilted her slightly, reaching deeper. She cried out his name, her whole body arching from head to heels as the power of her orgasm possessed her. His own release rushed up through his balls and swelled his already thick erection. Unbelievable pleasure tore through him. His. Hers. His body jerked and shook with the force of their joining, his shaft pulsing as his seed spilled into his beloved mate. "Avera!" he shouted.

Then the magic struck, racking his body and hers.

Pleasure swept over them in waves more intense than anything Devlin had ever felt in his life. Avera's inner muscles squeezed him in a tight rhythm, locking him deep inside her. Their bodies strained together. He couldn't stop kissing her as the essence of magic flowed through them, sealing the bond between them for all time.

Chapter Forty-Seven

Avera lay still, listening to the harper bird outside the window sing his ode to the dawn while pale light slowly turned the dark sky gray. Devlin's body spooned around her protectively, one arm wrapped around her waist, his hand tucked between her breasts. She smiled. Lying in his bed without a stitch on and no covers, she couldn't be warmer. The man generated heat like a space-heater.

Thinking about a space-heater made her think about electricity, which led to thoughts about electronics, which had her picturing the analyzers, computers, and centrifuges in her lab—things she'd never see or use again. That chapter of her life was over. What she had in its place was a vague outline of a hypothetical future she wasn't sure she could handle.

"Devlin," she said softly, not wanting to disturb the harper's serenade. "What if I can't do this, make all these changes, I mean?"

She felt him stir. Firm lips pressed against her hair. "Peace, me`surrasie. You don't have to walk this path alone. I will be right beside you. I swear I will do my best to make you happy here." His arms tightened. "You are more than just a prophecy bride to me, Avera St. John."

Her lips trembled and she blinked the sudden moisture from her eyes. She was glad he couldn't see her face. "I think that's what scares me the most. I'm not used to being anyone's anything. Now all of a sudden I've got a handsome barbarian prince I barely know, claiming I'm his everything. Can you blame me for being a little incredulous?"

"You think me handsome?"

The hopeful note in his voice made her smile, but she slapped his arm just on principle. "You are such a male."

He captured her hand, took it over her shoulder to his mouth, and kissed her palm. A slight shudder ran through her body.

"Yes, I am most definitely male, and no, I do not blame you for your doubts, Avera. All I ask is that you give my world a chance. Give *me* a chance." He kissed her shoulder. "My whole life, all I have ever desired was a loving mate to stand at my side. I never dreamed the very Prophecy I believed would take that possibility away would instead, grant my one true wish."

More tears clogged her throat, and she had to wait a moment to speak. "So, does this mean the Prophecy has been fulfilled?"

"Not entirely. There are other aspects to the Prophecy besides our joining, and even that will not be complete until we bind together in a formal ceremony."

"If that's your idea of a proposal, I think we're going to have problems."

His deep chuckle warmed her ear. The hand between her breasts opened wide, teasing both nipples. "I believe I can do better."

The duel sensations made her arch her neck. He nuzzled and kissed her, leaving chill bumps racing down her spine while something warmer kindled deep inside her. She moaned. "We've been at this all night. How can you still do this to me?"

"Starmates know no boundaries, *me`surrasie.*

There is no limit to the pleasure we can give each other."

No limit. She could almost believe him. They'd made love so many times in the last few hours, she'd lost count. Now she felt the wet heat between her thighs all over again, and the hard, glorious length of him growing against her backside. He shifted the leg he'd thrown over both of hers during their last nap, forcing it between her thighs, opening her to him.

"I've been meaning to ask you." She gasped and pushed back against him. "What does *me`surrasie* mean?"

"Ah," he said, nudging the wide head of his erection against her wet folds, "it means, 'my beloved', or in some dialects, 'my darling one'."

He slid inside her.

Avera arched her back as he reached down to raise her leg up higher, allowing him to thrust deeper, harder, faster. Pushed up and over the edge just as the sun of her new world broke over the horizon, she couldn't hold back her cry of pleasure. "Devlin! *Me`surrasie!*"

A word about the author...

Kathy Lane was born and raised in central Florida. She grew up running wild through orange groves and swamps, tagging after her older brothers when possible or creating her own imaginary adventures. Writing fiction has always been a passion for her so it's a mystery how she ended up working as an accountant.

When her sons grew up and moved out, she filled her empty nest with a computer and began writing again. She is a member of Romance Writers of America and her local chapter, Tampa Area Romance Authors. She is also a member of the Florida Writer's Association.

Kathy still lives in Florida where she gets frequent visits from her two sons, Joe and Jon, and her wonderful niece, Darelle.

Visit Kathy at
http:// www.kyrlane.com

Thank you for purchasing
this Wild Rose Press publication.
For other wonderful stories of romance,
please visit our on-line bookstore at
www.thewildrosepress.com

For questions or more information,
contact us at
info@thewildrosepress.com

The Wild Rose Press
www.TheWildRosePress.com